THE

SEVENTH

ROOM

Nicola Belluomo

The Seventh Room

Copyright © Nicola Belluomo 2024

All rights reserved.
No part of this book may be reproduced or used in any manner whatsoever, including information storage and retrieval systems, without the express written permission from the author, except for the use of brief quotations in a book review.

This book is a work of fiction. Any references to historical events, real people, or real places are used fictitiously. Other names, characters, places and events are products of the author's imagination, and any resemblance to actual events, places or persons, living or dead, is entirely coincidental

A catalogue record of this book is available from the British Library

ISBN: 978-1-0687141-7-7

Cover designed by
Holly Belluomo @nyx_designs

For Arthur, Holly and Sal

About this book

The Seventh Room is a fictional story woven around historical characters, places and events. For the reader's reference, at the back of the book is an index of the historical characters who appear in this story. Their interactions with the fictional characters are, naturally, invented, but the public statements and writings used in this story, such as Ludwig Beck's memo to the generals, are taken from first-hand reported evidence.

In two instances, the historical details on which The Seventh Room is based have been slightly smudged: the SOE was formed in 1940, but I wanted Tommie to be established as an agent in Paris before the Germans occupied the city in June of that year, so I hurried her assignment along a little. Also, in order to apply for the Kriegsakademie, Peter would have had to have experienced at least two years of active service in the German army, which would distort the storyline, so that detail was also blurred out.

Prologue

August 1944

All was quiet as he unlocked the pass door into the hospital wing and walked down the corridor. The floodlights were off again tonight, and, in the seventh room, staring through the window into the velvet blackness of the sky, he could almost hear the faint whisper of the dark moon as it passed through the night. The voice from the bed startled him out of his trance.
"What is it about that window that has you hypnotized night after night, Major Brandt?"
He pulled himself together.
"My apologies, Fraulein West, I had thought you would be asleep at this time of the night."
"I don't sleep too soundly now."
"Of course," he said, turning to leave. "I have been thoughtless. I won't disturb you again."
"Oh, you don't disturb me," she said lightly, "Not anymore, but I am curious about what you see through that window. I have watched you for the past several nights, staring out there."
Out there.
He was drawn irresistibly back to the void.
"The hospital wing has the best views in the castle," he said slowly, "and in this room, if one looks straight ahead, neither up nor down, it is possible to imagine that this castle

doesn't exist; that nothing exists." He stopped, and silence fell thickly.

"But for the past two nights there has been no moon to light the landscape," she said eventually, as though the last three words had not been spoken, "and yet you have stood there and stared out on... on what?" He could feel her eyes on him as he gazed out into the blackness, and in the absence of a response, her voice became conversational. "Some say that the new moon is a time when the darkest acts of men are conceived or committed, but you don't strike me as a man who enjoys contemplating the darkest acts, Major Brandt."

"The darkest acts of men originate within the minds of men," he said sharply, "not with the movements of the moon, or the planets, or the stars. There is no excuse to be made for our crimes." He paused, making a deliberate effort to erase the harshness in his voice. When he spoke again, it had been replaced by weariness. "It is not the window that draws me here, but the room itself. Frau Heller believes that this is a healing room; perhaps I am in need of healing."

Digitalis can strengthen a heartbeat or stop it. How you use it, and why... that's what matters

*1
The truth about herself*

London, 1938

The smoke inched up her legs, mouthing at her with grey lips, before blossoming into drab flowers that were snatched apart by bony fingers of wind. Her body jolted as the pyre beneath her imploded and opened up its maw, a vision of Hell gaping to receive her. She opened her own mouth to cry out the truth about herself, but the smoke thrust itself down her throat, and the truth was corrupted. A bright tongue of yellow leaped up, undulated lewdly before her eyes, then sank again to lick her ankles with a soft touch. A familiar touch. With a singing whine, the breath from Hell lifted her hair into flames as she stepped away from the stake and reached down to embrace the inferno.

"Tommie! Tommie, it's alright, wake up. I've got a pot of tea ready downstairs. Come on, open your eyes and see where you are."

She opened her eyes and saw. The rumpled comfort of her bed was around her like a grandmother's arms, but the hair at the back of her head was snarled into a matted clump from friction with the stake ... *not* with the stake, she told herself, there was no stake, and there was no pyre, just Kate kneeling on the bed beside her. "Are you awake?" she was saying, peering into Tommie's eyes, "What the hell do you see in those awful nightmares? No! Don't tell me!" She covered her ears. "You'll pass them on to me. For God's sake, you should talk to the doctor about this."

Tommie drew a cautious breath, but her lungs were not seared, and there was no smoke, just the clean scent of lavender from her sheets.

"I have spoken to the doctor," she said, "I went to see him last week."

"Really?"

"Really." She drew another breath. "Did you say something about tea?"

"It's downstairs. I'm not bringing you breakfast in bed, dreams or no dreams. So, what did the doctor have to say?"

Tommie reached around to the back of her head and explored the hair clump gloomily; that was going to take a lot of unpicking. Sliding her legs over the edge of the bed, she poked around with her feet and found the sanctuary of her slippers.

"What did he say? He said, 'Dear girl, the nightmares are quite clearly the symptoms of... mmm... a nervous disorder,'" she mumbled, mimicking the doctor's fusty tones as she pulled on her dressing-gown. "'Mmm, your parents' tragic deaths have left you quite alone in the world, unmarried and exposed to the vicissitudes of life. You have... mmm... nobody to depend on, and you are vulnerable. It's quite natural that you should be... mmm... anxious." Don't laugh, Kate, those were his exact words! It was like something from a Jane Austen novel!"

"Tch!" Kate shook her head, "Did you give him what for? Oh, hell, the toast!" She dashed down the stairs and across the living room to the kitchen.

"No, of course I didn't give him what for," Tommie said, following her friend, "Doctor Kent has been in the family for generations." She leaned against the door frame while Kate busied herself with setting the breakfast tray. "I just reminded him that I have a house – all bought and paid for – as well as a nice nest egg waiting in trust... and I make a liveable income of my own. I'm not vulnerable, I'm independent. I'm Mr. Darcy, not Elizabeth Bennet."

A quick tap on the living room window made her glance up, and she waved.

"Is that Will?" Kate said from the depths of a cupboard, "Grab him for me, Tommie, I've been waiting for a parcel from the printer. And give him some toast."

"More pamphlets?" Tommie headed for the door with a plate of toast. "Isn't London sick of pamphlets yet?"

"Cable Street was only last year, you know," said Kate acidly, "London was glad enough to have communists around then. Have some toast, Will," she called out to the postman as Tommie relieved him of the package. The postman shook his head regretfully, eyeing the plate.

"I shouldn't. I got it in the neck from Mrs. Butler last time, for leaving a buttery fingerprint on her electricity bill."

"Not Mrs. Butler of the Women's Institute?!" From the kitchen, Kate's voice sounded alarmed, "You didn't tell her who you got the toast from?"

"Nope," he called back, "I blamed it on my kids."

Tommie held up a slice of toast for him. "Bite," she said. He grinned, took a large bite, and went on his way.

Kate set the breakfast tray on the coffee table in the living room.

"Ah, tea!" sighed Tommie, "and you've made toast for me, too! Oh, Kate, you're a godsend." Toast... she wondered briefly if... but no; under no circumstances could the soul-satisfying smell of toast have inspired the dream-smoke, that rank, lung-choking, semi-solid mass that had clawed its way into her lungs.

Dropping herself into her favourite armchair, she made an effort to dismiss the residual tension that still held her muscles in a state of low-level horror. This house was her sanctuary; her hearth, her home and her castle. Others would call it – had called it – dowdy and drab, dated, dreary, old-fashioned and frumpy, but she was unapologetically content with it, from the ecru rose-print wallpaper to the slumped armchairs with their mismatched upholstery that had long since mellowed into a congenial truce with the rugs and the curtains. So why, in this safe harbour, did she find herself, night after night, hunted and brought down by these dreams?

"I'm going to the British Museum this morning, Kate," she said. "I've reserved some books in the reading room. If you're going into the Party offices, I'll walk with you."

"Good, you can help me to carry my bags." Kate settled into her own chair on the other side of the fireplace and bit into her toast, pushing aside the newspaper she had been reading. "I'll be catching the train straight after work…" She stopped short, "Oh! Tommie!" she said, carefully managing a mouthful of crumbs, "I can put off this trip to Oxford if you want me to stay with you. Because of the dreams, I mean. They've been coming thick and fast recently, perhaps you shouldn't be left on your own for a whole week." She shrugged at Tommie's exasperated glance. "Alright, just offering. So, what did the doctor have to say about your invulnerable speech? I bet that shook his faith in the world as it should be."

"Well, it helped him to remember which century we're in, because then he started talking about Doctor Freud's theories; he suggested that the dreams might be brought on by my not having a mother-figure to initiate me into womanly matters."

"Womanly matters?! You're a midwife! He knows you're a midwife, doesn't he?"

"Of course he does, and maybe he thinks that's part of the problem; I help mothers to become mothers, but I don't have a mother behind me to support me; I'm a dangling link in a broken chain." She paused for a moment, then shook her head. "So, that's it. According to Doctor Kent, Freud would say that my problems all boil down to my lack of a mother."

"Lack of a penis is more like it!"

"Kate!"

"Not you in particular; women in general!" said Kate, "And don't look so shocked, Tomasin West, you're always coming up with bits of pithy midwife wisdom, now it's my turn. I know about Freud; basically, everything a woman does and says comes down to the fact that she doesn't have a penis, and she really wants one. No! Don't be rude; you know what I meant! Honestly! Stop giggling, Tommie..." A spurt of toast crumbs fountained across the room.

***

The pavements were wet from the previous night's rain, and a waning moon sank through the fragile blue of the morning sky as they made their way into town. The world was as fresh as a London morning could be, but the faint tang of anthracite from somebody's chimney drifted across Tommie's soul, and the dewy morning seemed populated with spirits from another world; a man, walking his dog, held the leash awkwardly with his left hand because his right arm was missing. Another man swung along on crutches, with one empty trouser leg pinned up, and on the next street, the owner of the corner shop set out his sign, adjusting the sculpted mask that covered one half of his face. Any one of those men might have been her uncle.

"I didn't know you had an uncle," said Kate, taking Tommie by surprise. She didn't know she'd spoken aloud.

"I don't any more," she said. "I suppose, technically, I never did, because he died before I was born, killed in the great war. He was my mother's younger brother. She kept a box with all their letters to each other... and photographs. He was beautiful, Kate; you know how some men can be so outstandingly beautiful that it makes you catch your breath? His name was Thomas. I'm named after him. I wish I looked like him, I would be gorgeous!"

"Was he at the front?"

She nodded.

"At the Somme. My mother told me once that she hated knowing everything he was going through, but she read all his letters because they say a trouble shared is a trouble halved. Well, I think they got that calculation wrong; I think a trouble shared is a trouble doubled, because he was killed on his twentieth birthday, and now she knew what his death had looked like, how it had sounded, how it had smelled, how it had tasted. She couldn't escape it."

The letters inside the precious rosewood box had been explicit, and Tommie was silent for a moment, reflecting not for the first time on what that knowledge must have done to her finely-tuned mother.

Their relationship had always been tempestuous, but most of that was probably her own fault; her mother had been diaphanous and refined, and Tommie definitely wasn't. Now, looking back, she wondered how much of her mother's fragility had been the thinned-out substance of someone who knew about the Portuguese Man-of-War transparency of life... had seen through its allure to its trailing, killing sting.

Tommie had wanted to go to university to study philosophy, but her parents would not countenance a bluestocking in the family, and they held the purse strings. They had prepared a Tomasin-shaped place in society for her, presenting her with a genteel future that waited only for her to slip it over her shoulders like the finest fur stole.

She had been sent to a finishing school on a hill in Switzerland. She had battled against it.

"I don't want to be like you," she had raged – and she might even have stamped her foot – "You skate over the surface of life as though it's a frozen pond!" Her mother had smiled her perfectly chilled smile, and, with an uncharacteristic edge to her voice, unveiled for her daughter a precious pearl of enlightenment; "Being born burdens us with the duty to live, Tomasin, and this is how I bear that duty. Life is a farmyard, but we don't have to go wading through the pigsties and poking around in the abattoir. I choose to stay in the parlour and keep the curtains closed. Please respect that."

Duty and respect; they were odd, lumpy words to hear in her mother's cut glass tones, and they had embedded themselves in Tommie's thoughts. For the sake of duty then, she had picked her way disdainfully through finishing school – managing to get very little of it on her – and then, duty done, when she was of age, she had chosen her own path.

Surprisingly, her mother had swallowed her displeasure and had bought the house on Elizabeth Street so that Tommie could attend nursing school.

As they arrived at the museum, Kate shouldered her satchel and took her carpet bag from Tommie.

"I'll see you next week, then," she called as she crossed the road, "no more dreams, alright?"

"Alright," said Tommie, "Enjoy Oxford." She paused to gaze up at the crowning pediment, with its series of sculptures depicting the progress of civilization, and her eyes rested on the first two figures, the ones who meant most to her; a man emerging from the rock of the savage past, reaching out to a kneeling angel who held aloft the lamp of knowledge. Beside these two, the others seemed superfluous. She sighed and tucked her hair firmly behind her ears. The residue of her nightmare had still not entirely dispersed, and as she started up the steps her senses seethed like a basket of snakes waking up.

An ancient silence echoed from the soaring dome of the reading room as she waited at the issue desk and was handed a stack of books on witchcraft.

***

It was five o'clock before she managed to haul herself out of bed and into the bath, and close to six o'clock before she made it downstairs, debating whether to dig around in the kitchen or face whatever the hospital cafeteria had prepared for the night-shift.

She found Kate sitting at the dining table, still dressed in her suit, and with her evening meal, half-eaten, in front of her. On returning from Oxford, she had discovered that Tommie had not been alone with her nightmares – those had stopped, as though some angel had held aloft the lamp of knowledge – but she *had* been alone with a pile of books that made Kate highly uneasy.

The latest Communist Party pamphlet was lying next to her plate, but in her hands was the library's copy of The History of Witchcraft and Demonology, and she was holding the book in her fingertips as though expecting it to burst into flames at any moment.

"Tommie, listen to me," she said urgently, "You have to stop reading this stuff. Look at this; she read from the book, 'Hell seems to vomit its foulest dregs upon the shrinking earth; a loathsome shape of obscene horror squats huge and monstrous upon the ebon throne; the stifling air reeks with filth and blasphemy; faster and faster whirls the witches' lewd lavolta...'"

Pausing at the bottom of the stairs, Tommie lifted her eyebrows.

"Look closer, Kate, because there are layers in there; that's the author, Montagu Summers, insisting that real witches are living and operating amongst us, and getting away with it because they look and act like ordinary people. He says witches are a danger to society."

"Well, yes!" Kate poked at another page, grimaced, and read again, ""The Devil made her kneel down, while he himself stood up on his hind legs... and caused her to worship and invoke himself." This is bad stuff, Tommie; Edward says it's just the hobby of a bored bourgeoise debutante, but I think you're going too far now. It's bad stuff, and you should leave it alone."

A congenial relationship with her friend had come to hinge on them steering clear of this subject, so Tommie decided to make a quick exit and eat at the hospital.

"It's bad stuff, and it happened a long time ago," she said, crossing the room and grabbing her coat. "But it's happening again and I want to understand about it. What's happening in Germany today is happening because Goebbels is using the same sort of propaganda that led to the witch-hunts. And Mosley's trying the same thing in this country."

"I think we should clarify what each of us means by bad

stuff," insisted Kate, "You're talking about the witch-hunts, I'm talking about you getting obsessed with them. The bad stuff that's happening in Germany is happening in Germany. It doesn't affect us, and it's not our problem because we sorted out our own fascists in the Battle of Cable Street. The bad stuff that happened in the Middle Ages happened in the Middle Ages, and again, it's not our problem. You getting lost in this nonsense," she brandished The History of Witchcraft and Demonology, "is bad stuff that's happening to you here and now. It's going to affect your sanity, and that *is* our problem! Leave it alone. Witches and witch-hunts are history."

Tommie had one arm inside the sleeve of her coat, and she was almost out of the door. She knew she should ignore Kate's words, but she didn't.

"No, they're not," she said.

Kate closed her eyes tightly.

"What are you talking about?"

Tommie returned her coat to the hook and went over to the table, lowering herself onto the dining chair opposite Kate.

"It's *people*, Kate; people did those things... and people aren't some anomaly of history; they're always with us. They *are* us. See this book? The Malleus Maleficarum? Back in the Middle Ages, it was the witchhunters' handbook, commissioned by the Pope in 1484, but this edition..." she opened it and showed her friend the publisher's details... "was published here in London in nineteen twenty-eight. Nine years ago! It has been in print for well over four hundred years. These books – all of them – were published within the last fifteen years, and I borrowed all of them from our local library. And your friend there, Montagu Summers," she said, indicating the book in Kate's hand, "is still writing as we speak so no, Kate, witch-hunts aren't history."

"Well, maybe that's not such a bad thing," persisted Kate, "People need to be policed, and don't tell me that witches were just harmless old women, because in those books of yours they admitted to worshipping Satan. Look at the state our world is in! The last thing we need now is Satan worshippers."

"*Not* Satan! An antlered god – or a man wearing antlers."

"Yes, an antlered god... Satan."

"No! Horns are a symbol of deity that predates the Bible," said Tommie, "In fact, in the Book of Revelation, Jesus wears seven horns as a sign of his divinity." This was a calculated point; she had been amused to see relief in the eyes of her atheist friend when she saw the Bible appearing in Tommie's reading pile. "Seven horns," she repeated, "Seven; a sacred number. Horns; a sign of divinity. The antlered god of the pagans represented the connection between humans and nature, and the Christians couldn't stamp him out, so they commissioned artists to depict Satan with horns and animal features. Now, if the pagans wanted to follow their religion, it looked like they were worshipping Satan." She paused, "Twisting ideas and manipulating perceptions," she added, "it's how propaganda works."

Kate rolled her eyes.

"No wonder you're having nightmares."

"But I'm not anymore; I haven't had a single bad dream since I started researching this."

There was a nasty pause.

"What's that supposed to signify?" said Kate sharply, and Tommie floundered. She wasn't religious, and she didn't think she was superstitious, but through these dreams, religion and superstition had shoe-horned themselves into her life, along with a dreadful fascination for the power wielded by those who knew how to manipulate them.

If she answered Kate's question truthfully, if she spoke out loud the thought that had been bothering her, it might make it real. The words came out anyway.

"Look... right here, Kate; it says, "With regard to midwives, who surpass all others in wickedness...." In the Middle Ages, a midwife was automatically considered to be a witch."

Kate shook her head vigorously.

"I was afraid you'd start something like this. You're a well-trained professional, Tommie, you don't use eye of newt and snakeskin girdles to deliver babies. This is 1938, and a midwife is not a witch. *You're* not a witch. And you're not a danger to society."

"Neither were most of the people who were burned. And neither are the Jews, nor the homosexuals nor the communists... nor any of the groups that the Nazis are victimizing." Tommie reached for another book. "Joan of Arc..."

"Well, she's definitely history," snapped Kate, "And she wasn't a witch anyway, in the end. The Catholic Church made her a saint, and they don't do that to witches, so put all these books away, and leave it alone. Oh, for pity's sake, why are you giving me that look?"

"*Was* she a saint, though? Or was she really a witch? The Church couldn't squash her followers any more than they could squash the horned god. They'd failed to demonize her, so they claimed her – and her power and her followers – for the Church."

She pushed another book across the table to Kate. "Margaret Murray writes that Joan had received her visions at the Fairy Tree, a tree that grew over a spring held sacred by followers of the old religion. She had been known as the Maid of Orleans, and the Maid of France, and "maiden" was an honorific in a coven of witches; "Maiden" for a female role, and "Simon" for a male..."

"Simon?" interrupted Kate, curious despite herself. "Why Simon?"

Tommie frowned and shook her head, "I'm not sure about that. Maybe in reference to Simon Magus."

"Who?"

"Simon Magus. He was a charismatic, spiritualist-magician-type character who was mentioned in the Bible. But anyway; was Joan of Arc a witch or a saint? It's impossible to say, and, ultimately, it doesn't matter, because it was never about good and evil, it was about the authorities flaunting their power by driving a whole population to act en-masse, irrationally, and it's happening again in Germany; the same thing all over again. The witch-hunts are not dead and buried, Kate, and they never will be, as long as there are people. And I can't just sit around, waiting for them to bring this one to my hearth. I'm going to do something about it."

"Oh, for God's sake, Tommie!" said Kate in exasperation. "What are you going to do? You're not going to join the army nurses, are you?"

Tommie hesitated. She had signed up while Kate was in Oxford. But not for the army nurses.

"Something like that."

Kate stared at her, defeated, then shrugged her shoulders.

"Can I still rent my room from you?"

"Of course you can. I don't know how long I'll be away for, though." She reached across the table and picked up Kate's empty teacup. "If you were in Germany now, as a member of the Communist Party, you might as well be a witch," she said. "Does that make you evil?" She turned the cup in her hands, staring sightlessly at the tiny pieces of tealeaf that had escaped the net of the strainer. Fear warped Kate's face.

"You're not dabbling in witchcraft, are you, Tommie?"

The words flayed them both with shards of ice.

"No!" she said, shocked. "No, of course not! I just... I..."

They sat in silence, both of them astounded at the proximity and the severity of that ancient, unreasoning terror.

"You see, Kate? You see how it works?"

The witches hadn't been evil, and the devil wasn't... the devil, so why did the accusation frighten her? Because of the mindless surge of inhumanity that drives a witch-hunt to scorch the earth, and because of the distortion of life it causes. Because of the rage that made her want to fly screaming and flailing at the witchfinders for starting this all over again. Because of the suspicion that – just maybe – some of the witches had been a little bit more than harmless old women; maybe not all of them had stuck to healing. But mostly because, in the dreams, she had been stepping down into the abyss, reaching out towards the flames.

***

The distorted form of a man rose up before her, flayed raw and vibrating with violence. With evil. Her face was at the level of his navel, and this fact sucked her into a bone-exploding terror; was she on her knees before him? Looming above her was a malformed, goat-like face with long, rigid horns thrusting out from the top of its skull.

Fixing her with dull yellow eyes, the creature made a coughing, groaning sound, blew saliva from its lips, and pushed the tip of a horn into her shoulder. There was no pain, and this was bad; a sign of the Witches Mark, the brand of the Devil.

As it raised its head again, she saw, glinting in its forehead, a sign that she knew to be an ancient symbol; powerful, but newly debased. The creature raised its right arm, and Tommie woke up screaming, clutching her left calf where the muscles were seized into a rigid cramp.

It had been three weeks since she had returned the books to the library, but she had refused to examine her reasons for doing so, refused to confront the fear evoked by the accusation of witchcraft, and soon after that trip to the library, her sleep had become once again plagued by new dreams that writhed with disturbing, half-hidden images.

She was profoundly relieved that Kate wasn't in the house this time. She would not have been surprised to wake from one of these dreams to find Kate standing over her, brandishing a crucifix. Honestly, in the aftermath of this particular dream, Tommie was tempted to go in search of a crucifix for her own protection. Kate had been right; she should turn away from these sticky shadows and focus on real life.

She padded downstairs as the letterbox clattered and

delivered a manila envelope bearing the logo of the First Aid Nursing Yeomanry, the FANYs. It was time for her to ride out and confront the beast.

2
How do you feel about your father?

London, 1934

"How do you feel about your father?"

The eyes of a painted Russian nesting doll – a matryoshka – were watching him steadily from the corner of the desk, and Peter blinked.

"I beg your pardon?"

Captain Michael Hendry, DSM, glanced up from the file he had been reading.

"I asked you how you feel about your father, Mr. Brandt. I like to cut straight to the beating heart of any matter, but if you are uncomfortable with that approach, I can do it by the book. Something like this, perhaps..." drawing his face into a caricature of bureaucratic indifference, the man tightened his voice into a perfect, clipped, Noel Coward impersonation. "You have expressed an interest in joining Military Intelligence," he intoned, tapping the file with an officious finger, "And although these documents testify that you are a British subject with a British passport, I find that your late father was in fact German."

Pausing, he pulled a drag from his cigarette, and held it along with his breath, regarding Peter intently. "A German war hero, more to the point," he continued, releasing the accent along with the smoke. "Indeed, despite a childhood divided between rural Wales and some of England's most... influential educational establishments, you yourself speak German fluently. I'm sure you would agree that these two latter facts alone would necessitate a degree of circumspection on my part regarding your application."

Peter didn't offer a response. He was irritated, but he had prepared meticulously for this interview, and he would not allow the perennially thorny issue of his father to derail it. Across the desk, veiled by a haze of cigarette smoke and spiralling dust motes, Hendry continued to read from the file, and Peter listened as the man reviewed his academic career; Oxford, and before that, Eton, of course.

He had spent the greater part of his life in the presence of academics; men who held court in their booklined studies, droning on just like this, but he sensed that Michael Hendry was neither an academic nor a natural office-dweller. In fact, he seemed as out of place in his own office as the outlandish matryoshka. Out of place and about to jump out of his skin.

Curious now, Peter glanced around the room, searching for a context for the man. Without success. The only item that was not standard, square-edged, War Office issue was the matryoshka. A bottle of ink sat resolutely on the left-hand corner of the desk in defiance of the inkwell hollowed out in the customary right-hand corner, and all writing equipment was likewise positioned for the convenience of a left-handed man. There was a glass ashtray, piled high with stubs, each one smoked down to the last yellow pinch of paper, and it was from here, between the ashtray and the free-standing ink bottle, that the matryoshka watched him.

The small figure, with its gaudy headscarf, claimed his attention again. There were worn patches in the glaze, where restless fingers had pried. An uncanny breeze lifted the fine hairs on Peter's neck, and he sat up straighter, aligning his spine with the slats of the wooden chair.

"You are also fluent in several other languages," Hendry was saying, "Russian, French, and... Welsh." He paused.

"Welsh?"

"Yes, although I haven't made a formal study of Welsh."

"Why would anyone do that?" Hendry muttered, not quite under his breath.

Peter remained silent; this was one of his key skills, first deployed against playground taunts, and, latterly, against the jibes of Oxford's finest. Remaining silent would see him through this man's clumsy provocations, and then, perhaps, his application would proceed to someone more civilized.

"First class honours in Politics, Philosophy and Economics at Balliol," continued Hendry. "By all accounts you are an accomplished young man, a notably reserved individual who, for some reason, is anxious to work for British Military Intelligence. So, enlighten me; why have you chosen to make use of your very specific background in this very specific way at this… particular time?" He grimaced as though the question had left an unpleasant taste in his mouth, "There, that's the standard approach. Terribly stuffy. Far more agreeable to be direct, don't you think?"

"For some, perhaps, sir, but I would like to address the standard approach."

There was a sour silence before, with a coarse shrug of his shoulders, Hendry gestured for him to proceed. Peter delivered his presentation flawlessly.

"And your other reason?" Hendry had dropped the drone and was suddenly, unnervingly, attentive.

"My other reason?"

"You know," Hendry nodded encouragingly, "The *other* reason." Peter shook his head. "Your father, man! Your father! I want to hear about your father!" Dust motes swirled as Hendry waved a dismissive hand at the manila folder. "I have scant interest in files; a file shows me a skeleton, and I am not interested in skeletons. Everyone's skeleton is pretty much the same as everyone else's; a little more or less backbone in one than in another, perhaps, but otherwise identical. The flesh, on the other hand, the sentient body that touches, that feels the blood pulsing through it, that's another story altogether!"

He lunged forwards across the desk. "They say nobody will ever know you like your mother did, but they're wrong. If you join this organization, I will need to know you at least as well, although perhaps not as intimately, as your mother did." Without removing his eyes from Peter's, he took a drag from his cigarette. "I must be able to sense when you're about to stick a fork into the electrical socket, Mr. Brandt, so tell me about your other reason for wanting to join Military Intelligence."

The uncanny breeze had blown up into a cyclone, the barometer plummeted, and Peter dug his heels in.

"I'm sorry, sir," he said, stubbornly, "now you've lost me completely."

Hendry scowled.

"Well, either you're a liar or you genuinely don't know," he said grimly. "I'm not sure which of those two I like least, but in order to bulldoze this impasse, let me flesh out this blessed skeleton they've given me; you were raised by your mother and grandmother after your father discarded you and ran off to fight for his country. To be blunt, he chose Germany over you… that stings. Now your mother and your grandmother are gone, and you are naturally curious to learn about this man whom you never knew. Perhaps you ache to discover just what it was about this other country that could exert such an irresistible pull on a man. To live and die for Germany… could that be your Holy Grail too? Your raison d'etre?"

The old, familiar anger surged in Peter as the man's voice continued in a rapid flow of melodrama. Had he been invited to present himself – to reveal himself – to these people simply to indulge their arrogance in confirming his outsider status? He fought to catch hold of his hard-won survival skills, although right now they felt as useful as a wine cork bobbing alongside a drowning man.

"Perhaps," Hendry was needling, "perhaps your father's crusade is also yours; to unite your soul with the pounding heart of the Fatherland. To pull free from the apron strings of women. To stride forth into the dynamic world of men;

to learn about honour, vitality, all those masculine mysteries that have been withheld from you by the women who raised you."

"Captain Hendry!" Peter heard his own voice, sharp-edged and forceful, cutting through the monologue and leaving the air vibrating. Somehow his chair lay upended behind him, and he found that he was standing with his fists clenched on the scuffed surface of the desk in front of him. The torrent of words ceased as Hendry subsided into his chair with an airily dismissive gesture.

"Naturally, we would discover the truth eventually," he said coolly, "but I'd rather find out today than spend months training you for the other side."

"Captain Hendry..." Peter said again. He had quieted his voice, but it wasn't a serene quietness. He saw that Hendry recognized this, and was watching him with interest. Warning bells were sounding in his head, but remaining silent was out of reach now. "While I admit to a certain curiosity about my father and his values," he continued, and the words were pinched, working their way out from between clenched jaws, "I feel no desire to replace my nationality with his. And as for the apron strings and the dynamic world of men, I will tell you this much; I learned from my mother and from my grandmother an appreciation of honour and vitality, tempered with humanity, that makes a lot more sense than any of the puffed-up philosophies of certain men who have taken it upon themselves to enlighten me. And with respect, sir, I am familiar with Doctor Freud and his work, and I resent being subjected to a spectacularly amateur interpretation of his theories."

Hendry had not moved during Peter's outburst, but now he shook his head gravely, leaned forward, flipped the file closed, and sent it sliding away from him to come to rest against the matryoshka. He drew his hands together in a steeple, pressing his two index fingers against his lips, and his face split into a grin of triumph.

"Ha! I knew it! They told me after your screening that you were just another bored academic. 'A stuffed shirt,' to use their exact words, but it seems they were wrong! It's good to know you've got a pulse, man." He sat back in his chair again and regarded Peter frankly. "Good lord, though, we'll have to work on burying that righteous indignation a little deeper. It's not a common trigger in agents, but in your case it seems to be a fearfully easy one to pull." He chuckled again, "'With respect, sir, you're a spectacular amateur.' I like it! Instinct, Brandt, instinct!" he jabbed a finger at a spot midway between his eyebrows, "If you have it, listen to it. The only time I ever ignored mine... well, that's a story for another day. Alright, pick up the chair, and you can stop bristling. I don't need to know your secrets, I just needed to know that you have some. After all, that's what drives us, isn't it? Secrets." He stood up abruptly. "Let's take a walk along the river, I get edgy being cooped up in these blasted offices.

***

The Thames slid by beneath them, brown and sluggish in the mild afternoon light. Leaning on the parapet of the bridge, Hendry gazed across at the grimy walls of Westminster.

"There is no cohesive intelligence organization in this country, Brandt, did you know that?" He took a last drag on his cigarette and flicked it into the river, inhaling the smoke with satisfaction before allowing it to slide from his mouth, coiling around his words. "It's a writhing snake pit of jealousy and suspicion, a protean monster, self-consuming and dangerous. Absolutely unworkable. Tell me," he added, "what is your perception of the situation in Germany?"

This was home ground for Peter and he answered succinctly, finishing with the passing of The Enabling Act.

"President Hindenburg doesn't have long for this world," he concluded, "and when he dies, Adolf Hitler will inherit a government with no term-limits on its emergency powers, and a country that is re-arming, has left the League of Nations and has no civil liberties."

Hendry nodded.

"Remarkably concise, for an Oxford man," he said. "Yes, the Leash of Nations; a noble endeavour, but possessed of a fatal flaw; when the bad dogs slip their leashes, the good dogs remain tethered. 'Sit!' says Geneva, 'Stay!' and the good dogs sit and stay. Meanwhile, Mussolini savages Ethiopia, and Hitler bares his teeth at Czechoslovakia." He pulled a pack of cigarettes from his pocket and offered one to Peter, who declined. "Quite right," he said. "Filthy habit." Lighting one for himself, he scowled at the windows of Parliament. "Hitler is offering the German people a banquet of national pride, and our liberal statesmen are all sniggering behind his back, because his ideas are just so much naive quackery." He blew out a decisive stream of smoke, "But statesmen do not form the majority of the voting public, and Hitler is speaking directly to the hearts that do. No more big words, volks; he has quite simply promised to dismantle the vast conspiracy of Jews and communists, homosexuals, gypsies and sub-humans that is strangling the country. Now, what about Russia?" A sucking silence dropped into the lee of his words.

"Russia?" repeated Peter, disconcerted by the sudden switchback.

"Bingo!" cried Hendry triumphantly. "No, no, don't say a word. I've read your file; I know you know your stuff on Russia. That was just a little practical demonstration of my pet theory."

"Which is?"

"That the world is so wrapped up – quite understandably – in what's happening in Germany, that genial old Uncle Joe could have all of Europe under his boot before you could say 'Stalin who?' You won't be joining us at Military Intelligence, Brandt."

Peter was side-swiped.

"Because I hesitated over Russia?"

"Oh, Good Lord, no."

"Then may I ask your reason for rejecting me?"

"Yes, of course you may," Hendry said absently. Staring

out across the river at the glistening silt of the exposed banks, he seemed to have forgotten Peter's presence, and, still smarting from his pronouncement, Peter spoke sharply.

"What *is* your reason?"

Hendry blinked. "My reason? Ah, yes. Let's walk a little." He sucked the life out of his cigarette, crushed the stub on the iron railings, and lit another, heading upstream against the ebbing tide. Falling into step beside him, Peter noticed a slight irregularity in the man's stride – a hesitation as he came down on his left leg – but it didn't interfere with his vigorous pace, and, verbally, Hendry was back on track. "Did I tell you about the state of the intelligence organizations in this country?"

"The writhing snake pit, the protean monster?"

Hendry grinned. "Precisely. Hold onto that image, but now think of a pearl." With his pale blue eyes squinting in contemplation, he hesitated, then nodded to himself. "Yes, a pearl is the perfect metaphor, let's use that. One of the few items of lasting value in the ocean, Brandt, is a pearl. A pearl exists beyond the tiny tragedy of a fish's demise in the tentacles of an anemone. A pearl survives the feeding frenzies of sharks and the turmoil of changing tides. How does it manage to do this? Because it is a precious secret known only to the oyster that generates it." He paused and frowned. "Or is it a clam that produces pearls? I feel I should know that." He turned to Peter with a peculiar intensity. "Do you see my point, though?"

Peter fought to neutralize the caustic tone that had crept into his voice. "In the context of sea life, I believe you're correct, but perhaps – at some point – you will apply that principle to my particular situation?"

Hendry turned abruptly, and resumed his march along the embankment.

"Yes, I will," he said as Peter caught up with him, "and here it is; I want to be your oyster, Brandt. I want you to be my pearl." Peter halted in mid-stride. Hendry stopped too, but continued his line of thought. "I want to build something of value; something that can be preserved from the spiralling idiocy that threatens to confound us." Becoming aware of Peter's discomposure, he retraced his words and found the problem.

Chuckling to himself, he continued, "Alright, no more metaphors! I will train you as an intelligence agent, but only on my own terms; it must be an exclusive arrangement between the two of us. You must continue with your life as though you have been rejected for service with Military Intelligence – which indeed you have been – and we will work together in your free time. When the various intelligence agencies can agree to share their toys, you will be formally invited into the organization, but not until then.

"As a whole entity you are priceless to me, but if they get their hands on you at this point in time, you will be snatched apart like a piece of live bait." He turned to Peter and regarded him soberly. "It is my hope that you will agree to this, but if you decline I, of course, will deny ever putting such an absurd proposition before you."

***

So, how did he feel about his father? On the train heading back to Oxford, safely distanced from Michael Hendry's astute gaze, Peter fell to considering this. How did he feel about the heedless self-absorption that led a man – a soldier no less – to pluck a young girl from her home in the teeth of a war, stamp her with the enemy's mark, then casually drop her back there to raise her child – similarly stamped – in a hostile environment. How did he feel about that? Contempt. Condemnation. Disdain; his father could not have known that he was about to die, but as a soldier, and for the sake of his wife and son, he should have anticipated it.

'Secrets,' Hendry had said. 'That's what drives us.' Was this contempt for his father the secret that Hendry had probed for, then left for Peter to keep like a clam keeps a pearl? Probably not, because it was the other question that was of more interest to an intelligence officer; 'Why have you chosen to make use of your very specific background in this very specific way at this particular time?' The answer to that one was more convoluted.

He stared out of the train window. The glinting self-importance of the city had yielded to sooted brickwork and industrial sprawl and then, in turn, to an ordered, suburban symmetry. Soon he would be looking out on a gentle patchwork of green fields dotted with rambling villages, and staid county towns frothing with flower-stuffed gardens and window-boxes. If he should step off the train at any one of the interchangeable new-pin-neat little platforms – Eastleigh Halt or Cranham Grange, or Eastleigh Grange, or Cranham Halt – he would breathe the soft, summer air, inextricably braided with rose, geranium and lavender. If he rode the train to the destination on his ticket, he would alight into the antiquity of Oxford and feel the shadow of the university settling on his shoulders.

But he was in the process of shrugging off that shadow, along with the career in government or diplomacy that was its natural progression. Why? Because of the League of Peace.

And in a League of Peace – God grant we may –
Transform the earth, not patch up the old plan.

Words written in the trenches of the last war; a plea from the very mouth of oblivion. If Peter had a quest, its genesis was in reading these words in the poetry of Robert Bridges, so he had followed the prescribed path towards the creation of a league of peace, only to see that it led to a mirage of peace, recognizable, on closer inspection, as business as usual. Because of this desolate sense of riding the rails towards business as usual, and because he knew that something must be done, he balked at a life of doing no more than had always been done. And just as surely as he knew this, he knew that Hendry's shrewd eyes had read it in his face.

3
The forces that rustle and scuttle

London 1938

A delicate frost dusted the streets with glamour in the early morning light as Tommie found a ground-floor window and examined her reflection. The crushable, brownish uniform cap of the FANYs always seemed to her like a botched attempt at a flamboyant pie crust, and her skirt was creased from the train journey, but the tunic was acceptable.

She took the envelope from her pocket. Aside from her own name and address at the training camp, it was blank. There was no indication of the sender's organization, not even a return address, but this was the address given in the letter. She stared up at the unremarkable building in front of her and frowned. Why hadn't she joined the army nurses, or the RAF nurses or the Royal Navy nurses? Was it because the forces that she wanted to take on were the sort that rustled and scuttled unseen beneath the surface of the battlefields that those nurses served? Instead, she had joined the First Aid Nursing Yeomanry, and now she was fully trained as a driver-mechanic. She could fix and drive everything from ambulances to six-wheeled lorries. The fearsomely practical uniform – as fearsomely practical as a sensible skirt and thick stockings could be – would have made her mother blanche, and she had enjoyed getting elbow-deep inside stricken engines, but all the time, she had been looking one step ahead; and this was that step.

She had joined the FANYs because she had heard, on the hush-hush, that, for the right candidate, it could lead to meatier stuff; more yeomanry than first aid and nursing, and now here she stood, about to be interviewed for the meatier stuff.

The meatier stuff was the SOE; the Special Operations Executive, waggishly known as the Ministry of Ungentlemanly Warfare. They were the ones who took on the forces that rustled and scuttled beneath the surface – or maybe they *were* the ones that rustled and scuttled. It was a step into the unknown. There had been no advice about how to prepare for this interview; nobody seemed to know what 'the right candidate' for the SOE looked like. It was all very hush-hush.

She was five minutes early; five minutes to decide whether to take this step or walk on past the building. The city began to stir around her and the frost thawed, turning the pavements to quicksilver. She drew her fingers over her eyebrows, lifting them into an arch in an attempt to give her the illusion of wakefulness, and then there was nothing more she could do for herself, so she rang the bell and presented her letter to the doorman who read it carefully, then pointed her along an echoing corridor. She paused for a moment outside the specified door, and took a deep breath before knocking and entering.

The man sitting behind the scuffed and scruffy desk stood up politely, set down a gaudy matryoshka doll that he had been studying, and offered his hand.

"Good morning, Miss West. Please take a seat."

4
Parasite

London, 1935

"Russia?" Peter was puzzled, but Hendry was deep in his beer glass, and held up his hand for silence. The lunchtime rush had not yet hit the pub, and they were sitting quietly over a pint. Peter had attained a level of skill in armed and unarmed combat that had satisfied Hendry, and he was impatient for what was next. 'This commando training is usually taught by a team of experts,' Hendry had said at their first session, 'but we're doing it on the hush-hush, so I'm afraid you'll have to make do with me.' Peter had pulled his punches out of consideration for the older man, until he very quickly learned that this gallantry jeopardized his chances of surviving the training. When he made this observation, Hendry had grinned. 'Who do you think trained the team of experts?'

"Russia?" he said again, as Hendry put down his glass, "I understand that you have long-term concerns in that area, but surely at this point we're more immediately concerned about war with Germany?"

"Good Lord, no! Whatever makes you say that?" said Hendry lightly, reaching for a cigarette. "Yes, of course we are. But it's far more complicated than that. It always is, I find. By the way," he leaned forward confidingly, "the "w" word is strictly verboten in polite circles. Appeasement is the way to go."

"So, we're not gearing up for... for the 'w' word at all?"

Hendry threw him an old-fashioned look and told him about how Europe was like a series of ant colonies, and that because one of those ant colonies was becoming militant, everyone was getting antsy, and that, in diplomatic circles, there was talk of an alliance with a large colony of red ants.

"Only as insurance, of course," he added, "but looking to the future, I anticipate problems. That colony of red ants is, after all, extremely large and alarmingly dogmatic. You see what I'm getting at."

Peter nodded.

"You're more concerned about Russia than you are about Germany, and you need someone who speaks red ant."

Hendry smiled.

"Don't sell yourself cheap, Brandt," he said, "I have a dozen men who speak red ant. You are quite a different kettle of fish."

"So, you're sending me to Russia?"

"No. To Germany."

Peter sighed. Why was it that, with a top-flight university education behind him, he still found himself at sea in Hendry's world?

"You're sending me to Germany to spy on Russia? Wouldn't I be more effective spying on Russia from Russia?"

Hendry shook his head.

"Let's change the metaphor here," he said briskly. "Forget the ants. One of our big chiefs likes to talk in angling terms, so let's go with that metaphor. I am, in fact, a fly-fisherman in my spare time. Not course-fishing, I'm not the commando type; not a bait and tackle man... why does that sound like an unfortunate euphemism? Anyway, let's just say that it doesn't suit me to merely impale a worm on a hook and toss it into the water. Sending you to Russia would be like dropping you in the middle of the Atlantic Ocean in a row-boat armed with a child's fishing net. No, Peter, we'll be fishing for Russia in Germany, but not with a fishing net. I don't want sticklebacks."

"Is there a particular fish that you have in mind?"

"Admiral Wilhelm Canaris, the head of Abwehr – Germany's Military Intelligence," replied Hendry. "We're going to be parasites, you and I, Peter, we're going to suck on the enemy! Abwehr is a supremely efficient and well-stocked reservoir of intelligence on Russia, and in you I have found the perfect fly; the admirable admiral will not be able to resist you. No, Peter Brandt, it's not simply that you speak Russian, not even that you have German blood; it is that you are also well-educated, ethical and conspicuously honourable; precisely the combination of markings that appeals to this particular fish."

"And you don't think a British man joining German Military Intelligence in the current political climate would raise suspicions?"

"Not a British man; the rehabilitated son of a German war hero. And, yes, it will cause ripples for a while, but look at the climate we live in; Britain is sickly, and Germany is burgeoning. Why wouldn't a man with your parentage turn his back on Britain's shameful pacifism and her shoddy inclination towards socialism?"

Peter raised his eyebrows and Hendry grinned. Sitting up abruptly, he took a quick drag on his cigarette before perching it on the rim of the ashtray, a move which rasped oddly against Peter's senses; had he ever seen the man put down a lit cigarette? "Incidentally, old chap," Hendry said, his words simultaneously releasing the smoke and puncturing it into a dingy piece of lace-work, "you should know that I have been promoted. They're closing down the division, absorbing it into the 'establishment.'" His upper lip curled slightly over the word.

"Congratulations... Major Hendry," said Peter. "So, they've finally agreed to share their toys, and you're going to make an honest man of me. Will we be operating out of London?"

"Well, sort of. That is, everyone else will be, but not you. You won't." Hendry picked up his cigarette again, carefully sorting through his next words. "You see, Peter, you have never really been one of us and as it turns out, now you never will be." He turned the cigarette to examine its smoking tip. "The task I have in mind for you is not one that I want overseen by the powers that be. Do you catch my drift?"

"I'm nowhere near catching your drift," said Peter flatly. This was not strictly true; he was catching part of the drift – enough to know he wouldn't like the other part. Hendry grimaced.

"Let me be quite plain then. The project that I am about to suggest must be known absolutely exclusively to you and to me."

"I don't think I quite understand. You want me to go to Germany under no authority other than yours?"

"Not mine. Yours. You will be going to Germany under your own authority."

Peter stared at Hendry, finally understanding with a cold shock.

"The real thing?"

"Correct."

"You expect me to renounce my British citizenship and become German in order to spy on Russia – for your own private purposes – using the resources of what will, in reality, be my new country?"

"It will only be your country insofar as a parasite can be considered to be a part of its host. You will not renounce your British citizenship; that would draw attention to you from this side. Just claim your German birthright, but remain loyal to Britain."

Peter thought hard, and Hendry gave him time to do so, smoking quietly and waiting.

"But how will we communicate when the war starts?" he said eventually.

"Ah," said Hendry, with an odd little tilt of his head that

was the closest Peter had ever seen him come to expressing awkwardness. "We will communicate by post. I have post restante, of course, and other... resources, and I will be travelling to Berlin whenever I can, for as long as I can, and when that no longer becomes possible, we can arrange to meet in Switzerland; our sources assure us that Switzerland can be relied upon to remain neutral. Regular communication between us will be neither necessary nor advisable, but to answer your question fully; there will come a time when all contact between us must cease. At that point... well, I will see you after the war for a debriefing."

This last sentence dropped into Peter's mind so stripped of Hendry's usual rhetoric that he struggled to process it.

"And if we don't win the war?"

"Which 'we'?" Hendry said, returning Peter's gaze with demonstrably no intention of answering the question. Peter considered the proposition with the caution of someone examining a blown-out egg-shell.

"I will be reporting exclusively to you," he said slowly. "No one other than you will be aware of our... arrangement. There will be nobody to verify my identity if anything should happen to you."

Hendry's eyes had not moved from Peter's.

"The oyster and its pearl, Peter, the oyster and its pearl. I refuse to place either you or this project at the mercy of the short-sighted reactionaries in Whitehall. I am haunted by the faces that have perished unnecessarily, hanging from their damned red tape." A muscle in his jaw pulsed faintly. "I will not attach a safety harness to you, Peter. No safety net. No strings to snag and strangle you. You have to be alone and undetectable from this end as well as over there." The twirling dust motes waltzed silently.

"Only you." Peter said eventually, lowering his head to ease his thumb and forefinger down a line of tension that had suddenly set in between his eyes. "How is your health these days, Hendry?"

"My health is fine, Peter," Hendry said firmly. "Thank you for asking."

The bells of Saint Martin-in-the-fields sang softly through the open window, transporting Peter back to the eternal chimes of Oxford; to that neat, sequestered world, where people learned about how these things work.

"A parasite," he said quietly. "You couldn't come up with a more appealing image?" He sighed deeply. "How am I to survive, financially, until I get settled?"

Hendry closed his eyes fleetingly, then smiled and flexed his hands, cracking his knuckles.

"A troubled intelligence organization we may be, but not entirely ineffectual. It has been noted in your file that your father left a substantial sum in trust for his only son under the incontrovertible circumstance that you should assume German citizenship and take up residence in Germany. Were you aware of that fact, Peter? It would be understandable if your mother had neglected to mention it to you."

Peter shook his head. "I grew up a long way away from subterfuge and deceit. Of course I knew about the trust, but it might have been sitting on the moon for all I ever intended to claim it."

"You will need money for living until your claim on the trust is cleared, and I will provide that myself."

"Yourself?" said Peter, surprised.

"Well, I can hardly draw money from the government coffers and tell them "Mind your own business," when they ask me to account for it, can I? And I do have a little set aside for just such an occasion."

Peter smiled wryly. "How long could you possibly have been anticipating this occasion?" He stopped smiling. "Just how deep does your antipathy towards Russia go?"

A bleak light filtered through Hendry's eyes. He stared down at the beaten, scarred top of the table. "We have a pike waiting for us in the shadows of eastern Europe, Peter. If we neglect the big picture and throw everything we have into this battle with Germany, we may win, but we'll be on our knees, and whatever's left of Europe afterwards will become no more than fodder for the pike."

***

Anthracite, the king of coal, had brought his father across the sea to Wales. The grandson of a prominent Prussian family, with its wealth founded on industry, Hector Brandt had made his career with the General Staff, but he had been called to visit his family's interests in this land of gently undulating hills, this land that yielded wealth almost beyond value as its veins were bled to fire the arteries of industry.

Summoned by the siren call of riches, he had been bewitched by a vision. With hair as black as the treasure beneath her feet, with skin like milk, and eyes like the green of marsh pools, Lynwen Rhys had seemed to him a visitation from ancient times, from the legends of mighty kings and exquisite queens. A fitting bride for a notable son of Germany, a precious gem to mine, polish, and carry home to display, like a jewel, in a stately setting.

To Lynwen Rhys, the arrival of the elegant foreigner, and his unconcealed admiration for her, was an opportunity to leave the damp green hills behind and wear Sunday clothes every day, but when, shortly after Peter's birth, war loomed in Europe, Hector Brandt whisked his wife and infant son away from Berlin, back to the safety of this quiet place, and returned to Germany alone, to fulfil his oath to the Kaiser.

After his death, there had been a fractious exchange as Lynwen Rhys Brandt laid down the law to her mother regarding her son. She would not return to Germany when the war was over, but she would teach the child his father's language, and he would be made to understand, in defiance of the raging wartime propaganda, that his father's country was a great and noble nation. Furthermore, he would grow up well-spoken and well-educated. "Peter is to go through Eton and then on to Oxford," she said. "He will be raised as a gentleman, just as his father wished. Hector has provided for that. He was an honourable man and I will not dishonour him by defying his wishes for his son."

"Honour! What is honour worth if it spits on humanity and common sense?" her mother had muttered darkly. "The boy needs a home, not a children's prison and a lot of hot air." But she understood a promise, and when her daughter died in the influenza epidemic a few short years later, she held her little grandson against her comfortable bulk, saying, "Well, child, if you must endure posh-school nonsense in that flat country then you shall come home here every spare moment they give you. You will do well to know the mountain wind, and get some good honest dirt under your nails."

She came to understand that, although she had been right about the mountains and the dirt, her daughter had been right about the schools. Even running wild in the holidays, with scuffed knees and dirty fingernails, there was something intangible about her grandson that held him distinct from the other boys in the town. He had inherited his mother's coal-black hair, his eyes were the grey of the high mountain pools that are said to be fathomless, and there was an inner stillness about him that she recognized from herself, but the mantle of a foreign land wound unmistakably around his shoulders. *Hiraeth*

At an early age Peter had learned what it was to have the name Hun hurled at him, and when the playground battles escalated, he had hurled insults back, shouting that his father had been a fool to marry himself to common Welsh stock.

On days like those he would take himself off, beaten and bloody, to brood over what it was to be an outsider among others; to be *not one of us*. He taught himself how to fight hard and win those battles, and he did win. Every time. But he remained an outsider, and winning brought chill comfort when there was no friend standing at the victor's shoulder; only shame and guilt over that small, cheap retort about common Welsh stock – the only battle-colour he had had to fly – because his grandmother was his blood, and Wales had given him the only home he had ever known, and he loved it, but it didn't want him, or his name.

In later years, returning to this place, he had stood before the war memorial in town, reading the rows upon rows of Davies, Evans, Jones, Griffiths. He had learned about the Treachery of the Blue Books; about the parliamentary report of 1847, which noted that the introduction of the English language was necessary to improve the moral and material condition of the Welsh people. He had heard stories about the despised Welsh Not, and he had understood about the playground hostility towards an outsider with a German name and an English accent. The people he met on those later visits gently probed, listened, heard and saw him, and then drew him warmly in.

He would never become accustomed to how diminutive her house appeared to his grown-up self, because no matter how many times he returned to this place as an adult, in his mind its dimensions encompassed an eleven-year old's whole world. The air, though... The air still filled his lungs and his head with the breath of life itself.

He crunched up the unpaved lane towards the church and turned in through the gate, feeling the old leaden heaviness settle in his heart. Staring down at the grave, at the chiselled letters in the marble headstone and the still-fresh flowers in a china vase, brought by another visitor, he felt the soft wind buffeting him gently, like a sheet billowing on the washing line, and closed his eyes, remembering.

"I'll visit you often, Mamgu."

"You'll have your work cut out for you," she had replied, chuckling with the shreds of breath that were left to her.

"I mean, I'll visit your... your..." the word 'grave' wouldn't come. She had always been able to speak easily about such things, but he, at eleven years old, faltered.

"You'll not find me in any churchyard, Peter," she had said firmly, "I wouldn't be caught dead lying underneath an old pot of cut flowers." And, in sympathy for his confusion, she had explained; "At times like this it's kind to go along with other people's ways, because they'll be the ones left behind, and things will matter to them that no longer matter to those of us who are at peace."

This churchyard was not for her, he understood; it was

for others. Her hand had closed around his and squeezed gently, "I'll be with the living flowers, cariad," she told him, "Not the dead ones. With the rooted ones, not the cut. I'll be in the grass wherever you walk, and in the wind wherever you breathe. In this country or any other. So, don't you go catching pneumonia looking for me in that old churchyard. If you should want me, just be still for a moment, and you'll find me."

He had cried then, ashamed of his weakness in the face of her crisis, and she hadn't told him to hush, knowing how rare it was to see tears from her solemn little grandson. She had taken him one last time in her comfortable arms.

Later, when she died, he had not cried, but busied himself helping with the funeral arrangements. He had not cried since that moment, and although the memory still hung as heavily in his heart, he did not cry now, but turned and followed the lane uphill, on past the church.

The lichened stone of the churchyard wall gave way to bramble-tangled hedges, heavy with berries, like the long-ago berries that would burst in his hands, sending their purple-red juice trickling down his wrists, and set his grandmother tutting over fingers that would remain stained for days. Reaching the top field, he glanced around before self-consciously climbing over the gate. Mr. Davies Bryn Eglwys didn't hold with trespassers, and it was common knowledge that his wife watched over their farm through the eyes of the ravens, but even Mrs. Davies and the ravens hadn't been able to stop what was happening in the next valley.

Reaching the crest of the hill, he gazed down. Two miles below him the soft green had been torn open, like moss peeled from a rock, leaving a great, raw gash. Ugly iron structures poked out from the wound, their wheels spinning bleakly, drawing blackness out – coughing it out – from the occult depths.

Life renewed itself, he mused as the wind from the mountains, soft and wistful, not yet sharp with the certainty of winter, tugged and shoved at him. Life had been renewing itself since before the earliest memories of mankind, but this – he looked down on the carpet of black that crept up the valley towards him – this unnatural, accelerated destruction; was it possible for this damage to be absorbed?

And what of the other blight that loomed across the channel? Could that darkness be arrested? And if not, what then? Surely there must be a limit to the level of destruction that humans could wreak in this world and still find themselves enfolded in the embrace of life.

The valley behind him was still a rich patchwork of greens and golds, but was it enough to compensate for the destruction that lay before him? He turned his back on the darkness, closed his eyes, and leaned into the wind's embrace before stepping down into the valley.

5
Uniforms

Paris, 1941

"She was whoring for the Boche!" The receptionist's carmine-red fingernail stabbed at the page with the force of a nail hammering into a stake, and Tommie's brain juddered from its impact. The antiseptic air of the clinic was crackling with self-righteousness, but the doctor, Emil Franz, leaning his narrow body against a filing cabinet in the corner of the office, quietly sipped his coffee and pointedly ignored the dispute.

She knew she should follow his example, but the photograph of the young woman in the newspaper had done something to her. Even in the context of an occupied Paris where people could be dragged from their homes and shot in the street it had shaken her, because war should be about fighting the enemy, but this was personal. This was spiteful. Darker. Deeper. This was Paris turning on itself, even in the presence of the enemy.

The victim was a local girl who had been found lying half-conscious in an alleyway. In the photograph, she was surrounded by grinning men and women, and the graininess of the image did nothing to disguise the blood-filled egg that swelled up from one cheekbone to obscure her eye, or the crusted gashes in her shaved scalp, or the satisfaction on the faces of the patriots who surrounded her, leering into the camera lens with that awful righteousness, that vicious, oblivious righteousness, clinging to their skin like smoke. Tommie folded the newspaper and set it down in a gesture of moderation.

"But what good has this act done for France?" she said, aiming for a reasonable tone, "Petain's government is supplying the Nazis with census information to help them identify French Jews, and road crews are working to improve the roads so that German tanks can roll more efficiently across France. Wouldn't you say that they, too, are whoring for the Boche? Why not sabotage their efforts instead?" She caught the doctor's warning look and subsided, but the receptionist was gaining momentum.

"It is an insult to the memory of the men who gave their lives for France to see these women cavorting with their murderers."

"I understand that, Dorotea…"

"And it is a blow to the hearts of their mothers and sisters to see this sort of behaviour."

"I understand that too. But victimising these women…"

"She was whoring for the Boche," repeated the receptionist stubbornly, her faded lips compressing after the pronouncement. "Such women deserve what they get, and that goes equally for those libertines who run around with the men of the resistance. Bitches on heat, that's all they are. For every one of them that the Germans shoot, France is cleaner!" Her eyes skated over Tommie's face for a reaction to this, but Tommie had stilled herself. The receptionist was suspicious of her, and understandably so; what clinic nurse speaks finishing-school-perfect French? That had been a blunder, but it was too late to muddy her grammar now because, with the bloodhound nose of people like her everywhere, Dorotea had scented foreigner.

Tommie tucked the newspaper away in her bag, but that wasn't the end of it. Dorotea prided herself on being a respectable woman; she might hate the Germans, but she hated loose women more, and late that afternoon, when seventeen-year-old Yvonne Boudin, frightened, heavily pregnant, and poised to run, had stood in the waiting room, filling out her registration form only to be coldly ejected from the clinic, there had been a scene.

"That slut belongs in Drancy," Dorotea had announced, crumpling up the form and tossing it into the bin as the door closed on the young woman, "and if her brat turns out to be a girl, it can follow in its mother's footsteps, servicing the Nazis!"

Tommie's restraint flared and burned.

"If all of France thinks as you do, Dorotea, and we all turn on each other, God help us all, because you'll be seeing your grandchildren servicing the Nazis."

The woman's face twisted in fury.

"You'd better watch yourself, you little witch!" she spat, "Drancy is full of women like you."

"Nurse Pascal!" The door to the doctor's office whipped open just as Tommie was drawing breath for a response. "Please come in. I have a package ready for the Rue St. Jean. You may deliver it on your way home. Monsieur Arnaud must not be kept waiting for his insulin." Fuming, Tommie followed him into his office. "There are more important issues at stake here," he said quietly, when the door was closed, "you must not let her push you into indiscretion, Thereze."

"I know, Doctor Franz, but..." She stopped and gritted her teeth. He was right. And Dorotea's parting shot had put things into perspective for her. She watched as he lifted a battered leather bag onto his desk, reached inside with a specially modified steel tongue-depressor, and, with some effort, stretched one section of the seam at the bottom, lifting the base to reveal a hidden compartment. Taking a manila envelope from a drawer in his desk, he dropped it into the compartment, then pushed it closed and placed the medical supplies on top.

"Let's hope this goes some way towards alleviating the

disease," he said grimly as he handed the bag to Tommie. "As always, Nurse Pascal, take great care."

As she stepped out of the clinic, a storm of red banners on the corner of the next street announced another protest by the French Communist Party, which – in a mind-boggling inversion of priorities – was vehemently objecting to Germany's invasion of the Soviet Union.

Les Boches, that's what the French called the German soldiers; *cabbage-heads*, but it was no cabbage-head who had given the order permitting the Communist Party, marginalized by its own government, to function in France, knowing that this would generate disunity in the population.

Despite the influenza epidemic that was still decimating Paris, the protest was well-attended, and police officers were swarming, like wasps to a jam pot. Tommie stopped and turned back, but as she did so, two German soldiers, who had been heading towards the protest, moved to block her. Her skin prickled with the soft caress of a nettle as the senior of the two demanded her identification, waving his partner on towards the disturbance.

Putting the bag on the pavement by her feet, she reached into her pocket and handed over her papers. The noise from the crowd behind her was increasing, and the trouble promised to escalate, but the soldier's attention was stolidly fixed on Tommie. He found nothing amiss in her papers, and handed them back with a bad grace. Then his eyes fell on the bag.

"Du medecines," she told him, indicating her papers. "Je suis un infermiera. Eine krankenschwester."

Picking up the bag, he opened it, put his foot on a nearby bench, rested the bag on his knee and reached in. Fishing out bottles and vials and a caseful of syringes, he examined each one minutely. An acid fear swirled in Tommie's stomach as he leafed through the documents of the fictitious M. Arnaud. The name was a code, and the house at the address on the Rue St. Jean was vacant; Dr. Franz had given her the address for today's delivery verbally, but her skin was buzzing with nettle-rash, because now the bag was empty and the false bottom was beginning, in the face of this man's zeal, to look like a Boy's Own spy tool.

The soldier scowled, peering closely at the forms, and Tommie leaned in too. Suddenly she drew in a sharp breath and sneezed explosively all over the papers and over the soldier's hands. With a shout of disgust, the man backed away, and Tommie followed him, wiping her hands across her face, sniffing dismally and brushing at his sleeves, depositing influenza phantoms all over him. Cursing loudly, he flung the bag at her, threw the papers down, and pushed past her, heading towards the disturbance in the street ahead.

***

After delivering the package to Monsieur Arnaud's twitchy associates, Tommie found a window table at a local restaurant and sat, staring into her thoughts. Dorotea's words were echoing inside her head; Drancy, The Silent City. She shuddered. The receptionist was right, the internment camp at Drancy held many women like Tommie – women of the resistance – but nowhere near as many as the Jews who were being caught up in the Nazi dragnet.

She flinched away from the impotence; one small person couldn't stop what was going on, but to lose oneself in the enormity of it was to surrender to futility, and that was a step too far. Sighing, she took Yvonne Boudin's discarded registration form from her handbag, smoothed it out on the table, and made a mental note of the address. It wouldn't be a long walk.

When the waitress came to take her order, she glanced at the menu, made a face and ordered turnip soup. Making the face was important; she came from a land of stolid eating habits, and she *liked* root vegetables, but as part of her camouflage she had learned to complain about them. Poor Paris; the capital city of fine eating, condemned to a diet of root vegetables and emergency food. In a national crisis, any city is only days away from food shortages; that lesson had been learned more than once in history, learning how to avoid the national crisis in the first instance required more work.

Outside the window, the streets were growing quieter, and what had been an overcast day now put on a spectacular finale. The sinking sun released its fire into the darkening sky, and shreds of cloud burned like flaming torches over the uneven rooftops.

New figures emerged into the strange half-light, and Tommie watched as a cluster of young women; girls, really – not one of them older than Yvonne Boudin – entered the square from the far corner. Arm in arm and giggling, they gathered self-consciously on a bench nearby. She recognized the behaviour; any minute now... yes, here they were. A group of young men approached, drawn as iron filings to magnets, and, like a spark-plug firing, a flash of energy flew between the two groups. Tommie felt it; a charge of excitement passing through the collective bodies, then, like a forgotten dance from a forgotten century, the figures began to weave in and out of each other, the girls coquettish or shy, the boys alternately eager and tentative, uncertain and swaggering.

Like the little match girl with her nose pressed against a window, Tommie watched them as an outsider. But things were all muddled up, because in this story, she, the little matchgirl, was warm, and she had a meal in front of her, and they were outside in the cold, but they were still having more fun – were more vibrant – than she was. She frowned. When did *I* last sit on a bench and wait for someone interesting to walk by? There's no romance in me.

Taking a spoonful of her turnip soup, she re-grouped; but that's a *good* thing, because we're at war, and lightning-strike glances and spark-plug flashes have no part in war. And anyway, what they're doing isn't romance, it's biology. For pity's sake, girls, tuck it away in a drawer until it's over.

Faintly, from the square, a burst of laughter reached her, and she sighed. Until what's over? The war, or life? Life can be short, perhaps I should carpe diem. The little match girl died in her sleep on a doorstep, didn't she? I could die here, eating turnip soup. I'm not that much older than those girls – only by about seven years – but it seems so much more.

She shook her head irritably. No. She was doing the right thing. When war became inevitable, she hadn't gone out and draped herself over a bench, half-dressed in the freezing cold – alright, it was spring, but it was still bloody cold out there – she had tucked it away in a drawer and gone and found Hendry, because that was more important; she would not just sit back and wait for the enemy to set their boots on her hearth.

Across the square, a shop window lit up, illuminating a large noticeboard on the pavement. *Les Allemandes son Bienvenu ici. Deutsche willkommen hier.* And now she could see the bright colours of the girls' dresses, their neat little hats, red lipstick and rouge. The boys were in German military uniform.

"Pardon, Mam'selle, peut-etre j'asseyez ici, s'il vous plait?" The gruff voice startled Tommie, and its tentative, school-book French confused her momentarily. A man wearing the uniform of a middle-ranking officer in the Wehrmacht had approached and was indicating the chair across from her at the tiny table; might he sit with her? She stood up abruptly, sending her own chair crashing to the floor. The officer stared at her, then inclined his head apologetically. "Verzeih mir, bitte... Pardonnez moi, Mam'selle." He took a seat at another table and signalled for the waiter as she paid for her meal and left.

In the dark streets she walked quickly, with her shoulders hitched up around her ears and her nurse's scissors clutched tightly in her fist, making eye contact with nobody. All around her, rows of wrought iron balconies sagged drearily beneath elderly windows, but inside 423 Rue des Arbres, the apartment was fresh and clean. With a shy hospitality, Yvonne set a pot of coffee to brew on a tiny gas stove, and placed a plate of biscuits on the table.

"I haven't had anyone visit me for so long," she said,

"Not for a year, I think. Why is it that you will?"

"Because life goes deeper than war does."

The girl glanced across, unsettled by her sharpness, and Tommie scowled. Yes, the treatment of the young woman in the newspaper had angered her, but, for heaven's sake, the enemy had their boots all over France – all over Europe – and she couldn't for the life of her understand why girls like Yvonne Boudin would welcome them in. Why, then, had she committed herself to helping the girl? Because life is buffeted by circumstances, and people should not be sacrificed to principles.

She sighed. "You are pregnant," she said, more gently, "And you need someone to attend you."

"Attend me? You can help me? With the birth, I mean?"

"I'm a midwife."

And there it was; "I'm a midwife." Such a simple statement, but this was the genesis of the dreams that had sent her ricocheting into Hendry's office via the reading room of the British Museum.

The dreams had all been about the Burning Times, capital B, capital T; the witch-hunts. A time of mass executions, when anybody – not just old women who talked to their cats and laughed immoderately – could be accused of witchcraft and burned. Hanged first, perhaps, or drowned, often beheaded, but always burned. Men and women both, but mainly women. And Jews, of course, and communists and Muslims, and all the usual culprits; red-headed people, dark-skinned people, people with a cleft palate, people with a turn in their eye, foreigners, left-handed people, women who wore men's clothes. 'Witch' was just a convenient, catch-all term that covered multitudes of sins. Multitudes. Nine million people by the time it was all over.

And Tommie would have burned along with them back then; the Malleus Maleficarum had told her that. Man was made in God's image, woman was not. And midwives ministered to the unfathomable, unspeakable functions and strange tides of women's unholy bodies. Midwives not only worked beneath and beyond the parameters of the Church, they also flouted the fledgeling science of medicine. Midwives possessed knowledge that was sanctioned by neither the medical profession nor the Church. *Midwives surpass all others in wickedness.* And beneath it all – beneath the clinic nurse and the SOE agent – Tommie was a midwife.

***

On the way home from Yvonne's apartment, she allowed herself to think of Hendry... of the day she had walked down that echoing corridor and knocked on his door. 'Come in, and good morning, Miss West,' he had said, barely visible behind the twisting smoke of his perpetual cigarettes. His hand had penetrated the fug to place that painted matryoshka down on his desk next to an overflowing ash-tray. 'Please, take a seat and tell me why a midwife should want to join the Special Operations Executive.'

Why? Because when she had returned the books to the library, the dreams had started up again, advancing like currents under the Sargasso Sea, soughing closer each time. Then, crusted with flotsam from blasted civilizations, that last dream had swelled up, risen up, and surged right over her. She had woken from it with her nightdress twisted around her body like a barber's pole and an obliterating, impotent rage exploding inside her.

Enrolled in the FANYs, she had striven to be recruited for the SOE – variously known as the Ministry of Ungentlemanly Warfare, Churchill's Secret Army, and The Baker Street Irregulars after the address of their headquarters and, more poetically, after Sherlock Holmes' team of street-level intelligence gatherers. She could be ungentlemanly. And she had been top of her intake at marksmanship.

Why should a midwife want to join the SOE? Because the pyre in her dreams had been her own house; her modest, faded, comfortable little house, and that's where she set her boundaries; the world out there might get mangled, there wasn't a lot she could do about that, but her hearth was not to be touched. That's why this midwife had wanted to join the Baker Street Irregulars; because her hearth and her country had been under siege.

At their interview, Hendry had obfuscated. 'There's not much call for midwives or nurses in our business,' he had said blandly, 'perhaps you should stick to being the lady with the lamp; heroic womanhood and all that.'

Later, she realized that Hendry had already guessed at her convictions, and was playing her like a game fish, but he couldn't have known about the dreams, or Joan of Arc, or the uniforms. He wore a uniform, of course, and, at that point in time, so had she, so she hadn't explained her theory that uniforms camouflage the ticklish, lumpish, irregular forms under the surface, and make them look...well, uniform. She had sought out the people who train irregular people to defend their hearth without a uniform, and Hendry was one of those people, so she had told him about wanting to defend her hearth.

Now she looked around herself at a country that had been stripped of its uniforms; there was no army, no navy and no air force, just the uniforms of the occupying enemy, and a police force that was working shoulder-to-shoulder with them, winkling their own people out like snails from their shells, leaving them exposed for the carrion to feast on. The irregular people were there, under the surface, defending their hearth, and Tommie was with them, but there were no uniforms, and the lack of them left the whole country vulnerable.

***

Peering through the window of the treatment room into the courtyard behind the clinic, Tommie watched a few dirty gusts of wind flinging old pamphlets around. She pulled her cardigan tighter over her shoulders and warmed her hands under the hot tap before she approached the old man lying on the examining table.

"That's the difference between a good nurse and a doctor," he said, his speech muffled by the absolute absence of teeth. Louis Benet couldn't bear to wear his dentures, but he always carried them in his jacket pocket, 'just in case.'

Tommie smiled and gently removed the dressing from the man's ulcerated leg.

"What *is* the difference?"

"Eh?"

"What is the difference between a good nurse and a doctor?"

"Oh. Yes. You see, Doctor Franz is a good doctor and I won't say otherwise," the old man said staunchly, "But his hands are as cold as a dead frog, and as many times as I've told him, it don't seem to matter to him. Her out there, too," he added tipping his head in the direction of Dorotea's office, "There's been times when she's had to help out, and it's the same thing; her hands are as cold as a corpse. I've told her about it too; her hands, that is, but she's not one for listening to nobody. The last time the doctor sent her to help me, she touched me with her hands, and it was such a shock my hands just flew up in the air and knocked her glasses clean off her face!" The old man's thin frame vibrated with a wheezing chuckle and Tommie laughed. She finished cleaning his wound and secured the new dressing with a fresh bandage.

"Now, Monsieur Benet, you must get some exercise," she said, washing her hands with the pungent antiseptic soap. "All the cleaning and dressing in the world is not going to do any good if you don't get some blood circulating in those legs. Try going up and downstairs once or twice a day even when you don't need to."

The old man nodded politely, fished in his jacket pocket, slipped his dentures into his mouth and gave her a charming smile, removed the dentures and returned them to his pocket before shuffling out of the clinic.

The waiting room was empty except for a little girl of about nine years old, who was fidgeting nervously, polishing the toes of her shoes on the backs of her socks where they left streaks of street-dirt. From behind her closed window, the receptionist gestured to the girl, and she approached Tommie with an air of importance.

"Are you Nurse Thereze?" she asked, "I have a message for Nurse Thereze."

"Yes, I'm Nurse Thereze," Tommie said, "What is your message?"

The girl stood up on tiptoe to whisper into Tommie's ear.

"Yvonne's baby is coming."

***

Confinement, that's what it used to be called; a prim term for the dark, messy, painful and dangerous experience of childbirth. In ancient Chinese practice, a new mother would keep herself and her newborn confined for a month, isolated from the outside world, while they learned about themselves and each other.

Confined in the tiny apartment, Tommie attended to a flow of dammed words and punctuating contractions, because nobody else had allowed Yvonne to speak about Hans. At fifteen, Yvonne had been raped by an uncle, and, pregnant, she had been cast out by her family for the shame of it. Grim-faced nuns had taken her in, delivered a baby she never saw, found work for her in Paris and told her she was no longer welcome at home. But Hans... Hans had taken her to the Louvre even before he took her to bed. Hans had taught her about art, and Yvonne had taught him to speak French, and then he was gone, his division sent somewhere else.

When her baby was delivered, Yvonne took the child into her arms, "You don't have horns," she said softly. "You don't have horns and you don't have a tail. They lied."

***

"Monsieur Arnaud." Dorotea's summons received no response from the waiting room, and in the examining room Tommie hesitated, surprised, before placing the last roll of new bandage on the shelf. Monsieur Arnaud's people were not supposed to visit the clinic. She glanced into the waiting room at the same time as Dorotea poked her head through her window and glared at the patients sitting there. "Monsieur Arnaud," she said again, loudly. Five pairs of eyes sought the scuffed linoleum. The clinic had been open for ten minutes and the doctor was unaccountably late. "Well then," the receptionist snapped, withdrawing her head, "One less patient is a blessing."

At the far end of the waiting room the street door of the clinic swung open, slamming against the wall and causing the building to shudder. Dorotea's head appeared again, her face suffused with righteous wrath which curdled into white as a large man strode in, his uniform bearing the lightning-bolt insignia and two shoulder pips of a captain in the SS.

"Monsieur Arnaud will not be requiring his medication today," he said, placing his hand on the receptionist's head, pushing it back through the little window and sliding the glass shut. "He has been cured," he added, grinning around at the waiting patients. Tommie quietly closed the door of the examining room and slid the bolt, but the man's voice followed her, "Tell Nurse Thereze Pascal that she has a visitor... and tell her I'm not 'patient.'"

Tommie ran to the back door onto the alleyway, opened it, and collided with another large and tightly-packed uniform. She was handcuffed and manhandled back through the examining room. A shiny black boot was placed against the door she had bolted, and the door exploded into the now deserted waiting room. The SS captain turned.

"Ah! Here she is. No, Leutnant Brock, don't let those hands go too deep – you never know what you will catch. I've heard about these resistance women; you might as well fuck a whole brothel."

6
Guards, guns and clip-boards

Paris, 1942

Tommie's treatment under arrest had been almost perfunctory. Her involvement with the resistance had earned her solitary confinement in Drancy, but she was the last and smallest link in the resistance line, and the Gestapo wasted little time on her. She wasn't their problem anymore; an internment camp in Poland would sort her out. Until then, her cell in Drancy was a broom closet.

There was a bucket, which was emptied once a day, in the middle of the afternoon, when Tommie was escorted to a nearby toilet to perform that function, and there was a rug on the floor for a bed. She had been stripped of her clinic uniform – no indications of authority were tolerated – and provided with a frowsy black satin blouse and a heavy tweed skirt that reached almost to her ankles. She spent days and nights exercising to keep her muscles working, or huddled on the floor with the rug wrapped around her against the brutal cold.

Occasionally, she would be escorted outside to the yard, where she would see buses pulling into the yard, discharging their human contents, being loaded up with others, and pulling out again, like a newsreel playing over and over. It was done mechanically. Efficiently. There were clip-boards. Some of the clip-boards were wielded by the police in their dark blue uniforms, working shoulder-to-shoulder with the field-grey; the witch-finders may have been in charge, but they wielded an enthusiastic mob.

She thought of the Battle of Cable Street, when Oswald Mosely and his British Union of Fascists gathered to march through the east end of London, with its large Jewish population. The Metropolitan Police had been assigned to protect the fascist marchers, and their response went above and beyond the call of duty, as mounted charges and baton charges were launched against the hundreds of thousands of counter-demonstrators.

Ultimately, the march was rerouted, but while the anti-fascists celebrated their victory, the membership of the British Union of Fascists quietly increased. How would things play out these days, Tommie mused; for now, everyone knew who the enemy was, but if Hitler's Nazis managed to get their boots on British soil, would the British police work compliantly alongside them? Her impotence scorched her. She had ridden out like Joan of Arc to defend her country and her hearth, but how do you defend your country against your next-door neighbour?

Spring turned to summer, but any warmth in the world outside stood no chance of penetrating the walls. Then came the day when she woke and knew that something had changed. She stood up, stood perfectly still, and listened. Something was different. She turned sharply as the door to her broom closet was unlocked. In the doorway stood an SS lieutenant and a police sergeant, each bearing a clipboard. She was hustled out and down the corridor, down the stairs and into the yard, where a crowd of women were clustered around a waiting bus. Jabbed in the back, Tommie stumbled forwards, joining the women as a ring of rifles forced them onto the bus. Guards, guns, barbed wire, clipboards. There was no choice.

At Bobigny Station, too, there were guards and guns and

clipboards, but no barbed wire. This was her chance. Glancing over her shoulder, she backed up gradually, edging through the crowd, until, from the corner of her eye, a familiar motion pulled her attention; something warm and soft and reassuring. One woman had stepped aside, loosened her jacket, unbuttoned her blouse, and was nursing her baby. Tommie closed her eyes briefly. A seed of the future.

She glanced past the young mother, scanning the station for escape routes, but field grey and dark blue uniforms were everywhere. She stopped backing up. If she ran now, and if she wasn't felled by a hailstorm of bullets, where would she go? Paris was locked down. She looked at the train; cattle cars. Precious little hope of escape from there, but precious little wasn't none. A whistle was blown, and the police straightened up.

Tommie cast one more glance over her shoulder at Paris, and once again the young mother caught her attention. She was bending down to the suitcase at her feet, opening it and taking out some linens. She was kissing her sleeping bundle and carefully laying it at the bottom of the suitcase. She was replacing the linens on top, tucking them in tightly, closing the suitcase and clipping the clasps. She was standing up and calmly pushing the suitcase with her foot, pushing it behind a rubbish bin.

Another whistle blew, and the police stepped forward. Tommie shouted and turned against the tide of women pressing up behind her. She shouted again. The young mother heard her, saw her, and shook her head as she shuffled forwards with the women, leaving the suitcase behind. Tommie kept shouting. She didn't know what she was shouting, but she was shouting. Shouting and shoving, trying to plough her way through the women. Then the world jolted and went black.

***

She vomited before she even knew she was awake. Lying on her side, she hitched her sleeve up and wiped her mouth on her wrist. No point in fouling her clothes; skin could be washed, but wet clothes would be a death sentence.

Watching her sick seeping between the boards, she imagined it dripping onto the tracks below as the train lurched and rattled along. A fierce draught blasted her from a gap in the wooden walls, and eventually she forced herself to sit upright.

Only one face out of the countless faces in the cattle car turned towards her; the young mother met her eyes and did not look away, but Tommie looked away. She drew her knees up to her chest and then realized that she badly needed the toilet. There it was, in the middle of the car; a bucket. One bucket for... she didn't even want to count how many women there were. The bucket was only half full. Someone must have emptied it while she was unconscious, tipping it over to drain through the floor, like her sick. Now would be the best time to use it, before it filled up again. She wriggled out of her bloomers, approached the bucket and used it mechanically, shooing her mind away from the experience.

Returning to her spot, she forced herself to stare through the walls of the cattle car, picturing the landscape that they were passing through. She had no idea how long they had been traveling, but the sun was beginning to set behind them, which meant that the train was heading east. East, towards Poland. Towards those prison camps that people whispered about.

The suitcase would not leave her mind. It had been a small suitcase, but sufficient to contain hope and the end of hope. Tragedy and mercy tucked into one overnight case. Inevitably, her eyes found the still, upright figure of the young mother, sitting against the front of the cattle car, her legs tucked neatly to one side. Her eyes were blank, full of nothing, but they were fixed on Tommie, the only person who shared with her the knowledge of that tragic mercy. She watched as Tommie crawled across the car towards her, reared up on her knees, then sank down beside her and drew the mother into her arms.

The train rattled on fitfully, sometimes stopping, waiting,

and starting again. The day had disappeared. A night had disappeared too, dropping utter blackness into the cattle car, and now another day was passing, but something was happening. Two women were working away at something that was shining. No, not a something – a nothing. The shining thing was the late-afternoon sunlight, and the nothing was a hole in the wall where the side of the cattle car had rotted away. It was a small hole, not big enough for one leg to fit through, but the women were working on that, and the shining thing was getting bigger.

Tension blossomed in the car as more women joined in. One of the women was kicking at the edges, and another was scraping away with something – a belt-buckle – trying to weaken it further. Tommie leaned forwards, and beside her the young mother sat upright, letting her go. Crawling across the car, Tommie tapped the kicking woman on the shoulder, then turned, wedged her heels against a floorboard, and braced the woman's back with hers. Now the woman had purchase; something to lend force to her feet. Tommie couldn't see the progress, but a prickling excitement charged the air around her.

"Stop!" A voice was raised sharply on the other side of the car. "Stop it! You will get us all killed." Tommie felt the kicking woman turn.

"Killed?!" she snapped, "What do you think they're going to do with us when we get where we're going?"

"They are going to re-settle us," came the answer, "at least we will be alive. If we do what they say, and do it quietly, we will keep our dignity and our lives."

The kicking woman shook her head, and a brief flash of pity softened her face.

"When this train reaches its destination, we will have neither," she said, and turned back to her work. The other woman set her face into a grimace.

"I'm going to call the guards," she said. "You're risking all of our lives."

The kicking woman didn't turn around again.

"Someone, stop her," she said. Without hesitation,

someone pulled the scarf from around the woman's neck and tied it tightly around her mouth while others pinned her arms. The kicking woman nodded. "Anyone else want to call the guards?"

Tommie, with her back to the hole, could only guess at its progress, but suddenly the back that was braced against hers was no longer there. She turned just in time to see a pair of hands vanishing through the hole in the side of the car. It was a jagged opening, still only big enough for a medium-sized person to squeeze through, but one person had made it out, and a second was taking her turn, while a third woman worked on enlarging the hole, scraping with the belt-buckle, which had been left behind for the purpose. Even as she worked, the second woman squeezed herself into the hole, stretched her arms back over her head, and muttered something. A pair of feet positioned themselves against her shoulders.

"Oui?"

"Oui."

The feet shoved, and the second woman vanished through the hole. Another woman crept forwards, flinched away from the roaring, screaming void on the other side, and retreated. Tommie scrambled forwards, then turned back to the young mother. The light outside was fading fast now, and the cattle car was almost in darkness, but Tommie could just make out the shape of her, sitting perfectly still against the wall. There was a pale movement in the shadows – two pale movements – as the woman shook her head and gave a little wave. She had delivered her baby from the unthinkable life-death of those who should have been protected, and now she wanted no more of the world. This wild, desperate leap for life was meaningless to her.

Tommie inclined her head to the woman in a sort of salute, then turned and squeezed herself through the hole, blotting out the pain as the flesh was scraped off her legs and hips and waist. She surrendered herself to the force of the wind that whipped her sideways, until, finally, there was nothing of her inside the cattle car but her shoulders, her head, and her hands gripping the wood. A pair of feet braced themselves against her shoulders.

"Oui?" said a voice.

"Oui," she answered, and was ejected into the sucking void.

7
Germany is not our problem

Berlin, 1937

"So, you're clearly not Nazi material." Conrad was regarding Peter shrewdly over his coffee cup. "Of course, if you were of pure German stock instead of being tainted with English blood…"

"Welsh blood," Peter responded, "and not 'tainted'," he added quickly. Conrad laughed.

"And if you were a strapping specimen of gymnastic excellence," he continued, "rather than an enigmatic intellectual with a…" he tilted his head and regarded Peter critically, "reedy physique and merely adequate sporting ability; if not for those shortcomings, you would be gathered up into the bosom of the Party, willing or not."

Anticipating the direction this conversation was taking, Peter glanced casually around the room. Count Conrad von Heiden was renowned for not having a discreet bone in his body, but they had dined late, and the restaurant was mostly empty.

"It's no secret that I'm not one of Himmler's golden boys," he said, sitting back, "but when did you last look in the mirror, Conrad? What better advertisement for the flower of Aryan youth?"

"Think again," grinned Conrad. "My blood is as blue as my eyes, and they despise that. No, my friend, thanks be to God or Lady Fortune or whoever is responsible, neither one of us makes the grade. We are both flawed in the eyes of the Nazis; you because you think too deeply, and I because I am an aristocrat and, by that token, both morally and socially decadent."

Peter had slipped quite naturally into life at the Prussian Staff College, the Kriegsakademie, in Berlin, finding it not too different in its nature from the world of England's privileged sons. It was the pinnacle of military education in Germany, and many of its graduates went on to be selected for positions within the General Staff. Peter's father and Conrad's had been part of that tradition, and because of this, he had found himself embraced by it; an ugly duckling received into the society of swans. No longer 'not one of us.'

He signalled to the waiter for a fresh cafetière.

"When all is said and done, Conrad," he said coolly, "your attitude towards the Nazis amounts to little more than ingratitude, you know."

"Ingratitude?" Conrad responded sharply, "Do explain."

It had been a dull, rain-soaked week, and Peter was tempted to prod Conrad into the electrifying verbal fireworks that he could always be relied upon to produce.

"Well, thanks to National Socialism, when we graduate in a matter of weeks, we will assume leadership roles in an army that has been given back its purpose in life. So yes, Conrad, I accuse you of ingratitude."

Conrad rose instantly and vehemently to the bait. "I should be grateful to belong to an army that is swelling with empty pride?" he spat, "An army that is polishing its ceremonial sword at the prospect of having-at some phantom foe? Hitler promises to make Germany great again, but he is incapable of understanding what made Germany great in the first place. Rearmament?!" he snorted, "An army fights a foreign enemy and we have no foreign enemy; not even France or England can carry that honour. What is France today? What is England? They are two tired old men, still sagging at the knees after the last fight, and Hitler is shaking his fist at them like a lout confronting the doddering schoolmaster who caned him when he was a schoolyard bully. We mustn't become a lout, Peter. Hitler's thousand-year Reich is nothing more than a wet dream, and one day soon Germany will wake up with a mess all over the sheets."

Conrad's voice was harsh and Peter began to regret provoking him. "Alright, Conrad, simmer down, you're preaching to the choir here." He leaned forward and poured himself another coffee. "But you're wrong about the foreign enemy. Not France, and not England, perhaps, but there's something else coming, can't you sense it? Something even more threatening."

Conrad groaned. "Not Russia again!" He gave a hoarse cackle, "'By the pricking of my thumbs something wicked this way comes.'" You make an interesting weird sister, Peter, but you're so preoccupied with Russia that you can't see that the enemy is among us. No, not among us; he's squatting on top of us! He's puffing the people up with his hot air, and sooner or later the little prick will burst his own bubble and Germany will once more be the fart of Europe. We don't need Russia to squash us, Hitler will do it all by himself." He swallowed down the rest of his coffee and lifted his empty cup in a mock toast, "To our illustrious Fuhrer!"

"Conrad!" Peter's alarm was intensifying. He had put his friend into a dangerous mood.

"We are the last great hope for our country, Peter, it's up to us. I know where I stand, but what about you? What is your position?"

Peter felt himself tensing, raising his guard.

"You know my politics," he said quietly.

"No!" snapped Conrad, "Nobody does. You're a dark horse. You keep your opinions very close, and that's a wise tactic if you can do it. I can't. I want to know where you stand! I believe that you hate this plague as much as anyone, but I have never once heard you publicly denounce the regime."

"Publicly denounce...?!" he said, his voice rising, "Don't

you remember what happened to Otto Wells when he spoke out against the Enabling Act? We voted democracy out of existence when we voted a dictator into power. Did you somehow miss the significance of that?" He scanned the restaurant again. The staff were clearing the tables, and although nobody was looking in their direction, Conrad's words had been audible to anyone who cared to listen. He forced himself to lower his voice. "There can be no outspoken opposition. The government is not led by men of reason, and certainly not by men of honour. Their way is brutality and, for now, their way is working."

"Their way is working because it is cowing people," said Conrad, "People like you! Yes, I remember Otto Wells, and I remember his words on that occasion; he stood up to Hitler and said to his face, "No enabling act can give you power to destroy ideas which are eternal and indestructible." Did *you* miss the significance of *that?* You astound me, Peter. You're a good, brave man, I know this much about you, so why are you content to creep around, muttering behind your hand and glancing over your shoulder like some fieldmouse?"

Peter's own anger flared.

"Hitler holds the government by the balls, and the Brownshirts grasp the people by the throat," he hissed angrily. "Yes, ideas are eternal and indestructible, but voices aren't. Go ahead, stand on your soap box and wave your arms, and they will shoot you right off it without a second thought, and then what good will you have done for Germany? What good will you have done anyone?"

"Alright, alright!" Conrad held up his hands against the onslaught. "You're being cool and reasonable, as always, and you're damnably right, but how am I supposed to just stand back and watch my country being defiled? How do *you* do it, Peter? Ah, I know!" he added with a grin that didn't succeed, "you have inherited your mother's blood, and it is this English blood that remains cool in Germany's crisis."

"Welsh," Peter responded automatically. It would be better if the accusation were true, but it wasn't. Hendry's big picture, and the knowledge of the pike in the shadows, was all that kept him separate; kept him "not one of us."

In sombre mood, they left the restaurant. It was late, but the quiet of the evening was disturbed by the sounds of a commotion; angry, brutish voices and visceral thuds echoed off the walls, coming over the rooftops from the next street, and then the sound of skidding, scrabbling feet reached them from the alleyway that led from there. A young man had flung himself around the corner and was now speeding towards them, his shirt torn and spattered with blood from a long gash on his face. Catching sight of Peter and Conrad, he hesitated for half a heartbeat and then fled past them. With a heavy grunt another figure rounded the corner, using the wall to deflect his momentum and redirect him down the alley. The brown of his uniform was instantly recognizable in the fan of streetlight, and calculating his timing perfectly, Conrad planted a foot firmly in his path. The man's body launched itself in a trajectory that brought him to land, sprawling, not a body's length away from them. Wincing at the sound of the impact, Peter watched as he scrambled to his feet, cursing and spitting, and rounded on Conrad.

"Dog! I'll whip you until you whimper, you filthy cur!"

Conrad unbuttoned his tunic, pulled it off and tossed it to Peter.

"A dog, you say? Yes, I am a dog! A good German hunting dog who will stop at nothing until the last of you vermin is dangling on a fence with his neck snapped."

With a roar the Brownshirt ploughed into him and they fought viciously. Conrad, although outmatched in weight and muscle, had the advantage of intelligence and an education not lacking in traditional masculine sports, and he accounted very well for himself. He always did, Peter thought wryly, every time he picked a fight with one of Rohm's thugs.

Standing back, he kept a wary eye on the alley, anticipating the appearance of brown-clad reinforcements, but a sudden, strained silence drew his attention. Conrad was standing, arms spread and hands splayed open warily, because the Brownshirt, with his back to Peter, had drawn a flick-knife from his boot.

Peter draped Conrad's tunic over the wrought iron fence of the restaurant and quietly stepped forward. Grasping the Brownshirt's knife-arm, he twisted it quickly backwards and upwards until the man's fingers released the knife involuntarily into his hand. Maintaining the critical angle of the shoulder joint with his left hand, Peter held the knife up in front of the man's face with his right. The blade caught and distorted the cheerful lights from the restaurant's windows. The care that had been expended on whetting it was unmistakable. No matter how violent a man's soul became, Peter reflected, there would always be something – if only one thing – he cherished, and he guessed that, in this instance, this knife was it.

"Nice blade," he said into the man's ear. "Is it sharp?" With a quick motion he flicked the knife down to the man's throat, just beneath the jawline, and felt the angry resistance transform into a concentrated, careful passivity.

Grinning broadly, Conrad set about hobbling the Brownshirt with his own belt, then he pulled off the man's neckerchief and tied his wrists, removed his cap, rolled it up, kneed him in the groin and rammed the cap firmly into his gaping mouth. Peter shook his head at him. "Why must you put me in situations where I am forced to behave badly, Dieter?"

Retrieving his tunic from the fence, Conrad laughed. "Because I need to be reassured that there is a man of action lurking behind that damnably reserved façade," he said. "It's like watching Doctor Jekyll turn into Mr. Hyde. That knife-work was impressive," he added, circling an appreciative finger at the blade. "Very dark. I don't recall being taught that move at the Academy." Taking the knife from Peter, he tossed it down a storm drain and retrieved his tunic from the fence. "That's enough fun for tonight, Horst, let's get ourselves home."

***

The Tiergarten on a sparkling spring Saturday. The sun

was warm, the air was heavy with the smell of mown grass, and the ancient tree against which Peter sat raised its arms in salutation to the eternal sky, garlanded like a maiden with fresh new growth.

The remains of a picnic lay spread out before him, and at the far corner Conrad lay in the sun with his head pillowed in his fiancée's lap, drowsing as her fingers played in his hair. Next week they would graduate from the Kriegsakademie, and later in the summer, the countess von Heiden would host a ball to celebrate her son's engagement to Greta. Life was good.

In the shade of the tree, though, Peter was lost in unwelcome reflection. Sitting, sated and contented, in the easy company of good friends, the dishonesty of his position cast an uneasy shadow on him. If it were not for Hendry – and for himself – he might indeed be the born-again German that he professed to be. What if, under the influence of this exquisite day, he were to shake off that dichotomy and step into the sunlight?

He lifted his face to a periwinkle-blue sky almost obscured by an intricate lacework of leaves, and, seduced by the slow silence of the afternoon, he allowed his thoughts to drift. With his father's trust fund now sitting in his bank account, he could easily pay off Hendry's investment in him, and after that, thanks to Hendry's own scheming, there was no living person who knew of their agreement. How easy would it be to slip out from beneath the subterfuge of that half-existence and embrace fully this life that lay before him? *You see, Peter, you have never really been one of us, and as it turns out, now you never will be.*

He was Peter Brandt, son of Hector Brandt and he had – by all standards save his own – assumed his birthright. 'To live and die for the Fatherland,' Hendry had said. Was it possible that he had recognized in Peter something that Peter himself had missed? How tenuous was the thread that tied him to one country rather than another?

"The pensive Peter Brandt." Sultry and flirtatious, the voice brought him smoothly out of his reverie. "To others you may be an enigma, Peter, but I know your secret." Astrid, Greta's friend, lowered herself gracefully to sit beside him. "Shall I tell you your secret?" Her tone was playful, and Peter smiled.

"Do tell."

"You have been holding that beer glass for..." she consulted her watch, "ten minutes, without once raising it to your lips, and now it is warm, so I conclude that, even in the face of a far superior German beer, you are perversely longing for the dreadful, tepid stuff that the English drink."

He shook his head. "No beer is better than German beer," he said with deep conviction.

"An elemental truth. Nevertheless, there can be a certain comfort in familiar things – English beers for instance – however unpalatable they may be in the consumption."

"Unpalatable!" he drew in his breath sharply, "That's going too far. You wouldn't have said that out loud in the King's Oak." He lifted his glass and took a deep draught of the golden beer. "There! I drink deeply of Germany. Does that make you happy, Astrid?"

She smiled. "That will do for a start, but there is something else I wish to say." She picked a buttercup from the grass, twirling it between finger and thumb, and held it up to peer into its glossy depths. A faint golden reflection shone briefly on her forehead, but her playfulness had faded. "I believe we must drink deeply of life, Peter, but sometimes I feel that you hesitate over your own life. You hover, almost as if you are not entitled to plunge in."

She was watching him closely for a reaction, but he knew that the quick twist her words had wrought in his chest had not registered on his face, and he studied her in return.

With her soft, full lips, clouds of wavy blonde hair, and skin that a porcelain doll would kill for, Astrid was a beautiful woman, blonde and statuesque, almost as tall as himself. She had recently returned to Berlin from Oxford, where she had been studying the history of art, and together with Conrad and Greta, they had become a foursome, virtually inseparable. "If we hold life in abeyance," Astrid was saying, "if we resist it for one moment, it could be gone, and..."

He leaned forward, stopping her words with his mouth. "You are absolutely right, Astrid," he said, between kisses. "On a day... such as this, and with company... such as this, there must be no... parsimonious... sipping... at... life."

Drawing back and shaking her head, she regarded him through narrowed eyes.

"You're a fraud, Peter, and you're not fooling me for one minute. You never fully cast off that cloak of gloom you wear; you merely fold it up tightly and stash it somewhere deep inside."

He feigned horror. "Can this be? Has the earnest art historian defected to the pseudo-scientific ranks of psychoanalysis?"

"Peter, I'm serious!" she said, laughing.

"Serious?! On this glorious day? And cloaks of gloom, too. Shame on you!"

"Peter..."

"Astrid."

Astrid looked into his eyes, shook her head, and capitulated.

***

"I swear by God this sacred oath that I will render unconditional obedience to Adolf Hitler, the Fuhrer of the German Reich and people, Supreme Commander of the Armed Forces, and will be ready as a brave soldier to risk my life at any time for this oath."

The infamous oath was spoken by the eight standing here in the gardens of the Kriegsakademie; the eight who had been winnowed down from the hundred who had passed the entrance exam three years earlier, but this oath... this was a thing that every soldier – every soldier – had to speak.

"I trust you had your fingers crossed, my friend," Conrad grinned, his blue eyes unclouded. "Oath, my arse! Hitler might swallow the army, but I will be a legal worm burrowing through his intestines, eating him away from the inside out; a political assassin."

Grey dishwater trickled through the sludge in Peter's veins. He forced his voice into a level tone. "Political assassin? Conrad, what are you talking about?"

"Relax," Conrad laughed, "If you like, we can put more emphasis on "political" than "assassin", and when I say "assassin" I mean purely in the sense of his political career." Lowering his gaze too quickly for Peter's liking, he glanced around at the newly-minted officers around them. "So, what about you, Peter?"

Suppressing the echoes of Conrad's words, Peter shrugged. In spite of all the philosophical and ethical justifications he had explored in preparation for this occasion, the speaking of the oath had coated his mouth and his brain with a foul residue. "I still think the army holds the answer," he said shortly.

Conrad shook his head, suddenly urgent. "Don't fool yourself," he said, "For God's sake, I know how glorious that whole General Staff thing can seem; it's in my bone marrow, but all that's gone now. Perhaps for good."

"And your way is better?" Peter snapped. Conrad had chosen to turn his back on the army and make his career with the Reich Ministry of Justice. "The law is no more immune to Hitler than the army is. There is no clear path here, Conrad, and in the absence of a clear path, I choose the army."

Conrad stared at him unhappily. "Then promise me one thing, Peter, don't trust the generals. The army is like a plaster cast. Remove a plaster cast and the muscles beneath are wasted. The generals have no instincts of their own to hold them upright any more. Hitler is a madman and a criminal, but they will follow him because he is their Commander in Chief." Conrad's face was tight with concern. "Don't trust the generals with your life, Peter."

Greta had woven her way through the crowd in time to catch that last comment.

"There's such a thing as a time and a place, Conrad," she

said, amused, "and this is neither."

Conrad closed his eyes and pulled Greta into his arms.

"You'll be missing a big party, Peter," he said, "I'm going out with a noble bang. Fireworks, no less! Are you sure you can't make it? What cloak and dagger assignation denies me the company of my best friend tonight?"

***

Yes indeed; what cloak and dagger assignation had drawn him away from his closest friend on this day of toxic significance?

The taxi dropped Peter at the Eiserne Bridge, and he walked between the blocky wings of the Pergamon Museum, crossing the Court of Honour to the reception area, where Hendry was waiting on a bench, reading a pamphlet. He stood up as Peter approached, and shook his hand.

"Congratulations on your graduation, Lieutenant Brandt."

Peter smiled, pleased to see him despite the lingering disquiet from the oath. But Hendry always had a purpose for these meetings – and a good reason for the venues he chose – so he kept himself disengaged, not allowing himself to be ambushed, even as they stood, dwarfed, before the monumental Altar of Pergamon. Until, turning down a passage guarded by two large stone lions, Hendry stopped short. "Ah, this is what I came to see," he said with satisfaction.

Peter looked up from examining the stone lions, and his chest prickled like a fistful of sparklers. A blaze of cobalt blue stretched before him; a man-made canyon of ancient, blue-glazed stones, ornamented with golden, prowling lions that stalked towards him and then past him at shoulder height. Beyond this, at the far end of the blue avenue, a structure rose up, kicked a hole in his chest, and then reconstructed itself, brick-by-brick inside his ribcage.

"The Ishtar Gate," said Hendry softly, "and the Processional Way. The most powerful representation of the magnificence that was Babylon. Can you imagine seeing this structure rising out of the Fertile Crescent, six hundred years BC?"

Peter heard Hendry's words, marching like the footsteps of soldier ants beneath the unqualifiable resonance that the gate had struck in him. Like a cobalt tuning fork. "Ishtar was the goddess of war, love, sex and procreation," he was saying. "Also had a hand in music, joy, abundance, death and vengeance," he added. "Didn't leave much for the other goddesses to do, one would think."

"A goddess of war," said Peter, coming down to earth, "That always seems redundant, when men are so adept at the spadework."

"The ancients would disagree," said Hendry. "Think of Anat, Bellona, Freya, Durga, the Morrigan... And there's no more effective battle-cry than "God is with us!" By the way, Peter, slight change of plans; our trout has turned cannibal. He's hatching a plot to dethrone the chief trout."

There it was; the revelation. And he was ambushed. Peter stared at him in disbelief.

"Canaris? No, of course not!" He shook his head; that couldn't be right. The chief of Abwehr – German Military Intelligence – couldn't be plotting against Hitler. Hendry's elaborate imagery must be getting too obscure for him. "I don't follow you, Hendry."

"Canaris, yes," said Hendry firmly, "but for discretion's sake, let's use 'Trout,' shall we?"

Peter cast around, trying to assimilate the new information. "Trout! But that's excellent news! So why a change of plans? If this sort of activity is on the table, the whole picture changes. I can be there to monitor the situation; the army will overthrow Hi... the chief trout, and the problem can be solved in one blow."

Hendry's eyes could command the power of a steel rivet, and right now they were riveted to Peter's face.

"Germany is not our problem, remember?" he said, "Tell

me you remember the big picture, Peter, because that's what counts; not the icing, but the cake that's underneath it. We can't afford to be led astray by will o' the wisps."

"That trout is not what I would call a will o' the wisp," Peter said sharply, but Hendry had turned away to examine the painted brickwork of a golden lion. With his back turned, he shook his head emphatically. Peter tried to quell the bitter taste of disappointment that had risen in his mouth.

"So, what now? Where does this change leave me?"

"It has to be anticipated that the good admiral will, albeit with the noblest of intentions, sink his own ship," answered Hendry, squatting down to investigate what looked like a band of daisies beneath the feet of the marching lions. "We would wish otherwise, of course, but we have to be circumspect."

"You mean we have to assume that he will fail."

Hendry gave him an old-fashioned look.

"Blithe optimism is not a useful trait in our business, Peter. I don't want you going down with him, so you must jump ship in favour of another vessel."

"And after all that work you put into selecting the perfect fly for your fish."

Hendry smiled grimly. "There are other fish in the sea. But what sea shall we cast you into next? I have my ideas, and you must have your own, let's see if we concur. You go first."

"The General Staff," answered Peter promptly.

Hendry clapped him on the shoulder. "We concur!"

8
Riptides

The headquarters of the Army High Command in the Bendlerblock enjoyed fresh breezes from the Tiergarten, just one block away, but in the office of General Wilhelm Metelmann that morning, those breezes were not admitted.

Summoned to an audience, Peter stood, suppressing a stab of claustrophobia, in a muffled room of red velvet draperies that reached down in fringed and tasselled layers to a deep carpet. The man behind the desk finished a few notes, scrawled his signature with a fat, gold pen, and glanced up, squinting owlishly over thick spectacles, waiting for him to introduce himself.

"General Metelmann, sir, I am Lieutenant Peter Brandt. I understand that you wished to see me?"

Watery eyes scanned Peter's face and washed with recognition, then, heaving his bulk out of the chair, Metelmann swung himself around the desk with an intensity of purpose that caused various sets of Peter's muscles to review Hendry's unarmed combat training.

"Hah!" he exclaimed, peering into Peter's face, "Hector's son!" He grabbed Peter's hand in his meaty paw and pumped his arm in a vigorous handshake. "I knew your father, my boy. Dear God in heaven, it's like having him standing here before me."

Somehow Peter had not anticipated meeting someone

who had known – and who remembered – his father before his death over twenty years ago. He remained silent, but the general's voice carried with it the thickness of every layer of flesh that packed his neck, and Peter caught himself trying to clear his own throat as Metelmann launched into an homage to Hector Brandt, the noble soldier. "Your father was a brilliant military strategist and an honourable man. A fine man, a great man," Metelmann concluded, "Although I imagine you know very little about him. You were an infant when he left, no?"

"That is correct, sir; I have no memory of a father."

Metelmann's florid complexion deepened and his eyes bulged. Peter stood perfectly still, and watched his own words twisting in front of his eyes as the remaining air in the room vanished, inhaled by the carpet. It had been a petulant response to his prodigal-son reception in this country; to the chorus of voices which proclaimed that the privilege he now enjoyed – his whole existence, in fact – was at the behest of Hector Brandt, as though Peter had sprung, fully-formed, from his father's excellence, like Aphrodite from the head of Zeus.

He clenched his jaw. In this place, of all places, where his father was revered, he should have been prepared to swallow his reservations about the man. 'Righteous indignation,' Hendry had said, 'an easy trigger to pull.' Peter had fallen at the first hurdle.

A fictitious image had appeared in his mind at Metelmann's eulogy for his father; an image of his mother, very young, her hand resting on a suitcase as, with a brief glance at their sleeping son, Hector Brandt turned and walked away – a fine man, a great man. The uncomfortable silence had become harrowing before Metelmann spoke again.

"You were raised by your maternal grandmother, I believe," he said eventually. "I met her once. A very spirited person. She was of... Celtic blood, wasn't she?"

The air around Peter shifted in the approximation of a chuckle and Peter smiled involuntarily, a smile that had its genesis far from that opulent room.

"Yes, sir. She was Welsh, and very spirited."

Satisfied that he had found the culprit behind Peter's words, Metelmann regained his former benevolence.

"When a man hears the call of his country, Lieutenant Brandt, it is impossible for him to resist," he said, leaning back in his chair. "Your father responded to that call, but he fulfilled his duty to your mother by endowing her – and you also – with financial support and the dignity of his name. A woman can have no further claim on a man's soul."

"Yes, sir." said Peter.

"And now here you are, responding to that self-same call to dedicate yourself to your country." The general paused over a thought. "I trust that you yourself didn't leave any, er... encumbrances behind in England?"

"No, sir," replied Peter, hoping fervently that the audience was over. There was a discreet knock on the door that led into the next office, and an aide appeared wearing a fretful expression. Metelmann dismissed Peter with another vigorous handshake and Peter stepped out into the corridor, standing for a moment to draw breath.

Further down the corridor, two officers were making their way in his direction. One of them had seen him leave Metelmann's office and was now watching him curiously. It seemed that he asked his companion a question and, in response to the other man's reply, he observed Peter with heightened interest. As they approached him, Peter recognized the senior officer as General Ludwig Beck, the highly respected Chief of the General Staff. He paused and saluted the two officers, and as they returned the salute, Beck addressed him.

"Lieutenant Brandt, isn't it?"

"Yes, sir."

"I am General Beck, Lieutenant Brandt. I knew your father many years ago. You resemble him very much."

"So I have been given to understand, sir." He knew that his response had been impeccably polite, but the older man evidently detected the undercurrent of distaste in it and, puzzled, his gaze cut to Metelmann's door.

"You have been paying a visit to General Metelmann."

"Yes, sir. It seems the general was a friend of my father's. He was kind enough to tell me a little about the man."

Beck studied Peter's face in silence for a moment. "General Metelmann was a contemporary of your father, Lieutenant Brandt, as was I," he said slowly, "but your father was a very private man, and I would venture to say that nobody knew him personally. All that anyone could honestly say about him is that he was a supremely honourable man who loved his country above all else." He paused, and a look of intense speculation came into his sharp blue eyes, then he nodded at some internal conclusion. "Above all else," he repeated. "You have lived in Germany for how many years now, Lieutenant Brandt?"

"Just over three years, sir."

"And do you think that you can truly love Germany?"

The acute eyes were fixed on his and, with a sudden conviction that this man deserved honesty, Peter obliged.

"I see this country changing before my eyes, sir, and I know that it has changed greatly since my father's time, but where the spirit of Germany is intact, I feel privileged to embrace it. Yes, Herr General, I can truly love this country."

Beck smiled and the lines carved into his face relaxed. "Without a doubt, you are Hector's son." Once again, Peter could not hide a flicker of ambivalence, and once again Beck caught the expression. He darted a sour glance at Metelmann's door. "As I have said, Lieutenant Brandt, I will not claim to illuminate for you your father's character, but neither should you allow anyone else to do so." His stern mouth twitched with wry amusement, "What I will say, though, is that I used to watch your father escape from his conversations with Metelmann wearing the same, slightly sick look that I saw on your face a moment ago. Perhaps that will tell you something." He nodded. "I wish you the best, Lieutenant Brandt. I am sure we will meet again."

It was with gratification and a disconcerting sense of destiny that Peter received, some weeks later, his promotion to the rank of captain, and the order of his transfer to the staff of General Ludwig Beck.

***

"I don't believe you bought it!" Awe, disapproval and envy were doing battle in Conrad's face. "Maybe there's a touch of the rebel in you after all."

Peter laughed.

"Rebellion is a state of mind, my friend, a motorbike is just a motorbike."

Conrad circled the Pioneer admiringly.

"Maybe so, but Greta wouldn't let me get near one of these things. She wants me alive. My God, but it's a beautiful machine!"

Peter took out his pocket handkerchief and carefully polished a smudge from the engine of the machine. He knew, now, that Conrad was involved with a network of officers and civilians who were actively opposed to the Nazi regime.

"If Greta wants to keep you alive, she should take a closer look at how you spend so much of your free time," he said mildly. "And what about your mother? Anything… unseemly that you're involved in will impact her too."

"My mother?" Conrad laughed softly "Who do you think put together the guest list for Friday?" He shook his head. "No, they're fully supportive of our business. To be honest, I'm not sure about my mother, but I think Greta would rather see me in front of a firing squad than riding on two wheels."

And they were. Supportive of the resistance. Just how extensive the resistance was, and how committed, Peter was to discover at the engagement ball.

As he stepped through the door with Astrid that night, the air in the von Heiden house was sparkling like champagne. The banquet room was swirling with silks and lace, and a small orchestra was playing a merry Strauss waltz. There was no nod to modern times here; the whole scene might have been an echo from history. Peter hesitated and muttered in Astrid's ear.

"I'm not ready for this yet, let's find Conrad and Greta."

In the dark-panelled games room they found clusters of guests caught up in heated discussions, and made their way to the far corner where Greta was beckoning to them from a deep leather armchair. Leaning down to kiss her cheek, Peter turned towards an insistent voice, and recognized the speaker as Karl Friedrich Goerdeler, the former mayor of Leipzig.

"To paraphrase a great Prussian statesman," Goerdeler was saying, "Hitler 'has Hell in his heart and Chaos in his head.'"

A hand touched Peter's arm.

"We're supposed to be celebrating love and life, not doom and gloom," Astrid said with a wry smile, "I'll be in the ballroom." He watched her graceful figure disappearing through the door, until a familiar face drew his attention.

"That's General Erwin von Witzleben." Conrad had appeared at his side, "soon to be Field Marshal, so the rumours say, and in the far corner over there, that's Hans Oster from the counter-intelligence office. Ludwig Beck sent his regrets; he's not one for socializing, but you would know that already."

Beck? General Beck was involved in this? Peter's head swam as Conrad introduced him to his guests, Hans von Dohnanyi from the Ministry of Justice, who was Conrad's boss; Hans Bernd Gisevius, a prominent and outspoken lawyer; the brilliant young theologian Dietrich Bonhoeffer, and more... so many more. Here in this room was the nobility of spirit that had built Germany into the great nation that his father had loved and died for. Here was the dynamism and clarity of purpose that he himself had been searching for. And he must have no part of it, because of Hendry's big picture. He excused himself and left the room.

"Peter..."

Conrad had followed him to the hall. Peter lowered his

head and sighed.

"Conrad, I don't belong in that room. Not because I disagree with what you're all trying to do, but for reasons that I can't give you, I just can't participate." He laid a hand on his friend's shoulder, "For the peace of mind and productivity of the men in there I have to absent myself." Conrad regarded him soberly, then nodded and turned away.

Heading towards the ballroom, Peter hesitated again, and instead sought the peace of the drawing room. Outside, the night was warm, but old houses are always chilly, and in here a fire burned in the grate, its flickering glow dancing with the candlelight over countless portraits that hung from the walls. Family portraits. He sighed.

On his arrival in Germany, he had set out dutifully to trace his father's family, only to find that, in contrast with the high esteem in which the army held him, Hector Brandt had been considered an ill-favoured branch of his family tree. This state of affairs originated in a forbidden marriage, many years ago, when a daughter of the family defied her parents to marry a Belgian industrialist involved with the Antwerp-Cologne railway line.

When, two generations later, their grandson, Hector Brandt, took a commoner and a foreigner as his bride, his branch of the family was pronounced fit only for pruning, so when Peter turned up unexpectedly and introduced himself, the relief was palpable when he declined any claim on the family coffers, consented to the pruning, and took himself off, along with his unwelcome name, content with just the independently-acquired fortune of his father.

Incensed by this, the countess von Heiden had drawn Peter gently, by degrees, to her own home and hearth. He sighed again. Family.

On the wall, one portrait caught his attention, and, moving closer to study it, he saw a young woman with eyes the precise shade of Conrad's, sitting demurely for the artist. Her mouth was set in the conventional expression of solemn dignity, but in the eyes, there was the unmistakeable flash of character that he knew so well.

"My mother." He hadn't heard her enter, but the countess was standing in a whisper of taffeta at his shoulder. "Conrad takes after her, doesn't he?" she said softly. She indicated the portraits. "We were a big family once, but no more. This house was always full of people when I was a girl, but these are troubled times, and I have to be very selective when I put together a gathering like this one." She paused, watching his face, and there was a new guardedness in her eyes that tore his heart just a little bit. "My guests tonight are some of the people I admire and trust most in the world," she said quietly. "The company in that room is of one mind, and I think you know what that mind intends; does that... discomfort you?"

Impulsively he took her hands and held them firmly. "Your Excellency, I know of those men by reputation. I have listened to some of them speak, and I have read what others have written. My hesitation to join their cause does not come from a conflict of convictions, not by any means, but..." He found a half-truth he could offer her, "I have been in Germany for only a few years, and I feel that it is not my place to agitate against the government, regardless of how opposed I may be to its policies." He released her hands awkwardly and she smiled up at him, the guardedness gone.

"I thought as much, Peter. Did you know that your goodness shines from your face?"

His throat felt raw. This woman's kindness and warmth touched him to the core. Fumbling for a response, his gaze fell on the portraits. They were alive with the combined light from the fire and the candles.

"I never hear Conrad speak of an extended family."

She shook her head sadly. The Great War, the influenza epidemic, and a death in childbirth had left only herself and Conrad to carry the von Heiden name.

"When I find myself overwhelmed by the terrible things that are being done in this country," she said, "I look at these faces and imagine the way things will be once these horrors have passed." Her face brightened and she rested her hand on his arm, "Ah, Peter, imagine the children that Conrad and Greta will have." The fire sent out a burning ember that rebounded from the screen and fell into the tiled surround, fading rapidly to a charred black as they watched it together.

"There you are, Peter." Astrid had appeared in the doorway. "Would you mind terribly if I steal him from you, Your Excellency? My feet are just itching to dance."

The countess smiled. "I wouldn't relinquish him to anyone other than you, Astrid, but you must promise to take good care of him. Peter is very important to this family." She reached up and kissed him briefly on the cheek before pushing him gently towards Astrid and turning again to gaze at the portraits.

Tucking Astrid's hand into the crook of his arm, he led her to the ballroom, where a world of light and colour and swirling motion engulfed them. He felt her supple body adjust to his lead, and the evening passed in a blithe diorama. Lost in reverie, he realized he had missed a comment that Astrid had made, and there was a direct and penetrating light in her eyes, so he bent forward to catch her words.

"I said, now that Conrad and Greta are formally engaged, things will start to change," she repeated.

"Change in what way?"

"Well, people will be expecting us to announce our own engagement."

Peter missed his step, caught his foot on Astrid's and nearly stumbled. "Our engagement?"

Astrid laughed. "Don't look so terrified, I'm only telling you what other people will expect."

"And you? What will you expect?"

"Ah, yes. What will I expect?" Her expression grew serious. "Perhaps we should sit this one out." He followed her to a small alcove furnished with a plush couch. A manservant appeared instantly, bearing a tray clustered with champagne glasses. Astrid took one but Peter declined and waited to hear what she had to say.

"Peter," she began gently, "you know that I'm a modern

woman, and that I don't play the usual courtship games. On the other hand, I do like the familiarity of certain social forms, and I am ready for the next stage of my life. I want to be married, with children and a household of my own to run. She took his hand in hers, "I like you very much, Peter, more than any man I have met, and I want you to be candid with me..." She stopped and laughed quietly. "No. There's no need. I see it written all over your face."

"Astrid, I..."

She shook her head. "It's alright, Peter, you don't have to explain anything. Marriage is my goal and it is not yours." She smiled sadly. "I said I'm a modern woman, but here I am yearning for marriage, family, and tradition, and prepared to sacrifice a delicious romance for the sake of that goal."

Peter closed his eyes, and the countess' dream wound itself around him. All the good things he could imagine wanting were in this house; nobility of purpose, honour, family and traditions, a household where good friends would gather. What was there to stop him from embracing such a picture? In a year... two years, maybe, when the war was over – because it was inevitable that there would be a war – and if Hendry's plan succeeded... would a wife be able to forgive a husband who had deceived her so utterly about who he was and what he intended? No. The dishonesty would be too much.

On the other hand, if he chose to sever himself from that deception and become what he was perceived to be, he could marry Astrid and set up a household just like the one he was in now. Their children would grow up with Conrad's and Greta's. Hendry's plan probably wasn't even achievable. It would take just one step – a step that he was perfectly qualified to make – and he could have it all. Until the pike emerged from the shadows to savage that world. He shook his head and sighed.

"I will miss you, Astrid." He lifted her hands to his lips and kissed them. "I wish you great happiness in your life."

"And I wish you the same, Peter. I hope that you will

find a woman who can lift that cloak of gloom from your shoulders." She squeezed his hands, "For now, though, I'm not prepared to waste this perfectly lovely occasion in brooding. Will you take me to dance?"

***

Riptides were forming. Sinkholes and whirlpools gaped, swallowing people and institutions into the void of the Enabling Act, and Peter was unexpectedly thankful for Hendry's big picture, which allowed him to be not one of us; thankful for a purpose that insulated him – isolated him – from the quaking civilization around him.

Work kept him busy for long, full days that frequently stretched into late evenings. Ludwig Beck's staff would leave, and in the silence of the office Peter often found himself deep in conversation with his senior officer.

'A soldier should have no political agenda,' Beck would say firmly. 'His duty is not to question his orders, but to follow them to the best of his ability. If a soldier forswears that duty, he forswears his honour.' Yet Beck was involved in subversive activities.

From the orderly corridors of the Bendlerblock, Peter watched as the street-fighting tactics of the Nazis cut the legs out from beneath the army. It had started with naming Hitler in the oath; a bullet fired into the air by War Minister Werner von Blomberg – even Hitler had not dreamed that one up – but it would ricochet on and on into the future, and now Blomberg was to be married, with Goring as his best man and Hitler as a witness.

"I am to attend Blomberg's wedding tomorrow," Beck announced to Peter one Friday evening as he prepared to leave the office, "The man who has single-handedly compromised the sovereignty of the army, and I have to stand there and wish him well." He shook his head, "This decline will have to be arrested soon, or the damage will be irreversible." He buttoned his greatcoat and put on his cap.

"Surely you're not planning to walk home in this filthy weather, Peter, ride with me; I'll have my driver drop you off wherever you choose."

***

"He married a whore, for God's sake! Blomberg's bride used to be a whore." It was no more than a week after the wedding, and Beck had closed the door before making his announcement, conscious of the clerical staff in the outside office, although the information he delivered was already the delight of scandalmongers across Berlin. "She has a criminal record with the vice squad, and he allowed Hitler and Goering themselves to bear witness at the ceremony!" Overcome with outrage, Beck strode to the window and stared out across the city while his junior officers digested this information.

"Perhaps it will come to nothing," ventured Wagner, Beck's adjutant, who had often and openly demonstrated his distaste for Blomberg, "It suits Hitler nicely to have a spineless puppet for his Minister of War. The Fuhrer appreciates a good toady with no opinion of his own, and there's none quite like Blomberg; he won't want to lose him."

Beck's voice rose in anger. "It is unacceptable for the first soldier in the country to have a whore for a wife. We cannot have officers of the Reich making alliances with women of that kind."

"Unless it's on a purely professional basis," said Wagner glibly.

"No." Beck had collected himself, and he spoke now with quiet but unmistakeable determination. "There is no levity in this situation. As officers we must exhibit moral purity in our own behaviour and expect the same from our women. As German men, our duty to our families comes second only to our devotion to Germany." Peter twitched, and Beck, catching the movement, turned a searching look on him. In his senior officer's eyes Peter knew he was seeing the embodiment of his own father's moral values. Beck was watching him steadily. "What is your view of the situation, Captain Brandt?"

Unsettled, Peter responded to the question without filtering his thoughts.

"Minister Blomberg's... indiscretion has come to light only after the wedding, while the information was surely in Himmler's possession before the wedding took place. Now we face a situation where the leading soldier in the land, as you put it, sir, will certainly be dismissed, which begs the question; who will Hitler appoint as the new Minister of War?" He realized that he had answered the question as a politics and philosophy graduate – not as the General Staff officer that he now was – when Beck frowned, then sighed wearily.

"It is true that we are under attack from these people and their machinations, but we cannot allow ourselves to descend into the swamp of their political dealings. I'm sure that Admiral Canaris over at Abwehr will happily burn the midnight oil over this news, but the role of the General Staff is to advise the government in military strategy, not dabble in the politics of the gutter."

Within a week Blomberg was dismissed, and his intended successor, Werner von Fritsch, was immediately accused of homosexual offences, a charge brought by Himmler, using falsified evidence and a known criminal as a witness. It was like watching small children playing football, Peter thought bitterly; Hitler had taken possession of the ball, and everyone was running around the field after him, trying to get it back. The army was playing by the rules, but Hitler was both the referee and the captain of the other team.

As the institutional autonomy of the army tumbled like dominoes, Hitler's plan to occupy the Sudetenland region of Czechoslovakia became Beck's line in the sand, and when it became clear that Hitler would not be deterred from this aggression, Beck wrote a memo to Brauchitsch, the new commander-in-chief of the army, recommending that all of the senior officers threaten a mass collective resignation, to force Hitler to postpone the invasion.

'History will burden those leaders with blood guilt if they do not act according to their professional and statesmanly principles and knowledge,' the memo concluded. 'Their soldierly loyalty must end at the boundary where their knowledge, conscience, and sense of responsibility forbid the execution of an order.

'In case their advice and warnings fall on deaf ears in such circumstances, then they have the right and the duty, before the people and history, to resign their offices. If they all act together, then it will be impossible to carry out military action. They will thereby save the Fatherland from the worst, from total ruin.

'If a soldier in a position of highest authority in such times sees his duties and tasks only within the limits of his military responsibilities, without consciousness of his higher responsibility to the whole people, then he shows a lack of greatness, a lack of comprehension of responsibility. Extraordinary times demand extraordinary actions!'

For the chief of the General Staff to contemplate betraying his pledge, Peter knew, the impact of that betrayal on his sense of honour – his sense of self – must be ruinous. There was no mass-resignation of the generals, and suddenly Beck was gone, forced into retirement. The invasion of Czechoslovakia was unopposed by the army. But now the people faltered.

The peaceful annexation of Austria earlier in the year had been a victory for Hitler, but a second invasion in one year could not be ignored by France and Britain; Hitler's hubris would pitch Germany into a war that it would lose. Facing the spectre of this, the people's adulation of the Fuhrer faded.

Driving through Berlin in an open-topped car, he was exposed to the unthinkable; people along the route stood silent, and many turned away. It was the tipping point for Germany.

France blinked. Britain turned away. Berlin held its breath.

Germany tipped.

At the Munich agreement, Hitler stood on the world stage, triumphant, while France wriggled out of her treaty, and, together with Britain, agreed that Czechoslovakia should cede its territory to Germany. Anything to avoid war.

For Peter, it was like catching a cannonball in the chest; the craven shame of appeasement in the face of a bully. For the resistance, it was no less of a cannonball, because a coup had been poised for the moment that France and Britain declared war. Now, instead, the people were out in the streets, celebrating their Fuhrer's victory. Germany had occupied two neighbouring countries without a shot being fired. There was no other conclusion to be drawn; Europe was welcoming the Third Reich with open arms, and the old enemy was cowering before a superior force.

The humiliation weighed heavily on Peter as he and Conrad pressed through the crowds after work, heading for their favourite bar. Sick at heart, he steered the conversation away from the fiasco towards the urgent re-shuffling of the army brought on by the threat of war; he had received his posting to military intelligence.

"Abwehr? That's good," Conrad said, dropping himself into a chair, "you'll still be keeping company with the old crowd." Under Canaris, the staff of Abwehr were known to be disdainful of the Nazi regime. Peter shook his head.

"No, not Abwehr, they've assigned me to FHO. There's going to be an eastern division at Zossen, exclusively for gathering intelligence on the Soviets. Reinhard Gehlen will be commanding officer."

"Gehlen? I don't know the name."

"You wouldn't have any reason to. Gehlen is a dyed-in-the-wool soldier; unquestioning loyalty to the uniform. Nobody would even think to approach him about... about any other business."

"Ah, well. Cheer up," said Conrad clapping him on the shoulder, "You've got the Soviet Union; just what you've wanted all along. You'll be an Englishman in Germany, spying on Russia..." He stopped abruptly, listening to his own words, and Peter, staring moodily at his boots, hearing the quality of his friend's silence, closed his eyes tightly. Still shaken by Britain's humiliation, he wasn't prepared for this closer catastrophe. Raking his fingers through his hair, he lifted his face to confront his friend's shocked expression.

"You're a spy," Conrad's voice was flat and dull, and only Peter heard him. Holding his gaze, he stared back unhappily. The silence between them stretched out until the chair next to Peter's was pulled back with a harrowing scrape of wood on wood, and Heinz Wagner sat heavily.

"Are we getting drunk? Cheers to that."

As others joined them, Conrad, his face pale and pinched, glanced around at their faces. Finally, he looked back at Peter, his eyes filled with a hesitant optimism.

"Then you can help us with..."

Peter's heart was clay. "Germany is not our problem," Hendry had said. Mutely he shook his head.

***

The genius of Hendry's planning had presented itself to him over and over again during the following days; no amount of background checks on him would uncover any link with British Intelligence, but this was not what had kept him awake while Conrad considered his course of action.

"Will I turn you in?" Conrad said when they eventually met in the Tiergarten. "No. I might still beat you into pulp, but I will not turn you in. I have come to the conclusion that you are not actually working against the interests of Germany, and so I salve my conscience. He laughed sourly, "'An Englishman in Germany, spying on Russia,' I scored a bulls-eye with a wild shot! No, I will not turn you in, Peter. I would trust Beck and Oster and the others with my life; God knows I have already done so, but I will not trust them with yours."

FHO. And Gehlen. It felt as though the dispassionate hands of fate had placed him deliberately in the heart of

Hendry's plan, but nevertheless, at their next meeting, he was surprised to find that Hendry knew of Gehlen.

"FHO! Well done, Peter, I couldn't have engineered it better myself! Gehlen was once detained at Stalin's pleasure, and I understand he bears little affection for the Soviets. Well, you'd better get packing, then, because Chamberlain's little piece of paper is nothing more than kindling for the bonfire that Adolf is building, and I'd like to know that you are settled in before things start getting hot."

9
*Do I **look** like a prostitute?*

1942

The farm and its outbuildings had been visible from three fields away, stage-lit by the full moon, and Tommie's ingrained caution had surrendered to a sudden desire for sanctuary, so, finding a rotted-away section of the north wall of a barn, where a board had been wedged as a temporary fix, she crawled in.

The darkness inside was like a physical presence, thick and unyielding, but speared in places where the moon's light poked through gaps in the old walls. A ladder reached up to a hayloft which offered a better refuge, but once there, the static crackle of her movements through the hay strafed her nerves, so she settled down barely ten feet in from the trapdoor and curled up.

Here was shelter, a soft bed, and relative warmth, but her eyes wouldn't stay closed, so she lay watching the moonlight picking out a slowly-shifting kaleidoscope around her as inconvenient thoughts came crowding in.

She had no identity papers, and wouldn't be able to contact any resistance cells. She didn't even know what part of Europe she was in, and under Hitler's Commando Order, when she was captured, she would be shot. Well, looking on the bright side, in one way, her situation was quite liberating, because now she had an excuse to do what she had been inclined to do from the start; fly screaming and flailing, at the enemy. Metaphorically, of course. Or, ultimately, not metaphorically.

But first, she would put into practice the sabotage training she had undergone with Hendry's people; disrupting power lines, transport hubs, any part of the enemy's infrastructure that she could find. Then – when they caught her – *then* she would fly screaming and flailing at the enemy. Better that, than standing politely in front of a wall while they took aim.

In the darkness, she nodded to herself and settled deeper into the hay. The commando stuff would keep for tomorrow. For tonight, she had sanctuary, and she should make the most of it.

The three shocks happened almost simultaneously.

"No, you see... It didn't... I wasn't..." The voice came from a spot in the hay no further than five feet away from her, and her skin crawled with shock. "No, because..." The words were mumbled and fragmented; sleep talking.

The darkness vibrated with the violence of her heartbeat, and now came the second shock, rasping at her jangling nerves; the harsh growl of a military vehicle approaching. Across the yard, at the farmhouse, a dog started barking, its chain clacking as it lunged. This silent night was rapidly filling with noises.

The third shock; the words she had heard were English, and spoken, although sleep-muffled, with an unmistakably English accent. She turned for the trapdoor, but the Germans would be watching for figures running from the farm buildings, so however this was going to end, it was going to end in this barn.

She scanned the hayloft for hiding places. She could wedge herself into the corner where the roof met the wall; the soldiers would find the sleep talker and not look further. Of course, she could – *should* – climb down that ladder as the Germans walked in, and sacrifice herself to save the Englishman. That was her job, and it made sense, because in the long run – in the not so long run – she stood a snowball's chance in hell of surviving.

On the other hand, it was also her duty to try to survive... and there was sabotage to do, and the Germans would find the sleep talker anyway; they would hear him. She should save herself.

Edging past the Englishman, deeper into the hayloft, she prepared to tuck herself into the far corner, but some soft, stupid stalk in her chest was reaching out to him. He had to wake up, or he was lost. He breathed a deep sigh, the vehicle pulled into the farmyard, and something inside Tommie made a decision.

Cursing silently, she turned and crept back, her eyes working to pick out the dark shape of the man's body against the hay, then she stood, placed her feet astride him, and waited. The doors of the vehicle opened, soldiers clambered out, and under cover of the noise, she dropped, straddling the Englishman's torso with her knees, pinning his arms against his sides, and clamping her hands over his mouth. There was a brief attempt at a struggle, and his legs kicked wildly at the straw, but Hendry's training had been comprehensive, and she held him captive with little effort. Leaning down, she hissed in his ear.

"You were talking in your sleep – in English – and there's a German patrol outside. Lie still!" The man's legs stopped kicking as the last of the doors closed and the voices of soldiers rang out in the farmyard. Tommie froze, listening, then leaned down again and whispered fiercely against the side of his face, "Can I let go of your mouth? Will you stay quiet?" The man gave as much of a nod as he could manage with the pressure she was exerting on his face, and she removed her hands. Thankfully, he remained silent, focusing on the threat from outside, but in the fragmented moonlight Tommie could see the glint of his eyes as they flickered from the soldiers' voices back to her own face.

A woman's voice, slow and reluctant, had joined the party outside. Dragged from sleep, the farmer's wife did not appreciate being forced to unlock her barn. Shushing the dog, she complained as the soldiers searched below, poking at the straw bales with their rifles, but Tommie was listening to something else; someone was climbing up the ladder.

She closed her eyes as fear burrowed fungus-caked fingernails into her mind and squeezed. The two of them were there, in plain sight, positioned right under one of the moon's spear-thrusts. There could be no escape from this, and now it was obvious what she had to do. Catching the Englishman's eyes, she put a finger to her lips, made the "stay" sign, and turned towards the trapdoor.

A loud moan came from the man, and he rose up from the hay, tipping her onto her back and launching himself on top of her as she had done to him. Grabbing her wrists and pinning them, he buried his face in her neck.

"I'll do the talking," he muttered, "Don't speak, but play along."

At the sound of the scuffle, the soldier on the ladder shouted and picked up his pace. The sound of rifles being primed echoed in the barn below, and Tommie turned her head away from the trapdoor as a round helmet and a handgun appeared. The Englishman let go of her wrists, raised his arms above his head and yelled, "Nein! Nicht schiessen!" A tense silence fell. He shook his head and cursed bitterly in German. Tommie followed the gist of his appeal; "God damn it. Can't a man have a little fun? I'm not doing anything wrong. The girl is willing, ah! God, is she willing! I've spent half my pay to make it so, and this is what I get? Don't shoot, please; all my papers are in order and I have them right here. With your permission..." He reached cautiously into his jacket pocket and pulled out some carefully folded papers. "Five minutes," he said bitterly, handing them over, "all I needed was five minutes and we'd have been alright."

The soldier snorted. "Five minutes, you say?" Taking the papers and pulling out a flashlight, he studied them, calling back down the ladder, "Did you hear that, Schultz? Five minutes is all he needs. Just like you!" He tossed the papers back to the Englishman. "For God's sake, lad, take your time about it, and show the girl why Germany will conquer the world!" He started to descend the ladder amid cheers and shouts of laughter from below, but then he stopped and glanced back, "Fraulein?" Tommie's heart thumped painfully and she felt the Englishman tense. The soldier's voice came again, insistently, "Fraulein?" His flashlight was trained on her face and she shielded her eyes with her hand before she turned to him, squinting into the beam.

"Ya?"

"Do you also have your papers in order?

"Ya, Herr Leutnant," said Tommie in a small voice, and patted the tweed skirt, reaching feebly for non-existent papers in a non-existent pocket. The soldier snorted again.

"'Ya, Herr Leutnant,'" he mimicked in a falsetto. "No, fraulein, stay as you are... at ease," he grinned, and started down the ladder, calling out to the Englishman, "Try to last more than five minutes, lad; after this little interruption you'll have to make it better than just alright!" He disappeared into an ocean of catcalls and animal noises.

As the scuffle and thump of boots receded, the Englishman lifted himself carefully off Tommie and helped her to sit up. They sat in silence, listening to the sounds of the soldiers climbing back into the truck. The farmer's wife called up into the hayloft, her voice muffled in the dusty air.

"You two, whoever you are, make sure you are gone by morning." She bolted the barn door, evidently assuming that the intruders would leave by the same way they entered, and after a moment there was a distant thunk and a click as the farmhouse door was closed and locked. The truck's ignition grated, failed, grated again and reluctantly fired, driving the farm dog into a frenzy.

Still inclined to hold her breath, Tommie glanced at the figure sitting next to her in the hay. There was a pale gleam in the darkness that suggested blond hair, but the rest was a shapeless mass in the gloom. The snarl of the truck as it made its way along the dirt track towards the main road was reluctant to let silence descend, but the farm buildings were asleep again, and finally Tommie allowed herself to breathe. The Englishman peered at her through the darkness.

"Where the hell did you come from?!"

"Where the hell did *you* come from?!"

"Well, yes, but me being here is not exactly far-fetched, is it? There are bucket-loads of servicemen ducking and dodging around Europe right now. Not so many unaccompanied Englishwomen – and certainly not this far east."

She hesitated. "Alright, but you go first; I'm guessing RAF? Downed air-crew?"

"Yup. Flight Lieutenant Simon Leigh," he said brightly, offering his hand. Tommie smiled weakly and shook his hand.

"Tomasin West. And, by the way, 'The girl is willing, ah, God, is she willing'? You're lucky I'm not a nice girl, or I would slap your face."

"Oh. Yes." The Englishman's voice was contrite. "I apologise for that. But, to be fair," he added hotly, "You really *aren't* very nice. Why did you have to jump on me like that? You scared the living daylights out of me." He pressed his hand against his chest, "My heart is still going like the clappers!"

"Well, if I'd woken you up gently with "I say, old chap, are you English?" you'd have knocked me six ways from Sunday."

Leigh nodded. "Alright, but you still haven't told me what the devil an English girl is doing hiding in a barn in Germany."

In Germany?

"I wasn't in Germany this morning... yesterday... two days ago..." she said, disorientated. How many days had she been on that train? "I was in a prison in Paris. They put me on a train heading east, and I decided to get off."

"Why were you in prison? And why did they put you on a train?"

"It was a cattle-train."

A world of silence fell.

"You're Jewish?"

"No. Most of us... them... *us* were, but not all. Some of

us were just classified as undesirables."

There was an indrawn breath.

"You're a prostitute?"

"No!" she squeaked. "For pity's sake! You could have gone with "Gasp... You're a communist?" or "Gasp...You're a criminal? a drunkard? a beggar? a homosexual?" Why would you assume prostitute? Do I *look* like a prostitute?" She saw his eyes flick down to the black satin blouse. "Well, ok, the blouse... but would a prostitute wear this skirt? No, I was a nurse, *am* a nurse, and I was working in a clinic in Paris, with false papers, and I got caught." She closed her eyes against the thought of what had been waiting for her at the end of the train-ride, of what was still waiting for the other women, and turned away from it. "What about you?"

"I got shot down over Belgium, and they stuck me in a prison in Saxony," he said simply. "I escaped a fortnight ago, and I've been on the run since then."

His voice had a pleasant, low-pitched burr, and Tommie's thoughts drifted. How nice it would be to settle back down into this nest of scented hay, talk quietly together and forget about the world. No. She stood up, wincing. The burning rawness of her scraped legs and body lowered her spirits, and the unanticipated pleasure of Leigh's company faded with the prospect of moving on into the void.

"Well, I'm not going to push my luck by staying here for the night," she said briskly, "I'm going to get moving. Good luck, Flight Lieutenant Leigh, and thank you for your performance tonight. If it wasn't for you... well, thanks." She shook his hand and made her way down the ladder.

Ten minutes later, hearing footsteps approaching at a run on the dusty lane behind her, she dropped into the ditch at the side and risked a glance as someone hurried past. It was the Englishman. She called to him softly, and he skidded to a halt, peering into the dark for her.

"I was thinking that we could travel together," he whispered, helping her out of the ditch, "we could pool our resources."

"I don't have any resources."

"Your body is resource enough."

"I told you, I'm not..."

"No! I didn't mean that! I meant you can be my wife."

She couldn't resist.

"Oh, Simon, this is so sudden. I don't know what to say."

In the moonlight his face went even paler, then darkened.

"Very funny. You know what I mean; the Germans will be looking for a lone airman and a single woman; if we're a couple, they'll look right through us. I think that's what happened back there in the barn, because how would an escaped prisoner find the opportunity for a roll in the hay? What do you think?"

What did she think? The official SOE Manual, *How to Be an Agent in Occupied Europe* – and she still smirked at that title – was clear on the protocol; *The agent, unlike the soldier, who has many friends, is surrounded by enemies, seen and unseen. He cannot even be certain of the people of his own nationality who are apparently friendly. The agent must, therefore, remember that, like primitive men in the jungle, he has only his alertness, initiative and observation to help him.*

So, should they pool their resources?

"Ok."

***

She woke with the fuddled confusion of someone who has slept more deeply than they meant to. There was a battered leather workbag lying in the flattened area of grass beside her, and she had been covered with a workman's jacket that had been dyed an amateur shade of brown. Drawing the sleeves of the jacket around her, she curled up under its warmth.

When she woke again, she saw the Englishman approaching through the trees. He had been washing in the stream they had crossed last night to get into the wood, and was drying himself off with his shirt.

She sat up and watched him as he walked through the

dappled early sunlight. His hair was blond; a clear, uncompromised blond, and his skin, although pale, still carried a memory of gold. She tried not to stare; Flight Lieutenant Simon Leigh was an astoundingly beautiful man. Like an angel, she thought, then shook her head; no. Angels have a stillness about them. A sadness. Angels are remote and lonely. She knew this to be true. Simon Leigh was too vital and vibrant to be an angel.

He had reached the clearing and was tucking his damp shirt into his waistband. His eyes were an unusual speedwell blue, fringed with enviable lashes, his hair, darker where it was still wet, clung to his neck, and his cheeks were dusky from the cold water. Definitely too vibrant for an angel. He caught her staring, and she blushed.

"I was just picturing you in RAF blue," she said, to cover her embarrassment. He nodded and sat down beside her.

"How did you sleep?"

"Surprisingly well, thank you. How is the water?"

"Bloody freezing. It'll wake you up alright." He narrowed his eyes as she gathered leaves from a plant that was growing near his workbag. "What are you doing?"

"This is soapwort," she said, "If you crush the leaves, you can use it like soap."

He looked at her doubtfully, "I don't know about that."

The stream *was* bloody freezing, and she knew she shouldn't squander the precious heat that huddled in her core, but it would take more than a quick splash to clean away the cloying grime that clung to body and soul, so she stripped and plunged into the water, sucking in her breath with shock. Peeling off her bloomers under cover of the water, she gave them a good wash, wrung them out, flung them onto a shrub on the bank of the stream, and was out again very quickly, drying herself as well as she could on the tweed skirt. She pulled on her bra and nylon slip for decency, and examined her clothes.

Fortunately, the skirt had been tough enough to survive her exit from the train, but one cuff of the blouse was tattered; it would have to be rolled up to avoid drawing attention, although that would expose the livid lacerations on her arm. Tattered was the lesser of two evils, so she buttoned the cuff around her wrist. Her stockings were a different story; they were shredded, which always looks disreputable, so she used them to tie up her hair.

Dressed again, and shivering, she flapped her bloomers quickly in the air, then left them hanging on a tree, hoping they would dry before she had to start walking in them. In the clearing, the Englishman sat, cross legged on the grass, examining the contents of his rucksack. As she approached, he took off his jacket and threw it to her, and she pulled it on quickly, before it lost the warmth of him. Spread out on the leaf mould next to him lay a document with his photograph, bordered by his fingerprints and bearing the name Hans Claus Ritten. Tommie's mind lurched.

"What are those?!" she said sharply.

"My travel papers," he said, grinning up at her, "Hans Claus Ritten, plumber, at your service."

She glanced down at the photograph again, at his image, etched in patches of black and white, then stared at him, and the world righted itself again. She had been transporting packages every day since she had been in France, but she had never seen the documents inside them, and never met the people they were destined for. Now she was facing a real man behind a forged identity, and the experience shook her with its intimacy.

"Why?" His question startled her. "Do you have real ones? In your own name?" He paused, suddenly sober in the face of her confusion. "You do have papers, don't you?" When she didn't answer, he stood up slowly, a look of horror on his face. "You mean to tell me that you have no documentation at all? Nothing?" His voice was rising, and he hushed himself hastily. "Have you even got money? How were you planning to eat? For God's sake, you'll be lucky not to get shot as a spy. How did your escape officer let you get away with it?"

"Escape officer?" She felt suddenly foolish. Exposed and ridiculous. "What sort of prison do you think I was in?" she spat, "A country club for displaced gentlewomen? I jumped out of a train, for God's sake!"

He shook his head wildly.

"But where were you planning to go?" he persisted. "Assuming you can get to a neutral border by sheer, impossible luck, what happens then? Do you think they'll say "Congratulations! Such pluck. Let me lift the barrier for you"? Shit! What are we going to do?"

"*We* are not going to do anything," she snapped. "It's not your problem. And can I remind you that it was your idea in the first place for us to travel together? But you're right; I am a liability to you – not a resource – so I'll just say goodbye now."

"No! That's not what I meant."

"Isn't it? Then what could you possibly have meant?" she closed her eyes and took a deep breath, forcing the shrillness out of her voice. "Alright, even if it's not what you meant, you have to admit that it's the truth."

"I can't let you just go off like that. What will happen to you?"

"That's not your concern. And nobody *lets* me go anywhere. And we can't stay together the way you suggested; the first time we get stopped I'll be arrested, and your precious papers wouldn't be able to explain why you were with me." *Why hadn't she made that decision last night?* "It was nice meeting you," she said. "Really nice – and I wish you all the luck in the world." She reached out to shake his hand, and he took it, but kept hold of it, and shook his head.

"No. Wait a minute." He watched her in silence, his blue eyes troubled. Finally, he swallowed hard. "It takes more than clever documents to survive an escape, you know. I've been on my own for ten days. Last night I was supposed to be staying in a hotel room in Gottingen. I have the money and I have the correct travel documents; I could have been sleeping in a real bed last night, but a woman in the grocery store there was kind to me, and for a moment, I almost convinced myself that she could see who I really was, and wanted to help me. Almost... I almost told her. Instead, I walked out and kept walking, right out of the town, to avoid the temptation. Sometimes things are just meant to be; if I had stayed in Gottingen last night, I wouldn't have met you in that barn. Will you stay with me? Please? We can share this food, and I've got money to buy more. We'll work out some story about your papers."

Tommie closed her eyes. She was a walking liability; it was only a matter of time before she was picked up and put in front of a firing squad. She had rehearsed the moment in her thoughts several times, although, somehow, she felt that the imagining was only going to be a pale imitation of the real thing. But that was her story. This beautiful, sweet-natured airman standing before her should have no part in it. Of all the countless servicemen she had helped through Monsieur Arnaud's escape line, now that she was going down in flames, did Simon Leigh deserve to be hitched to her burning chariot?

She drew a long, shuddering breath. He was lonely, he said. He hadn't spoken to anyone in ten days. She was lonely too, and she had been locked in that broom closet in Drancy for longer than ten days.

"What food have you got?" she said.

"Potted meat and crackers."

"Alright, I'm yours."

They followed Leigh's intended route, and made good progress, even after stopping to eat a quick lunch. It had been two days since Tommie had last eaten, and when Simon pulled a red and white gingham bundle from his rucksack, laid it down on the ground, and opened it to reveal a package of crackers and a tin of potted meat, she had to force back the tears.

It was going to be a much colder night than the one before, and when they settled down to sleep, Tommie buried herself under a mound of last year's leaves. She pulled her legs up inside the tweed skirt and forgave its frumpy ugliness for the warmth it offered. The satin blouse had no such redeeming qualities, and she was curled up tight against the cold when Leigh sat up suddenly in his own leaf pile.

"Listen, Tomasin,"

"Tommie."

"Tommie? Ok. Listen, Tommie, please don't think I'm trying it on, but I'm perishing, so you must be too. Why don't we huddle up together?"

"Good idea," she answered eagerly, and made space for him in her leaves, but he hunched his shoulders, looking suddenly uncomfortable, and she stopped, confused.

"The only thing is," he began hesitantly, "I'm married. Newly married. Just six months, and it may sound quaint, but I don't want to be unfaithful to Mary, my wife." He faltered and stopped, and Tommie watched him in silence, unsure of how to respond.

"So, you're giving me fair warning to keep my hands off you?" she said eventually.

There was an embarrassed silence and she fished around for a way to resolve the awkwardness. "You are an exceptionally beautiful man, Simon," she said, "and if you catch me staring at you, there's nothing more to it than me admiring your beauty. Looking at you washes away some of the ugliness that I've seen. How about this for a solution; I'll promise not to climb all over you, if you promise not to climb all over me, because that's important too. The consequences for me would be a bit more tangible than they would be for you."

"Oh, God! I'm sorry. Oh, what a..."

"No, it's alright. It was very brave of you to say what you were thinking, and very honest, and those two things are far more important to me than... well, let's call it chivalry. Now, shall I shuffle over to you, or will you shuffle over to me? Is there an etiquette here? I've got the biggest pile of leaves."

He laughed and shuffled across the space that divided them, bringing his leaves with him. After a few self-conscious attempts they managed to achieve a comfortable, yet not too-familiar proximity, but sleep evaded them, and they fell to talking.

Twenty-five years old, and married to the girl-next-door, Simon was a navigator with a bomber crew flying the new Sterling bomber. He had signed up with the RAF to smash the Germans, he said, because the prospect of the Nazis marching over peaceful countries was intolerable. And now Britain stood alone against the threat.

Britain didn't stand alone, she pointed out; London had become known as 'Miniature Europe,' because of all the governments-in-exile it hosted, and it was common knowledge that more enemy aircraft had been shot down in the Battle of Britain by the indomitable Polish 303 squadron than by any other unit. He brushed this off. An Englishman's home is his castle, he said, and if the Nazis marching across Europe was intolerable, he could find no words to convey his horror at the thought of them setting foot on British soil. Where Mary was.

Listening to him, she remembered how simple it had seemed to her to ride out and confront the enemy who was threatening your hearth and your country, because the enemy was indisputably out there, and your hearth was your hearth. Yours alone. Indisputable.

Your country, on the other hand; your country was not yours alone. Who gets to define the enemy of your country? In the Battle of Cable Street, the fascists had battled for the good of their country, and the anti-fascists had battled for the good of their country, but it was the same country. Who gets to decide the interests of their country? The people who vote. The Germans had elected Hitler, and now he represented them, but what of the people who hadn't voted for him?

The chill of the night gave way to a milky morning, which opened up into a glorious day, and the countryside lay before them, peaceful and quiet. Keeping to country lanes and avoiding towns, they made good progress, and at noon they left the road and settled down behind a hedge to rest and eat. Spreading the gingham cloth on the ground, Simon set out some new treasures; early that morning, he had walked alone into a nearby town to buy a loaf of fresh bread and a piece of cheese as well as more potted meat and crackers.

Before them, on the other side of the gingham cloth, lay a sweeping field sown with winter wheat, still feathery, but turning a soft gold. The sky soared blue above them, and into it a lark levitated in stages, higher and higher, alerting the world to their intrusion on her landscape. Tommie followed her into the void and found that, as long as she ignored the war around the edges, she was perfectly happy in that moment. When she looked back down again, Simon was holding a small envelope. He let his eyes rest on it for a moment, then opened it, took out a photo, and handed it to Tommie.

"That's Mary," he said. She had heard all about Mary last night. They had known each other since they were twelve years old, but he hadn't really *seen* her until they were eighteen, and then she had refused to date him because she didn't want to be just his next conquest – there had been many conquests. But Simon also hadn't wanted Mary to be just another conquest. He was tired of conquests, and he wanted to have Mary at his side forever; his wife, his rock, the mother of his children. Winning her over had taken absolute commitment and a lot of patience, and he had never worked out what he had done to change her mind, but it had changed, and she had married him, and now...

She handed back the photo, and he tucked it into its envelope and back into his breast pocket without a word. Brushing the crumbs from his jacket, he took out a pack of cards, selected the four aces, carefully peeled the diamond-patterned backs from them, and put them together to form a home-made map. Muttering to himself, he studied it.

"The last major road was, what... five miles back, and we've got at least eight miles of meandering lanes in front of us before the next town. I wish we could just cut right across the fields, but we'd end up getting shot by a farmer..."

And that's when everything changed.

"Simon..."

"Two people trudging..."

"Simon!" Tommie was on her feet now, staring past the wheat field.

"What? What's wrong?"

"Those hills... the small, smooth hills, like eggs..."

"Yes, eggs in a basket," he said, "They're drumlins. Don't you remember secondary school geography?" He paused, thoughtfully, "But that's not right. They shouldn't be here. Not in this landscape."

"And they're... cracking, or something. And there are things moving around them." She shuddered, "Like headlice..."

She knew precisely what she was looking at. She didn't need to read the expression that stiffened Simon's face, but she was leaping giant steps ahead of this discovery, and she needed to think carefully while he followed his own reasoning.

"Shit!" he said savagely, "They're hangars. Camouflaged hangars. The things you saw moving must have been camouflaged vehicles." He consulted the map, tracing a finger across the pieces, and glanced back at the plain in front of them. "There should be train tracks running east-west down there, but I see no sign of them. My only guess is that the tracks have been camouflaged too, which means they're important." He fished out his train timetable. "No public rail service across the plain... trains terminate at Gehren and at Saalfeld." He groaned and carefully began to conceal the map and gather up his papers, slipping them into his pockets. "That's it, Tommie, we're sunk. What's down there must be some sort of industrial or military complex. We have to get away from here.

"But not together," she said firmly, "Because anyone who has seen us near whatever that place is, could report us, and now they'll be looking for a couple."

There was a brief argument about this, but common sense prevailed, and he nodded, staring bleakly at her.

"I'm going to miss your company, Tommie. For God's sake, be careful." Wrapping up the gingham bundle, he pushed it into her arms, ignoring her protests. "I can buy more, you can't. Alright, it's pretty much academic at this point, so ladies first; which way are you going to go?" She pointed in the direction they had come; it was his route, and he should continue to follow it. And she had other plans. Giving her a quick, tight hug, he turned and climbed over the gate into the lane.

The miniscule activity across the plain gave her goosepimples and she turned away from it, watching Simon instead, as he turned left onto a farm track, a solitary figure in the clear sunshine. Then she turned back to the headlice eggs.

She had been sent to France as a courier, and that had annoyed her, because others had been assigned to more exciting roles, but she had followed her orders dutifully. Now, however, the courier role was over, and this was her chance to do what she'd been trained to do; commit sabotage.

Of course, her sabotage training had involved explosives, a team, and painstaking planning, whereas under current circumstances she had nothing more than the clothes she crouched behind the hedge in. What she was about to do would be a ham-fisted attempt at disruption, because she had no equipment, not even a watch. It would be a ham-fisted attempt, but it was better than creeping around the countryside, consuming the last of Simon's rations until she was, inevitably, discovered.

Simon. She sighed. Well, at least he was safely out of her unhinged orbit now, and, soon after watching his already dear figure disappear around the corner of the lane, she had seen what she had been expecting; a convoy of three cargo trucks snaking along the road, making their way towards the compound. Then, across the plain, approaching from the west along the camouflaged tracks, a freight train had appeared and slowed to a stop somewhere behind the hangars.

After the first train, others had arrived at regular intervals, one from the west and one from the east. She guessed that the trains were being loaded and unloaded behind the hangars, and the trucks were synchronized to the arrival and departure of the trains. Convoys arrived, were admitted through the security gate, and drove around behind the hangars. An hour later, they departed, their engines labouring under a heavier load, and within minutes, another three approached from the opposite direction and turned into the lane towards the compound. Like a well-oiled machine. She smiled. Thanks to her FANY training, she knew more than a little something about machines, and thanks to her SOE training she knew about disabling them. Mentally, she cracked her knuckles.

The black blouse and tweed skirt weren't terrible in terms of camouflage, but the red-checked cloth was a bit eye-catching, so she rolled the food supplies up into a cylinder with it, and tied it out of sight around her waist under the blouse.

Creeping along behind the hedgerows, she made her way towards a tight bend in the road just before the approach to the compound's security barrier, squeezed through the hedge, and wriggled herself into the tall grass and cow parsley on the verge.

She had watched the routine carefully for two hours now, and she knew that while the first two trucks were waiting to be admitted, the third was out of sight of the security gate, around the bend of the lane.

Right on time, here came her convoy; Opel Blitzes, she noted with satisfaction – Hendry's people had provided a Blitz for practice. Two vehicles passed her, and as the third one rolled to a stop, she scurried across the lane and scrambled under its running board.

Clinging to the underside of the truck, she could hear voices exchanging information, then the truck passed through the barrier and around the back of one of the hangars before jerking to a stop. Three sets of doors opened and slammed shut, and the drivers' voices diminished.

Easing herself down to the ground behind the cover of a wheel, she scanned the area. Only thirty feet away was a tall, chain-link perimeter fence, topped with the ubiquitous barbed wire. An irrelevant part of her winced at the thought that she was, once again, inside a compound, but the active and buzzing part of her confirmed that the trucks had been parked out of sight of the guard post. The drivers had disappeared into a low, windowless building next to the hangar, and teams of workers in blue overalls were occupied at the rear of the trucks, loading ammunition crates from flat-bed trollies onto the trains, and transferring jerry cans from the train onto the trucks. From the weight of the jerry cans as they met the floor of the truck, and from the oily fug in the air, they were full of fuel.

She heartily wished that someone had left a boiler suit lying around, but she would just have to hope that everyone was too absorbed in their work to notice a little woman in a hideous skirt and frowsy blouse slipping into the cab of the truck. The toolkit in the foot-well of the passenger side yielded exactly what she needed, and she quickly unbolted the transmission coupler, tucked the appropriate spanner into her bra, and slid under the chassis. Under cover of the loading and unloading, it was a simple task to reverse the gear linkages of the truck. The tricky bit was to get back, unseen, into the cab, bolt the coupler back into place, and get out again.

Trickier still was judging her timing; after the loading was finished and the men had wheeled the flatbed away, she made a quick dash from the truck to the train, and then a sprint across the platform to the last car of the west-bound train. The timetable was precise; the west-bound train would depart five minutes before the east-bound train, so she would be out of the compound when the driver of the third truck started his engine, put it in what he believed to be first gear, and reversed it – loaded with fuel – into a train loaded with munitions.

Clinging grimly to the undercarriage of the west-bound train, approximately ten inches above the tracks, Tommie didn't hear the explosion, but she watched with satisfaction as an oily column of smoke rose, churning, into the sky behind her.

***

The potted meat and crackers lasted her three days, and when she had licked the last cracker crumb from her lips, and kissed the gingham cloth in thanks to Simon, she had tied it around her neck as a scarf, and walked. In those three days, with the assistance of a pair of wire-cutters and a few tools liberated from the Opel's toolkit, there had been a bit of clandestine tweaking to the infrastructure of a town here or there, until the evening when she had been stopped and questioned and arrested in a deserted country lane.

She reached back for the memory of the light as it had shone on the young wheat that day... as it had shone on Simon. She imagined him being welcomed with a handshake and a cup of tea into neutral territory; anything to take her away from the contemplation of what lay in her future. It was a lonely feeling to face a death that nobody would know about. She wondered what they would do with her body.

The staff of the prison had treated her cordially, bringing her a bowl of thin soup, and water to drink. There was a wooden cot bed with a straw mattress, and she had slept well, but the next morning, as she sat on the edge of the cot, she had visitors.

10
The swastika in his forehead

Heavy footsteps sounded in the corridor, a key grated in the lock, the cell door opened, and a young, fresh-faced man wearing the uniform of an SS lieutenant stepped in and stood smartly at attention. Another figure appeared in the doorway, reached up to remove his peaked cap, and, for Tommie, everything went dark as the swastika on the cap badge remained in place, gleaming in the centre of the man's forehead.

She scrambled to her feet, choking on a smog of fear, and the officer smiled.

"How gratifying that you recognize when respect is due." He coughed hard, winced, and cleared his throat, spitting phlegm into a handkerchief. Gesturing at the cot bed, he cleared his throat again. "Please, fraulein, be seated." As he handed his cap to the fresh-faced lieutenant, the darkness around her dispersed, and Tommie lowered herself shakily to the mattress. "I am Major Otto Steiger, and this is Leutnant Blauser," he said, bringing a chair over from the corner of the room and seating himself in front of her. "And please don't insult my intelligence by introducing yourself as Thereze Pascal, because the family of the real Thereze Pascal has been questioned by our intelligence services in Paris and you have been exposed as an imposter."

Taking a folder from Blauser and flicking it open to

reveal her passport and identity papers, he spread his hands in a gesture of reason. "In view of this, may we be permitted to know your real name?"

"My name is Tomasin West."

"And what organization are you with?"

"I work... worked for the Clinic St. Marie"

"Don't play stupid, I said which organization? Military Intelligence? Naval Intelligence?"

She gaped at him. "You think I'm a spy?"

"You have been working under an assumed name with forged papers, this in itself qualifies you as an enemy agent."

"No, I'm just a nurse. Thereze is a friend of mine. She lives in London now, and she gave me her passport. She said she would be afraid to ever go back to France now, so she had no more need of it."

"This is a professionally-produced fraudulent document, bearing your photograph."

"I have a friend who works at a printing firm."

"And your boyfriend, where is he?"

"I don't have a boyfriend."

"The English airman you were with in the barn, where is he?"

She was outraged. "I have never been in a barn with a man!"

He drew a paper from the folder, and studied it. His fingers were yellow; a heavy smoker, perhaps, but the yellow was in the nailbeds, and evenly distributed on each finger, not concentrated on the first two fingers. Out of habit, Tommie glanced at his face. The skin was sallow and the wrinkles around his eyes were oddly accentuated, as though outlined with a fine brown pen. She looked closer. Yes, the whites of his eyes were very slightly tinged with yellow. Gall bladder disease, and understandably so; the man was well into his fifties, and his uniform was stretched tightly around his stout torso. Instead of ending in a jawline, his face seemed to slide into a fleshy sack under his chin, overflowing the stricture of the collar.

He slipped the paper back into the folder. "I have some

more questions before we take you to be... processed. You were discovered and captured on the road between Salzgitter and Holle, is that right?"

"I don't know where I was. I have stayed away from towns and major roads."

"What have you been doing in the days since you escaped from the train?"

"I have been walking, sometimes sleeping."

"And in your considerable travels have you come across this man?" He drew the paper out once more from its folder and handed it to her. In the grainy photostat of a photograph she recognized the image of Simon Leigh, dressed in a neat RAF tunic. She squinted and looked closer before shaking her head and handing the paper back.

"He must be very handsome to look so good in such a poor photograph. Does that paper give his address? I might look him up after the war." She was breaking the rules, but somehow, acknowledging Simon's beauty and a hope for the future gave her comfort.

Steiger smiled grimly. "His address? I really don't think that matters. I would defy the young man himself to find his home in the rubble that the Luftwaffe have made of England."

***

Back in the lobby, Blauser turned to Steiger.

"What now?"

"Now we take Fraulein West for a ride. I know the prison where they are holding this airman; it's Josef Renger's hidey-hole. She can pay the young man a surprise visit, and if he shows the slightest sign of recognition when he sees her, then we'll know where we stand. Everyone is running around looking for four people. Nobody believes me when I say that the couple in the barn were the same two that were seen near the munitions plant near Leipzig. But let them believe that I was mistaken; that she is nothing more than the clinic nurse who escaped from the cattle-train. Let them forget all about her. That suits my purposes best."

Blauser was careful to keep his face and his tone neutral.

"So, we take her there for a visit, then what?"

Steiger smiled. "Then nothing... we leave her there."

"You're letting her go?"

"Hardly. That dreadful castle is supposed to be escape-proof... although this young man plainly disproves that, but either way, that's not my immediate concern."

"What I mean is, you're not going to interrogate her further?"

Steiger glanced at him sharply. "Perhaps you were anticipating working on her yourself? Put those thoughts away, Blauser, we have no need of her. She was never a significant source of information, just a courier. If it were not for her little cross-country jaunt last week, she would be serving in a Reich brothel right now, but after what she saw near Leipzig – whether or not she understood what she saw – she can't be entrusted to the shoddy security of a brothel. Yes, I know!" he snapped as Blauser opened his mouth to speak, "I know what the Commando order says. I know I should put her in front of a firing squad, but I despise these agents, these rats that breed on the margins of a battlefield. And for a woman to undertake such work? She is an aberration. An occult, underhanded creature. A bullet is wasted on her, a slow poison is better. Besides, I am in need of a little entertainment, and I shall have it; why waste her, when I can have her own men dispose of her so much more creatively?"

"In that case, why an officer's camp?" quibbled Blauser, "Wouldn't one of the stalags be more effective for the purpose?"

Steiger sighed. "Think bigger, Blauser; be more ambitious. If we put her in an other-ranks camp, and a thousand squaddies tear her to pieces, would that be surprising? No. And in some quarters, it might even be perceived as a sordid thing for us to have done. If we deliver her into the custody of British officers, though, and she suffers the same fate at their hands...oh, the dishonour!" He chuckled, "And to cap it all, I can't imagine anyone who would enjoy the joke less than the prudish Josef Renger."

***

Stepping into the large staff car, Tommie had been awed by its spacious and luxurious interior; even shackled at the wrists and ankles, she was comfortable. Soon enough, though, the sensation of being driven in a rear-facing seat had made her queasy, and the rich smell of the leather upholstery was compounding the effect. She leaned her head against the window, but a calculated movement drew her attention as Blauser inched along the opposite seat to position himself in front of her. His eyes drifted over her body, depositing a slug trail on her nerves.

She sat up straight and returned his gaze with a stony expression. Sliding his hips forward to the edge of the deep seat, he leaned forward and laid his hands on her knees.

"We have a long, boring trip ahead of us, fraulein, why don't we find a way to keep ourselves amused?" He glanced across at Steiger who stared at him for a moment with distaste, then turned and fixed his gaze out of the window.

Blauser smirked. "Major Steiger would be more than happy to keep his eyes averted, and I can certainly remove those shackles for you – the ones on your ankles, at least," he grinned, and Tommie's skin prickled. "So, what do you say? Wouldn't you like to make a comparison between British men and German men?" He tilted his head speculatively, "Plenty of French men have been there too, I would imagine. Yes, a little exercise in comparison; I believe you will be pleasantly surprised." When she gave no reply, he shrugged indifferently. "Your compliance is not necessary. Women are the spoils of war; it is a gratuity upheld by centuries of military tradition, so I will take my due either way." He smiled and let his thumbs slide downwards between her knees.

Tommie's feet jerked up in a sharp, convulsive movement, and she watched as the sculpted features registered the impact and twisted in horror.

Hearing the thud of Blauser's knees hitting the floor of the car, Steiger whipped around to see his subordinate huddled, writhing and coughing on the floor. He turned a murderous expression on Tommie and she returned it in kind.

"Why do you look at me like that, Major Steiger? I have fulfilled centuries of military tradition; I have spoiled his war."

The back of Steiger's hand connected with her cheekbone, and her face exploded in a flare of pain as her face hit and bounced off the window.

"Get off the floor, Blauser," he snapped. Leaning back into his seat, he turned to stare once more through the window. "You would do well to remember that move, fraulein," he said, "you will have need of it where you're going."

Tommie had never in her life been hit like that. She didn't consider her commando training to be in the same vein, and she sat, subdued, staring out at the landscape.

The endless farmland was eventually interrupted by a small, grey, provincial town which squatted alongside the road and then was gone, but now the road was taking them up the lower slopes of an odd outcropping of rock, and, glancing over her shoulder, she saw that the top of it seemed to metamorphose into a towering castle. No glorious Rhine palace or quaint Alpine schloss, the structure was as plain as its surroundings, and equally charmless.

Blauser turned to her with an unpleasant smile. The drive had taken just under an hour, and he had recovered from his extremity, although his complexion was still pale and pinched.

"You may have evaded *my* attentions, Fraulein West," he said, his voice grating with spite, "but I defy you to survive what awaits you in there." He indicated the castle with a nod of his head. "There are approximately four hundred men in that castle, many of whom have not had a woman for years. It will take more than a little nimble footwork on your part to outmatch so many men. Let me see… at least one to hold each arm, and several more for each leg, while the others impatiently wait their turn, becoming more and more aroused at the sport." He lowered his hand to his crotch. "Witnessing a woman's domination – her humiliation – excites a man like nothing else, and what one man has conquered becomes the next man's right, and the next and the next, and after that – after a woman has allowed herself to be used in such a way – she is a creature to be reviled, and will be handled accordingly." Blauser was breathing hard now, and pinpricks of sweat were oozing from the pores above his exquisitely chiselled top lip. "But look, here we are. You shall soon find out for yourself."

The car had pulled up beneath the gatehouse of the castle, and the guard standing there snapped to attention before turning to open the heavy gate. The car rolled into the centre of a large, cobbled courtyard and stopped. Steiger, suddenly invigorated, adopted an attitude of bluff bonhomie, opened up the door and stepped out.

11
Her own kind

1942

Pacing the courtyard of the commandantur, Peter listened to the shouts of a no-holds-barred football game echoing from the adjacent prisoners' yard, and the exuberance pulled at the edges of his mind the way that sunshine calls to a schoolboy confined in a classroom.

On such a fine summer day, all humanity yearns to be outside in parks and on village greens, celebrating life, but instead the world was at war and here he was, with the sound of his footsteps echoing around a stone courtyard, waiting to greet one of the most loathsome men he had ever met.

Now a senior staff officer, stationed at Zossen, an efficient communications centre sunk in the depths of a pine forest south of Berlin, Peter's primary task was the gathering of intelligence from Soviet prisoners held in the camp at Dabendorf, and for that purpose, he had been billeted nearby in this castle, which was in use as a prison for allied officers.

From the peace of the Tiergarten and the neo-classical grace of the Bendlerblock, to the dripping forests of Zossen and a glowering, stone-cold castle; the pre-war world appeared to him now like a distant hill-top catching the last, poignant glow of a setting sun.

In the other yard, a many-voiced bellow rang out, and he glanced up. The interior of the castle was segmented by what the castle staff called the seam; a stone wall that cleaved it into two chilly, misshapen wells. The commandantur courtyard was larger and marginally more well-favoured than the prisoners' side, and graced with more sunshine if the cloud cover allowed. Window boxes fixed to the walls tumbled incongruously with flowers, but no such incongruity occurred in the prisoners' courtyard; squatting on the other side of the seam, it was an echoing stone beaker. In the height of summer, the sun wouldn't touch its stone cobbles before mid-morning, when it briefly became a crucible, and in winter it was an ice-box.

Another noise interrupted his thoughts. From the inner guardhouse he heard a voice raised in anger; Kessler's voice, he noted without surprise. Kessler was a particularly surly character with an inadequate command of his temper, and it was rumoured that his exemption from active duty had been approved on psychological grounds. Too violent to be trusted with a weapon in battle, Peter thought sourly.

Standing in the doorway of the guardhouse, Kessler was shouting into the face of a heavy-set, middle-aged woman who was standing her ground before him, with defiance knitted into every muscle. Peter made his way over to them.

"What is the meaning of this behaviour?" he demanded sharply. "Sergeant Kessler, I consider it unacceptable for an officer of the Reich to address a woman in this way."

The sergeant gaped at him. "She is a cleaning woman, Herr Major, and she is insolent and unmanageable. I demand that she be fired immediately."

"You demand, sergeant?"

The sergeant backtracked hastily. "Sir, I had meant to say that I will demand of the housekeeper that she be fired."

"I see." Peter turned to the woman, "And what is the nature of your transgression, Frau...?"

"Heller," the woman answered. "My name is Frau Heller, sir." Her colour was high and her nostrils were pinched and white, but she spoke in level tones. "I had just finished sweeping the guardhouse when Sergeant Kessler called me back. He told me to wait while he finished his cigarette, then he dropped it on the floor, although there was an ash-tray to hand. He ground it out and told me to sweep it up. I took exception to this."

Kessler snorted. "You took exception! You are a cleaner. It is your job to clean floors. If I tell you to sweep up my cigarette then you sweep up my cigarette." His face was livid, and a vein showed, grey and swollen, in his forehead.

"Sergeant Kessler," said Peter quietly, "as a German man you are expected to demonstrate respect for all German womanhood. Is it not Party policy to honour the mothers of Germans? You will find that your own mother carries a card which reads "Protecting the mother is the noble duty of each member of the German community." That means it is your duty too."

"But, Herr Major, my mother is a biddable woman who knows her place and keeps to it. This woman is a scold who does not know when to still her tongue out of respect for a uniform. Surely there comes a point at which a man's obligation to his duty is neutralized."

Peter closed his eyes briefly as this statement echoed hollowly in his head.

"That's an interesting philosophy, Sergeant Kessler, he said. "As it happens, we are expecting Major Steiger for a visit at any moment. You must discuss your theory with him."

The man's face twisted into a mask of fear. "No, sir. I was speaking in anger. I see my mistake now. Please accept my apology."

"*I* am not due an apology, sergeant, but I think that an apology to Frau Heller would serve to demonstrate your acquiescence to the Fuhrer's policies."

Kessler slipped from fear back to his natural ill humour. He opened his mouth to protest, and hesitated; Peter had allowed his face to become still and calm. Stiller and calmer than usual, and he watched as some little-used instinct in the sergeant understood the intention behind it. Kessler swallowed with difficulty and turned to the woman.

"In compliance with the Fuhrer's policy towards German motherhood, I apologise for my rudeness to you."

"Thank you, sergeant, and I promise always to address you in the same tone with which you address me," she replied levelly.

"There!" Peter smiled beatifically, "Now you may both return to your duties, secure in the knowledge that the Fuhrer's wisdom enlightens our lives even on such an elemental level."

Stiff with outrage, Kessler turned on his heel and stalked back into the guardhouse with as much hostility in his bearing as he dared to express. Frau Heller didn't spare the man another glance, but Peter found that she was watching his own face intently.

"Frau Heller?"

The woman's gaze veered to his left, where the double gates were opening to admit a large black staff car.

"I must get back to my work," she said, "but I thank you for your mediation, Major Brandt." She disappeared into the commandantur, and Peter turned to the car, which had pulled up nearby and was purring quietly, its Nazi insignia battling the irregular breezes of the castle. The door opened and Otto Steiger stepped out.

Peter flexed his shoulders and crossed the courtyard as Steiger flashed him a broad smile.

"Major Brandt, good morning. But I was expecting to see the commandant of this delightful establishment. Has Colonel Renger assigned his house-guest to meet-and-greet duties? I would consider that to be squandering the talents of such a highly-skilled intelligence man."

Peter gave him a thin smile. The commandant had not even remotely entertained the thought of greeting Steiger himself; he would have snubbed the man by sending Friedrich Hamm, his second in command, but Hamm was on leave, and to send a still more junior officer would be a dangerously heavy-handed slight. Peter was effectively a guest in the castle, but from an intelligence point of view, documenting a visiting prisoner was good practice, and the opportunity to deliver Renger's snub to Steiger in person was a bonus.

"Colonel Renger will join us at his convenience," he said smoothly. "Meanwhile, I understand that you have someone for me to interview?"

Steiger registered the insult with a narrowing of his eyes, then turned to the open door of the car and gave a brief nod. A young woman, shackled at the wrists and ankles, appeared in the doorway, squinting up at the walls of the castle. In the next instant she was propelled forcefully out of the car by a booted foot, and landed hard, sprawling on the cobbles. Cold disgust welled up in Peter, and he went to help the girl, taking her arm as she struggled to her knees.

"Bist du verletzt, fraulein?"

With a hiss she pulled her arm away from him. "So, you want to be next, do you?" she spat.

"You're British!" In those two words, surprise stripped away the veneer of his German accent, whisking him back to the King's English, and he saw the girl's eyes widen. He turned to Steiger, who was watching with an expression of mild amusement.

"Was ist das, Steiger?"

Steiger laughed and answered him in English.

"'What is this?' he asks! This, Major Brandt, is a woman – of sorts. I understand that you lead a limited life in this god-forsaken spot, but can it be that you have forgotten so much? Ah, but of course!" he added, spreading his arms to encompass the castle, "Locked away with all these naughty public-schoolboys, why would you need women?"

"Why is she here, and why do you have custody of her? Foreign nationals are still under the jurisdiction of the Wehrmacht, I believe, and not subject to SS attentions."

"Foreign *servicemen* are under the jurisdiction of the Wehrmacht, Major Brandt. In this you are correct, as usual, but this foreign national qualifies as an enemy agent, and that affords me the right to investigate her as I see fit."

"A spy?" Peter said incredulously, casting his eye over

the odd little person in front of him. Dressed in a thick, shapeless, tweed skirt that reached almost to her ankles, and a torn black satin blouse, she wore a red and white check gingham scarf tied around her neck, and shoes that might once have been sensible, but were now split, flapping open and just short of disintegrating altogether. She had struggled to her feet without his assistance, and stood glaring at him.

"Don't be fooled," Steiger was saying, "she may look like an insignificant, shabby little thing, but she has quite a kick to her."

A sudden, animal roar erupted from the football game in the adjoining courtyard, and the girl flinched, stumbling sideways at the sound. This was a spy? She looked to be not much more than twenty years old, her small figure was anchored to the ground by the shackles, and her face bore the evidence of rough treatment. Behind her, Blauser, the latest of Steiger's lieutenants, was emerging from the car to stand, pale and stiff, stooping slightly from the waist in a posture that every man knows the origins of. Steiger was looking his man up and down critically.

"And now, Major Brandt, if you wouldn't mind offering us the primitive hospitality of this castle, I think Lieutenant Blauser here would be most grateful."

"First you will remove the girl's shackles."

"They should stay on," Steiger said lightly. "She's a tricky little piece of work."

"The shackles come off. Unless you want to carry her through the castle."

Steiger's face froze briefly in anger, then he concealed it, smiled again, slipped a hand into a pocket, and tossed the keys to Peter.

"You're such a humanitarian, Brandt," he said, bringing a cavilling tone into his voice, "a deplorable quality to suffer from. It's a significant flaw in your character." The smile slipped as Peter released the girl's wrists, but he offered no further argument. Kneeling at her feet to free her ankles, Peter tossed the key back to Steiger, flung the shackles at Blauser, then stood and gestured towards the commandantur.

"Please, if you would come this way."

Two years of living at the castle had not endeared him to the place. In its history, it had served variously as a monastery, a convent, and a lunatic asylum, and its stones had not forgotten.

Passing the administrative offices, he paused at an open office door and spoke briefly to a large, blonde woman in a grey wool uniform, who put down the papers she was sorting, and joined them.

"Frau Hess will serve as a chaperone," he announced, and caught a glance of derision between Steiger and Blauser.

The room he had chosen for the interview was bare, square and plain, its stone floors uncarpeted and its walls unplastered. A narrow window, heavily barred, occupied the centre of the back wall, looking out onto an abutting façade of more grey stone.

During the castle's years as a lunatic asylum, this room had served as a detention chamber for the more severely disturbed of its inmates. It did not require heightened psychic sensibilities to detect the clammy horror that permeated the walls, and Peter felt confident that Steiger would understand that he was as welcome as this cold reception implied. Steiger flashed him a look that confirmed this, then opened his briefcase and handed Peter a manila folder. Peter took it.

"There is a washroom across the hall, gentlemen," he said. "Fraulein Hess, perhaps you would escort the young lady to somewhere where she can freshen up."

Crossing to the window he glanced through the papers in the folder. The evidence supporting the girl's involvement with the French resistance was irrefutable, and yet, in one of those inexplicable quirks of circumstance that jinked, flickered and evaded the inevitable, she had not faced a firing squad. Instead, she had been put on a train destined for one of those infernal camps. So why was she here now? He read further, glanced at the photostat tucked into the back of the folder, and nodded to himself.

He declined to look up as he heard Steiger and Blauser return from the washroom and settle themselves, muttering quietly, into the chairs either side of the coffee table. He heard the girl's footsteps, scuffing in the disintegrating shoes, marshalled by the heavy clack of Fraulein Hess's heels, and then, when the door opened again, he lifted his head to greet the man who entered.

Josef Renger, the commandant of the castle, wore a perpetual expression of mild bewilderment, as though the complexities of his position defied his comprehension, but in truth he was an efficient administrator who deftly juggled the complex politics and practicalities of the prison. A career soldier, he rarely took the trouble to conceal his intense distaste for the Nazis, and now, as he caught sight of the girl, he hesitated, puzzled, before turning an expressionless gaze on Peter. Peter returned the gaze in kind before he spoke, holding his silence just long enough to allow a curdled awkwardness to squeeze into the room.

"Colonel Renger," he said eventually, "I believe you know Major Steiger of the SS, and this is Lieutenant Blauser." The men greeted each other stiffly. Peter turned to the girl. "And this is Tomasin West, believed to be a British spy. Fraulein West, please allow me to introduce Colonel Josef Renger, the commandant of this castle."

"And our other guest?" Steiger interrupted, impatient with the niceties.

"Will be here in due time," replied the commandant coolly. "I believe that Major Brandt, in his capacity as intelligence officer with FHO, has some questions for your prisoner. This interview will, of course, be noted on our records."

Steiger looked as though he might refuse, but cold arrogance took over. Renger took a seat in the far corner of the room, and Peter crossed to the centre table, and drew out the chair that faced the door, inviting the young woman to sit. Taking the chair opposite her, he glanced down at the file. "Your name is Tomasin West?"

"Yes."

"You are British?"

"Yes."

"And an agent of the British government."

"No."

He lifted his eyes to her face. "You were in France with forged papers, passing as... Thereze Pascal."

"I wanted to live and work in France, and I could not get papers by legitimate means. Thereze is a friend of my family's. She gave me her papers."

"A friend of your family's? Yet her family, when questioned, had no knowledge of you."

"Perhaps they were afraid of reprisals. Reprisals are very common in France these days."

She said no more, and he set the file down on the table. What purpose could possibly have been served by British Intelligence sending this young woman into France in the path of the war? She should be pacing a hospital ward, nursing wounded servicemen, falling in love, planning her wedding... anything other than sitting in this room at the mercy of Otto Steiger.

With the exception of the marks on her cheeks, she did not appear to have been beaten yet, but under the jurisdiction of the SS she faced intolerable treatment and a violent death. He studied her frankly. There was a quaint formality in her posture as she sat with her hands together on her lap and her head erect. Under his gaze she sat up straighter and pushed her hair back behind her ears.

The vivid red weals on her cheeks promised to ripen into large, purple bruises, and her eyes... he frowned. The pupils had expanded suddenly, forcing the living hazel of the irises to retreat, pursued by blackness. They seemed to be focusing fractionally inside his brain, and a strange expression occupied them – surprise or curiosity – as though she recognized him, or knew about him.

"Fraulein," he said sharply. The girl blinked and her eyes regained their focus. He took a quick breath and bent his head to the file again. No, it was impossible that she could know of him. "After your escape from the train you passed near Kirchheim," he continued coolly, "Is that correct?"

"I don't know."

"Then which direction did you take?"

"I think I travelled south."

He sighed heavily. It really made no difference now; nothing could extricate her from Steiger's hands.

The door behind him opened, and he heard the chink and rattle of crockery as an orderly passed him, dressed in a white jacket, carrying a large tray. The smell of good coffee wound through the room, and the girl's eyes followed the orderly's progress as he set the tray down and positioned place settings for Steiger and Blauser, before proffering a serving plate of pastries.

His mottled old hands shook slightly from the effort of concentration as Steiger took a large, cream-filled pastry, then added another to his plate and settled back comfortably. Blauser lifted an eyebrow and muttered under his breath. Steiger impaled him with a look. The orderly moved on to serve the commandant, and the girl's eyes followed the pastries until they were out of sight, then her throat constricted as she swallowed and stared fixedly at her hands.

Inclining his head gravely to the commandant, the orderly made his way around to Peter's elbow, and Peter turned his best charming smile on the girl.

"How do you take your coffee, Fraulein?" She looked up from her hands, startled.

"Coffee?"

He took a perverse enjoyment in the surprise that rippled her blank mask at his challenge. They both knew the cardinal rule; refuse all succour offered by the enemy, and in the face of her hesitation, he advanced.

"No?" he said lightly, "Perhaps you would you rather take tea?" A recognition of his provocation registered in her face, followed by indecision and then a stubborn defiance.

"Thank you, Major Brandt, I would like coffee, with milk, please."

His smile widened, and he gestured for the orderly to set

a place for her and serve coffee. It was real coffee, freshly made. Evidently the kitchen staff were keen to indulge the men who rode under the SS ensign.

"And a pastry too," he said indulgently, lifting the serving dish and silver tongs from the tray. "Please, allow me to make a selection for you. I insist that you try the sweet cheese Danish – it is my personal favourite – and then, perhaps, a slice of Bienenstich," he added, indicating the pastry with the serving tongs. "Yes, most definitely, you must try the Bienenstich; filled with vanilla custard and topped with a crust of almonds and honey." He set the cheese Danish on her plate and then placed the tongs and the serving dish deliberately on the table in front of her. "No, no, no," he waved away the orderly, who had reached out to retrieve the dish, "These are for Fraulein West. I am interested to see which ones she will select for herself after she has sampled my recommendations." The waves of silent outrage emanating from Steiger brought him a warm sense of satisfaction.

Turning to address the girl again, he saw a slight flush colouring her cheeks as she bit into the pastry, and his puckishness subsided. He stood up, crossed the room, laid the file down on the windowsill and bent over it, feigning deep concentration. Let her enjoy her coffee in peace; he shuddered to think what awaited her when she went on from here in Steiger's custody.

Reading the account of the couple spotted near Leipzig, he glanced again at the photostat that was tucked into the back of the folder. This was the trap that Steiger had set for his prisoner, but Peter's curiosity had been drawn by another detail in her history. When he finally straightened up and brought the file back to the centre table, the girl had finished her sweet cheese Danish and was eyeing the Bienenstich.

"I see in your file that you attended a French woman during her childbirth," he said conversationally, returning to his seat opposite her and handing her the serving tongs.

"Yes, I did."

"Are you qualified to perform this procedure?"

"There was no alternative," she said, transferring the Bienenstich to her plate. "Yvonne could not find anyone else willing to help her because she was known to have… to be… to have consorted with a German soldier."

"So I understand. Nevertheless, a desire to help is not a certificate of obstetric competence, yet you not only brought the woman and her child safely through labour and delivery, but, as noted here, provided her with a professional level of post-natal care. Where did you learn the skills you employed?"

She did not reply immediately, biting into the cake to delay answering, and when she did, she spoke carefully.

"I have had some experience of assisting women during childbirth."

"How so?"

"I am a nurse, Major Brandt."

"That, also, is understood. However, in Britain, as in Germany, it is not a nurse who attends women in childbirth, but rather a midwife. Are you a midwife?" A hiss of indrawn breath came from the other side of the room. Steiger was staring at the girl as though seeing her for the first time. Peter glanced curiously at the SS officer, then back at the girl who was sitting perfectly still, wilfully ignoring Steiger's reaction. "Fraulein?" he prompted. She lifted her eyes to his and held his gaze for a long moment, but her expression was unreadable.

"Yes, Major Brandt, I am a midwife."

He nodded and glanced back down at her file.

"Do you make a habit of offering aid to enemy sympathisers?"

"I offered my assistance to a woman who otherwise would have faced childbirth alone and afraid; an unnecessary and dangerous experience."

"Nevertheless, a British spy in occupied territory…"

"A nurse, Major Brandt," she interrupted, "I was employed as a nurse."

"Yes, of course. A nurse," he replied. He tapped his fingertips on the table, allowing his eyes to focus on some spot outside the room. "Still, I can't think that your actions were well-considered under the circumstances. In fact, I would go so far as to say that you were impulsive. That your actions jeopardized your position, whatever you claim that to be; spy or nurse."

Now her eyes and voice and face were pebble-hard. "Each one of us must answer ultimately to their own conscience."

A knock sounded at the door. Blauser rose and opened it, nodded briefly and stepped aside as a figure was unceremoniously propelled into the room.

Peter was impressed; if he hadn't been watching the young woman's face closely, he would have missed the fleeting fraction of a moment when she reacted – a single pulse of light from a lighthouse – before dousing it and glancing away again. Not that it mattered, he thought grimly, as Flight Lieutenant Leigh's voice rang out, clear and incredulous, in the expectant room.

"Tommie? *Tommie!*"

Stepping forward, he was roughly restrained by his guard as Peter sighed, closed the file, and rose from his chair. He glanced across at Steiger, anticipating a smirk, but instead, the mask of sophisticated cruelty had dissolved into frank astonishment.

Covering his confusion almost as rapidly as the girl had shut down her own reaction to Leigh's appearance, Steiger rallied, banishing the effect so swiftly and completely that Peter blinked, but for that one moment, the man's face had been illuminated, as though the sun had burst through a stained-glass window.

A strange disorientation settled on the room as Steiger picked up his briefcase and turned towards the door.

"Well, that concludes my business here," he said shortly. "Auf wiedersehn, fraulein."

Renger, who had been stewing silently in his chair, rose up like the Leviathan, roaring in fury. "You are not leaving her here!"

"Oh, but I am. Yes, I am," Steiger grinned. "There is no

better place for her. She has been identified as a spy by her good friend over there," he added, tilting his head towards Leigh without making eye contact. He wagged a finger at Peter, "You see what happens when you feed a stray, Major Brandt? It becomes impossible to get rid of."

"I refuse to accept custody of this prisoner," insisted the commandant, his voice shaking with anger. "There must be an alternative."

"I could take her outside and shoot her," said Steiger lightly. "Or I could shoot her right here." Setting down his briefcase, he slid his hand gun from its holster and, cocking the trigger, he strode across the room and pushed the barrel against the girl's forehead. In the corner of the room, Leigh gave a strangled shout and then a grunt as the guard drove the butt of his rifle into his chest.

Tomasin West's eyes fluttered closed briefly, then opened again. She drew a deep breath, but otherwise remained perfectly still, staring past the gun, past Steiger's shoulder, into the distance. Watching her face, Steiger smiled. "But that would make such a mess in this lovely room," he continued, without lowering the gun. "What do you say, Herr Commandant? It's your call." It was clear from Renger's face that, from his point of view, this might be considered a reasonable option, but he remained silent. Steiger shrugged, lowered the gun and tucked it back into its holster. "And is it not fitting that she stays here with her own kind?"

"They are not her own kind," snapped the commandant, "They are men; she is a woman."

"Better still," Steiger countered, "You will make yourself very popular with the prisoners; providing a little something for their... their stiff upper lips," he said, laughing.

"I will not allow it!" shouted Renger.

Steiger spread his hands, openly enjoying the other man's rage. "But this is a perfect opportunity to advance your career, is it not? We all know how Herr Goebbels loves a propaganda coup; I can see the newsreel footage now: The Enemy's Dishonour! British officers fall on their defenceless countrywoman like a pack of starving wolves." He cocked his head at Renger, "There could even be a financial bonus for you if you were so inclined; a discreet little room off the prisoners" courtyard... I understand being a madam is quite a profitable concern!"

Leigh stepped forwards again, earning himself another blow from the rifle butt. He stopped short, cursing, but kept talking.

"Look, what is your name? Major Steiger? Putting her in here contravenes the Geneva Convention. Tommie, tell him you won't stay."

Steiger stared at the Englishman, and again Peter saw astonishment in his eyes. That Leigh would be reckless enough to confront the man so forcefully was, indeed, astonishing, but he suspected that Steiger's reaction was of a different nature entirely.

The girl was shaking her head.

"Believe me, Simon," she said sourly, "you might as well appeal to Major Steiger as a gentleman."

Steiger grinned. "Fraulein West knows how things stand. A word of warning, though; she knows a few fast moves, doesn't she, Blauser?" He faked a punch at Blauser's groin and laughed as the young man doubled up. In the corner of the room, the commandant's face was livid.

"Am I to understand that I have no say in this matter?"

"On the contrary, Colonel Renger, you may say as much as you wish, and I feel certain that you will, but I can assure you that no one will be listening. No one who matters, at least." With a shocking suddenness, Steiger dropped his mask of congeniality, his face snapping shut like a bear-trap, "But be sure, Herr Colonel, not to misplace Fraulein West. The entertainment value that I personally derive from this situation is merely incidental to the reason for her presence here. She must under no circumstances be allowed to escape."

When no response was forthcoming from the commandant, Steiger nodded curtly, flashed another hollow glance at Leigh, and left the room without looking back.

The door closed behind him, and Renger cursed angrily. "What are we going to do with her?" he cried. "In God's name, where are we going to put her? Where? This castle is full of men!" He turned to Peter in despair. Peter shook his head and pressed his thumb to his forehead, shielding his eyes with his hand.

The situation was unthinkable, of course, and he sympathised with Renger's predicament, but he was puzzled by Steiger's actions; Hitler's Commando Order, signed by the Fuhrer himself, was explicit; any foreign agent, armed or unarmed was to be annihilated either in battle or in flight. *To hold them in military custody – for example in POW camps, etc,* the order stated, *even only as a temporary measure, is strictly forbidden... I shall hold every officer* answerable to a *court-martial who neglects or behaves contrary to this command.*

He glanced inside the girl's file again. It had been neither stamped nor signed by the Gestapo, and it was anybody's guess whether this would end up being a good thing for Tomasin West, or a bad thing, but either way, Steiger was already in contravention of this order, and that was worth knowing.

"I wish I could offer a resolution, Herr Commandant, but I find myself at a loss," he said, glancing at his watch, "And I must prepare for a meeting, so if you would please excuse me." He handed the file to the commandant, who assigned one guard and Frau Hess to remain in the room with the girl.

"A chaperone!" he moaned to Peter as they left together. "I am the commandant of this castle. I will not be made a pimp!"

***

It was a little less than an hour later when Tommie saw the door open again to admit the castle's commandant, along with Simon and a man who wore the uniform of a Royal Army colonel. She was relieved to see them, but they approached her warily, as though she were a feral animal.

The commandant introduced the army officer as Colonel Gregory, the senior British officer at the castle. Gregory shook her hand with old-fashioned civility. His grey-blue eyes regarded her from a face that was crumpled and lined, but comfortably so. Beneath well-established laugh lines, and creases that spoke of habitual contemplation, the man had a quiet dignity and an aura of personal authority that Tommie found herself submitting to willingly, like a lost child in the presence of a responsible adult.

He informed her that she had been assigned a room in one of the dormitories occupied by British officers, the only alternative – and an even more unacceptable one – being that she should be confined to a room in the commandantur.

"I anticipate that you will conduct yourself in a modest manner, is that understood?" he concluded.

"Yes, Colonel Gregory. I promise that you will have no trouble from me."

The commandant shook his head mournfully.

"How I wish I could believe that."

***

"You're letting them foist a bawdy woman on us, sir?"

The men of her assigned dormitory – about twelve in all – were staring at her in silent incredulity, but the scrawny one, dressed in the remains of a navy uniform, was volubly outraged. "We all know the drill, you strumpet," he snarled. "The Hun sets a woman like you to weaken a man's defences and before you know it, he's babbling out secrets like a fool."

"What secrets?" she said.

"See? There she goes already!" the man squawked.

Simon threw her a reproachful glance, and she tried for a penitent expression, but the man reminded her of a cross between a chihuahua and a rat as he darted at her and retreated, his top lip drawn back.

"Eric, calm down," said Colonel Gregory quietly.

"She's a bawdy woman, sir. They told us we'd be up against them."

"I'm not a bawdy woman."

"A bawdy woman would say that, wouldn't she!"

"So would a non-bawdy woman," said Tommie reasonably.

Simon sighed.

"What Eric means is that the Germans have been known to use... lewd women to undermine captured prisoners."

"I know what he meant, Simon, I was being flippant. And, alright, this is probably not a good time for being flippant, but look at me," she said, spreading her arms and letting her tattered sleeves flap. "I don't make a very good lewd woman."

"That's alright, love, you can practice on me," grinned a bright-faced young man wearing the battle-dress and Rising Sun badge of the Australian army.

"Alluring women, then," Simon amended, flashing the Australian a hard look. Tommie shook her head.

"Don't you think they could have found a more alluring woman for their purposes?"

"They wouldn't need to. Men in our position aren't exactly going to be picky." The malicious drawl came from a thin man wearing a spiv moustache and a much-repaired army uniform.

"That's enough, Watley." Colonel Gregory said wearily, "Gentlemen, I am aware that it is a highly irregular and undesirable circumstance for Miss West to be billeted here, but, while you are entitled to your reservations about the situation, I would ask you to approach her with meticulous courtesy, and I don't think I have to lecture you on maintaining the decency of which Major Steiger seems to think us incapable. If it helps in any way, I would also inform you that Flight Lieutenant Leigh is acquainted with Miss West, and assures me that, to the best of his knowledge, she is a member of the First Aid Nursing Yeomanry, and, until her capture, had been working in

France."

"So, she's already been in your trousers, eh, Leigh?"

"That's offensive, Eric" snapped Gregory, "Like it or not, this situation has been imposed on us, but I won't tolerate that sort of unpleasantness." He turned to Tommie, "You will need... well... supplies," he said awkwardly. "Soap, toothpaste and a towel. Lieutenant Bainbridge is our acting quartermaster, and he will help you out with that." He gestured to a very large, dark-haired man wearing a Canadian Army battledress jacket and a kilt. "Doug, the usual rules apply; any basic needs that can be met by our resources must be met." Bainbridge nodded, and Gregory turned back to Tommie, "My rooms are in the senior officers' quarters, Miss West, please consider me accessible at any time if you should need to see me." He swept a severe glance over the company before disappearing through the door to the courtyard.

Nobody moved. The officers remained in position, staring at her with frank suspicion, and then a voice, grating with hostility, inserted itself between them.

"You are not welcome here." A heavy man with a body like a flour sack was standing slouched against the bunk next to the outer door, watching her coldly. Unlike the other officers, who wore an eclectic combination of mismatched but recognizable uniform pieces, he was wearing a coarse sweater of a brownish colour, and shapeless trousers. "We are prisoners in this castle," he continued, "And the last time I looked in a dictionary, the definition of "prisoner" is one who is held against his will. You, on the other hand, seem content to be here. I can't speak for my fellow officers, but I find that suspicious."

As a demonstration of open-hearted hospitality, this welcome left a lot to be desired, and Steiger's move – a blatant violation of Hitler's Commando Order – was worrying, but she hadn't seen a British uniform since she had scrambled off the Lysander in France so long ago, and when Colonel Gregory had stepped through that door in the commandantur, she'd felt a powerful surge of belonging.

That surge receded now, but even so, an odd sensation was germinating in her like a tree that puts out buds in February, half-remembering something half-forgotten. She was remembering what it was like to have a hearth.

The men drifted away, and Simon showed her a cell-like room, measuring about five paces in length by four paces wide. There was a wooden bed with a thin mattress pad beneath a barred window in the left wall, and in the facing wall, a wardrobe stood next to a wash basin. It wasn't the broom closet in Drancy, and it was hers.

"I've swapped my bunk for Watley's," Simon said, awkwardly, "so I'll be right outside your door."

Tommie smiled.

"Thank you, that's good to know." She glanced through the doorway into the men's dormitory, and pushed the door closed. "I have some resources to share with you now, Simon," she said, reaching inside her blouse to where her waistline had become strangely lumpy, "...and no – it's not my body." She drew out the gingham cloth, laid it on the bed, and unfolded it to reveal the remaining three pastries which she had claimed from the serving plate in the commandantur.

When Frau Hess had tried to stop her from taking them, she had spat at the woman like a wildcat hoarding a kill; "Major Brandt said they were for me!" This was indisputable, and the woman had backed off reluctantly, watching with frank disdain as Tommie took the gingham cloth from around her neck, wrapped the treasures in it and tucked them out of sight.

Simon's eyes widened as he saw the hoard.

"I know I should have refused them," she said, "But for pity's sake, look at them, Simon!" He did look at them, and then back at her. "Oh! Oh, no!" she said, horrified, "Don't think... *please* don't think I did anything to... earn them. Major Brandt gave them to me to spite Steiger."

Simon looked at her oddly, then nodded and gave her a quick hug. "I'll make us a cup of tea."

Later, sitting beside him on the bed, with a cup of tea in

her hand and the cakes on the gingham cloth between them, she nudged him with her elbow.

"So, did they foist a bawdy woman on you when you were captured?"

12
The greatcoat

The quartermaster, Doug Bainbridge, had led her to a door in the far corner of the men's dormitory, which he unlocked with a key hung around his neck on a length of string, revealing an Aladdin's cave of supplies.

She selected soap, toothpaste and a toothbrush, a bottle of men's shampoo, and then, joy of joys, on the next shelf down she saw several neatly ordered piles of underwear. Men's underwear, naturally; woollen and manly, but underwear nevertheless, and warm. She had only the peach rayon bloomers she stood up in, and they weren't going to see the war out. She glanced shyly up at Bainbridge who shrugged, "All basic needs, Colonel Gregory said."

Self-consciously, she took two pairs of underpants, one to wash and one to wear. Turning to follow him out of the room, she paused. The shelves on the opposite wall held uniform pieces, neatly ordered by service and size.

"If you've got these new uniforms here, why don't the men wear them?" she asked.

"You mean instead of the rags they've got on?" he said dryly. It was true; some of the officers were turned out as smartly as was practical under the circumstances, but most were sloping around in a scruffy assortment of clothing barely recognizable as uniform. "They all have decent uniforms," Bainbridge said, "they wear them on special occasions, but on an everyday basis, they dress like scruffs to show their contempt for the Germans." He gestured at the shelves, "This stuff comes in the Red Cross parcels."

Tommie thought about that. "In that case, would I be allowed to wear something from here?" she asked. "I feel a bit conspicuous in this skirt..." She stopped short, and he held her gaze steadily while she very carefully didn't look down at his kilt.

"It's not a skirt," he said.

With Gregory's approval, she was allowed to choose a new wardrobe. It wasn't easy; hers was evidently not a common body-type in any branch of the armed services, but Bainbridge supervised the process with stoic patience, and eventually she found herself in possession of a pair of battle-dress army trousers, with webbing gaiters to seal the bottoms against the cold, a white wool sweater and a Denison smock that acted as a wind-cheater and, satisfyingly, gave her the outline of a camouflaged haystack.

Better still, in addition to the men's underpants, she now owned two pairs of long johns, two pairs of heavy wool socks, and two long-sleeved cotton vests which, along with a muffler, neutralized the itch of the wool sweater.

When she had finalized her new wardrobe – and no shopping trip in London had ever given her such a warm glow – she folded the unwanted items neatly, and handed them back to Bainbridge. He took them, then held out his hand again.

"I'll take your clothes then, Miss... the skirt and the blouse. The shoes, too; I might be able to fix them. In here, you'd be better off wearing flying boots in the winter, daps in summer." He tilted his head, looking down at her feet, "Women's size eight?"

"You want women's clothes?!"

"You never know what could come in useful," he said impassively. "Size eight, then?" Vanity urged her to claim a size six, but he was right, and he knew it, so she nodded. "Your bra too, please," he said. She stared at him. He stared back. "If you want to be inconspicuous, this is what you'll need," he said eventually, reaching up and taking a roll of wide bandage and two safety pins from the top shelf. Then, considering something else and avoiding her eyes, he reached up again, and placed two pieces of cotton flannel in her hands, and more safety pins. Makeshift sanitary supplies. She swallowed hard.

Turning to leave, she glanced down at the shelf nearest to the door, at a man's cardigan, hand-knitted in a deep moss-green wool, with simple cabling up the front. It reminded her, with a pang, of peacetime evenings, and families sitting together listening to the radio. For a quiet, timeless moment, she was curled up with a cup of tea and a book, on her favourite chair, in her comfortable, faded living room. Without a word, Bainbridge placed the cardigan into her arms and ushered her out of the room.

She was offered the exclusive use of the shower room for ten minutes, and a temporary barricade of three chairs was placed across the door as a precaution against accidental trespass.

In the dormitory, Simon addressed the other officers.

"Listen, drop the hostility. I know some of you think she's a mole, but I'm telling you she's not."

"It's well out of bounds," said Keith Barnes, an army lieutenant, to nobody in particular. "Having a woman in the men's quarters is an insult."

A dark chuckle drew their attention to the bunk nearest to the shower room, where a figure lay stretched out on his back, his head resting on his crossed arms, studying the bed boards of the bunk above him.

"What's so funny, Allenby?" said Barnes, instantly angry. Allenby smiled.

"All of you. You're like an elephant skooching into the corner when a mouse shows up." He levered himself onto one elbow and regarded Barnes coolly. "How many men are in this castle now?" he said, "It has to be close to five hundred, but they throw one tiny little woman into the mix and you're all cowering against the walls."

"Nobody's cowering!" snapped Barnes, "and if you're trying to make a connection with your own situation, don't flatter yourself; we shrink away from you because you're an abomination – an appalling, humiliating corruption of a man."

Simon sighed.

"Simmer down, Keith, and let me say my piece before she gets back out here. I'm not saying you should accept her as one of us, just as one of ours."

Watley grunted and bit off the thread he'd been using to darn a sock. "You mean we should see her as a sort of mascot, right?"

"Well, sort of, I suppose, yes."

"I knew it. I never met a flyboy who didn't want to mount the squadron's goat."

There was a communal indrawn breath, and then Simon launched himself at Watley.

When Tommie emerged from the shower room, dressed in the uniform pieces, she found the dormitory churning with brawling men. Colonel Gregory was standing in the main doorway, hands in pockets, and Tommie edged carefully towards him. They watched the action together for a moment, then she turned to him. "Aren't you going to do something about it?"

"By that, do you mean stopping it? Not on your life! They have to fight someone. If they can't fight the enemy, it might as well be each other." He caught her expression from the corner of his eye. "You wouldn't understand," he added.

A subtle but discernible vibration made itself heard then. Faintly studded with distant staccato bursts, it got louder, gradually undercutting the turmoil in the room. Gregory, his head cocked like a hunting dog, nodded.

"This should provide a timely diversion."

"Bombers," Tommie said, "and anti-aircraft fire." They stood back, and within minutes the officers had disappeared, scrambling down the stairs to the courtyard.

It was only then that she became aware of a figure sitting on the bunk next to the shower room. She must have sidled right past him when she made her way towards Gregory.

It was the tension in his face that she noticed first as he turned towards them, and next it was his eyes; a striking pale green against olive skin. In those eyes, as they flicked from her to Gregory and back, Tommie recognized – beneath and beyond the impotent bleakness of captivity – a distinctive unhappiness that was familiar, but so alien in this context as to be unidentifiable.

There was a momentary, shared silence, and then Gregory's voice, quiet and level, acknowledged the man.

"Everything alright, Sam?"

"Perfectly fine, sir," came the quick response.

Gregory nodded.

"Miss West, this is Captain Sam Allenby," he said. "Sam, I hope you will welcome Miss West, and try to discourage any mean-spirited behaviour towards her from the others."

"As you say, sir," replied Allenby coolly. "Welcome, Miss West."

Unsettled by the man's off-handedness, Tommie responded awkwardly, but Allenby had already stretched himself out on his bunk with a languid motion, and was staring at the slats of the bunk above him.

The distant crumping of the bombs was louder now, and she turned to Gregory.

"Will they bomb the castle?"

"No, we are not a target. They know we're here. They will have been bombing either Berlin or the Junkers factory at Leipzig, but this castle seems to lie on a flight path, and we occasionally get a stray dropped in the area."

Following Gregory to a window onto the courtyard, where they could see the men shouting and whistling and cheering the droning aircraft on, she saw Simon standing quietly, watching the squadron fly over. Even from here she recognized the wistfulness in him.

***

She had been glad to get rid of the questionable blouse and the lumpish tweed skirt, and with the bandage wound around her chest she felt contained and secure, but more could be done.

As a woman's crowning glory, her straight, dark-brown, shoulder-length hair had always been a disappointment, stubbornly resisting pin-curls, victory rolls, and every beauty-salon treatment available, but now it was problematical for different reasons, so she approached Watley about it.

Watley, who made a respectable business cutting hair for the other officers, balked at her request.

"I'm not a ladies' hairdresser."

"I don't want a ladies' hairstyle," she said, "I want a man's haircut; the same one you give the others."

"I don't give everyone the same haircut!" he snapped, "I'm not an army barber, and these are not enlisted men. I don't shear them like sheep!"

"I'm sorry," she said meekly, "I didn't mean any offence. Please, will you give me a masculine haircut? Any one you like."

Watley's eyes flickered.

Picking up a chair, he carried it into the centre of the shower room and gestured for her to sit. He arranged his tools on a small table next to it, then, without a word, he busied himself, snipping and clipping with scissors and doing something alarming with a razor.

When he had finished, Tommie stared at her reflection in the mirror he held up for her. The impulse to cover her head in shame was powerful. Clipped tightly up the back of her neck, around her ears and at the sides of her head, the haircut had shorn every hint of femininity from her. The effect was rather more pixyish than masculine, but it was in no way feminine, much less bawdy or alluring.

"I told you you wouldn't like it." Watley's voice was smug.

"I wasn't planning on liking it," said Tommie stiffly.

"You gave me exactly what I asked for. With that skill, you could make a fortune in women's hairdressing after the war."

"If that's what women will want to look like after the war," Watley growled, cleaning his tools, "the Germans can shoot me now. And you can sweep up your own hair. I'm not an orderly."

She nodded.

"Where can I find a broom?" she asked, but Watley had clearly exhausted his tolerance for her. Picking up the chair and table, he left the shower room, brushing roughly past Sam Allenby who was leaning against the doorjamb, watching them. Allenby absorbed the assault without surprise, and swayed, unperturbed, back into position, observing the scene with a fascination that unnerved Tommie.

He took in the crescent of discarded hair that formed a dark fringe around where the chair had stood, and then his green eyes explored her head and her newly-exposed ears and neck. In the face of his poise and self-possession she felt graceless and raw, and she returned the stare belligerently.

"Where can I find a broom?" she said sharply. Allenby's eyes met hers then, and after a moment's hesitation he tilted his head, indicating a broom closet in the corner of the room. Grabbing a broom and a dustpan, she swept up the hair and tipped it into a bin.

"You don't mind?" His voice was cool, almost insolent.

"Mind?" Tommie said.

"You don't mind looking like that?"

Tommie flinched at the casual cruelty that somehow stung more than Watley's rudeness, and hoped the twist of humiliation hadn't shown in her face. Turning away from him, she returned the broom and dustpan to the closet.

"It's safer," she said, flatly.

"What about the things they say to you? The insults, the meanness? Don't you mind that?"

She had been at the castle for a week now, and the backhanded comments hadn't slowed. She shrugged.

"It's better that way; hopefully they'll be less likely to... you know."

There was a contemplative pause.

"And you don't want to... *you know*?" A touch of amusement edged the mimicry, but curiosity had quickened in his green eyes.

"No," she said. "No, I don't."

At that moment Simon appeared and positioned himself solidly against the other jamb of the doorway, fixing Allenby with an openly hostile glare. Allenby repaid the look with the languid insouciance of a cat, and then turned back to Tommie. The mockery in his eyes had resurfaced, flaring into a wicked smile, and he raised an eyebrow at her, tilting his head towards Simon.

"No?"

"No."

Catching the interaction, Simon glanced across at her, and his face twisted in shock.

"Shit, Tommie! What happened to your hair?"

"Watley gave me a haircut."

"The bastard!"

"No, I asked him to!" she said quickly, flashing a sour glance at Allenby, who was laughing quietly into the corner of the room, "It's part of my camouflage."

Simon pursed his lips, studying her hair with something oddly like resignation in his eyes, then turned an obscure expression on Allenby. Allenby shook his head.

"Don't give me that look, Simon; it was already a fait accompli when I turned up." Simon's expression hardened and Allenby grinned. "Alright, I was just leaving."

***

"You might want to stay away from Allenby, you know." Simon's voice was awkward, aiming for casual. They were walking the circuit of the courtyard together the following day, and she glanced at him, waiting for an explanation. He met her eyes and shrugged, "He's a bit of an odd one."

She nodded.

"I've noticed. Not malicious, though. Provocative, but not malicious."

"No, not malicious. Just odd. But..."

"But?"

"Well, just be careful around him. I wouldn't want you to get hurt, and I imagine he's a bit of a ladies' man – given the opportunity."

She laughed.

"A ladies' man, Simon? I don't think that – even given every opportunity – he's a ladies' man."

Simon gave her a sideways look. "You know about... about that sort of thing?"

She smiled.

"I've heard about it, yes." She covered her mouth with her fingertips. "Now you know I'm not the nice girl you thought I was."

"No, I know you're nice. I'm just not sure if you're right about Allenby; he has never openly... you know." He shrugged. "I mean, Ian and Don don't bother to be discreet about it, and there are plenty of others who... but, collectively, we just don't notice it. And we certainly don't talk about it. And then there's Gabe and Ken..."

He left the sentence unfinished, and Tommie nodded. Ken Parr, a young lieutenant in their dormitory, was inseparable from Gabryel Zan, a captain from the Polish contingent. They would pace the courtyard together, run circuits of the exercise field together, and spend hours reading or talking together. Always together.

She liked Zan. A cheerful, easy-going man with quick, dark eyes, he was a study in perpetual motion, and when his ready laugh filled a room or rang from the stone walls of the courtyard Tommie would see the tension in the faces of the other men ease for a brief moment, but he had a volatile temper that would erupt unexpectedly when others took his good nature for granted.

"He's been beaten up for it a few times," Simon was saying, "Zan, I mean, for... well, you know. Maybe the Poles aren't as relaxed about it as we are. It's probably because of the public-school system in England."

Tommie fought briefly to ignore this cue, and failed.

"They teach it in the public schools?"

"No!" he snorted, "but the environment invites it; all boys in a dormitory together, no girls around to catch their fancy. It's bound to happen."

"Don't you think they would still choose to be with boys even if there were girls around?"

"Well, maybe some of them would, but others aren't too fussy, they just want to..." He made a piston motion with his fist, then remembered who he was talking to and blushed furiously. She made a point of not noticing.

"So, Allenby has never... formed an attachment with anyone here?" she said curiously.

"No. Not one that anybody has ever known about."

***

For Tommie – as an alternative to Steiger and a firing squad – life at the castle was a gift horse with its mouth open wide for inspection; she had shelter, a place to stay, and people – with reservations – to talk to. But she could never escape.

She thought of the documents Simon had carried under the name of Hans Claus Ritten; somewhere in this castle, men were working away, producing similar documents and plotting devious escapes, but she wasn't trusted. Conversation fell silent when she passed by, and without support, she wouldn't make it past the castle walls.

Blauser's prediction of rape was an ever-present possibility, but as the days passed it was diminished by the strangely civilized structure and routines of the place.

The rank structure imposed by the armed forces was intertwined with, and sometimes complicated by, the far more ancient pecking order of social privilege, which divided the British contingent invisibly into those officers who had attended the best public schools, and those who had joined the services – as Simon put it – on their own merit.

Officers of the Commonwealth countries, and Robert Pickman, a US army captain who had been captured in the first days of his battalion's fighting in Tunisia, stood on the sidelines of this field of play. As did Tommie. She watched while – unbelievably to someone not long out of Drancy – regular meals, skimpy and basic perhaps, but regular, were cooked and served to the officers by orderlies, many of whom were British servicemen recruited from other-ranks prison camps.

These other-ranks servicemen, who were housed in separate quarters in the castle, also worked in the laundry, and some were employed privately to serve as batmen to those officers who insisted on maintaining the standards to which they had become accustomed before their capture.

The prisoners, several hundred of them, were kettled into the prisoners' side of the castle, and locked into their quarters each evening. At three daily appels or headcounts, they had to present themselves as on parade in their national contingents, but other than that, they were free to wander the rabbit warren of stairwells and dormitories.

Tommie's position at these appels – presumably in response to Steiger's threat – was at the front right-hand corner of the British contingent, before the alphabetical listing, with Allenby on her left, and Bainbridge next to him.

Each day, unless escapes or bad behaviour had incurred a withdrawal of privileges, the officers could sign up for a walk to the exercise field below the castle. Heavily guarded, and surrounded by a chain-link fence topped with rolls of vicious barbed wire, the field nevertheless offered priceless space and fresh air, as well as allotments where the prisoners could grow vegetables, but the castle itself was a stone-built pressure cooker with a disc of sky above to vent the tension.

Today, on a sap-rising late-spring morning, the walk was

at capacity, and the crocodile of prisoners passed in fine spirits through the outer gatehouse and along the high dirt road that skirted the foot of the castle's west wing. The road was fringed by a thick hedge beyond which the hill fell away sharply to meet the plain.

After several minutes of walking, Tommie caught an unregulated movement and saw a figure break from the column and scramble up and over the top of the hedge.

Chaos erupted. Jostled and shoved, and all but trampled by shouting, cheering men, Tommie strained to catch sight of the fugitive, but the hedge formed a dense, green screen. Now the prisoners were leaping around, waving their arms and doing their best to obstruct the guards, but silence fell abruptly as the guards on the castle side of the crocodile lifted their rifles and released the safety catches.

The column was hustled along the path a few yards to where the hedge gave way to a simple wire fence, and the guards on that side began to fire down the hill. The man was in full sight now, scuttling down the slope, swerving wildly from side to side.

"Fool." Watley's voice, tight and low, came from behind Tommie's shoulder.

"He hasn't failed yet," said Bainbridge calmly, "He could still be a hero."

Beside her, Simon was silent and tense.

"Who is it, anyway?" demanded Watley, "I can't make him out."

"Padier," answered Bainbridge, his eyes following every move of the running man, and now, beneath his level tones, Tommie could hear the tautness in his throat. "I should have guessed he'd do something like this. He's been out of sorts lately, saying odd things... I should have said something to Lambin; maybe he could have talked to him."

Shots were ringing out now from the lower windows of the castle, and Tommie could see more guards running to line the main road between the castle and the town, rifles raised. Tension twisted in her chest as Padier, crouching low, dodged this way and that, occasionally stumbling and rolling down the slope.

Another volley of shots sounded, and he fell forward and lay still, his white cotton t-shirt marred by a random pattern of tufted red holes.

With the final volley, Tommie shuddered and closed her eyes, wrapping her arms around her body, then she staggered, knocked off balance, as the guards shoved and pushed the crocodile into an about-turn to head back up to the castle.

"Fool," said Watley bitterly. "The man's been jumping and twitching like a lunatic. It's a suicidal idiot who makes an attempt when his nerves are in that condition."

There was no reply from Bainbridge.

Escape. Her first instinct on being thrown into Drancy had been escape. Being transferred from there to Bobigny… being herded onto the train, all had meant only one thing to her; an opportunity to escape, but in this place, the solid walls of the castle had closed unyieldingly around her.

The level of preparation that had gone into Simon's Hans Claus Ritter papers, and the planning of his escape route were meticulous, they represented the burning purpose of the men here, and that fragile hope of escape was the only thing that kept them sane. But for her, the hope of escape was non-existent. Suicidal.

She could still feel the blunt nose of Steiger's handgun against her forehead, and the futile curiosity that had possessed her in that instant, about whether she would be able to feel the bullet entering her brain. She was a little disappointed in herself; it seemed that her fire had gone out.

***

"Stupid! You are not welcome here and you're too damn stupid to understand that!" George Selby was shaking with suppressed fury. He had been strangely elated since Padier's ill-fated escape – almost triumphant – proclaiming that Padier had chosen enlightenment over imprisonment, but the elation had soon given way to a sullen sourness.

Tommie had sensed pressure building up in him for some time, and now she had released the floodgates by entering the kitchen at the moment he lost patience with the strange contraption that she guessed was a still.

"Stupid!" he shouted again, pointing a buckled metal tube at her, "A doughy, lumpen potato!"

"Hey!" The interruption was from Gabryel Zan, who had thrust his head around the doorway in response to George's outburst. "Hey. Hey. Hey. No!" he said again, waving an angry finger at George. "No 'stupid.' No 'potato.' No! Be nice."

"It's alright, Gabe," said Parr, appearing behind him and taking his arm to draw him away. "She's a big girl, she can look after herself."

"No! No big girl; little lady," protested Zan. He shook his head vehemently at George, "You no good man! No talk like that to lady. British officers lucky. Got lady to look after. Be careful of little lady."

"Yeah, George," came Harry Shaw's Australian drawl from the other room, "be careful of the little lady!"

George flapped a contemptuous hand at Zan. "If you like her so much, why don't you take her to your own quarters?" he snarled. "Except you've got no use for her, have you?" he added unpleasantly, "so mind your own business. Get lost."

"Thank you, Gabryel," said Tommie, "That was nice of you."

"Nice... nice... nice" sneered George as, scowling darkly, Gabryel allowed himself to be led away by Parr. "Yes, let's make things nice for the little lady. You've set up house in your little room over there and you're happy as a lark, like bloody Cinderella, twittering with her birds. *Only those are happy who never think.* That's Emil Cioran, the anti-natalist philosopher, one of the most clear-sighted men ever cursed with birth."

"Ante-natalist philosopher?" said Tommie, momentarily diverted by a bizarre image.

"Anti-natalist - with an 'i'," snapped George. "Opposed

to being born. Opposed to birth. He's talking about the nature of life itself, but I find it particularly relevant to the nature of woman; only those are happy who never think."

Opposed to birth. She filed that away for further consideration, but right now the unfairness of his accusations rankled.

"There's a choir here, a prisoners' orchestra, and a theatre group," she pointed out, "all organized and presented by the prisoners. You have a gramophone and a pile of records. Some of the men offer art and language instruction, you yourself run a philosophy group, and on Friday, for pity's sake, they're putting on a cabaret. A cabaret! You can't tell me that they're not trying to make their time here more tolerable."

"Those are pastimes for men who want to maintain the fitness of their minds."

Tommie had been excluded from those pastimes. She had borrowed and read several books from the castle's library, but, frustratingly, their pages reminded her of the greater treasury of learning that lay beyond the scope of the prison library.

"I want to maintain the fitness of my mind, too," she said tentatively. "What do you say, George, would you let me join your philosophy group?"

"God help us all, a bluestocking!" George snarled. He turned away angrily and then, assessing the acoustic properties of his position in the doorway to the officers" room, he drew a deep breath. "I will not cast my pearls before swine," he thundered.

Tommie nodded, smiling grimly.

"Damned if I think, and damned if I don't! Good Lord, George, you are a piece of work, aren't you?"

"Out of the way! Clear the way!" Don Philpott came flying into the kitchen from the dormitory, sliding his thin form between George and the doorframe. "The Red Cross packages are here! Where's a pair of scissors? Oh, for God's sake, George, get out of the way!"

Within minutes the officers" room was fully occupied,

and the contents of the precious parcels were set reverently on a blanket on the floor. It was mid-summer now, and the backlog of winter supplies had finally arrived.

There were twelve pairs of army issue woollen socks, four pairs of army trousers, four pairs of army combat trousers and an RAF greatcoat. These service-issue supplies were supplemented with civilian offerings of clothing, knitted blankets and a rubber hot water bottle, as well as cigarettes and food items including tinned meat, tinned milk, chocolate, raisins dried egg powder and margarine.

When these supplies had been meticulously shared out – and, after some vehement protest, Tommie had been equally included in the distribution – the officers began a lengthy bartering process.

The civilian garments had been immediately claimed by Bainbridge, who, Tommie guessed, was in charge of escape-related supplies. She had entertained herself more than once with speculations about how her bra might assist in an escape attempt.

Casting her eyes over the garments still on the blanket, she glanced down longingly at the chocolate in her little pile, but there was something she wanted more.

"I don't know exactly how this works, she said hesitantly, but if I put all this back into the pot, can I have the greatcoat?"

From his position, squatting on the far side of the blanket, George rose up like a cobra about to strike.

"Out of the question!" he roared, "I will not see the uniform demeaned."

Silence reigned for a few heartbeats, and then was overthrown by a single word.

"Demeaned?"

The usually silken tones of Sam Allenby's voice sounded as though they had been shredded with a dull blade.

Unfolding himself from his place, cross-legged on the floor at the corner of the blanket, he stood to face George across the remaining items. His olive skin had paled by several shades, revealing a spattering of coffee-coloured freckles trailing over the bridge of his nose. "The female gender demeans the uniform," he said, "Is that what you're saying, George?" His words were clipped, and delivered with a calculated subtlety that underscored the vehemence in his eyes. "She would demean the greatcoat by virtue – perhaps you would say vice – of being a woman; is that what you're saying? It's of no consequence to you that she has been put in here because she was risking her life to save the lives of servicemen like us? That perhaps she saved the lives of men whom *you* sent into battle? This means nothing, does it?" he persisted, and now his voice was blistering with suppressed anger. "Because you feel that what's more important – here and now, in this castle – is that a woman is prohibited from wearing the uniform, because..." he paused, segregating each word with biting precision, "because she would demean it. Is that what you're saying, George?"

He stood perfectly still while George glared across at him warily. "Do you not understand that the uniform – all of our uniforms," he continued, "represent a duty – a covenant – to serve and protect our country and our people? What is that duty worth if we hold the uniform itself to be too precious to honour the duty it represents? You should be willing to take off your own uniform and offer it to someone in need of it; that's your duty as a serviceman, Captain Selby."

In the ringing silence Tommie watched Allenby's face as the anger in his green eyes burned down to a cold scorn. "Women demean the uniform," he said again, turning the words over on his tongue, tasting them.

Glancing around the room with the air of a man becoming aware that he has revealed more about himself than he intended, he drew a long, slow breath, and then deliberately exhaled his intensity along with it. The familiar, supercilious tone returned to his voice, along with a practiced indifference. "Have you taken a look at yourself in a mirror recently, George?" he said carelessly. "You are hardly qualified to get on your high horse about the uniform when you comport yourself like a floor mop."

"That's beside the point," snapped George, "I am entitled to wear the uniform; she is a civilian."

"Oh, belt up George," said Watley, unwrapping his bar of chocolate and biting off a piece. The soft, thick sound dispersed the tension in the room. "Can't you just let us appreciate this moment without having to listen to your pomposity?" he added, rendered magnanimous by the chocolate, "I say let her have the greatcoat."

"Absolutely!" Allenby seconded heartily, "After all, is it even possible to demean an RAF uniform?" A storm of foul language from the RAF officers greeted this provocation, and Allenby tutted disapprovingly. "Gentlemen, please!" he scolded, gathering his supplies and heading for his bunk, "there are ladies present. And you, Flight Lieutenant Leigh, I'm shocked – shocked – that you would subject your lady to that sort of profanity from the mouth of her champion!"

"Why would you forfeit your whole stash for the greatcoat, anyway, Tommie?" put in Pickman curiously, "it's the middle of summer."

Tommie shook off the thrall of Allenby's words. "I don't like being cold," she said shortly, "And I want to be prepared for next winter."

And, while this was strictly true, what was truer was that Allenby's words had echoed in a small, stranded place inside her which badly wanted to believe that the uniform still represented at least the intention of honour, duty and service. She had believed this when Colonel Gregory had taken custody of her, and although the ideal was badly tarnished in the avatars standing before her now, it persisted for her, and it manifested itself in the greatcoat.

"Well," said Donald Taylor, climbing stiffly to his feet, "As far as I'm concerned, she can have the coat, as long as the old man says it's ok."

"Can I assume that, by "the old man", you are referring to me?" Colonel Gregory had wandered in, unnoticed. Taylor winced.

"Sir."

"Then the old man concurs with Captain Allenby's point," continued Gregory smoothly, "We are all sworn to serve the crown, and – by default – the crown's subjects. The trading details are for you to sort out amongst yourselves, but Miss West has my authority to wear whichever pieces of uniform she finds useful."

***

It was cabaret night in the castle, and the auditorium of the theatre was at capacity.

With plenty of free time on their hands, and recreational equipment supplied by the Red Cross, the prisoners had been able to muster a surprising pool of musical and dramatic talent that performed on a wildly sliding scale of exhibitionism and skill.

Tonight, there had been chamber music, poetry readings and a violin solo, and now a jazz band was giving a lively performance, fronted by their band-leader, a Belgian army officer.

After two upbeat numbers, an entirely unexpected figure stepped out from the wings and joined them; a cabaret singer, gliding across the stage to a swell of cheers and whistles from the audience.

A vision of beauty, gleaming in the smoky air, she illuminated the auditorium as though a window into heaven had been blasted through the grey rocks of the castle. Her polished skin shone softly against the folds of a vivid scarlet gown, and Tommie's lungs, acting independently, drew in a long breath.

"Ah, she's beautiful! How did they get a cabaret singer to perform here?"

She was vaguely aware that Simon was watching her closely.

"You don't recognize him?" he said.

"Him?" she said, glancing at the band-leader, "No, I mean the singer."

"Yes, the singer; that's Sam Allenby."

There could be no response to that revelation. Tommie sat and stared as, riding the audience's roar of appreciation, the band broke into a moody rendition of Comes Love, and Allenby's silken voice – warm velvet now – replaced forever in her mind Helen Forrest's jazzier tones.

The spotlight, operated from the rafters by Robert Pickman, followed the singer, bathing her in smoky light as she descended from the stage with impossible grace and drifted across to the front row, where the senior officers of all the contingents sat. Slinking along the row, she trailed a seductive hand over knees, bestowing a smouldering glance here and a lifted eyebrow there as she sang.

"Comes a rainstorm, put some rubbers on your feet. Comes a snowstorm, you can get a little heat. Comes lo-o-ove..." Reaching Colonel Gregory, she lifted her hand and stroked his face tenderly with a single fingertip, "...nothing can be done."

Caught in the spotlight, the contours of Gregory's rugged cheeks peaked into a smile.

As she lost herself in Allenby's performance, Tommie stifled the inconsequential battle that was being fought inside her. A small, excluded, perpetually disregarded and squashed part of her suddenly yearned to be gorgeous like Allenby. Instead, here she was, wearing battledress trousers and a camouflage jacket, with her hair cropped into a short-back-and-sides, *don't you mind looking like that?* and there was Allenby, being what Tommie should be being – and he was being it better than she had ever been it.

Her mother would be mortified; Tommie was the only woman in the room, and the entire audience of men was enchanted by a man in a dress.

More troublingly, here she was, yet again, an objective observer of the bright flare of attraction... well, this was definitely not the time or the place for her to work on that. Let Sam Allenby enjoy those games – he was clearly born for them. She sighed and allowed herself to sink into the glamour of the performance.

Allenby's shoulder-length, dark hair, burnished to a rich gleam, swept down in a lustrous wave to brush fine, bare shoulders, and the scarlet fabric, glowing in the spotlight, draped the slender figure in sinuous folds.

At that moment the cabaret singer lifted her eyes from the row of senior officers and swept her gaze languidly over the audience, snagging on Tommie, who found herself caught, enthralled, as Allenby gave her a lazy wink, "Comes lo-o-ove, nothing can be done."

13
Men get funny where women are involved

Peter leafed through the paperwork in the file before him. Each page bore the signature of Reinhardt Gehlen. These were the documents he had selected to copy for Hendry, but tonight Gehlen was working late in his office across the corridor, and there was no legitimate reason for Peter to be making copies of these particular papers. He would have to wait until his senior officer left. He slid the documents under the blotter and leaned back in his chair. At that moment, the lights went off in Gehlen's office, and the general appeared, glancing over his shoulder at Peter as he locked his door.

"You're frowning, Peter, anything in particular, or just life in general?"

"Life in general, sir."

"Aren't you overdue for some leave?"

"I have arranged a few days in Switzerland next week."

"Switzerland indeed! Gehlen laughed, "What is that English expression now? A bus driver's holiday?"

Peter smiled. "A busman's holiday," he said.

"That's the one! Busman's holiday. Won't that be a busman's holiday for you, Peter? Keeping company with shady people in Switzerland? Well, come and see me before you go, I have a few items you can deliver for me while you are there. I will make it a real busman's holiday for you! Was there anything you wanted to discuss before I leave?"

"Just one thing, sir; Viniski and his men are asking if there is any progress on the Vlasov movement."

"It's treading water, that's all I will say. I know several of my officers are highly committed to it," he paused and sighed, "notably, Wilfried Strik-Strikfeldt, but until the word comes from above, all we can do is keep treading water."

"You do not share that commitment?"

Gehlen shrugged. "The movement is referred to as "Vlasov's Army," what leader is going to foster an army that bears someone else's name?" He shook his head, "To Hitler it is no more than a propaganda exercise. I predict that the whole structure will fall like a house of cards when it is ultimately put before him for approval."

Peter watched Gehlen's face carefully, and attempted to keep his tone neutral as he responded to this. The Russian prisoners who were collaborating with their German captors to undermine Stalin's regime had martialled under the captured Red Army general Andrey Vlasov, and believed that they were training to be deployed as an independent unit against the Soviets.

"But Viniski and his men have been assured the program is viable," he said, "And we are actively recruiting Red Army soldiers to the cause, knowing that, if captured, they will be summarily executed by their own side."

Gehlen glanced at his watch. "I really must go. Can I offer you a lift anywhere?"

"No, thank you, Herr General, I have my motorbike."

***

Checking into his hotel in Geneva, Peter smiled as he read the message that had been left at the front desk for him. A certain Herr Klamm requested the pleasure of his company for lunch.

He found Hendry waiting for him at a table that was tucked away in a secluded corner of a modest restaurant. A trolley bearing a selection of cold meats, cheeses and breads was already positioned nearby, and he guessed that this was going to be one of Hendry's quick working lunches.

"Very functional," he commented, glancing around at the drab decor, "I think I deserve better."

Hendry grinned and stood to shake his hand.

"You know what Switzerland is like," he said, carefully ignoring the briefcase that Peter placed under the table at his feet, "too many cloak-and-dagger types skulking around. It doesn't pay to be ostentatious." Casting his eyes over the expensively tailored uniform and highly polished leather boots standing in front of him, he sat down again. "I can see that you have become accustomed to... better."

Lowering himself into a chair, Peter scanned the room casually for eavesdroppers, but Hendry had chosen well, and the restaurant was very sparsely populated. Presumably, all the cloak-and-dagger types were somewhere else being ostentatious.

"Well, if I have to be a parasite," he said coolly, "I want to be a well-dressed parasite."

"Well-spoken too," observed Hendry, lighting up a cigarette, "More Prussian than the Prussians; a perfect Teutonic *dic*tion," he added, flashing Peter a toothy grin. "How is our little Miss West doing these days?"

Peter's head whipped up.

"She's one of yours?"

"Splendid, so she has kept mum."

Peter shook his head in disbelief. "I'm not even going to ask how you know that she's in the castle, but in God's name, are things really so bad that you have to recruit young girls to the cause? She had her whole life ahead of her, and now look where she is."

"We didn't recruit her; we didn't need to, she came to us," said Hendry, unmoved. "Just like you did. She was zealous. Exceptional at marksmanship, too. The trainers had a nickname for her; 'Tommie-get-your-gun', they used to call her."

Peter frowned.

"And yet you sent her over as a courier... a clinic nurse."

"Ye-es, I wasn't wholly confident about putting a gun in her hand; she really was very zealous. I remember her particularly because she put me in mind of Joan of Arc. Small and determined, propelled by some mystical force." An odd, pensive line creased his forehead as he lost himself in a thought.

Peter was also quiet. The rich scent of the coffee was conjuring up the memory of the young woman facing up to his challenge over the pastries, and with a strange ripple of interconnectedness he reflected that, in accepting the coffee that day, she had been defying not only his own challenge, but also the training she had received from the man sitting across the table from him now.

"Small and determined," he said. "Yes, that's her."

"And don't disparage the courier role," added Hendry, "it probably saved her life; it seems the Gestapo didn't think it necessary to shoot the messenger. Others have had different fortunes," he added grimly. He took a sip of his coffee. "I must admit, I'm glad she's with you, I wasn't happy to hear that she'd disappeared from Drancy. One thing puzzles me, though; why *is* she with you? Why is she in that castle, in the name of all that's reasonable?"

"Reasonable has nothing to do with it," said Peter, staring through the window at a mountain, eye-wateringly etched in the sunlight. "She was spotted near a sensitive establishment over by Leipzig, and a certain Otto Steiger of the SS – an especially peculiar specimen of the breed – decided that instead of arranging another tedious firing squad, it would be more amusing to dispose of her by throwing her into the lions' den and broadcasting the ensuing disgrace."

Hendry hissed through his teeth.

"I might have guessed the SS were behind it. They are a rum lot, I must say."

"And they don't come much rummer than Steiger," Peter said, slipping briefly and enjoyably into idiom. "That man would give even Hitler the willies."

"I'm assuming that the lions haven't obliged?"

"Not as far as I've heard." In the castle, his office looked down over the prisoners' courtyard, and he occasionally saw the girl there, walking circuits with Leigh, or with the army captain, Allenby. Her hair had been cropped into a boot-camp haircut, and she wore a shapeless mix of uniform pieces. "So far, she seems to have done a good job of camouflaging herself and putting herself out of bounds," he added, "let's just hope things stay that way." He paused, thoughtfully. "Is it at all possible that she knows who I am?"

"No. Not possible at all," Hendry said decisively. "Why do you ask?"

Peter shook his head, dismissing the memory of the girl's eyes, almost eclipsed by black pupils, staring, puzzled, into his.

"Just something about the way she looked at me on the day she arrived at the castle," he said, "almost as though she knew me, but couldn't quite place where she knew me from."

Hendry was watching him closely. "You do understand that you can't introduce yourself to her?" he said. Peter blinked at him, and he shrugged. "Well, you never know. Men get funny where women are involved."

"Really, Hendry? Is that your philosophy for the ages? 'Men get funny where women are involved'?"

"It is an eternal truth, Peter. If you don't know it yet, you will one day."

"We do *have* women in Germany, you know," said Peter dryly, "Some of them are quite spectacular. I haven't been doing without."

"Good to know!" said Hendry heartily. He looked at his watch and stood up. "Well, I wish I could stay longer, but I'm afraid I have to run. I'll try to stay in touch."

Peter stood and shook his hand. "One more thing, Mr. Klamm," he said. He had no idea why Steiger had sidestepped the Commando Order, but he would not leave the girl at the castle indefinitely, and when he took her from there it would be lights-out for her. "About Miss West and that establishment…" He narrowed his eyes, bringing the file to his mind, "ten miles north of Leipzig, it was, and five miles east of the railway tracks – perhaps you might make it all worth her while?" Hendry raised an eyebrow pointedly and Peter ignored it. "Nothing obvious, of course, just a few residual bombs jettisoned in the area after a raid; serendipity. Nobody over here could make any connection to her – or to me – it happens all the time."

"And how would I explain to London where I got the intelligence from?"

"You're good at explaining," Peter grinned. "Just keep hurling metaphors at them until they give you what you want. Don't forget your briefcase."

14
A sort of innocence

"Mind if I join you?" Without waiting for a response, Sam Allenby fell into step beside Tommie and proceeded to walk along in silence, his fractal green eyes wandering over the assorted population of the courtyard, giving every indication of being indifferent to her company.

"I've been meaning to congratulate you on your performance in the cabaret," said Tommie after a while. "It was quite outstanding."

Allenby smiled.

"Thank you. And I've been meaning to ask you something. I suppose it's a continuation of our earlier conversation about you not wanting to... you know." Again, there was that faint mockery in his eyes. "Can we continue to be candid?"

Tommie snorted.

"It seems to me that you are in the driving seat there, Captain Allenby."

He nodded, as though her response would have been inconsequential either way.

"So, a hundred women cloistered together for the sexual pleasure of one man would be termed a harem, yes?"

"Tssss!"

He spread his hands and painted an injured expression on his face.

"You said we could be candid!"

"I don't believe I did. But I have to admit, I'm intrigued to find out where this is going."

"Good. Well, last time we spoke, you implied that if this castle were a harem in reverse – if these men were all assembled here for your sexual pleasure – your response to them would be non-existent; that of a eunuch... a female eunuch."

Tommie grimaced.

"Not a pleasant image."

"And not entirely accurate," admitted Allenby, "because a eunuch has been surgically liberated from the pertinent organs. You haven't. Presumably," he added, glancing quickly at Tommie. "Is that something that can be done?"

Tommie looked into the smooth face and saw nothing more sinister there than a consuming curiosity. "I'm not sure if it can be done or not," she said, "but it hasn't been done to me. Why are we having this rather uncomfortable conversation, Captain Allenby?"

"Why not?" Allenby said airily. "We've got nothing but time on our hands, we might as well talk. So, why the vow of chastity? And is it really feasible under these circumstances? After all, most women who take that vow tend to be nuns, cloistered with other nuns, not with virile, sexually frustrated men."

Tommie gave an incredulous laugh and pinched the bridge of her nose, but there was a seductive appeal in talking to this man who had no regard for boundaries.

"You do realise, don't you?" continued Allenby, sweeping a comprehensive arm at the other officers, "that, with this little lot to choose from, you would be the envy of the women back home. I hear that a good man is hard to come by these days... if you will excuse the expression. You wouldn't even need to descend to the level of bawdy woman; you could pick just one item from this little buffet and make him your own if you were so inclined. And please don't think I'm offering," he added with a lazy smile, "I'm really not offering."

Tommie glanced up at him. His tone was, as usual, cool and detached, but in the shade of his peaked cap the pale green eyes were a cauldron of indecipherable thought-processes, and unexpectedly she found that she wanted to dip into that cauldron.

"We could be here for years," Allenby was saying. "Are you really not going to have sex with anyone? Despite the bountiful opportunities?"

"I can't."

"Can't?" he replied, acerbically. "It's difficult to imagine a circumstance in which that assertion would be less true. So, let's be more precise in our vocabulary, shall we...?" He tilted his head, waiting for her to respond.

"Alright, then, I mustn't. Won't. Can't allow myself to."

"Why not?"

"If I got pregnant..."

"Pff!" Allenby rejected this point as negligible with a dismissive wave of his hand. "There are ways to have sex without getting pregnant. You know that. You're not a child."

Tommie stopped and turned to face him.

"No, I'm not a child," she said sharply, "And I know that when a woman has been had by one man – whether voluntarily or by force – other men perceive it as an insult to their manhood if she then declines them. And men tend not to behave well when their advances have been rejected."

In Allenby's eyes, she recognized an uneasy acknowledgement of her point. He nodded darkly. "Very astute. So, is that it, or is there more?"

"I don't want to open myself up," said Tommie, without having intended to offer more. "You become vulnerable when you open yourself up, and this is not a safe place in which to be vulnerable."

Now she saw, clearly exposed in Allenby's eyes, a keen understanding. Something in her response had addressed a question that he badly wanted answered. His voice was muted, and stripped of the familiar silken undertones. "Does honour come into the equation at all?"

"Honour?" she said, blankly.

"Honour or its antithesis – dishonour."

"Into what equation?"

"Into your intention to be chaste while you are here. I'm not talking about *their* honour; I know all about that." He waved a hand peevishly, as though that line of debate had been explored at great length. "I'm interested in *your* perspective, *your* honour. Do you believe that, as a woman, it would be somehow dishonourable for you to engage in sexual activity while you are here? As though it would prove that your honour is insufficient to overcome desire?"

There was a deeply rooted, ingenuous urgency in his question, so she was willing to approach his question honestly.

"You're asking if I'm keeping myself... chaste out of an abstract sense of honour? It's difficult to say," she said slowly, "because the issue of vulnerability eclipses everything. But if vulnerability wasn't a problem, would it seem dishonourable to... to...?" She rubbed her eyes, "No, it's no use, I can't even imagine it. Just having a relationship like that in this place, well, it would be... uncomfortable."

"Uncomfortable?" said Allenby, turning away irritably. "No, I can see that there's no correlation. After all, you're a civilian."

Tommie found herself alone, feeling inadequate.

***

"So, chastity – in the face of so much opportunity – possibly for years on end; it's just not sustainable. Alright, alright, I know, we must agree to disagree about that, but..." Allenby spread his hands, indicating the population of the courtyard.

The days and weeks were passing greyly, but in the perma-gloom of life at the castle, Tommie's conversations with him glittered like unmined diamonds.

He was ruthless in his pursuit of whatever information

he was seeking, and would often appear beside her on a circuit of the courtyard, reviving a train of thought as though it had not been interrupted by hours or even days. It was like being observed by a cat; he was aloof, seemingly disinterested, yet clearly possessed by the need to know that leaves feline footprints in newly-laid cement.

"But just for the sake of conversation," he pressed, "if you did weaken, who would you choose? And, again, please understand that I'm not putting myself forward. So, who would it be? You've taken sweet Simon off the table, and I can't imagine why that should be."

Tommie scowled up at him. "You don't accept Eric's assertion that I've already been in Simon's trousers?"

Allenby spat out a laugh. "Even Eric doesn't really believe that, it was just a knee-jerk reaction; every man imagines that every woman is out for his valuables. Even when he has nothing of value to offer."

"What makes you so sure that Simon's off the table?"

"Because there's no fire between you. Not even a spark. You might as well be two puppies from the same litter, huddling up for comfort." He frowned, "Why is that? Is it because he's out of your league? Or have you got your eye on someone else?"

Tommie caught his sideways glance, and knew that he was observing her reaction to his insensitivity, but there was something else in there too; something carefully concealed.

She realized that she was equally curious about him, and the more he strove to provoke her, the more he revealed about himself. That comment, though – *he's out of your league* – that comment whisked her back to her childhood.

In the presence of her parents, she had always felt like a changeling; a goblin child, gracelessly rebelling against their ways, scorning their elegance and poise.

Her mother had been as lithe as a thoroughbred, tall and willowy, with the alabaster skin, sloping shoulders and passive muscle-tone prescribed by the fashion magazines. Her father had been shorter, but dapper and dashing. Tommie was a pit-pony; small, sturdy, and naturally endowed with saddle-bags.

Her parents had emerged from their war – the mud-coloured chrysalis of the Great War – like airy, filmy butterflies, dancing, always dancing and partying. Tommie had ridden off to her war like an ersatz Joan of Arc, with the voices of long-dead witches in her head.

They had one thing in common, though; all three of them bore the knowledge of the death of the boy who lay curled up inside that mud-coloured chrysalis; the young man whose death had left her parents with only each other to love. She had read their letters to each other, kept safe in that beautiful rosewood box, but life couldn't be kept safe, and it shouldn't be kept in a box.

"So, who will you choose?" Allenby said.

Tommie pulled herself back to the present, retraced the conversation, and shook her head wryly. That's right, he was playing matchmaker.

"Who's your type?" he persisted, "Big, bluff Bainbridge? Too much like a huge, rather disconcerting teddy bear, perhaps. Dour Watley, then; some women can't resist a man who treats them badly... not you? Good. Umm... Cute young Ken Parr? You'd have to fight Zan for him. How about Robert Pickman – fancy being a G.I. bride? Or Colonel Gregory; are you drawn to an avuncular man? Quiet, reserved, self-contained, unimpeachably proper. Handsome in a faded, comfortable sort of way. The man at the top. Are you drawn to authority? A father figure? Are you a daddy's girl?"

The patter stopped here, and Tommie saw that Allenby was watching her intently. Somewhere, buried in that run of speculation, lay the nucleus of his curiosity, and he was waiting for her reply.

"Captain Allenby, this is a prison, not a debutante ball," she said primly. "I'm not looking – and I will not look – at any of these men as men. I have no answer for you."

***

"I study women, you know." He had drifted up to stand next to Tommie, his boots a hand-spread away from her hips, as she sat reading in the courtyard. She was leaning against what was known as the seam; the wall that separated the prisoners' courtyard from the commandantur courtyard. There was a particular spot in this wall where her spine slotted into an indent, and where two cobbles were missing, leaving a convenient dip – two convenient dips – that cradled her where it mattered, and she had discovered that she could sit quite comfortably there. "I blend into the background," continued Allenby, "and observe their behaviour when they don't know they're being watched. Women are fascinating."

Glancing up, Tommie studied his face. With his high cheekbones, smooth olive skin and pale-green eyes he was strikingly beautiful, but in a very different way from Simon. Simon was open and golden, like sunlight on a field of sunflowers, but Allenby was complicated, veiled and mesmerizing. She ran her eyes pointedly down his elegant body.

"If you think that you can go unnoticed by any woman, you are deceiving yourself," she said. The green eyes rested on her thoughtfully, then he dropped down to sit next to her.

"No, really, I can. Not when I'm in uniform, of course, but when I camouflage myself, I'm in."

"Camouflage?" said Tommie blankly, "Oh, no! Please don't tell me you dress up in women's clothes and go in amongst them!"

"Not when there's even the slightest possibility that I could be recognized."

"That's really not what's wrong about that."

"Well, I wouldn't get far dressed like this, now, would I?" he said reasonably. "The whole point is to learn about how women interact among themselves when there isn't a man around."

"There has to be a word for people who do that."

"I don't do it in a sinister way," he said, unconcerned, "I

do it out of an academic interest. People say men are predatory like wolves, but women have predatory down to a fine art. There are the blatantly predatory women – the man-eaters – at one end of the spectrum, and at the other end there's the woman who wants only one man, even if that man doesn't want her – or can't or won't have her." He sighed deeply. "She only wants that one man, and if she can't have him, she watches him and starves." He paused and glanced at Tommie. "Is that you? Is there one man you wanted that you couldn't have, and that's why you've made a vow of chastity?"

"No, Sam, the answer is still because I don't want to be vulnerable."

***

"I am a woman."

Tommie found that she was staring at Allenby, and had been for a while, listening to the concussive silence that echoed his words. It was so resoundingly obvious. How had she not known it until now? He had folded his frame to sit, cross-legged next to her, leaning against the seam, and now his green eyes were watching her as someone who has pricked somebody with a pin and is waiting for a reaction. Tommie arrived at a finely-faceted, brilliant clarification of the connection that had developed between them, and her voice wriggled out of its paralysis.

"Oh!" she said joyfully and with monumental inadequacy, "Oh, I knew... Well, I knew something! Oh, how lovely!"

Allenby's eyes widened. "You believe me?!"

Confusion hit her like a bucket of water thrown by a circus clown, the bright colours of short-lived joy turning dishwater grey and swilling coldly down her body, exposing a stinging, betrayed hurt.

"You're not?" she said, weakly. "It was a lie? You're not a woman in a man's uniform?" She scrambled to her feet, angrily. "That was cruel."

"Cruel?!" Allenby's hand shot out to grab her by the arm. He whipped himself to his knees and yanked her down beside him. "You have no idea what cruel is," he snarled. "You think I'm a homosexual – it's why you feel safe with me – but I'm not. I should have been born a baby girl, just like you were, but by some unholy error, a boy's body was clamped around me instead, and it kept growing with me. All my life I've had to look down at myself and see it happening, like a living nightmare. And puberty..." The word saturated his face with disgust, and Tommie found herself pitching forwards into the dark well of his pain. "Can you imagine looking down at yourself; you, I mean – Tomasin West – and seeing a man's body where yours should be? Penis, balls, unwanted erections, wet dreams, a beard, even a man's smell... everything. I've had to live with that all my life. And now you come along with your pathetic camouflage – your adorable little dressing-up game – and you pretend to be a man. But they know you're a woman, and they behave with you accordingly. You are out of bounds; cordoned off. You even have your own little Wendy house in the corner. You're playing den-mother for the Lost Boys, and when this war is over, you'll go back to your Darling house, but for me the shutters are closed."

His face twisted out of shape, "You must think this is one big harem for me, like it could be for you if you wanted it that way. *Do* you want it that way? Do you want to be in amongst them, every day? To be around when they fart and piss and shit?! To listen to them masturbate? Every night! To have them all around you when you take a shower? Every... bloody... time? Do you want that?" he snapped, "No, you don't! Nor do I! And for the same reason; they are men – I am a woman.

"You have Leigh to be your champion, but I'm on my own. I have no sweet Simon to fight them off when they get horny." He paused, breathing hard, and now his olive skin was hectic. "It's like living in a nightmare," he rasped, "and it's been like that my whole life, so don't talk to me about cruelty."

Some indefinable sound made them both look up to see Simon standing over them, frozen in shock.

Allenby's eyes blazed at him. Tommie had once seen a fireball of copper sulphate compound produced in the school laboratory; its green inferno would have been eclipsed by those eyes.

She watched as Simon acknowledged the fireball, inclining his head fractionally, then he looked pointedly at where Sam's hand was still gripping Tommie's arm. Sam let her go with a muttered apology and they both sat back down on the cobbles.

"Are you alright, Tommie?" Simon said quietly.

"Yes, I'm fine, Simon. Thank you."

The stilted civility after the passion of Allenby's explosion was surreal, but Simon nodded, then shot Allenby a warning glance, and walked away. After a moment, Sam unfolded his legs.

"Don't leave," Tommie said, quickly.

He palmed her off contemptuously, and before she knew what she was doing, Tommie reached up, grasped his wrist and elbow, twisted his arm smoothly behind him, and brought him back down to the floor. He hissed in surprise and sat, staring at her.

"A nurse with the FANYs, were you?" he said after a moment. "A little more 'yeoman' than 'nurse,' I'm guessing." He nodded reflectively, "I did wonder how you managed to survive on the run for longer than Simon did. And he thinks he's looking after you. How sweet!"

"He *is* looking after me," said Tommie stiffly. "I need him."

Allenby studied her for a moment.

"Yes, I imagine you do; you need him to remind you that there is still beauty in the world."

"And loyalty," said Tommie stoutly. "And innocence."

"Well, I think I just blew the innocence out of the water."

"Not that sort of innocence," Tommie said. "The sort of innocence that believes that the world is made up of good guys and bad guys, and we're the good guys because we do good things and the enemy are the bad guys because they do bad things."

Where had that come from? From Paris; from watching the French police herding humanity onto a cattle train. And from brooding over the Battle of Cable Street. She should be doing a better job of asserting her national loyalties.

Sam watched her, frowning.

"And you have lost that innocence?"

"It's hard to hold onto when you've seen what the good guys are capable of." She shrugged, "I'm sorry about the… the move."

"You mean the commando move?" said Allenby pointedly, rubbing his elbow. *Her* elbow, Tommie told herself; her elbow.

"Yes, the commando move; I knew it would be… awkward to ever reopen the subject if you walked away, and I want to hear what you have to say."

"So, you're going to interrogate me about my gender and my sexuality," said Sam flippantly, "just how ideologically ambivalent are you? And speaking of interrogations," he added… *she* added. "Do I get to interrogate you? One woman locked in with hundreds of men, and the only one you allow to get close to you holds that honour because he offers you nothing more masculine than beauty, loyalty and innocence. And then you get all coercive when you think some form of female companionship is going to be denied you – however contorted that definition of "female" might turn out to be. What an odd little woman you are."

"I don't think that's odd at all."

Allenby considered this for a moment.

"No. Actually, you could be right about that," she said. "I was thinking like a man. Force of habit."

Her voice was heavy with unspoken words, so Tommie waited.

"I wasn't mocking you, by the way, when I said "you believe me," Sam continued haltingly. "What I meant was *you believe me*. Yes, I know, it sounds the same, but what I was trying to say was... well, that nobody has ever believed me before; believed that I was a girl. Nobody. Not my mother, not my father... although I can see now why it would be harder for them. Nobody would believe me. It was like being tied up in a straitjacket that nobody else could see. And, alright, maybe you thought I was telling you that I'm like you; physically a woman, pretending to be a man – which I'm not – but even so... you did, for one split second, see me as a woman. Can you still do that?"

There was a rawness in the pale green eyes now, flinching, ready to dodge back behind the veil. The privilege of what Sam was offering her reached Tommie's scrunched-up heart like spring rain on a crocus bulb. She nodded.

15
Diamonds in the Dark

Simon had become increasingly preoccupied with some secretive project which involved Doug Bainbridge and Donald Taylor, and when Tommie did manage to grab him for a walk around the courtyard, he seemed uncomfortable with her, preoccupied and withdrawn. A rodent-like scratching began in her mind; Bainbridge and Taylor were the escape committee, one of the things that she was not supposed to be aware of.

Her heart clenched when she thought of Simon on the run again, and then twisted with guilt for wanting to hold on to him, to keep him safe in prison with her. For her, there would be no chance of survival out there, but she had no right to hold onto Simon.

She became increasingly glad of Sam's company, and every conversation with her was like wandering in the depths of a diamond mine, spotting muted gleams here and there in the rock.

"I know it must be a bit back-to-front for me to say this to you," Tommie said cautiously, tugging at her army trousers, "but it feels so liberating to walk around as a man."

Sam laughed lightly. "Sweetie, you looked more like a man the day you turned up here in that hideous skirt."

"Really?" Deflated, Tommie looked down at the

Denison smock, "Well, it worked for Crighton in mess three. He didn't notice that I was the woman he'd heard about until I opened my mouth."

"Is that so? And how long can you go without opening your mouth?"

Tommie turned a sour look on her.

"Oh, well done!" grinned Sam. "Anyway," she continued, "it's not just the uniform that keeps them off, it's also the fence that you put up around yourself; closed for business. But be careful, because there will come a time when that won't work, when it doesn't matter what you look like, and the barriers you put up... well, a stag in rut doesn't even feel the fences it tramples." A dark tension invaded her usual liquid movements, and she fell silent for a moment. "Besides," she said abruptly, shaking her head, "a man is what half of them are aching for... and what at least half of the others would settle for in a pinch, and if this castle isn't a pinch, I don't know what is! It's a good thing there are no more pink triangles being handed out."

"Pink triangles?" Tommie said blankly.

"You don't know about the pink triangle? Well, you must know about the yellow star."

Tommie winced, "Yes, of course, but a pink triangle... Oh! Oh, no! Is that... do they do that?"

"Oh, yes, we had a big scene here a few months ago; there was a guard, Rickert I think his name was – he's not here anymore – he was a hard-liner, and unpopular with everyone, staff as well as prisoners, well, one day he just walked up to another guard, Hage, one of the more... amenable types, and pinned a pink triangle on him, in front of everyone in the commandantur courtyard, on the other side of this wall, then threatened to report him to the authorities.

"He must have thought doing it like that – publicly – would make it impossible for Hage to cover up the accusation." Sam smiled grimly, "He was wrong! They all turned on him – the German staff who were there – turned on Rickert.

"There was a hell of a racket; shouting, shoving, punches thrown. Hamm was called in, but the thing just escalated, and then Brandt descended on the scene like an avenging angel, like Saint Michael... that's the one with the sword, isn't it, because the way I pictured it, he went striding in there, wielding a sword. He was bellowing like a bull about people who pin patches onto people – Brandt was, I mean. We heard every word. Said he wouldn't have the commandant's authority undermined and the reputation of the castle smeared, and that if anyone thought it their duty to follow the new national culture of finger-pointing, then they had better make sure that they themselves were absolutely innocent of everything or he would find out about it.

"Then he announced – on the spot – Rickert's transfer to another post. There must have been some significant dirt on Rickert because he didn't turn up for duty the next day, and we never saw him again."

Tommie considered this for a moment, remembering Steiger's comment to Brandt on her arrival at the castle; 'Locked away with all these naughty public-schoolboys, why would you need women?'

"Well, I think Brandt is a homosexual himself..."

Sam laughed a hollow laugh.

"Ho! No, he is not!" she said emphatically.

"No?"

"No. You seem surprised by that. What makes you think he is?"

"Something I heard another German officer say to him."

"Wishful thinking," snorted Sam.

"But after what you've just told me, why are you so sure he isn't?" asked Tommie.

"Because I know," said Sam crisply, "I've sounded him out."

"You've... ?!"

"I was angry and hurt... about something. I wanted to behave badly, and after listening in on that scene I felt quite soft about Brandt, so I let him know it."

Tommie stared at her, astounded.

"What did you say? What did you do? Where...?!"

"Don't look at me like that, I didn't proposition him like some streetwalker, I just gave him a... significant smile, and raised an eyebrow."

Tommie was transfixed by the image her mind conjured up. "What did he say?"

"He didn't say anything. Just looked at me with those... oh, those moody eyes, and shook his head. Just a discreet *No, and let's say no more about it*, sort of shake of the head. Made me feel like a lady; a lady who has been just a touch too forward, perhaps, but still a lady. My knees turned to chocolate, but there was nothing to be done. If he's not that way..."

"I still think you're wrong about that."

"I'm not wrong!" Sam insisted. "He said no to this..." she spread her hands, palms facing outwards, framing her body.

"Then he's honourable," said Tommie firmly. "Or sensible – or both. He's a General Staff officer, Sam, and you're a prisoner. He wouldn't risk his career... no," she laughed at Sam's expression, and spread her own hands, mirroring Sam's gesture. "Not even for all of that!"

She knew this stuff; Hendry's lecture on Germany's military forces had been comprehensive.

"General Staff officers are a breed apart. For them, honour and dignity are everything," she said, recalling the officer who had approached her at the café in Paris, and who had retreated politely and respectfully when she rejected his attentions so gracelessly. He, like Brandt, had worn the double bars of the General Staff on the collar of his tunic. Sam was watching her, amused.

"Oh, sweetie, do you have a crush?"

"A crush?" she said, struggling to extricate herself from the memory of the officer and the sexual frisson of the young people in the square. The question of her estrangement from the spark-plug charge of life sat in a dark corner of her mind like a snarled-up ball of yarn pushed into the bottom of the sewing basket, waiting to be sorted out at some point in the future, when the time was right. A crush? Beyond those double bars, she couldn't recall anything about the man; she hadn't even seen him as a man, just as a uniform.

"A crush on the tasty Major Brandt," persisted Sam. "Could it be that honour and dignity and moody eyes are what it takes to get your locked-up little heart beating?"

"No!" said Tommie, shocked. She pushed the tangle back down into the bottom of the basket. "I'm just telling you what I know about the General Staff; that they are rooted in a code of ethics that serves their country and their people – not the politics of whichever government happens to be in power at the time. I would like to think our military follows the same principle. You would know about that."

"I would," agreed Sam, regarding her thoughtfully, "but most nurses wouldn't. Where did you learn all that? In Resistance School?!"

"On the streets of occupied Paris," answered Tommie smartly, mentally tucking Hendry's lecture into a back pocket and turning a shield against Sam's searching look. Sam acknowledged the shield with a smile. "Anyway, the point is," said Tommie, "...What *was* the point? Oh, yes... I still think Brandt is homosexual, and that he turned you down for reasons of honour."

"They pin a black triangle on lesbians," Sam said, inconsequentially.

"I didn't know that," said Tommie. There was a pertinent silence, and she looked up to see Sam regarding her intently. She returned the look blankly.

"Do you have anything to tell me?" Sam said, soberly.

"About what?"

"About the way you look at me sometimes. Adoringly."

"I *do* adore you. Oh, I see. Well! But not like that – I don't think," she said, frowning. Sam smiled, watching her through her eyelashes, and Tommie shook her head. "Haven't you got enough on your hands with your own difficulties?" she said, "without turning me into a lesbian?"

"Turning you into a lesbian," laughed Sam, "now there's

a challenge!" She cracked her knuckles, "Tomasin Sackville-West! Yes, let's do it. We've got nothing but time on our hands."

"You would make me fall in love with you?" said Tommie reproachfully. "That wouldn't be fair, because you're in love with someone else."

Sam's smile vanished. "What makes you think that?"

"You told me yourself; you said you were hurt and angry, and that's why you toyed with Brandt. Don't worry, I'm not going to pry," she added quickly, "Privacy is too hard to come by in here. Anyway, to get back to the subject; I adore you because you're good company. Simon's good company too, and I love him to bits, but he's a man, and some things have to be explained to him – and then he blushes. You never blush. And if I look at you adoringly it's because you're gorgeous... and you wear that uniform so well," she added, wholeheartedly, "better than any man. And I know I can feast my eyes on you without inviting any consequences."

Sam's smile had returned. "Better than any man? Better than Leigh?"

"Army and RAF... apples and oranges."

Sam laughed.

"Well wriggled-out-of! Alright, I'll let you off the hook for that." She leaned back luxuriously against the stone wall. "Maybe you like a bit of both, then, because you adore me, and I am a bit of both. And even if you've blocked out all our lovely compatriots here – which definitely argues for the lesbian theory – on the other hand, you have noticed the tasty Major Brandt, which argues for the straight side."

"I have not "noticed" him!" said Tommie, "And I certainly don't have a crush on him. If anyone has a crush on him, it's you, Sam; "tasty" was your word, not mine. I've only noticed that he can be kind."

"Oh... kind," said Sam with a cabaret-sized wink, "Yes, he is kind; devastatingly, broodingly kind. I, too, have noticed that!"

"Anyway, that would be fraternizing."

"Nothing wrong with a bit of fraternizing," said Sam lightly. She was silent for a moment. "They're all men under their uniforms, Tommie. Even the General Staff officers," she added with a sideways smirk, "A good man or a bad man; you can't tell by the uniform. Except for the SS, of course, no man puts on that uniform with noble intentions."

"Then where are the boundaries?" mused Tommie. "Look what's going on in the world out there. Civilization is being pulled apart by its aversion to differences, yet here, in this castle – in this crucible – people will turn a blind eye to homosexuality, and there is even a bit of mutual respect between enemies, both of which would cause untold trouble out there in the world."

"It's because most people in this world just want to live and let live, but when some hard-liner comes along and poisons the well, people feel pressured to polarize and take a stand that they wouldn't otherwise have taken. When you don't really like foreigners in your country, and suddenly you've got a government who says that you're right to feel like that, and yes, we *should* get rid of them, and suddenly everyone around you is saying it too, then what was once a private little prejudice becomes a national movement."

Tommie nodded.

"And suddenly we're on wheels, going downhill with no brakes."

"But locked up in here, we are steeped in each other, and we can't escape noticing that we're all just human beings. That's not to say that everyone here is a paragon of tolerance," she added. "Some of the guards hate us with a vengeance – understandably, because we're bombing their cities to bits – and some of *us* hate all Germans because their government led us into this war. Our lovely Simon has that tendency himself; he sees them as being of the genus enemy – like sparrows and sparrowhawks; no common ground."

Tommie nodded again. She herself had ridden out, all fired up and ready to battle the enemy, and under the influence of that fire, she would have fallen on the enemy and torn them apart with her teeth and nails, but where was that fire now? The enemy was all around her, but none of them really deserved to be torn apart, and all of Hendry's training was going to waste.

What had Sam called her? A den-mother for the Lost Boys. She glanced up.

"What about you, Sam? It's my turn to interrogate. You say I'm an odd little woman for keeping myself away from the men, but what about you? You're full of talk, but I don't see any action."

Sam was silent for a moment, then she smiled a slow smile.

"Would you buy the 'honourable' thing in my case? Or is that exclusive to General Staff officers?" she said slyly. "Or, how about one of your own excuses…" She set her face into a prim expression and mimicked Tommie wickedly, "'I can't allow myself to be vulnerable.'"

***

"'Shouting at the Lord in impotent defiance,'" Tommie said suddenly. Sam stopped in their circuit of the courtyard and stared at her. Tommie stared back. "It's from The Well of Loneliness," she said.

"I know where it's from."

"It's what I thought about when you told me about what it was like to grow up in the wrong body."

"Yes, I'm getting the reference. I'm just surprised that you've read the book."

"It was banned in Britain, not in France."

"Nevertheless, of all the books you could have read, I'm intrigued that you sought that one out."

"Isn't everyone curious about something that the authorities say they shouldn't know about?"

"Everyone? No. Not even most, I would say. Maybe a few." She walked on. "I've seen you reading Thomas Hardy and George Eliot, but I wasn't expecting you to quote from The Well of Loneliness. They can do surgery for it now, did you know that?"

Tommie took a moment to catch up.

"Surgery?"

"For people like me. There was a place in Berlin before the war; an institute for sexual research, and a surgeon in Munich helped an artist called Einar Wegener to become Lili Elbe." She grinned, "Wouldn't that be a great burlesque name! Anyway, the Nazis tore the institute down, but at least they paved a way for the future, and gave us hope. By the time I found out about that hope, I was an officer, and the war was brewing, and I had to put it on the back boiler for the duration. Because if the other side wins... well, Hitler's utopia is not a world that I want to live in, so I chose to fight that utopia using the hand I've been dealt."

She sighed. "After the war, who knows? I love my career, but I wouldn't be able to have any of it if I tried to force everyone to accept what I really am. I'm a good soldier, Tommie, but I can only be that because I've been double-stamped; I'm a man... in a uniform." She laughed bitterly, "I've even passed the physical, for God's sake! Better still, I'm an officer, with a medal, climbing the ranks. You know where it says in the Bible, 'To those who have, more will be given'? Well, I think they edited that. I think it originally said 'To those who have a penis, more will be given.'" She paused and frowned. "And I don't think they meant more penises will be given. Can you imagine how many religious conflicts must arise from slipshod editing! Anyway, believe me, the army needs people like me; people who understand it. People who know that it must be trained to behave itself around innocent people, but it also has to be allowed to be a guard dog, because it's no use to anyone if it's castrated and kept on a short chain."

"Can one person do all that?"

"One person is all I am," Sam said soberly, "I can't do more than one person can do, but I won't do less, just because there is so much arrayed against me." She clenched her jaw. "I have to get back to work."

***

It was belting down with rain outside, and the air in the dormitory was thick with the fug of damp clothes. There was a hasty whistle from Halstead, but before illicit projects could be concealed, the door from the courtyard stairwell opened and closed.

A solitary figure stood there, glancing around as the officers stared back. He wore an RAF uniform, and his skin was the colour of coffee.

"Flight Lieutenant Joshua Jones," he said.

Halstead looked him up and down and snorted. "Looks like the RAF is scraping the bottom of the tar barrel."

A generalized uncomfortable twitch passed through the room at his words, but the new officer answered smartly.

"Well, if the first string is skulking over here, waiting for everyone else to win the war for them…"

Halstead reached him first, but Jones floored him easily, and then fought off two more contenders before Simon and Bainbridge managed to restore order.

Tommie brought out her first aid kit and approached the newcomer. He had a split lip, and there was a gash over his left eyebrow that was bleeding freely.

"Why does he get looked after first?" snapped Halstead, who had come out of the fray worse off.

"Because those are the rules of hospitality," said Tommie, "and because I don't like you."

Hearing Tommie's voice, Jones stared at her.

"Are you a woman?" he said, cautiously.

"Yes, I am."

"Do they know that?" he said under his voice, indicating the other officers with a tilt of his head.

"Yes, they know."

"Do you… um…?" he said, managing to communicate the rest of his question with surprising clarity and no words.

"No, I don't."

He looked at her doubtfully.

"How do you manage that?"

"We pretend she's a man," said Sam from behind her shoulder, "it's not too much of a challenge."

Simon pulled up a chair and sat in front of Jones while Tommie worked. "Where have you come from?" he said bluntly.

"Cranwell," Jones responded, equally bluntly.

"No, I mean which prison camp have you come from? Laufen? It's usually Laufen. Why have they put you in here?"

"Same reason they put *you* in here," Jones' voice hardened, "it's an officer's prison. And I'm an officer, just like you."

Simon shook his head irritably, and Sam stepped in.

"I think what Flight Lieutenant Leigh is trying to say, in his usual obscure way, is that this is not just any old oflag, it's a sonderlager, a special prison for serial escapers. A bad boys' camp."

Jones pursed his lips and nodded.

"And I can't possibly be a serial escaper," he said, "because although I might be able to get around under cover of darkness without needing to black my face, I'm not much use in daylight. Don't worry; I've heard them all."

"Back to me... and let me be unobscure," said Simon, giving Sam a sour look, "You're obviously not a serial escaper; you would stand out in a crowd anywhere in Europe, so no escape officer would waste resources on you. But it's not my job to debrief you, you'll have a chat with Colonel Gregory in a minute, all I'm asking is, were you brought straight here, or have you been in other camps?"

Jones shrugged. "I've been in a few," he said. "I don't always play nicely with the other children, so I suppose that makes me a serial bad boy."

Jones was an engineer with one of the crews that had been assembled to fly the new Avro Lancasters, and Tommie could see the hunger in Simon's eyes, and hear the eagerness in his voice as they spoke the mystifying shorthand of the RAF.

She was glad of the new energy that animated Simon,

but as the days passed, those conversations evolved to include Doug Bainbridge and Donald Taylor, and Tommie guessed that Jones had been recruited onto the escape committee as someone who would not, himself, be escaping.

Escape activities were something that she carefully declined to notice, but she couldn't avoid noticing the conspicuous cloud of frustration that hovered over Taylor and Simon, and even Sam, after Philip Cooper, a navy captain from one of the other dormitories, was discovered, curled up in a knot under his bunk.

"It's those damn mouldy potatoes they serve us," he had moaned when Colonel Gregory asked Tommie to take a look at him. "I don't need a nurse, I just need a good fart."

"You go ahead, Phil," she'd said dryly, "but it'll take more than a good fart to sort this out."

Cooper had been rushed to a nearby hospital, and was returned to the castle's hospital wing a week later, minus his appendix, and suffering from a wound infection which would enforce a lengthy recuperation. This was when Tommie became aware of the cloud of frustration; winter was bearing down fast, and she guessed that an escape attempt by Cooper had had to be postponed until the following spring. Why this concerned Simon was something that she refused to dwell on.

On Cooper's return to the castle, Tommie was recruited to clean his wound and change the dressing twice a day.

Entering his room in the hospital wing on the first day, she halted abruptly in the doorway, staring out of the window at the view. It was not by any standards picturesque, but the plains, stretching into the distance, russet and ragged with bare trees, were wide open and breathing the wild breath of autumn, and a corresponding window opened up in the shell that she had built around herself. Glancing up, Cooper ran his eyes over her with no enthusiasm.

"They couldn't have put you in a nurse's uniform?"

She turned away from the window.

"You should be less interested in the nurse, Captain

Cooper, and more concerned about the sharp scissors that she's about to apply to your groin."

He grinned. "Ohh, say 'groin' again."

Shortly after Cooper was discharged back to the dormitory, she overheard Donald Taylor and Doug Bainbridge debriefing him in the kitchen annexe.

"... limited. And 'limited' is optimistic," Cooper was saying, "Brandt patrols there every night."

"Brandt?" said Taylor, "Why would a senior officer be doing sentry duty? And he's not even on staff."

"It's not sentry duty. My guess is insomnia. Every night I was there, he came drifting down that corridor like a ghost. I was ready to take him down if he tried anything on with me... you know, but all he does is pace."

"Timing?"

"Random. Sometimes two o'clock-ish, sometimes three o'clock-ish, sometimes one o'clock-ish... No wonder that Frenchman got caught last month; by the time you hear the door at the end of the corridor being unlocked, it's too late to cover your tracks."

***

Winter squeezed a little tighter. The prisoners' choir was given permission to perform a carol concert in the courtyard at midnight on Christmas Eve, and Tommie stood on her bed to look out of her window and pick out Sam's face below. Listening to 'Silent Night' lifting into the sky above the castle, she heard voices from the adjacent courtyard singing in harmony; 'Stille Nacht,' and her heart stirred in the darkness like the wings of a moth.

Apart from that, Christmas was a spectral mime of the traditional festivities; a wretched shadow-play of the light of hope and the defeat of darkness, and afterwards, in the new year slump, the long, dark hours seemed only to grow longer.

Many of the prisoners became withdrawn and morose,

others seethed and twitched like a flea-infested dog, or flew into sudden, explosive rages. These flashes of temper, like water flicked onto a hot frying pan, reminded Tommie of the anger the burning dreams had inspired in her; an anger which now seemed to have been smothered by lethargy.

In an attempt to stave off despair, the officers immersed themselves in hobbies or study. Bainbridge read, ploughing steadily through new titles that arrived in the prisoners' library, where Tommie would come across him in her own search for books. Occasionally he received a new title sent by his wife, which he added to his personal library. All books coming into the castle for the prisoners had their covers removed for security reasons, and Tommie would watch him lay his hand gently over the stripped spine and the exposed title page before starting to read.

Robert Pickman was forever drawing. Today, Sam was sitting for a portrait, and Tommie was keeping her company while Pickman sketched, until they were interrupted by a commotion outside in the courtyard.

Sam beat the other officers in the scramble for the windows, Pickman threw down his pencil and threw up his hands, and Tommie ducked into her own room and stared down at the scene in the courtyard below.

The Polish officers – apparently the whole contingent – were racing around the courtyard, dressed in nothing but cotton vests and underpants, chasing each other with tin beakers of water, flinging the contents at each other and shrieking as they were targeted in kind.

Buckets of water had been placed at strategic points around the courtyard for the purpose of refilling the beakers; this was organized and pre-meditated exuberance. The weather had harkened back to the bitterest days of February, and the scantily-clad Poles were the only occupants of the courtyard other than the duty sentries, some of whom were openly enjoying the spectacle, while others were looking on with disdain. The windows and stairwells were jammed with allied officers watching from a comparatively warm and dry vantage point, and rude comments and the sound of cheering echoed from the walls.

"What on earth is going on out there?" said Tommie, coming back into the dormitory, "They must be freezing!" From her prime position at the window, Sam threw her an incredulous glance.

"Oh, Mumsie, is that really all you're getting from this?" She turned back to the spectacle, "It's Smigus Dyngus, and they're not cold," she called over her shoulder, "they've got the sap rising in them. Spring is coming, and each one of them has got a hot little furnace burning inside. You'd better hope they'll keep themselves under control at the dance next week... or not!"

"It's what?" Tommie said to the room in general.

"Smigus Dyngus," said Bainbridge, who was stretched out on his bunk with a book, indifferent to the commotion. "It's a pagan fertility rite overlaid with a thin veneer of Easter Monday." Bainbridge had read Divinity at Oxford.

"Oh. Ok, but why are they throwing water?" said Tommie, "and are they hitting each other with branches?"

"Yup," said Bainbridge, "I'm told they traditionally whip young women with pussy willow branches. Propriety forbids me from going into that one too deeply, but the water represents life and the renewal of life; ritual cleansing, baptism, washing away the old life and rising to the new, all that sort of stuff. Think about it; at this very moment, the Catholics are celebrating Mass in the chapel, and they, too, are tossing water around. Not having as much fun, I would imagine, but not getting so cold."

"That's what the dance is all about next week," said Sam, leaving the window. Tommie had been intrigued to receive a formal invitation to a ball hosted by the Polish contingent. "It's part of their Easter celebrations, and we're politely requested to dress up for it. Actual dresses, I mean; ballgowns! Not Simon, of course... unless he wants to, but Ian and Don and myself –and you too – we all get to be honorary women for the occasion! Sorry about that, Robert, I'll sit still now; is this right?" She resumed her pose, then slid her eyes sideways to Tommie, "So, tomorrow, let's go and pick out our dresses. I'll show you around the wardrobe."

***

The backstage room that housed the wardrobe resembled a boudoir.

A large cheval mirror, draped with gauzy scarves and a black feather boa, dominated the back wall, and an ornate vanity table with another mirror was tucked into the corner on the left. A throb of colour pulsed in the right-hand side of the room where a rack of gowns, picked out in a shaft of rare light from a high window, glowed in the gloom like semi-precious stones in a mine.

"Where did all this stuff come from?" said Tommie, drifting over to the dresses. The rich colours touched her unexpectedly, like an echo from another existence.

"Trade," said Sam, joining her. "Bainbridge is a wizard. Chocolate and cigarettes are more valuable than glad rags out there these days, and the commandant allows it because having an active theatre troupe scores highly on the Red Cross reports. Plain clothes wouldn't pass security, but these..." she said, selecting a cloth-of-gold evening gown and holding it up against herself, "Well, anyone trudging through Germany in this is going to be conspicuous, however well he might wear it."

Don joined them briefly, saw Tommie sitting at the vanity, poking tentatively at the greasepaint, and took her in hand, transforming her face with consummate skill.

"No, no, no. Don't blot the lipstick; don't mute yourself. Broadcast your sex! Women might be doing men's work these days, but if they don't want to look like men, they need to do something dramatic. The eyes are too subtle, so it's all up to the lips. The lips are the mouthpiece for the sex organs, and they say 'I'm still a woman down there – where it counts!'"

Staring at herself in the mirror, Tommie watched her

eyes widen in alarm.

"But I don't want to be broadcasting my... my lips under current circumstances!"

"Not out there, perhaps," grinned Don, inclining his head towards the courtyard, "But you're in the theatre now, darling. And the theatre is all about fantasy."

"Yes; fantasy," agreed Sam dryly, as Don hurried off to attend a French lesson, "Let's really challenge fantasy, and try to make you look like a woman, shall we? The scarlet dress is mine, though."

Slipping effortlessly into the dress she had worn for the cabaret, Sam turned her attentions to Tommie, and Tommie submitted, shyly unwinding her chest band and allowing herself to be crammed into a clinging, cobalt-blue satin dress with a plummeting neckline. They disagreed about the amount of cleavage that she should reveal, and Sam – and the dress – won. With a peroxide blonde wig over her still-short hair, and with cherry-red lipstick, the overall effect was that of a Hollywood siren.

They were standing side-by-side in front of the cheval mirror, examining the result, when the door behind them opened and they turned to see Robert Pickman entering from the auditorium, bringing with him a young American serviceman.

The two men stopped short and stared, and Tommie stared back; it was the first time that she had seen a new face arriving at the castle, and there was an indefinable strangeness about the experience. To her, the newcomer seemed outlandish, brought in from the separate world outside, and she found herself wondering if there was a corresponding apartness about the inhabitants of the castle that was perceptible to outsiders.

The young American, meanwhile, was coming to terms with the far less nebulous, far more definable strangeness of the two people standing in front of him. There was a bemused silence all round – except from Sam, who preened herself seductively.

"Who is this, Robert?" she said in her richest, smoothest

tones. Pickman didn't answer immediately, he was staring at Tommie and looking almost as confused as the young lieutenant. "Robert," chided Sam, "where are your manners? Please, introduce us."

"Er. Er..." Pickman said eventually, "er, this is second lieutenant Harold Crozier, transferred from Laufen. I'm just showing him around."

Sam advanced, sashaying smoothly in the scarlet dress, moving like a steam locomotive on oiled rails. "What a pleasure to meet you, Lieutenant Crozier. Welcome to our little chateau."

Crozier gazed on the vision before him. "Are you ladies here for... for... for...?" he stammered, lowering his eyes inevitably towards Sam's nether regions.

"Yes," said Sam, smiling her crocodile smile.

"No!" said Tommie.

"For... for... for entertaining the troops, you mean?" Sam said, with merciless mimicry. "Is that what you were trying to say, Harold? Then the answer is yes."

"The answer is no," insisted Tommie.

"Speak for yourself, sweetie," said Sam archly, "I am highly entertaining."

Tommie couldn't help noticing that, while the newcomer was in thrall to Sam, Robert Pickman's eyes were fixed on her own body, travelling like a tourist in a new world, lingering over the curves that had been liberated from the chest band only to be compressed into the disputed cleavage, and finally settling wonderingly on her face. Her face! She was broadcasting her sex!

She pulled off the wig and wiped the back of her wrist across her mouth. Catching the movement, Crozier's eyes widened in horror, and a shudder passed through his body.

"Are you both *men?*"

Sam summoned high umbrage. "How dare you?!"

"I'm sorry, ma'am," the young man said, addressing Sam in painful confusion. His eyes flickered back to Tommie, "It's just that... well, everyone knows that British servicemen like to wear women's clothes, and... well, it's not for me to judge, but I need to know what's what."

Tommie winced and braced herself for an earthquake following this slur on Sam's beloved army. She sent an urgent look across at Pickman, who returned the look blankly; the removal of the wig had jolted him from his bewitchment, but he was still disoriented. Sam was not. Sublimely dismissive of the fact that she was, in fact, a British serviceman dressed in women's clothes, her eyes flashed.

"Lieutenant Pickman, this man needs to be told what's what. Will you tell him what's what," she said, ominously, "Or shall I do it?"

"He'll find out soon enough," said Pickman distantly. Then he registered Sam's tone, and pulled himself together. "Oh! Right! What's what. Yes," he amended hastily, "Lieutenant Crozier, let me introduce you to Captain Sam Allenby and Miss Tomasin West, usually known as Tommie."

"Captain Sam Allenby, and *Miss* Tomasin...?" said Crozier, grasping at straws. "So, 'Tommie' is a lady, and er... 'Sam' is a... a... a..." he ventured, his eyes darting from Sam's gorgeous form to Tommie's disarranged glamour. Pickman rolled his eyes.

"Tommie is a lady pretending to be a man," he said shortly, "Although, clearly, not at this particular moment. And Captain Allenby is a man who occasionally pretends to be a lady. A lady cabaret singer. And it's not *all* British servicemen who do this, Crozier," he added hastily, "but you should understand that it's generally considered to be quite acceptable." He sighed. "I wish they'd got Burgess Meredith to cover this one."

Crozier nodded, and now his face bore a fixed, waxy expression.

"But which is which?" he ventured. "Which one is Tommie?" Tommie raised her hand. "You're Tommie, and you're a real woman?"

"Yes."

"Ok. Got it," he said, clearly unconvinced. He turned to

Sam, his eyes drifting irresistibly once more over her glorious outline. "And you're... a captain in the British army? A... man?" Sam rewarded him with a juicy wink and Crozier turned hastily back to Tommie as the lesser of two evils. "So, why are you here, in this castle, if you're a woman?"

"She's a civilian," said Pickman, "The SS think she's a spy, so they threw her in here as a sort of social experiment."

Crozier frowned.

"Why didn't they just shoot her?"

Sam snorted and Tommie scowled at her.

"There are times when I think that might have been preferable," she said, sourly.

"Right," said Pickman briskly, turning towards the door, "I think we're done here. Come on, Crozier, I'll show you the canteen."

Crozier followed him, then turned back to throw an apologetic glance at Tommie.

"Sorry, er... ma'am – about the shooting you comment," he said, "That wasn't polite."

Tommie shrugged.

"Don't worry about it," she said, "you're not the first one to have made the point."

"Be sure to attend the cabaret on Friday, Harold," cooed Sam running her eyes over the young man with her best bodacious smile, "I'll be looking out for you."

"Yes, ma'am... Captain Allenby, sir," said Crozier, blushing furiously.

Sam laughed, letting the sound swirl, hot-chocolate-rich and deep, in her chest.

"Well done, that man, for covering all the bases!"

***

On their circuit of the courtyard the next day, Tommie and Sam passed Crozier, who was talking dispiritedly to Watley. Sam paused to greet him.

"Good morning, Lieutenant Crozier."

"Sir!" said Crozier instinctively to the three stars on

Sam's shoulder then, puzzled, he glanced into Sam's face and, with a creeping suspicion, to Tommie. As a blurry recognition dawned, he raised curious eyes to Sam's face again.

"Captain Allenby?" he said.

Sam smiled, and Tommie saw the Captain Allenby who led a company of soldiers.

"Yes, Lieutenant Crozier, and, regarding yesterday," he said, "do you notice that I'm in uniform today?"

"Yes, sir"

Sam nodded. "I play fair when I'm in uniform."

***

Wearing a sensible dress and her cabaret heels, Sam was concentrating on sliding her feet in a slow, slow, quick-quick, slow rhythm. "Teach me to do it backwards and in heels, Tommie, please," she had wheedled that morning. "I have to practice for the dance, and we're running out of time. Phil said he'll be my practice partner."

"Gladly, Sam, but... why with Phil? He's always so unpleasant to you. Surely Simon will partner you?"

An odd expression had flickered across Sam's face like a fast-moving cloud-shadow over an open landscape, there and gone. "It's complicated," she'd said. So, partnered by Simon for demonstration purposes, Tommie was wearing a dress and dancing shoes borrowed from the wardrobe, because Sam had insisted on it. "You can't teach me to dance in heels if you're wearing flying boots and battle-dress."

The gramophone sat on a table next to a stack of records, and Cooper was holding Sam at arm's length, with a scowl on his face, manoeuvring her around the floor, until she gave a sharp squawk, and Cooper pulled irritably away from her.

"Let's change the music," he snapped, "How about "Your Feet's Too Big." Better still, let's change partners. Come on, Simon, let's see how smooth you look dancing with mine." He crossed the room to the gramophone, and Simon glared darkly at him, but relinquished Tommie and took Sam in his arms. Cooper set the music playing again, and returned to partner Tommie.

He was taller than Simon, and she felt an immediate sense of otherness in dancing with him; a heightened sensitization. Not an attraction or a desire, but a hum of otherness – a biological reaction.

Watching her face, Cooper switched from the formal dance hold to the more intimate hold, sliding his arm to the small of her back, and drawing her closer to him. A soft wash of heat rose in her, and she became suddenly aware of the flimsy drift of the sleeve against her arm, and the flow of the skirt around her legs, contrasting with the solidness of Cooper's uniform. She felt feminine, he felt masculine.

She had to put a stop to this. Swinging precariously towards a fit of the giggles as naval terminology filled her mind, she told herself to drop anchor and send up a distress flare. This rogue heat had nothing to do with the rather insufferable Phil Cooper; it was nothing more than... than otherness. Biological otherness. She latched onto this understanding, drew a deep, slow breath, and composed herself.

Across the floor, she could see Simon and Sam gliding together, a perfect match. The dysphoria that had been evident and so out of place on Sam's face when she was dancing with Cooper had vanished, and she swept gloriously around the floor, perfectly in step with Simon. Tommie heard her voice, teasing, as they danced past.

"I know what you're doing, Simon – and why you're doing it." Simon's face stiffened, and a warning light flickered in his eyes. "But I'm going to enjoy the hell out of it anyway," Sam added, freeing her hand from his and flicking the top button of his tunic, "and I'm going to make sure that you do too." She leaned into him and whispered something into his ear. He lifted his head and laughed, the ready blush flooding his face and making his blue eyes flash.

Tommie felt Phil's hold on her stiffen, and she glanced

up to find that he too was watching them, his expression suddenly sharp and alert.

In the corner of the room, the door to the courtyard swung open, and a French officer strode in. He hesitated, his eyes assessing the scene as the music ended.

"If you want to dance, you have to bring your own girl, Joliet," Cooper called, releasing Tommie and heading for the gramophone again.

"I have my girl," said Joliet. He walked over and took Tommie by the wrist, then grunted as she bent his fingers back, breaking his grip. Cursing and massaging his hand, he stared at her, and his eyes narrowed. Sam laughed.

"Wrong, Joliet," she said, side-stepping Cooper as he reached out for her, "That's not your girl. That's my girl." She took Tommie in her arms and whisked her across the floor, taking the lead effortlessly. Joliet watched them for a while, then left, scowling, as Cooper stepped in and reclaimed Sam.

The music started again, but now Simon was distracted as they danced together.

"Have you had enough?" she said, "Do you want to sit out?"

He shook his head. "No. I'm loving this. It's... lovely..."

"But?"

"But..." His eyes were troubled. "This must be appallingly bad form, Tommie, but would you mind if I pretended that it's Mary I'm dancing with, not you?" His voice cracked, and he pressed his hand against his breast pocket where, she knew, he always carried his photograph of Mary. "God, I wish it was her I'm holding right now."

Her heart twisted.

"Only if you don't mind me pretending that I'm Mary too." He frowned unhappily, and she shook her head, "Just so I can feel what it's like to have someone longing for me."

He held her eyes for a moment, then nodded.

"So, just to be clear," he said soberly, "you'll understand that if I sniff your hair, or... hold you against me, or..."

She winced.

"Simon, you really do say the sweetest things in the clumsiest ways! Just do whatever you want, within the bounds of decency, and I'll understand."

He nodded and slid his arm around her, pulling her in tight, and she tucked her head against his neck, breathing in the shaving-soap scent of him.

***

The Smigus Dyngus ball was the affirmation of light and joy and life that had been missing in the flat days of that stretched-out winter.

The musicians, stationed on a dais at one end of the theatre auditorium, played their hearts out, mixing traditional and popular tunes, and the dancing didn't stop.

Ian, wearing an unnecessarily frothy pink gown, Don, in a green sequinned dress, and Tommie in a cobalt blue creation, danced with a string of officers, and Gabryel Zan danced with Ken Parr all night.

Simon was there as Tommie's unofficial chaperone, and Colonel Gregory, who was good friends with Henryk Norek, the senior Polish officer, was attending to oversee the propriety of the occasion for his men. They had both agreed to stand down in favour of the Polish officers, but Tommie looked up at one point, when the music slowed to a sedate waltz, to see Sam dancing in the arms of Colonel Gregory, listening intently as Gregory – unusually – did most of the talking, speaking soberly, his face close to her ear.

16
A transcendent sigh

She had fallen asleep on her bed, reading, but, waking up, she knew instantly that it was more than just the residue of an afternoon nap that prickled in her brain. An oppressive weight bore down on the castle, and the air had a heavy, thick texture, as though its entire population – staff and prisoners alike – had been suspended in aspic jelly.

She washed her face and brushed her teeth slowly, in no hurry to investigate the cause of the heaviness. When she eventually opened her door, the dormitory was almost at capacity, but ominously silent. Gregory was heading out.

"I have an audience with the commandant," he announced to nobody in particular.

Tommie drifted towards Simon's bunk. She had never seen him wearing the expression that now set his face into dark channels of anger. Sam was sitting in a chair nearby, her normally languorous posture seized into a rigid tension. It was a room full of sleepwalkers sharing the same dream.

"What's happened?" she asked warily.

Sam looked up, her head moving with the mechanical motion of an automaton. Her face might have been carved from teak, and the light in her eyes was flat and cold. This interaction was between Captain Allenby and a civilian.

"The German army has discovered a mass grave in the

Katyn forest near Smolensk. More than four thousand Polish officers. Shot in the back."

Tommie's mouth opened, but no sound came out. She must have mis-heard. *Four thousand?*

"It came through the grapevine," Sam added, "but it looks as though Colonel Gregory is about to be given the news formally."

Tommie floundered.

"No. Because who would follow that order? To shoot them in the *back* – so many men? Who would follow that order?"

"Soldiers!" Sam snapped, "Soldiers, airmen and sailors. Servicemen follow orders. The officers – the ones who give the command," her voice hardened, "they are responsible not only for those deaths, but for the nightmares that will haunt their men for the rest of their lives." She turned sharply. "Simon…" A tense glance flew between them.

"I know, Sam," Simon muttered, "I know."

Colonel Gregory returned half an hour later, striding through the officers' room and shutting himself into his own quarters without a word. After ten minutes, his door opened and he addressed the room briefly.

"The news that we all heard today has been confirmed by the commandant. Further to this, the entire contingent of Polish officers in this prison is to be handed over to the custody of the SS, and transferred out." He paused as, through the open window onto the courtyard, a piercing cry echoed; Ken Parr had spent the morning in the Polish quarters with Gabryel Zan.

At the sound, Gregory closed his eyes briefly, then continued.

"This is an order that the commandant feels to be incontrovertible. The other senior officers and I have protested most vehemently, and will continue to do so, but the order comes from the highest levels, and we must be prepared to accept that it will be complied with." He met the eyes of each man in turn, "It should not be insurmountable for you all, as servicemen, to understand that outrage is also running high with the Germans regarding today's news. Notwithstanding the... difficult history between Poland and Germany, this atrocity is a desecration of military honour. Disquiet about the transfer of Norek and his men to SS custody is to be expected, and the situation in this castle is volatile. Please be cognizant of that and behave accordingly. Thank you."

As anticipated, all appeals for the reversal of the order were refused, and on the day scheduled for the departure of the Polish contingent, the prisoners assembled in the courtyard for a regular appel... except that it was like no appel that Tommie had ever witnessed.

All officers turned out as for parade, wearing uniforms that were, if not immaculate, then certainly close to it. When the headcount had been completed, the Polish officers, standing at the innermost side of the courtyard, were called to attention by Henryk Norek.

With perfect parade-ground precision, the men stiffened, and when the order was given, they marched forwards, performed a razor-sharp left turn and marched past the ranks of the other contingents, who, on the order of their senior officers, gave a salute.

A corresponding movement caught Tommie's eye, and she swallowed hard as she watched some of the German guards, of their own volition, join the salute.

The doors into the commandantur courtyard swung open, and a transcendent sound breathed across the two courtyards – a sound that was somewhere between a hiss and a sigh – as the entire off-duty military staff were revealed there, standing to attention, with Renger, Hamm, Brandt and Henning at the head of them.

Through the open outer gates, Steiger could be seen waiting by his staff car, along with four garrison trucks and a troop of SS guards.

Led by the commandant, the castle staff snapped a salute as the Polish contingent marched past them. A military salute, Tommie noted; they had honoured Norek and his men with a military salute – a salute given by a soldier to a soldier – not the prescribed, politically-weighted Nazi one. Such significances seemed to her like a faint pulse in a body left for dead.

The gates of the courtyard swung shut behind the Polish officers, and a hollow silence reigned.

Colonel Gregory stood as though turned to stone. The senior officers of the other contingents dismissed their men, but Gregory remained in place, and not a single British officer moved. Tommie saw Sam's eyes settle on him with a shadow of concern deepening their green, and after a long moment Gregory turned sharply and dismissed his men. He met Sam's gaze momentarily, but then his eyes slid past her and his expression altered.

One figure remained unmoving as the officers drifted away; Ken Parr, in his position at the back of the ranks, was still standing stiffly at attention. His eyes were fixed on nothing, and his slight frame swayed slightly as Pickman patted him awkwardly on the back. On the other side of Sam, Doug Bainbridge turned to watch as Colonel Gregory approached the young man and spoke to him quietly. Parr nodded crisply once or twice but maintained his parade-ground rigidity. Gregory rested his hand briefly on Parr's shoulder and walked away, throwing a significant glance at Bainbridge.

"Come on, son," said Bainbridge, walking over to Parr and putting a gentle arm around the boy's shoulders, "Let's get you inside. I'll make you a nice cup of tea." At his touch, Parr's eyes squeezed shut, the corners of his mouth pulled down, and Tommie saw his chest catching, heard the sharp, sobbing puffs of breath escaping from his clamped lips.

Tommie had been unsure, as the Polish officers marched out, if she had imagined that transcendent sigh passing over the courtyard, but she heard the echo of it in Simon's voice as he approached her through the dispersing officers.

"That was the commandant putting Steiger on notice that everyone in this castle knows he's responsible for what happens to those men," he said. "Not only did Renger deny Steiger entry into the castle to take custody of them, he made sure that he witnessed the formal send-off."

"It appears that the Wehrmacht is still fighting for its existence and its honour," said Sam, breaking out of her reverie.

"Who were those three men in Russian uniform, standing behind Brandt?" Tommie asked. "That wasn't a sight I expected to see; Russian uniforms in here... and on the other side of that wall."

"It's supposed to be very hush-hush," said Sam, "But Henryk Norek knew about them and tolerated them. They're brought here regularly to work with Brandt. The rumour is that they are leaders of the Russian soldiers who have deserted to work with Germany against Stalin's regime. That sounds about right to me; I can't think of any other reason why they would be here, and the Polish officers must be of the same opinion or there's no way they would have stood for them being there today."

***

A splash of warm weather arrived like a miracle, and the entire population of prisoners migrated to the courtyard, to lounge or stroll in the precious sunshine. Even Colonel Gregory had shunned his room and his reclusive habits, and was sitting over a chess board with the senior French officer.

For Tommie, this was a perfect time to take a shower without having to enlist Simon as a gatekeeper. Taking the towel that somebody had left draped over the doorknob of the shower room, she opened the door and went in.

A stench of testosterone and sweat gusted out of the room, along with another element that she couldn't quite identify. Keith Barnes caught sight of her and lifted his hand to his mouth, which was swelling and turning an ugly blue.

"Get out!" he snapped. She backed away, but stopped as the figure confronting Barnes turned around and, seeing her, slumped.

"Go away, Tommie." Sam's voice was strained and

unfamiliar.

Tommie's insides lurched. She had trespassed on a private scene. Mortified, she remembered the towel that had been draped over the door handle.

"Get out!" barked Barnes again, stepping towards her. "Get out of here, you stupid, fucked-up little lesbian."

"Lesbian?" she said weakly, glancing, wounded, at Sam. Sam shook her head.

"No," she said quickly, "That's just what a man calls a woman who doesn't respond to him." Now Tommie saw the blood that was flowing from a gash in her temple, and the large, shining lump high on her cheekbone. "What was it that you called me just now, Keith?" Sam said, turning back to Barnes, and her voice turned harsh. "It wasn't quite as nice as "lesbian" was it?"

"I called you a cock-tease," spat Barnes.

Cock-tease. Tommie was a pillar of salt. In the face of obscenity – in the skin-crawling understanding of what she had walked in on – she found that she couldn't move, and now she recognized the other element in the room that had come along with the stench of testosterone... Fear. A bolt of electricity passed through the soles of her feet, fusing her to the spot and splitting every cell of her body.

"Oh, Sam!" she said. Her voice was low and flat, and her throat had thickened to the point where she thought she would choke. "Oh, no, Sam."

Sam stared at her.

"No!" she snapped. Whipping back around to face Barnes, her face turned savage. "I have *never* made myself attractive to you. I have *never* come on to you. I..."

"Don't, Sam!" Tommie croaked. "Don't answer to him!" She turned to Barnes. She knew she was shaking - she could feel herself shaking - all the way down to her hair follicles. She was shaking so violently that she could see her own body vibrating. He saw it too, and smirked. She closed her eyes and drew a deep breath, "You don't get to take what you desire by force, just because you desire it."

She had spoken quietly, but Barnes' smirk vanished.

"Oh, shut up, you whiny little bitch," he snapped, "This is men's business. You know nothing about men."

"I'm learning fast."

"You think so?" He advanced on her.

"Don't *touch* her!" Sam's voice was a snarl. Barnes wheeled around, slamming his left fist into her face, and she flew across the room. He turned back to Tommie.

"You think you've learned about men, do you?" he said, "Have you learned about this yet?" He tapped her face lightly with his fist, "And this?" again, a little harder, just hard enough to turn her face to the side. The side where Sam was sprawled, dazed, but struggling to get to her feet. She fell still when she caught the look on Tommie's face, and shook her head.

"No, Tommie, don't do it. He's violent, and he's strong. Just go."

"'Don't do it, Tommie, he's violent.'" minced Barnes in falsetto. "Don't do what? Don't take me on?" He laughed, a sharp bark of a laugh. "Because you're a lesbian in a uniform, you think you can fight me? Tell me, does hitting a lesbian feel the same as hitting a woman?"

"I don't know," said Tommie. She had stopped shaking. "Why don't you give it a try?"

Barnes hit her again, harder this time, and she grabbed his wrist, taking his momentum and pulling him off balance. Bringing his arm downwards, she twisted it, bracing the elbow joint against itself, and swung the weight of her upper body down onto it. Barnes shouted out and froze in an attempt to keep his wrist, elbow and shoulder joints intact. Tommie held the pressure for a moment, then released the grip and swung her elbow sharply backwards, listening to the crack as Barnes' nose broke.

She stood back then, reining in her anger hard until it sat back on its haunches with its muscles bunched, ready to leap.

"Sam said no to you, didn't he?" she said quietly, "He said no, and he kept saying no."

Barnes grinned at her with bloodied teeth and took a step

forward.

"Yeah, well, he should have said yes. It would have gone better for him... Much better."

Tommie let go of the reins. Barnes fought back viciously, landing a few bone-jolting blows, mainly to her chest and trunk, where they wouldn't show; he must be experienced at this, she realized, and the understanding fed her anger, but eventually he lay curled up, coughing and retching, on the stone floor.

Shrugging off the spreading pains in her body, she jabbed a boot into his ribs.

"Well, look at that, Keith. I *can* take you on," she said, "And it's not because I'm a lesbian in a uniform, it's because – in the words of an even meaner bastard than you are – I know a few quick moves."

Sam stepped forwards and kicked Barnes in the crotch.

"Bastard!" she snarled. Her voice was harsh and raspy, and her face was knotted with rage. "Bastard, bastard, bastard! Filthy bastard." With each word she stepped around him, kicking him from every angle as he twisted to avoid the assault. Tommie reached out and gently took her arm.

"That's enough, Sam. You don't want to cause internal damage."

"Yes, I do! I *do* want to cause internal damage... and external damage too. I want to damage it so badly that they have to cut it off. Make them castrate him!" but she stopped kicking and walked away. "You should have stayed out of it," she said stiffly, over her shoulder, "I didn't need your help."

"That wasn't for you," Tommie said, "it was for me."

Following Sam into the still-empty main dormitory, she led her into her own room and sat her on the bed, closing the door firmly and taking the first aid box from the closet. Kneeling in front of her, she set out some cotton wadding and a few jars of ointment on a clean cloth on the small bedside table.

"I hate being hit."

Tommie looked up at the tone in Sam's voice. She was staring into the middle distance. "I would have been able to fight him off, I've done it before, but that's not the point. I hate being hit," she repeated, and her rich voice was distressingly flat and colourless. "I know that sounds stupid, because nobody likes being hit, right? Wrong. Boys – men – don't mind being hit, as long as they're hitting too. This is just the way things are. Girls don't like being hit, and boys are taught never to hit them. Hitting girls is a big taboo, strictly enforced. But boys are allowed to hit boys. It's publicly tutted over, of course, but privately it's understood that boys must be boys."

She paused and drew a deep breath. "You heard what Edward said that day when everyone was fighting, the first day you were here; "They have to fight someone. If they can't fight the enemy they might as well fight each other." It's natural, you see; it's the way of things. It makes sense."

Sam's voice was thin and threadbare now, and Tommie understood that she was picking away at the stitches that knitted her together; seizing a loose end of yarn and unravelling it into a crooked filament. In the quiet of the room some siren call was echoing thinly, summoning her, back through a spiral of similar, recurring acts of violence in her past. "But to me it doesn't make sense," Sam was saying, "Hitting, I mean. It didn't make sense then and it doesn't make sense now. I didn't want to hit anyone, and I didn't want to be hit. I knew I was a girl, but the adults said I wasn't; they said I was a boy, and they let me be hit. I had to toughen up, they said."

Her eyes closed briefly, then flinched open again; the instinct of a vulnerable creature in a world of predators. "The boys knew I wasn't really a boy, of course, and they hit me more because of it - they didn't understand it, so they hit me. That's what boys do when they don't understand something.

"I tried to do what was expected, I tried really hard; I hit back, but I wasn't good at it, so my parents sent me to boxing lessons. My instructor told me I hit like a girl." The muscles of Sam's face formed the shape of a laugh, but there was no sound. "I wasn't a boy Tommie," she choked, and the honey voice was a ragged, desolate whisper "But they wouldn't let me be a girl. I was nothing."

Tommie watched as the spiral slowed, stopped and reversed, and the inconceivable pain corkscrewed relentlessly up from the past, dredging up a lifetime of confusion and pain and fear, and spilling the result of it out over her torn, swollen face. "I don't like being hit."

Sam's voice caught, broke, and slid into a wild, wordless howl of pain and fear and betrayal, crying out for protection and a sanctuary that had never been there.

Climbing onto the bed, Tommie set her back against the wall, and opened her arms wide as Sam, rigid, shuddering, and keening, scrambled after her and clung to her. Stroking the heavy, ebony hair, gently combing Sam's hot scalp with her fingertips, and freeing the strands from her wet face, she looked down and contemplated the obscenity of those same wounds on a child.

Some time later a tentative knock on the door woke them from their reverie. Sam groaned.

"Tell them to go away."

Tommie opened her mouth, but Simon's voice reached them first, sounding worried.

"Tommie? It's me… and Colonel Gregory. Are you ok? Is Sam in there with you?"

At the mention of Gregory's name Sam stiffened, sat up, and shuffled to the edge of the bed, straightening out her uniform and smoothing her hair.

"Yes, Simon," Tommie called, following her lead, "We're both here. Just give me one second." She hissed at Sam, "No mention of the commando moves."

Sam nodded.

"Did you get hurt? I should have asked…"

Tommie shook her head and positioned the bedside table with its ointments within reach.

"No. Too much adrenaline flowing."

Picking up a soft wad of cotton, she knelt on the floor in

front of Sam, who froze suddenly, turning horrified eyes on her.

"Everyone must have heard me crying," she whispered, glancing up at the open window onto the courtyard. Tommie shook her head and brushed the swollen face with her fingertips, taking the tears and transferring them to her own skin.

"They heard a woman crying, Captain Allenby." She kissed Sam gently on the forehead and saw her eyes react, shifting like marsh pools when someone approaches. Then, throwing a hunted glance at the door, Sam gestured urgently for the evidence of her tears to be erased.

Quickly, Tommie dabbed the unbroken areas of skin with iodine for appearances; the painful treatment would be performed in front of witnesses, she thought, grimly. She lifted her eyebrows, and Sam nodded.

"Ok, Simon, you can come in now," she called, "And Colonel Gregory, of course."

When the two men opened the door and stepped self-consciously into the room, she was at work, gently touching an iodine-soaked pad to the swollen graze on the cheekbone. Sam winced and blinked, and her eyes watered.

"Sorry, Sam," Tommie said. "This will make your eyes all bloodshot and puffy for a while." She glanced up. Simon searched her face and she saw his throat constrict.

"I've heard there was a fight," Gregory said. He was tense and stiff, but his voice was as calm as always, and casually solicitous. "Nothing too severe, I hope, Captain Allenby?"

"No, sir," answered Sam crisply, "Just the usual nonsense. I gave as good as I got, but Miss West got a little upset and she took a few blows, trying to intervene."

"Tommie?!" snapped Simon.

"It was nothing," said Tommie, "It's not the first time I've been in a scrap. I'm a bit of a tomboy. I'm fine."

"Good, good," said Gregory, clearly unconvinced. He watched closely as she tended to Sam's face. "What's your assessment, Miss West? Anything to be concerned about?"

Tommie hesitated and Sam's eyes fixed on hers sharply.

"I don't think there are any fractures to the facial bones, Colonel Gregory," she said tightly, "and the cuts will heal in their own time. There will be scars," she added heavily, and her voice thickened and wobbled as she glanced up at Gregory, "but the new scars will just blend in with the old ones."

The shadows in his face told her that he understood exactly what she was saying, and there was pain in the understanding.

There were to be no consequences for the incident. Sam had insisted. It was nothing more than a fight between two officers, and Captain Allenby had given as good as he got.

17
I have a copy of Metamorphoses

An unlikely, trembling optimism surged as spring opened up and the air filled with the scents of lilac and hawthorn. In the following weeks, a handful of escapes were attempted by other contingents. All failed, but no attempts were made by the British, and Tommie could see that Doug Bainbridge was – by his standards – edgy.

One day, as summer rolled in, she noticed him glancing up absent-mindedly at a family of jackdaws who were chacking and fussing somewhere high up in the cluster of roofs.

Except Bainbridge was never absent-minded.

"They're making a hell of a racket, aren't they, Doug? It's enough to make anyone wonder what's going on up there," she said, inclining her head towards a guard on the far side of the courtyard who was showing an acute interest in the roofline. "It's only because their young ones are fledging," she added, "Once they're strong enough to make it as far as the west wing, it will get a lot quieter around here; if anything disturbs them after that, they will just take off without a word."

Bainbridge gave her a keen glance. "I'm very interested in birds," he said, "how long will it take them to fledge?"

"They've been working on it for a while, so, any day

now."

Bainbridge nodded. "Will you let me know when it happens?"

"Will do."

It was two days before the fledglings reached the west wing, and the sound of their chacking now echoed more distantly from the courtyard of the commandantur.

Bainbridge's face shed its tension in favour of a stony determination, and Tommie felt waves of pins and needles passing over her; the prospect of life in the castle without Simon was bad enough, but she was haunted by the memory of Padier running, swerving, jerking, falling.

She flinched and pushed away the thought of bullets tearing into the golden skin of Simon's back, ripping him apart.

***

The morning sky was a singing blue, and had been for more than an hour by the time the early appel was called. From her window, Tommie watched a flock of swifts wheeling and squealing above the castle, their scythe-like silhouettes almost invisible in the void, and released her heart to go soaring with them. Below her, the movements of the guards were now so familiar that the courtyard seemed like just any street-scene in any town she had ever been in.

She dressed quickly, and opened her door to see Simon glance up and make his way hastily towards her, hopping as he pulled his uniform trousers on over his pyjamas. He was not a morning person, it was usually a battle to separate him from his mattress in the mornings, and she stared at him in surprise.

"Don't look around for Sam, and don't react," he said under his breath. Turning back to grab his tunic from his bunk, he shoved his feet into his boots, took her sleeve, and drew her towards the door.

Tommie had already assumed her poker face, but it was

hard to keep her expression neutral as Tom Currier from mess number three casually took Sam's place next to her at appel.

Muzzling the klaxon wail that was winding up inside her heart, she maintained a blank expression as the guards completed their count, conferred, became concerned, and performed an agitated recount. When a voice that wasn't Phil Cooper's answered to his name, she began to understand about the dance lessons. A guard paused in front of Currier, held up Sam's identity photo, looked once, then twice, then shook his head, pulled Currier roughly out of the line, and hustled him over to the table. A shout went up.

"Captain Samuel Allenby."

Tommie's poker face folded, and she glanced over her shoulder at Simon, who met her gaze solidly, his blue eyes reflecting her distress back at her, along with a trace of something else that she could not interpret.

Tension was escalating in the courtyard, the nearest guard shouted a command for her to keep her eyes to the front, and she turned back into herself. Her chest felt like bronchitis. There would be no more teasing, candid conversations, no melted-chocolate laugh, no curious, green-eyed interrogations, and the disasters that she had feared for Simon now transferred themselves to Sam, except now they included harrowing images of songbirds, scooped up in the trappers' misting nets or glued to birdlime in their migration across the Mediterranean.

It seemed that the whole day passed before the appel was dismissed, and then, from the other side of that empty space, Bainbridge turned to her.

"I have a copy of Metamorphoses. Ovid, not Kafka."

The man's direct and unfussy approach to conversation had long ceased to unsettle Tommie, but she was puzzled by this statement. She looked up at him.

"Oh."

"Ovid can be a bit exotic, but if you're interested, you're welcome to borrow it."

"Oh!" she said again. "Thank you, Doug, I would love

to read it."

Bainbridge nodded. "I'll leave it on my bunk for you."

Simon came and, without hesitation, put his arms around her. She leaned against him, pressing her face into his shoulder.

"I thought it was going to be you."

She felt him shake his head.

"No."

"Nice work, Leigh," said Watley passing by, "Eliminate the competition, eh?"

"Fucking shut up, Watley," came Pickman's voice behind her.

"How are we going to know what has happened to her, Simon?" she said.

"Gregory will be informed if... if something goes bad, but otherwise, Sam and Phil will get word to us once they are safe. In the meantime, we try to forget about it."

"You don't forget Sam Allenby."

Simon released her abruptly. "Sir," he said to Colonel Gregory, who was standing there, holding an envelope and looking as though someone had stepped on his foot. He handed the note to Tommie.

"Captain Allenby left a note for you, Miss West, to be handed over after he left."

Tommie took the envelope and read the note inside.

Sorry to leave you like this, sweetie. Stay strong, and take good care of Simon – you're going to need each other. See you on the other side.

Love,

Sam.

"If it's not too personal, might I be permitted to know what it says?" Gregory asked hesitantly.

"Of course," Tommie said. She handed the note to Gregory, then glanced up at him curiously as he read. Something that had been tucked away in her thoughts, like an actor waiting in the wings, sidled into the conscious part of her mind; Sam had quoted Gregory's words after Barnes' assault on her. 'You heard Edward,' she had said; 'Edward,' not 'Colonel Gregory,' or even 'Gregory.' Tommie had never heard anyone else use Gregory's given name, and in view of the expression in his eyes now, that unconscious slip explained so much.

"Thank you." He handed the note back to her with a quick twist of his face that should have been a smile, and walked away. Tommie turned to Simon, who was watching his senior officer's departing back with a thoughtful expression.

18
Malki

Peter watched Conrad's fingers drumming an irritable beat on the table-top. His friend's natural buoyancy and optimism had been whittled away over recent months by an oppressive understanding of the private maze that Hitler had made of the legal system, and at times he seemed overwhelmed by the enormity of what he stood against.

They were having coffee with Greta at a street café in defiance of the damage that the RAF and the Americans were wreaking on Berlin.

"I remember telling you that joining the General Staff would put you in Hitler's pocket," Conrad said, glancing up with a brittle smile at Peter. "Now I find myself in exactly that position; Hitler has the entire legal system in his grip. It's as though he has seized for himself every stick of dynamite in the whole damn country, and whenever he wants to make a turn that doesn't legally exist, he merely blasts a hole and goes where he wants."

He stretched out his legs and kicked irritably at a nearby chair. "We too have dynamite in our hands, but it's old, and the spark keeps snuffing itself out, or maybe it's damp because Hitler's pissed on it. Damn it all to Hell!" He directed one more kick at the chair and threw his head back to stare up into the powder-blue sky.

Greta shot a worried glance at Peter, and then her expression softened as her eyes focused on something behind him. He turned.

A little girl, no more than four years old, was running between the tables, humming happily and occasionally stopping to perform an unsteady twirl, while her mother stood nearby, deep in conversation with another woman.

The child was wearing a powder-blue woollen jacket over a dress of white cotton that was trimmed around the hem with Alsace lace, and she had discovered, to her joy, that the skirt swirled out when she spun around. Her exuberance was infectious, and the three sitting at the table were captivated, lost momentarily in a world that could be made joyful by a twirling skirt.

The little girl alternately spun and ran, and as she rounded the table where they were sitting, she twirled one more time, became dizzy, took a couple of unsteady steps sideways, and tumbled over near Peter's feet. He got up and kneeled down in front of her. Sprawled on the floor, she lifted her head and frowned. In her dark eyes he could see a solemn consideration of her options – to cry would mean being clamped to her mother's side, and the end of her fun.

"Is she alright?" said Greta, leaning over the table.

"She's fine," he answered, slipping his hands around the small figure and gently lifting her to her feet. "You're indestructible, aren't you, little princess?"

The child's dark hair, all glossy, shining curls, tumbled forwards over her face as she peered down, assessing the damage to her knees, then she looked up at him, wide-eyed and solemn, and he saw that, beneath the jacket, the tiny bodice of her dress was obliterated by a large, sulphurous-yellow fabric star. His mind lurched, and he felt himself sway, but the child stood, unconcerned, in front of him, studying his uniform curiously. A small, plump finger reached out and touched the eagle on his chest.

"Bird," she said, and watched his face, waiting for his approval of her linguistic skills.

"Malki!" The girl's mother was suddenly there, her voice

shrill, and her face ghostly pale. Without a word, her head lowered, she grabbed the child's arm and hurried away, her heels clacking a staccato heartbeat on the paving stones.

Still kneeling, Peter watched as the little girl turned to look back at him and wave with her free hand; a child's wave, the fingers curling and uncurling from the soft palm.

"Wait!" he shouted, stumbling to his feet. Fairly dangling from her mother's grasp, her legs working bravely, Malki was hurried along and hoisted up onto the step of a tram car as it rattled away to disappear around the next street corner.

Peter stared after them, his fingers cramped and stiff, like winter branches, around the void left by the child. He brushed the dust from his knees, and turned back to the table. Greta was sitting rigid and pale, the knuckles of her right hand gleaming through the tanned skin as she clutched the arm of her chair. Conrad was staring at the paving stones with a strained expression. In the stark sunlight, shadows that Peter had never noticed before showed up under his friend's eyes, and lines pulled the darkened skin taut.

In silence they finished their coffee and left.

***

"Malki?" Conrad's voice was incredulous, "Peter, I thought I had become accustomed to your peculiar eccentricities but it seems I was wrong. Please tell me you are joking."

Peter shook his head wildly. The yellow star had burned itself into his brain.

"Not joking. For pity's sake, Conrad, you've always wanted me to leap into action but I wouldn't do it. Now everything has changed. I'm ready to leap. They could come for her tomorrow... or tonight."

"*Nothing* has changed, Peter! After all my efforts to make you understand where it was going... and it took a snip of a girl to open your eyes?"

"I didn't see it!" He heard the distress crackling in his

voice, "I didn't see it." Yes, it had taken a snip of a girl to open his eyes, and his eyes had not closed all night long.

He had known what was going on – of course he had, everyone knew – but he hadn't *known* until now; until he had seen it in the obscenity of a yellow star on a small dress, and understood. They had all deplored the corruption of politics and law and ethics as it happened, wringing their hands over the mess, so why had they – why had *he* – not seen the small lives that were being mangled in the machinery? His brain was boiling.

"I was so caught up in... in the big picture. Conrad, please, there must be something we can do."

"Yes, there is! We can be logical about it, but for the first time since I've known you, it seems that logic is outside your sphere of interest; you would rather go door-to-door around the streets of Berlin searching for –"

"Birth records, that's all I'm asking you for. It's quite simple, I can arrange visas for them from my end."

"Simple is precisely what it is not. For one thing, there are probably as many Malkis born in this city each year as there are Helgas, or were, until..."

"She got on a tram car headed towards Kurfurstendamm."

Conrad shook his head.

"Where maybe she lives, or maybe she doesn't. Maybe that was just the first tram that passed by. Maybe she got off after two stops and got on another tram... or more than one. And even that is immaterial. Peter, listen to me, you don't understand how things are; any reference made to the personal records of Jews must be cleared by the SS. Haven't you heard a word I've been saying these past months, or is it just that you didn't believe me? The Nazis don't want the Jews to leave; Hitler's afraid they're going to siphon off half of Germany's wealth. Jews cannot leave Germany, and their best hope inside Germany is to slip through the net, a feat which, so far, this little Malki and her mother seem to have accomplished.

"If she is a mischling – with a German mother and

Jewish father – she might be left alone, but she might not. Would you draw attention to the existence of this child? Would you tell the authorities about her?" Conrad's voice cracked and failed.

"Canaris has done it," Peter persisted, "Dohnanyi too. I can get access to…"

"You are not Canaris, Peter, and they haven't figured Dohnanyi out yet, but they will if we don't take them down soon. Canaris leads a charmed life, and I wouldn't want to put yours to the test. Even Hitler doesn't know which team the admiral is playing for – everybody just really hopes he's on their side. Canaris is an enigma, and he plays fast and loose, but it would strain even his remarkable powers of persuasion to pass off a toddler as one of his spies." He shook his head emphatically, "No, Peter, it has to be a coup. Then everything changes." He barked a short, bitter laugh, "And it turns out that you're in a better position to act on it than I am. I heard that Hitler told the Minister of Justice, 'The only man I fear is Beck. That man is capable of acting against me.' Breaking the oath and breaking the law; that's the only way things can get done. Join us, Peter. In all good conscience, what else is there to do?"

Hendry's big picture was suddenly out of focus. Right here, right now, the big picture was a little girl daubed with a yellow star.

Peter joined.

He found himself plunged into an odd, cobbled-together organization of military personnel, civilians and civil servants. Preparations for a coup were at an advanced stage; the seemingly unassailable edifice of Hitler's regime was to be taken down quickly and efficiently, and replaced with a transitional government led by Beck as Regent. There was even a constitution written by the irrepressible Goerdeler.

To Peter, however, the plans resembled a large family sharing one bed and one blanket, each one tugging the blanket to themselves. Some were even advocating for a return to monarchism, but the most contentious sticking point was what to do with Hitler; assassination, arrest and execution, or trial? Conrad was infuriated by the steadfast opposition of the members of the Christian Kreisau Circle to the killing of Hitler.

"Each to his own conscience, Conrad," Peter remarked after a particularly rancorous meeting.

"Oh, yes, of course, conscience above all else!" replied Conrad sourly, "Kreisau want a shining future won by good Christian virtues, but Jesus didn't have to deal with Hitler." Lost in his own thoughts, Peter didn't respond, but he caught the sly glance attached to his friend's next comment.

"It's good to see you following in your father's footsteps, though."

"My father's footsteps?" he said, frowning, "What are you talking about?"

"Quite simply, that if your father hadn't been killed in the last war, he would have been Ludwig Beck."

Peter recognized the puckish gleam in his friend's eyes, and, preoccupied with the implications of the meeting, he shook his head and responded vaguely. "But my father *is* dead, Conrad. Ludwig Beck is not my father."

"Come on, Peter, he might just as well be. Look at the two of you; both reserved and brooding, excruciatingly moral, and damnably cautious. Face it, you and Beck could be father and son!"

Peter sighed. "Not only is my father dead, he died when he was not much older than I am now, so I will never know what his footsteps might have been."

"Beck has a daughter, you know, I could introduce you..."

"Conrad, listen to yourself!"

***

"Mam'selle Tomasine, I have a proposition for you." The man who had come up quietly behind her, and was standing too close for comfort, was Joliet, one of the handful of French prisoners who supported France's government under occupation.

France's mangled politics frequently fuelled violent altercations in the French quarters, and although he and the other followers of Petain formed a small minority, Joliet invariably emerged from the fray having inflicted more injuries than he had received.

Dark haired, with a sallow complexion, he was muscular and heavy, even after more than a year of prison rations. She remembered his proprietorial grip on her wrist at the dance practice in the theatre; remembered the primal urgency she had felt to break that grip.

"This is my proposition," Joliet said now, lowering himself to sprawl against the perimeter fence as she was digging in her allotment. He gazed up at her boldly, "Don't answer me before you have heard me out. I have been thinking that you and I should enter into a mutually beneficial arrangement. You grant me the use of your body and I will offer you not only my own considerable skills in that area, but also my protection from the advances of other men. What do you say, Tomasine?"

She declined, politely. "I will not be engaging in any such activities while I am a prisoner at this castle."

He smiled.

"I anticipated this answer, but you must be realistic. How much longer do you think you can have a choice in the matter – a solitary woman among so many men? I could protect you. I am being practical, of course, but if you want to hear it in romantic terms, I would be your champion. You see, as a French man, while I am most partial to femininity when it is dressed in skirts and fragrant with fine perfume, I can be amenable. And in my dreams, I remember you in that dress, dancing in the auditorium not so long ago."

Tommie continued to turn the soil with the fork.

"If you cast your mind back to that day, Lieutenant Joliet," she said, "you will know that, should it be necessary, I am quite capable of protecting myself."

"Not *should* it be necessary, Tomasina, but *when*, because it will happen, I can assure you. Even your thin-blooded countrymen will sooner or later feel the need, and who will defend you then? That milky pup, Leigh?" he laughed and shook his head, "A very pretty boy, but a boy nonetheless, and not a wise choice of champion, I think. You will need a real man while you are here, and it appears that I am the only one who has been man enough to come to you with such a proposition."

Reaching into his shirt pocket he drew out a pack of cigarettes, took one and offered the pack to Tommie. When she shook her head, he shrugged coarsely and tucked it back into his pocket, retrieving a lighter in the same movement. He lit his cigarette with thick, yellowed fingertips, stashed the lighter and drew deeply on the smoke. Slouching comfortably against the fence, he narrowed his eyes.

"You and I are in an enviable position, Tomasine; we can enjoy the rest of the war here in relative safety and comfort."

Tommie thought of Emil Franz, and Monsieur Arnaud's people, who had risked their lives – most likely lost their lives – in the fight to liberate France. And here was Joliet, planning to enjoy the war in comfort. After a moment she realized he was waiting for a response.

"Oh, I'm sorry, Joliet," she said, "I stopped listening to you after I said no the first time."

His face hardened. "Come now, girl, have you no blood in your veins?"

"Not for that purpose, no."

He threw his head back, laughing harshly.

"Of course, 'no;' you're a dead-fish English girl with no more heat in her than there is in a bucket of water."

The flash of anger that struck Tommie at this crude insult flared brightly. She allowed a flame to kindle and burn cold; a bucket of cold water was exactly what Joliet would get from her.

"French women know how to love," he continued, "the wine of life is in their blood, and even now, with the Germans striding over France, they surrender themselves to life." He paused and sucked on the damp end of the cigarette paper, his eyes unfocused and his fingers curling into claws as they held the stub to his lips. "The Germans are the victors," he said with a shrug, picking a thread of tobacco from his tongue, "the survival of the fittest is the way of all life, and there will be no more French blood spilled."

"Except for the blood of those who fight on for the freedom of their country."

Joliet dismissed this with contempt.

"Rebels and dreamers who are making life difficult for those of us who choose to live in reality," he said flatly. "So, what is your answer, Tomasine?" He looked up at her, squinting into the sun, "What do you say to my proposition?"

"No."

He cursed, pounding his fist into the turned earth. "The forces of life cannot be denied; the dynamic and the passive, those who take what they want and those who yield it to them!"

Tommie drove her gardening fork into the ground, missing his fingers by less than an inch. Snatching his hand away, he scrambled angrily to his feet, and she squared up to face him.

"France did not yield!" she spat. "Petain yielded France, and I saw the shame and humiliation that his betrayal caused. But you should remember, Joliet, that I am British, and I will not yield." It was all she could do to keep from wincing at her own words, but Joliet leaned close to her and she turned her face away from his pungent, tobacco-sour breath.

"Understand this, Tomasine," he said hoarsely, "Yield or don't yield, I myself am one of those who takes."

She stared at him, registering the threat.

"And you think that in this place, surrounded by so many of my countrymen as you put it, you will be permitted to take me by force?"

He smiled.

"Many of these men have not had a woman for several years; when they see me getting what they have missed for so long – when they see the opportunity that lies within their grasp – do you think their own manhoods will not swell with lust? It will be quite a party, Tomasine, and from what I have heard, it is an opportunity that has been sanctioned by Steiger himself."

She couldn't block Blauser's voice from echoing in her mind; *witnessing a woman's domination, her humiliation, excites a man like nothing else can.*

"Think on it some more, cheri," said Joliet softly, "you might find that my proposition for exclusive rights is more to your taste." He strolled off, whistling, and Tommie stood for a while, staring through the fence at the trees beyond.

"Was that Joliet talking to you just now?" Simon had been running laps around the wire, and he flung himself, panting, on the grass nearby. "What did he want?"

"Oh, nothing much," she said lightly, "I don't understand half of what he says."

He nodded absently and propped himself up on his elbow to look at her.

"Can I ask you a bit of an odd question, Tommie? It's just that... well, I wouldn't ask, but it's been bothering me. A lot. And... well, you're a straightforward sort of girl, and I thought you might take it in your stride."

"Of course," she said. She knew that something had been gnawing away at him since Sam's escape, something that was coloured with what seemed like guilt, but she hadn't wanted to pry. She brushed the soil from her hands and sat beside him, "What's on your mind?"

"How long can a woman go without needing to have sex?"

"Ah! Well..."

"I mean, I was wondering about Mary. You see, people say that nice girls don't really like sex. That they do it out of duty. You know... lie back and think of England and so on. But Mary really enjoys it. We both enjoy it... enjoyed it... together. But now I'm not there, will she be able to... to do without it? To stay faithful to me? I suppose that's what I really want to know. I mean, I know you can't possibly tell me for sure, but as a woman you can tell me if it's likely. Can I reasonably expect her to? Perhaps I should just not think about it. What you don't know can't hurt you, and all that. God knows there's nothing I can do about it anyway."

He rambled on, searching for an answer, his blue eyes flinching from painful images until he sank back on the grass with a groan, "Ah, Tommie! I had everything, and now I've got nothing. No purpose, no dignity. I can't fight for my country, and I'm not there to keep my wife satisfied, and while I'm sitting here rotting away, who knows what's happening at home? And Watley keeps talking about how the Americans are there now. I mean, that's like putting a herd of bulls into a dairy farm. And what happens when I get home... *if* I get home? Should I just not ask questions, and accept that things might have happened... that things *will* have happened? Because we all have needs."

He sat up and stared at her, his blue eyes pleading for an answer. And what answer should she give? *Don't be daft, Simon, what woman would be unfaithful to* you*?* That wouldn't do, because, beneath his puppyish naivete, an emotional wisdom was developing in Simon, and patting him on the head with empty reassurances would betray that wisdom. Besides, he had clearly been following this path over and over, like a rat in a maze, for some time now, and he would keep following it unless he had a credible reason not to.

"Well, what about you, Simon?" she said slowly. "A man has needs too."

"Oh!" he said, startled, "I'm alright, thank you, Tommie; I wasn't asking..."

"No! I wasn't offering!" she said quickly, "I just meant that you must be coping with your own needs somehow."

He blinked and pushed his hands into his pockets, his face darkening to a russet blush.

"Well, a woman can do the same thing," she said, reassuringly. "I mean, obviously not the same thing; what I mean is..."

"I know, I've heard about the broom handle," Simon said harshly. "But it's not the same thing as having another person to touch, to hold onto. Can a broom handle be enough, in the long term?"

"A broom handle? Oh, for God's sake, Simon, don't listen to Watley! If you're going to pay any heed to that jackal you might as well strap yourself into a straitjacket right now." Simon's face twisted in confusion and misery, and she sighed.

She had overheard the conversation; 'Letter from wifey?' Watley had said, seeing Simon tucking Mary's latest letter back into its envelope. 'Newly married, aren't you? Tough luck. I've seen it happen before. You've just got them into the swing of things, given them a taste of what's on the menu, so to say... a hint of the possibilities, then, poof, you're gone. How long has it been now, Leigh? Too long, I'd say. What's a girl to do? You'd better hope she's got herself a good broom handle, or it's going to be party time for the postman and the milkman. And now the Americans have turned up...'

She knew that Simon had learned to use his fists to disabuse men of the impression that his pretty-boy looks made him a pushover, and she had seen him in action several times now. Pickman called him Scrappin' Simon. There was a reckless abandonment about him as he threw himself into fights, barely even acknowledging punches that jolted his body in a way that made Tommie fear for his internal organs. This was why she hadn't told him about Joliet's threat.

Watley had been thoroughly disabused on this occasion, and Simon had earned himself two days in solitary confinement, which had only served to isolate him with his fears and Watley's words.

Recognizing the effect of those two days of tortured contemplation in Simon's face now, she took his hands in hers.

"Mary will be able to take care of her own needs," she said gently. "Of course, it's not as satisfying... it's not the same as... I mean, it doesn't make up for... well actually, sometimes it can. I mean, sometimes it can be better than the real thing, because, well... But that's not true of you and Mary, I imagine. Not that I imagine you and Mary... you know..."

Floundering in an eddy of inappropriate currents, she glanced up at his face, but he was still picking his way through her words, and hadn't yet followed her down that particular rabbit hole.

"What I'm trying to say," she said quickly, before he could catch up, "is that the physical need is one issue; the emotional thing is quite separate. It's *your* body she wants, Simon, so she will sort her*self* out rather than find somebody else to do it for her."

She drew a deep breath and took the plunge.

"Look at me, for example; I've got more opportunity here than any woman could want, but it's not right for me, so I ... I don't indulge." The wave of relief that washed over Simon's face told her she had given a good answer. She knew that she had no right, any more than Watley had, to project pictures into Simon's mind, but Watley's poison had to be neutralized, and whatever Mary Leigh was doing in her husband's absence, no good would be served by him fretting about it.

Simon lay back down on the grass, weaving his fingers into a shield in front of his eyes, and Tommie sat quietly beside him. She wanted to conjure up a bubble that would, for this one moment, insulate them from the world, but the sweet scent of new-mown grass was drifting over from the town on a soft breeze, the spring sky was pierced by the bubbling cry of a lark climbing high above the plain, and she knew that there was no such thing as insulation from the world.

"What about you, Tommie?" Simon's voice broke into her reverie. His hands were now cradled behind his head and he was regarding her frankly, "How do you handle it?"

"Oh! Well..." She blushed hotly.

"What? Why are you blushing? Oh! No! That's not what I meant!" Now he was blushing too, but he battled his way out of it. "I didn't mean the broom handle thing, I meant the emotional bit... you know; romance. Like you said, you're living in close quarters with hundreds of men..."

"Which is very far from being romantic, believe me!"

"Point taken. But aren't you ever tempted? By any of them? Am I being too personal?"

She laughed, rocking backwards and forwards on her crossed legs. "Too personal? I think the ship has sailed on that, Simon. We're venturing into girl-talk now. God, I've missed that since Sam left!"

"You talked to Allenby like this?"

"You really wouldn't want to know the sort of things we talked about."

"Does that mean I can ask you about stuff like this?"

"Yes. There will be limits though!"

"Alright, then; so how do you deal with the temptation? How do you stop yourself from being attracted?"

She considered for a moment. "I don't look."

"That's it?" he echoed, incredulously, "You don't look?"

"Yup. I don't look," she said with a shrug. "I switched myself off the day they put me in this castle. As far as I'm concerned, every man here is transparent; a disembodied voice. I don't see them. It has to be that way. I can't afford to be attracted any more than I can afford to attract. Think about it. It would be a disaster."

He looked at her dubiously.

"Well, yes, I get that. But in practice, that's not how it works, is it? I don't think an attraction is something you can just block."

"Of course it is. It's a state of mind. I've been doing it for years, because..." she hesitated. Because why? Why *was* there no spark-plug charge? Was her connection to the battery of life broken? "...because the war was coming, and that was more important," she finished weakly.

He shook his head, frowning.

"No, I don't believe that. I don't believe you can be immune to attraction. It's like that song Sam used to sing; 'Comes love, nothing can be done.'"

Sam. Her heart contracted.

"Well, it's worked for me so far, but if you're right I could be in trouble."

They sat in silence for a moment, then she smiled, "I'm glad we met before I got here, otherwise I wouldn't be able to see you either. As it stands, I can look at you as much as I like. I can use you for companionship and the occasional hug, and the rest..." she flashed him a grin, "I can sort out for myself."

When the prisoners were marshalled onto the road for the walk back to the castle, Tommie took with her the first swede of the season, along with a few runners of pennyroyal that had reached into the exercise yard from the ditch outside the perimeter fence. *Pennyroyal for menstrual cramps, bronchitis and asthma.* How did she know that? It must have filtered into her consciousness during her midwifery training. There had been a few of those – fragments of old remedies using the common names of medicinal plants... names that had been used to persecute the witches; 'eye of newt and toe of frog, wool of bat and tongue of dog.'

She was examining the swede with satisfaction when a pair of hands reached out and tried to pull it from her grasp. She pulled back and clutched it to her chest. The guard reached out again and she shielded it, speaking in reasonable tones, hoping to coax him into good will. Instead, he grabbed at the swede, prying her fingers from around it, but as each finger was pried free, she clamped it back again.

The other prisoners, always ready for a session of guard-baiting, began taunting the man and egging Tommie on. She didn't want to be responsible for that, but she knew that if she let the swede out of her hands, she would never see it again. The guard's face turned an angry red, and he got rough, grabbing at the vegetable with one hand and shoving at Tommie's shoulder with the other.

The uprising was escalating, and the column of prisoners was spreading into an amorphous rabble on the road.

"Was ist hier los?"

The new voice, crisp and authoritative, brought the confusion to an abrupt end. Brandt was sitting astride a motor bike on the road behind them, having been forced to a halt by the milling prisoners. Nobody had heard the bike's approach over the noise, and she knew that, to everyone's mild embarrassment, the whole scene resembled nothing more than a playground ruckus interrupted by a teacher. She was mortified to have been the instigator, but the guard, anticipating an advocate in Brandt, launched into a tirade from which Tommie recognized a word she knew.

"Contraband?" she said through grated teeth. "It's a swede! *Mein* schwede!" She turned to Brandt, "It's just a swede, but it's my swede. I grew it, and he has no reason to confiscate it!"

Now we're like children, bickering in front of a parent, she thought, annoyed. Brandt was watching her, his expression neutral.

"If Sergeant Walthausen seems puzzled, fraulein, perhaps it is because you have claimed ownership of a Swedish national," he said, "The word you are looking for is steckrubengemuse."

She felt herself blush, but the injustice still rankled. "Thank you," she said coolly, and turned back to the sergeant. "*Mein* steckrubengemuse."

"Where did you grow it?" Brandt asked calmly, dismounting and pulling the bike onto its stand. The guard broke in with a string of agitated accusations: this prisoner had requisitioned a piece of Reich land inside the exercise compound, where she had proceeded to grow all manner of plants... He finished his story and stood, stiff with righteous indignation.

The prisoners were quiet now, some of them covertly admiring the bike, others, including Simon, taking advantage of the delay to study the exterior of the castle and its grounds.

Spotting this, and ordering the guards to cover the party for any breakouts, Brandt turned to Tommie.

"Sergeant Walthausen makes the point that everything going into the castle grounds must be inspected, and he feels that a vegetable should not be considered above suspicion, so perhaps, fraulein, you would be so good as to submit your swede for inspection, and if it proves innocent, I see no reason why you should not be allowed to take it with you." Piqued by the faint mockery of his tone, Tommie scowled. He held his hands out for the swede, she surrendered it, and he passed it to the guard.

The wind drew strands of hair across her forehead, and she lifted her hand to brush them away, catching a faint scent of pennyroyal from the stems she held. Brandt noticed them, and gazed over her shoulder towards the compound.

"You have an allotment in the exercise yard? What do you grow there?"

"Swedes, cabbages, carrots, onions, leeks and some herbs; this is pennyroyal."

"Pennyroyal?" He narrowed his eyes as though the mention of the herb had triggered a memory. "Is that for eating?"

"No, for medicinal purposes; for menstr... for the men. For bronchitis, asthma, and pain relief."

"I see. And does Doctor Henning know that you are using these preparations?"

"Yes, he does," she said, with defiance sharpening her voice. He nodded, then lifted his head and breathed in.

"Woodbine," he said, surprising her with his use of the traditional English name for honeysuckle, "I have never noticed that scent on this road before. Do you have that growing in your allotment too?"

"Yes," she said shortly. It was a wild form of woodbine, and its sweet, heavy scent had the power to sustain a withered soul. Risking punishment, she had reached through the fence, pulled up some rooted sections, and transplanted them into her plot, training them along the wires.

"And what do you use woodbine for?"

"For keeping the soul alive." She had not meant to be so direct. There was a pause.

"Of course."

They turned as the sergeant approached. His expression

was spiteful as he held his hands out, proffering a small pile of roughly-hewn chunks of swede.

From the corner of her eye Tommie saw an unexpected flash of annoyance pass over Brandt's face, and he glanced at her, clearly anticipating another outburst. For a moment nobody spoke, then she took the remains of the swede and thanked the guard sweetly.

"Thank you, Sergeant Walthausen, chopping swedes makes my wrists ache terribly. Next time perhaps you would be good enough to peel it first."

Brandt stared fixedly at the decimated vegetable.

"Ist die steckrubengemuse sicher, Feldwebel Walthausen?" he said.

"Ja, Herr Major, es ist sicher."

"So, it seems that the swede is truly innocent, fraulein," he said. "You may take it into the castle. Now, gentlemen, please stand aside so I can pass."

As the officers shuffled over, Simon rejoined her and frowned.

"What happened to your turnip?"

"It's not a turnip," she said. "It's a swede. A steckrubengemuse."

19
A stone angel

"F14s! Yee ha! Give 'em hell, Yanks!" Jim Palmer's unfailing enthusiasm for all things military rang out above the drone of the aircraft that were marching heavily across the patch of sky above the courtyard. It was mid-afternoon, and the men were queuing patiently in the far corner, where letters from home were being distributed. The sight of the ominous silhouettes passing overhead was familiar now, and Tommie barely glanced up from where she sat, cross legged against the seam, but the all-encompassing vibration of the bombers – winged bringers of retribution – resonated strangely with her reading. She was lost in Metamorphoses, wandering in a garish world where the Furies, goddesses of vengeance, punished the crimes of mankind. She heard Bainbridge's voice as he passed by, talking to Joshua Jones, and she called out to him.

"Doug, what – or where – is Tartarus?"

Bainbridge paused.

"Tartarus is where the vilest, most unimaginable monsters are incarcerated by the gods and subdued by Tisiphone, the chief of the Furies, to be released and deployed when required. Keep reading," he added, moving on, "you'll get the gist."

Sure enough, on the page in front of her, Tisiphone was

walking, preparing to deliver retribution.

Tisiphone seized a torch steeped in blood, put on a robe all red with dripping gore, and wound a snake around her waist, and started from her home; and with her as she went were Grief, Dread, Terror, and Madness too with frantic face.

The world was white when Tommie sat up. Nothing was there, just white air, a cotton-wool silence, and herself.

Am I dead? *Why* am I dead? What happened? Hearing her own thoughts, loud in the muffled silence, she felt a flash of fear, half-expecting to look up and see Tisiphone walking, but the lurid colours of Ovid's imaginings were notably absent from her surroundings. Everything was white here.

So, a different afterlife then. Something a little less exotic. Heaven, perhaps? If it's white, it must be heaven. Then the white air seized and squeezed the tiny, fragile air sacs of her lungs, and she doubled up in a violent fit of coughing that engorged her face, leaving the skin stretched tight and pulsing.

When the hacking and retching had ceased, and her eyes felt like they were going to explode, she sat up and stared at the backs of her hands, at the swollen grey worms of her veins. Not dead. Not heaven.

Disinclined to move, she sat and watched dust settle on her eyelashes. As long as she didn't breathe too deeply, it was peaceful. More dust settled, and a white shape began to materialize out of the whiteness some distance away from her, its slumped outline distinguishing it from the geometric, blocky landscape that lay between them.

Curiosity compelled her to investigate, and the world crunched beneath her knees, scraping at her palms as she crawled over fractured stones through a gap in the ruins of a wall that loomed ghostly around her.

The shape that had called to her was a white figure, draped in white. An angel. Her thoughts performed a switchback, so, this *is* heaven. And another switchback, *not* heaven, because it was a fallen angel – a stone angel – toppled from its pedestal and lying crumpled awkwardly on the ground. At this point, a full-colour memory intruded on the whiteness, and she stepped into it.

As a young girl in boarding school, newly fourteen years old, and granted lunchtime liberty privileges, she had taken a path into town that led, by virtue of a kissing-gate, through a churchyard. There, on a low pedestal in the preternaturally dark shadow of an ancient yew, had stood a stone angel. With wings lifting gracefully and arms reaching out, frozen in infinite compassion, he grieved over the afflictions of humanity.

Long moments of her liberty had been spent in that quiet graveyard, gazing up at the angel, drinking in the pure stillness of the stone face, and she had come to understand that, by their nature, all angels must be lonely; watching over their human charges but forbidden to touch. Forbidden to comfort. Then, one clear morning in April, with the scent of lilac in the air and the pulse of spring swelling in the earth, she had left the path, stepped into the shadow of the yew, climbed onto the pedestal, stretched up on tiptoe, and kissed the stone lips. The lips, naturally, had been cold and unresponsive, and she had sunk back down on her heels with her romantic little heart chastened; angels were not to be kissed.

That full-colour world receded, and Tommie's thought-processes, veiled and fuddled again by whiteness and dust, perceived something not quite right about this angel in front of her; fallen stone angels shatter or break – they don't crumple. And there was something familiar about the angel. A name appeared before her, pinned to the white air like a note on a bulletin board.

Major Brandt.

Another full-colour slice of memory returned, and in it she remembered Major Brandt – remembered that he had been shining, or glowing, or gleaming or... or something. She had not been able to pin the phenomenon down at the time, but now she understood; Major Brandt is actually an angel. A real one, not a stone one. That must be why he had given her coffee and cakes. She swallowed, tasting the coffee and the cakes through the grit and the dust.

Sitting back on her heels, she gazed at the angel, but something was making her uneasy now; the still, calm face was peaceful. Too peaceful. And the white was all wrong too. Major Brandt shines, and yet here was Major Brandt, lying crumpled in front of her, white but not shining. White like a plaster angel, lacking even the subtle life of stone. There was some urgency here, but she was hard pressed to think what it might be.

Another note appeared on the bulletin board; *Perhaps fallen angels need to breathe just like the rest of us*.

A sense of satisfaction animated her aimlessness; she could help him do that. She had learned how. Leaning forward she cautiously opened the angel's mouth – shockingly red in the midst of all the white – check for obstructions to the airway; none. Tilt the head back to open the airway; done.

She took a deep breath and pressed her mouth against the mouth. Warm. She breathed into the angel with all her strength, compelling it to accept her breath. The white chest rose and fell. That was good. Three more breaths, then she took her hands and crossed them on the critical part of the angel's ribcage, locking her elbows and throwing all her weight onto them. One, two, three, four... she lifted her hands, leaning down again towards the mouth, and froze, staring at her handprints in the white dust. Field grey handprints.

Enemy.

The deaf silence in her ears thinned out, giving way to a uniform whistling. The man, no longer an angel, lay there, as still as before, but her grey handprints on his chest shrieked and gibbered at her, hurling shards of context in her face. This is the enemy. These are the boots that mustn't reach your hearth. She turned and crawled away, but something was dragging at her heels. What good reason did she have for leaving this man to die when she could breathe life back into him?

Enemy.

The word flung itself at her again, propelling her farther

away from him; its truth was right there in the field grey patch over his heart. But who gets to define the enemy? Her teeth crunched on the grit from his mouth, and she paused, searching the flapping shreds of her memory for the wrongs committed by this enemy – wrongs that would warrant a death sentence – and found none. Instead, she found cakes and coffee and a blessed salvation from Steiger's sinister presence. Steiger! Now there was a man she could leave to die, but this man?

She turned back. Brandt lay as still as before, his angel's disguise penetrated now by her grey handprints on his chest. Sam's chocolate voice came to her. 'He was very polite, even quite kind. Made me feel like a lady.' Brandt had made Sam feel like a lady.

Tommie turned around, crawled back, knelt down again and drew a deep breath, fighting the snagging of her lungs. Breathe. Push, push, push. Breathe. Push, push, push. She was getting dizzy, but there was still no sign of life in the man. Weakness perched like a vulture on her shoulders, and she shook herself to dislodge it. She started again. Breathe. Push, push, push.

The man coughed suddenly, just once, then sucked a shrieking breath into his lungs and convulsed in a fit of coughing. Tommie sat back, light-headed, then reached over his juddering body, and pulled him onto his side. She took off her cardigan, turned it inside out to enclose the grit that clung to it, and tucked it under his head, pillowing his face from the sharp rubble.

The cotton-wool silence inside her head was thinning fast now, and sounds were crashing in on her from every direction, an aural jigsaw puzzle with most pieces missing. There was a garbled shouting. It was harsh and loud, and, pressing her palms over her ears, she glanced up.

A face came at her, red and angry, its mouth screaming words she couldn't understand, and beneath the face she saw a rifle, all grey gunmetal and tenderly polished woodgrain. 'Mauser Karabiner 98K,' Jim Palmer had said just last week, his voice loaded with grudging admiration as he had eyed a sentry's weapon. 'One of the best military rifles ever made. Nine pounds of metal and wood.' Watching absently as the nine pounds of metal and wood swung at her, she registered the impact in the centre of her forehead and felt herself launched backwards, her arms and legs, rubber-like, following behind. When she hit the ground, she sat up reflexively as diamonds, cold and sharp, wedged themselves under her eyelids and sparkled excruciatingly.

Now a new voice was shouting angry words, but this second voice brought with it gentle hands that swept away the warm blood that was seeping into her eyes and congealing around the diamonds with a deeply unpleasant sensation.

"Fraulein, I have to attend to Major Brandt." She recognized the quaintly formal English of the prison doctor. "His condition is more urgent than yours at this moment, but I promise I will be with you as soon as possible. When you get to your room, please lie down quietly and have them put cold compresses over your eyes until I come."

A guard was summoned to help her, and, grateful for some instructions to follow, she set about obeying them, but now she had to try to stand and, even less likely, walk. Another guard appeared, and she was half-carried over the rubble. At one point in this undignified process, she saw something familiar, and dug her heels in, pulling the guards to a halt; Metamorphoses was lying in a small crater in the rubble. One of the guards bent down, picked up the book and pushed it into her hand, and then, somehow, she found herself at the bottom of the steps leading up to the British quarters. Orders were shouted up the stairwell, and suddenly Simon was beside her, cursing.

"Bloody, bloody, *bloody* hell! They ought to shoot that animal, Kessler. Christ, Tommie, I thought you were dead. You must have been within yards of where that sodding bomb fell. The seam must have shielded you. Oh, for God's sake, why did you have to go and help Brandt? I swear, Eccles was trying to get out there and kill you. Ah, Jesus, Tommie, I thought..." His voice broke, and the flow of words stopped as, with the assistance of a stony-faced Bainbridge, he carried her up the stairwell, into her room, and laid her on her bed.

Immensely relieved to be there, because she had doubted that her head would fit through the doorway, she handed the book to Bainbridge, who took it, flashed her an unreadable glance, and walked out without a word. She watched Simon's face as he fussed around her, clumsily dabbing at her forehead and building a pile of blood-soaked rags on the floor. She could hear his voice, but she was finding it difficult to make sense of his words, so she smiled at him while her eyes, two throbbing, lacerated hard-boiled eggs, gradually closed up.

As the world disappeared into darkness, she clutched the mattress, fighting the onset of panic. At some point, the doctor came and spoke to her. He had brought crushed ice, wrapped in a towel, which he laid gently on her forehead, and then he lifted her gritty eyelids to shine his torch into her eyes, an experience that was many times more painful than the Mauser Karabiner 98K, and for which he apologized sincerely.

Somewhere far behind him, voices were raised in anger. She could hear Simon in the centre of the uproar, and wondered if he was still holding Eccles back from trying to kill her. The doctor's voice was closer, soothing and reassuring, so she focused on that.

"Good. No damage done there."

"No damage you say, doctor? When I regain my eyesight, would you kindly allow me to check your credentials?"

The doctor chuckled.

"There is no damage to the functioning of your eyes. I will put a dressing over them to help protect them until the swelling goes down. Leave the dressing in place at all times, and I will return tomorrow to check your progress."

"Doctor Henning?"

"Yes?"

"*Will* I regain my eyesight? Right now, all I can see are

diamonds."

The doctor patted her hand.

"Enjoy the diamonds, fraulein," he said gravely, "within a day or two you will be seeing grey stone walls again."

With a growing awareness of the ripe bag of shit that was hitting the fan in the background, Tommie hesitated before speaking further, but what had been done was done, and wouldn't be undone by pretending she hadn't done it.

"How is Major Brandt, Doctor Henning?" she said, "I didn't get to tell you, but he had stopped breathing and there was no pulse. I had to resuscitate him."

"Major Brandt is still unconscious, but out of danger, I think. He has been taken to a hospital in Berlin for observation, and I am going to visit him now. Oh, and I am returning your... your *this*." His English failed and he put the cardigan into her hands. There was a pause before he added, soberly, "Fraulein West, I want to thank you for what you did out there, it was very courageous of you. Major Brandt is a friend of mine, and without your intervention he would have died today."

***

Peter caught sight of Henning approaching across the clinical expanse of the ward. With a surge of relief, he sat up and threw back the bedcovers, swinging his legs over the edge of the bed. "Thank God you're here, Karl, would you please tell these doctors I'm fit to be discharged?"

"Absolutely not, my friend. You need to be here."

"Damn! Karl..."

"You were dead for a moment, Peter," Henning said sharply. "Thankfully you seem to have suffered nothing more than a severe concussion from the blast, but that alone is sufficient to keep you on bedrest for a day or two. You weren't even conscious yesterday afternoon when I came to see you. Anyway," he continued more lightly, "You should consider yourself lucky to be here. The bomb that put you in here also put an end to the boiler that serves the commandantur. We are without hot water, and will be, they estimate, until at least next week."

Peter drew his legs back onto the bed, unwilling to acknowledge that, in sitting up, he had almost swung, with the impetus of a gyroscope, to sprawl helplessly, top to tail in the bed.

"I'm sorry, Karl," he said, "I haven't even thanked you. You saved my life."

"Not I, my friend, not I. It was the kleine fraulein who saved your life."

"The kleine fraulein? What the devil is that supposed to mean?" Peter's lungs, throat, mouth and nose seemed to be lined with sandpaper – rough side inwards – and every breath he took rasped on his nerves. "For God's sake, do I look like a man who wants to be solving riddles right now?"

Henning grinned. "No riddle, Peter. The concussion must have scrambled your brains as well as your temper. As it happens, I was in my office when the bomb hit. By the time I reached the courtyard – and by the time the guards stopped taking aim at anything that moved – you had already been resuscitated. It was the kleine fraulein, Fraulein West, who gave you what the English so sweetly call the kiss of life."

Peter stared at the doctor in silence. He felt certain that, at some point in the events leading up to his presence in this hospital, an elephant had trodden on his head, but for some reason, nobody wanted to mention this. Moreover, he suspected that things were being explained to him several times before he was able to understand them.

"Fraulein West?" he said cautiously, any dependable sense of reality evading his grasp, "What was she doing in the commandantur?"

"She wasn't in the commandantur. Neither were you. According to the sentries, you had just returned from Zossen and you were in the outer courtyard when the bomb hit."

"Then why was she in the outer courtyard?"

"There was a bomb, Peter," the doctor said patiently, "a

bomb fell on the castle, demolishing the seam. For a while there was no such thing as an inner and outer courtyard. They are building the wall up again, of course, and quickly, but immediately after the explosion the two courtyards were as one under a field of rubble, and Fraulein West crawled over the rubble to get to you."

Peter shook his head and wished he hadn't.

"Why the devil would she do something like that?"

"She's a nurse. She couldn't do otherwise, but I believe that she has been given plenty of reason to regret it." Peter relinquished the fight for clarity, and allowed himself to sink back into the pillows while Henning continued. "As you can imagine, the British officers took great exception to her actions. When I went to see her yesterday, they were being quite cruel about the whole incident, saying that I should take her away with me; that she'd be more useful in the commandantur and so on."

Peter gingerly touched his fingertips to his burning eye sockets. "Then I must remind them who their real enemy is. How long will I have to stay here Karl?"

***

After three days of disgrace over the resuscitation of Brandt, Tommie's presence was being thinly tolerated, and she was sitting on her blanket on the floor, leaning up against Simon's bunk, when Eccles, who was doing watch duty at the window, called a warning. Scrambling to squirrel away their illicit projects, the officers glared at Tommie, who obediently lowered her eyes.

The room settled into a suspiciously innocent calm as she heard the door open, but then an odd, surly quality in the silence caused her to look up again. Like a field full of cows, the officers were staring at the doorway, where Brandt stood, scanning the room. Smiling broadly, he addressed the room in jovial tones.

"Good afternoon, gentlemen. Dreadful weather, is it

not?"

The men turned to scowl at Tommie, all their hostility resurrected, and with a mulish defiance, she responded, matching the man's jaunty manner.

"Good afternoon, Major Brandt, I am glad to see you have made a rapid recovery."

Behind her, she heard Simon's hiss of exasperation as Brandt inclined his head towards her in acknowledgement.

"Thank you, fraulein. As it happens, that is the reason for my visit; I am given to understand that I owe my recovery to you. That, in fact, I owe my life to you."

The silence in the room was deafening, and Tommie hesitated, wrong-footed.

"It was my professional duty as a nurse," she said awkwardly, "Anyone with the same training would have done the same."

"Oh, I think not," Brandt insisted, stepping into the room. "I can't imagine that anyone else here would have extended the hand of solidarity towards the enemy."

"Solidarity?" she said.

"No, Major Brandt, *not* solidarity," said Bainbridge loudly, swinging himself off his bunk, landing weightily, and planting himself squarely in front of the German. "Tommie's not an enemy sympathiser, she's a soft touch, that's all." The two men were matched for height, but Bainbridge was built like a brick outhouse, and Brandt wasn't. "She has the instincts of a nurse," Bainbridge continued, sweeping a cold stare around the room, "that's the only reason why she did what she did."

Brandt stepped casually around him and approached Tommie with an attitude of insolent familiarity. Behind her, on his bunk, Simon sat up, bristling. Brandt ignored him.

"Is this true, fraulein?" he said, with an affected, plaintive tone in his voice. "Is it true that there is no more significance to your actions than that you are a... a soft touch?" He was standing over her now, too close, and Simon rose to his feet, radiating menace. He was neither as tall as Brandt, nor as heavily-built as Bainbridge, but

Tommie knew how explosive his temper could be. Still sitting cross-legged on the floor, she wrapped a hand around his ankle, and answered carefully. "I acted out of duty and humanity, Major Brandt. Some would say misplaced humanity."

"She's not a sympathiser," repeated Bainbridge, who had quietly brought himself to stand at the German officer's left shoulder. Not liking being towered over like this, Tommie stood up. She was still towered over, but not by so much. Brandt glanced over his shoulder, acknowledging Bainbridge's proximity.

"My mistake," he answered coolly. He turned to address Tommie again, and she saw his expression change as he caught sight of the livid scar and the purpling across her forehead. The artificial affability evaporated, and his grey eyes hardened to slate. "Was this retribution?" he said, speaking so softly that she barely heard him, and remained silent. He spun around and yelled into the room, his voice rasping. "Was this retribution?!"

"You should ask sergeant Kessler to answer that question, Major Brandt," answered a quiet voice. Colonel Gregory was standing in the doorway of his room. Brandt turned towards him, swaying slightly on his feet.

"Sergeant Kessler did this?"

"Yes, he did," piped up Eric, smugly, "Tommie saved your life, and Kessler brained her for it. Saved us the effort."

Brandt stood in silence for a moment, then he looked down at her again and reverted to his usual, neutral tones.

"I thank you for the humanity you showed me, Fraulein West, and I bitterly regret that you were mistreated for that humanity." He left without another word.

20
An Englishman and his spitfire

Conrad's voice over the telephone was unexpected in the middle of the day, and Peter stiffened, anticipating the news that the coup had been launched, but it was only an invitation to join a gathering at the nearby estate of a family friend. He would have liked the excuse to ride the Pioneer there, but Conrad, who had taken to taunting him mercilessly about what he called his country seat, insisted on picking him up in his staff car, and seeing the castle for himself.

Arriving early, he was escorted to Peter's office, finding on the way a wealth of material with which to torment him. Giving up on work, Peter tidied his desk and led his friend back through the corridors.

"How can you tell me that you have nothing to offer a bride?" Conrad exclaimed, sweeping his arms up in a grand gesture as they skirted the cordoned-off main staircase where workmen were still clearing the rubble left by the bomb. Peter smiled sourly. The structural damage to the west wing meant that he was obliged to lead his friend through the pass door that opened into the prisoners' courtyard, and he braced himself for the commentary on that. "What woman wouldn't jump at the chance of being the lady of this manor!" continued Conrad, ostentatiously brushing dust off his suit. He had taken great exception to Peter's break-up with Astrid.

The sentry at the bottom of the stairs opened the pass door for them, and Peter stepped out, colliding clumsily with Tomasin West who was walking by. She yelped as he stepped on her foot, although it must have been from surprise rather than pain, considering the sturdiness of the flying boots that had replaced those flapping shoes.

"Forgive me, fraulein," he said, taking her arm to steady her. From behind his shoulder, he heard Conrad's voice, still mocking.

"Fraulein? Peter, I thought I heard you say 'fraulein,' can it be that you *have* found a chatelaine for your castle? Ah!" Conrad saw the girl and lapsed into silence as his eyes took in the shapeless figure in the roll-neck sweater and army battle-dress trousers, not quite obscured beneath an RAF greatcoat. The weather had turned bitterly cold again, and she wore a woollen balaclava pulled over her head, leaving only her face exposed.

Finding his voice again, Conrad grinned and switched effortlessly into English.

"So, Peter, this must be your guardian angel. Please, introduce us properly. No, I insist," he added as Peter demurred. Peter sighed. His friend's visit to the castle was turning out to be more aggravating than he had anticipated.

"Fraulein West, this is a friend of mine, Count Conrad von Heiden. Conrad, this is Miss Tomasin West." The incongruity of the introduction made his still-bruised brain wince.

"It is a great pleasure to meet you, Fraulein West," Conrad said, "For now I can thank you for saving my good friend's life." He smiled, twinkling his eyes in a way that Peter had seen him do a thousand times. "My compliments, my dear, your camouflage is outstanding. From a distance one would easily mistake you for a small, scruffy British officer, but moving closer, one understands that to stand at any distance from you is to be grievously cheated."

Peter watched the interaction uneasily. So far Tomasin

West had managed to disguise herself amongst the prisoners, like a stage prop painted to blend into the backdrop. Her potentially volatile presence at the castle had, thankfully, gone without incident, and now his friend's flirtation was jarring.

Studying the girl more closely, Conrad paused, his eyes narrowed, and he shot Peter an odd, interrogative glance that promised a shedload of taunting to come.

"How strange, Peter, that you should have neglected to mention that your guardian angel is quite so beguiling," he said.

"Conrad!" Peter said, warningly.

"Quite enchanting," Conrad continued. "Yes, indeed, fraulein, on closer inspection you are undoubtedly... a woman."

A faint blush coloured what could be seen of the girl's face. Conrad smiled, and Peter, who had witnessed too many of his friend's effortless conquests, turned away, irritated. After all the training she must have received from Hendry's people, to fall so easily for this patent charm offensive... when she responded, though, her voice was snake-soft, and modulated to an ominous pitch and he turned back, listening with interest.

"Why, how kind of you to say so, Your Excellency," she said, "But let me assure you that the circumstances don't exist under which I would permit your closer inspection. Good afternoon, gentlemen." She turned and walked away.

Conrad stared after her, aggrieved.

"I used to be irresistible," he said, "Where did it go?"

Peter laughed.

"It hasn't gone, Conrad," he said, "any woman with half a brain would have been weak at the knees. Perhaps it was the astonishingly inappropriate circumstances..."

Conrad's face cleared and he jabbed a finger into Peter's chest.

"Ha! That's it! Now I understand why you are so aloof with the ladies. Or should I say... with *other* ladies." He mimicked Peter in a seductive baritone, "'Forgive me,

Fraulein.'"

Peter led him through the gatehouse into the outer courtyard, and the heavy door swung shut behind them. "What are you talking about?"

"The fraulein."

"What about the fraulein?"

"That small English miss. She has captured your heart!"

Peter stopped short.

"Conrad! You're talking about a prisoner!"

"So what? So what?" Conrad waved him into the waiting staff car. "Yes, of course, that is it. My God, you Englishmen; you render your lives so chilly. In the brooding, nineteenth-century gothic novel of your mind, you want that girl. Desire? No. Desire is too passionate a term for a nondescript little creature like that, but you most definitely want her. You are Mr. Rochester to her Jane Eyre! Rather than embrace a warm, red-blooded, charming woman like Astrid, you have burned that bridge in favour of a fierce little shrew! No, Peter, I will say it; when we go out on the town you are reticent with women. Distracted. I had wondered if, perhaps, you were inclined another way, but no, I don't think that's it."

He hesitated, then fixed Peter with a direct look.

"You do know, don't you, that it would be alright with me if you were... you know... otherwise inclined."

Feigning incomprehension, Peter offered him a puzzled frown – there were subtler ways of winding up a friend than those Conrad employed.

"Not with *me*," Conrad continued hurriedly, "I didn't mean it would be alright with *me*. But as your friend... if you were... well, you know... that way, it would be alright with me, if you see what I mean."

"Thank you, Conrad," Peter said dryly, "Astonishingly, I do see what you mean." He mirrored Conrad's earnest expression back at him. "And it would be alright with me if you were... well, you know."

"Quite!" said Conrad robustly, "I'm glad we got that cleared up. Now, let's get back to the subject; you and your castle and your formidable little fraulein. Peter, you are such a romantic!"

"*I'm* a romantic?! And *my* mind is a gothic novel? you should be *writing* gothic novels! No, my friend, no," Peter laughed, "don't fool yourself; this is not about me, this is about you! This is about you trying to deflect attention from the fact that, despite having deployed all your notorious charms, you have just, as the Americans would put it, struck out."

But Conrad was not to be diverted from his course; he had discovered a fresh and intriguing source of material with which to bait Peter, and he was keen to explore it.

"So, is she your type? That little spitfire back there? How appropriate; an Englishman and his spitfire. She couldn't be more different from Astrid, but I saw past the disguise to the woman underneath. Is this someone whom you would take dancing, or sit with in a coffee shop, or invite to a picnic in the Tiergarten?"

"She's a prisoner, Conrad."

"That's not what I asked, Peter, I asked is she your type?"

"She's a prisoner."

Conrad shook his head, waving a finger in denial.

"Ah, but she is not *your* prisoner, Peter. True, she is a prisoner in that castle, but you are not a prison officer. You are not *her* prison officer. She is not your charge."

"Still, ethically –"

"Even ethically, even given your excruciatingly rigid ethics, these… interesting circumstances may be a barrier to action, but they are not a barrier to love. In fact, to someone of your cool and contrary nature, they might even be a heady aphrodisiac. You mustn't act, so instead you sit here and you brood and you pine for that diminutive, cross-dressing doll. And that's no hardship for you; it suits your personality! But let's put that issue to one side. I simply want to know if this particular girl is your type. Alright, alright," he flapped his hands at Peter, "don't say it again – I know; she is a prisoner. I dispute it, but I acknowledge your point. But let's say she wasn't a prisoner? Imagine for a moment that little Fraulein... what is her name again?"

"Fraulein West."

"So, imagine for a moment that Fraulein West is the daughter of a good German family – God forbid that Germany should ever produce such a graceless shrew – and actually wears women's clothes. You meet at a glorious ball at her parents' mansion; there are chandeliers, rousing waltzes, a moonlit stroll in the fragrant rose garden. She has her sights trained on you – has, in fact, been angling for you, trying to land you for long months now. Her parents approve, and there is no moral or ethical obstacle whatsoever to your romance. Now, tell me... what do you think of her?"

Peter made his friend wait for an answer while he appeared to consider, and at length allowed a vague ambivalence to drift across his face.

"She seems like a nice girl."

Conrad threw himself back in the seat with a groan.

"Ah! God! We're fire and ice, you and I, Peter. Fire and ice. How am I supposed to tolerate your phlegmatic English behaviour? I see now what I must do for you, my friend. I hereby make it my mission to teach you how to throw caution to the wind and take life by the horns!"

***

The meeting was a gathering of hotheads, this much was clear to Peter from the moment he walked into the hall.

The progress of the coup was plagued by loose ends that writhed like the snakes on the head of the Medusa as she turned to face them. Most troubling of those loose ends was General Friedrich Fromm, who had committed himself to the resistance only as far as agreeing to support whichever side emerged from the fray still standing.

Surprised to note the presence of several of his colleagues from FHO in the room, Peter watched and listened. The earth was quaking and shifting beneath their feet, and

Fromm's non-committal commitment opened wide the fissure that they straddled. Erich Lohse, one of Gehlen's officers, was at the end of his tether.

"We need Fromm's involvement! He is chief of armaments, and commands the reserve army."

"Our need does not dictate his actions," pointed out Braun, another of Gehlen's officers, but a more cautious man. "We cannot trust Fromm."

With that issue unresolved, they turned to the next item on the agenda; Hitler was to be visiting the eastern front the following week, and the possibility of planting a bomb on his plane was discussed.

"But nobody can get a bomb near him," said Conrad wearily. "Because a hissing fuse cannot be silenced."

"There is an explosive that uses a silent detonator." All faces turned to Peter as he spoke. "The British have been manufacturing a plastic explosive for several years," he said into the hush, "The firing pin and the detonator use a corrosive chemical, not a fuse."

"Oh, excellent!" sneered Lohse, "All we have to do is to cable Mr. Churchill to send us a bomb."

"You may do so if you wish, Lohse," replied Peter coldly, "or you can keep your mouth shut long enough to learn something. Britain supplies the explosives to the Russian commando units, and when the commando units fall into our hands at FHO, so do the explosives. I can have some for you by the end of the week." The silence in the room deepened.

"How are you going to do that?" asked Lohse curiously, "access to that area is restricted." Peter sat back deliberately in his chair.

"I will get access." From his desk in the corner, Braun spoke, shaking his head reluctantly.

"Then you will be involved, Peter – officially, I mean; on paper – and Gehlen doesn't want his officers implicated in this."

"And yet here I am, and here you are, and Lohse too."

Hidden tactfully behind Braun's words was the

reluctance of senior members of the resistance to allow Peter a significant role, for fear that, if everything failed, his British background would be used to brand them as puppets of the enemy. The men here this evening, though, were the revolutionaries of the movement, and their world was disintegrating, so Braun agreed to put the plan forward, and by Thursday of that week Peter called in at the man's office and placed a brown paper package in his hands.

***

The acknowledgment of failure came indirectly, impotently, with the absence of news. Eventually, on the Friday, he learned what had happened; the explosives had been stowed in the cargo area of the aircraft, and the chemical fuse had frozen during the flight, rendering the device useless.

21
Frau Heller

A full-contact, all-contingents football game was in progress, and the guards were looking on with a rapt hunger, like spectators at a bare-knuckle boxing match. The seam had been requisitioned for one sideline, and a wall of onlookers formed the opposite sideline, encapsulating the attention, if not the noise.

A belligerent wind snatched at Tommie's greatcoat as she cast around for somewhere to sit. There was a secluded corner behind the coal house, but as she ducked into its shelter, an unpleasant snaking sensation slithered over her shoulders. She shrugged her arms out reflexively, but the noose of braided sheet fabric tightened, trapping her elbows against her sides. A hand clamped itself over her mouth, and her head was gripped, vice-like, by someone behind her. Twisting inside the balaclava, she tried to bite the hand, but her mouth was crushed closed. Someone came into view. Joliet. His face was set, and he muttered under his breath as he kicked her feet apart and stepped between them. She pulled her legs back, levered herself on the man behind her and, bracing one foot on Joliet's hip, she drove the other into his face, sending him sprawling into the courtyard. He scrambled back to her and swung his fist. The world lit up like a flash-bulb and then went dark as the prisoners roared.

***

Glancing down from his office window onto the prisoners' courtyard and what resembled a riot more than a sport, Peter felt the echo of that riot thrashing underneath his ribs. Every effort to overthrow Hitler's regime was being swatted aside. He had jeopardized both his own position and Hendry's big picture in the name of the resistance, and he knew that he would do so again, given the opportunity. Others had risked even more, but it was beginning to seem that destiny really was arrayed against them.

On the far side of the courtyard below, a figure stumbled backwards into view. Hardly an anomaly in all that turmoil, and yet, somehow, it *was* an anomaly. An unpleasant prickling of his scalp made him turn and sprint out of his office, down the stairs, and through the pass door.

The clamour in the courtyard greeted him like a physical presence, surging dangerously as he crossed the field of play and burst through the far wall of spectators. And then he could see too clearly what was happening just ten yards away, behind the coal house. Pulling his gun from its holster and flicking off the safety, he fired one shot into the air, and advanced. The game ended abruptly as the prisoners dropped to the ground.

The man who had been supporting the girl from behind released her and ran, letting her head and shoulders fall to the cobbles with a thud, but the other knelt between the girl's legs, fumbling at her trousers and reaching for his own fly buttons. Walking steadily forwards, Peter spoke into the echoing silence.

"Stop now, or I will shoot."

There was no reaction, and Peter took aim and cocked the trigger, then hastily turned the gun's nose to the sky as the man flung himself down on top of the girl, glanced over his shoulder and grinned, spitting blood that streamed from a broken nose. Tomasin West had put up a fight.

"That's right, at that angle and proximity your bullet would pass through both of us," he said, jerking his head at the girl. "Ask her; is that the ending she would choose?" He finished unbuttoning his trousers and reached for himself. "Come on, be a gentleman and let me have this one pleasure. Believe me, after all this time, it will last only a few minutes, but right now it seems like a good way to die!"

Fifteen feet away now, Peter stopped, crouched and took aim again from a lower angle, levelling his pistol at the Frenchman's head, but the man had whipped a straight-edged shaving razor from his boot, had flipped it open, and was holding the blade to the girl's throat.

Peter froze as the edge rested on her skin, scoring fine slashes that turned crimson and bled. Catching the direction of his gaze, the man nodded.

"I don't think you want to see the little lady's throat explode all over my shirt, do you? So, let's make a deal. Why don't you just stay right where you are while I do what I have to do, and then you can have me." He laughed harshly, phlegm rattling in his throat, "Then you can have her too, for that matter. Or am I the only man in this place with the balls to fuck a real woman?"

The girl was beginning to regain consciousness. She moaned quietly, turning her head from side to side, and Peter winced as the skin of her throat brushed against the blade, opening up deeper slashes.

He turned his eyes back on his target, keeping his pistol levelled at the Frenchman's head. The blade was in the man's left hand, while his right hand, mottled with the strain, was splayed on the cobbles, supporting his weight. Sweat was running down his face and trickling into his eyes, which were rapidly swelling and bruising, and with no free hand available, he was blinking and twitching to shake off the drops. Peter watched and waited until, with a reflexive movement, the man raised his knife hand to wipe his face.

The hand never reached its goal. The sound of the gunshot, fired so close, jolted the girl's head to one side, and the razor fell, bouncing off the lapel of her greatcoat as the man's body pitched sideways, spraying blood in a crimson arc that steamed in the chill air.

"Tommie!" The shout ricocheted off the castle walls,

battling with the echoes from the shot. Glancing over his shoulder, Peter saw that the duty guards had penned the prisoners into the far end of the courtyard, but in a gesture of compassion, someone had allowed Leigh through, and he was approaching slowly, moving cautiously with his arms raised and fingers splayed.

Peter turned back to the girl as she shuddered and stared around, her eyes wide and dazed. She struggled to sit up, but her arms were tied to her sides by a length of sheet-rope, and her legs were pinned by the body of the French officer. Still on his knees and with his gun in his hand, Peter made a move to help her, but the fear and rage that flooded her face froze him in place. With a fierce twist of her trunk, she pulled herself into a sitting position and wriggled herself out of the greatcoat, which fell to the ground, still encircled by the rope.

Leigh's voice called out to the girl again, more softly now, and she turned towards him like the needle of a compass finding magnetic north, but when she saw what was behind him her expression evolved into pure terror. The prisoners, bovine in their curiosity, were edging towards the scene, and the guards were unconsciously giving ground.

From his position – his head on a level with hers – Peter saw what she saw, and heard her response; a long, low growl coming from deep inside her, rising in pitch until her voice was a feral scream of fury. With frantic lunges, she wrenched herself out from underneath the corpse, and propelled herself, shuffling and scrambling backwards, to the shelter of the courtyard wall where she screamed again, eyes wide and teeth bared.

Peter stood then, and turned to face the prisoners. This was not a moment for words; holding his gun out at arm's length, he swept it silently across the wall of faces, and the guards herded them back. Leigh, who had stopped dead in horror at the girl's scream, ignored the gesture and tried again to approach her. He spoke her name gently but, with her arms clutched across her chest, she sank lower behind her knees and shook her head mutely.

A recollection drifted across Peter's mind then, like a strand of gossamer bearing a fledgeling spider of a memory; a girl had come to his grandmother's house once. Wrapped fiercely in the arms of her mother she had come, looking just like the girl who was huddled in front of him now; torn, shocked and trembling. His grandmother had taken them both into her own arms and into her house while he himself was sent to town on an errand. Young as he was, he had understood that there are times when only a woman can help a woman.

But where was he going to find a woman in this place? The administrative staff? Frau Hess? No, it couldn't be just any woman. His grandmother had been no ordinary woman.

At this thought he nodded to himself, glanced around the courtyard and called to the nearest guard,

"There is a woman who cleans the offices in the commandantur, Frau Heller is her name. Tell her what has happened and ask her if she would please come here immediately." Then, remembering something, he hastily called after the guard, "And be sure to speak respectfully to her. I will hear about it if you don't."

He turned back to the small figure crouched against the wall. In her backwards scramble, one of her flying boots had come off, and he saw the outline of her foot, swamped inside a military issue sock, the heel of which was sitting halfway up her calf. Conscious of looming over her in her vulnerability, he squatted down again. Ten feet to his right, Leigh was also hunkered down on the cobbles, his gaze fixed on the girl, who remained huddled and silent. They waited.

He became aware of Frau Heller's arrival before he saw her, and as he turned and watched her approach, he knew he had acted well. The woman was middle-aged, comfortable and matronly, yet there was something about her that held her apart. In defiance of the current, tightly-tailored styles, she wore loose, shapeless clothes that gave off a faint, elusive scent of herbs as she moved; thyme, sage and lavender. She did not offer an acknowledgement to

Peter, passing between him and Leigh without a glance.

Beneath the whisper of her movement, he could hear her muttering softly in German, but as she approached the girl, she spoke clearly in English, and in the surreal silence that lay over the courtyard, Peter saw the girl's head lift up from her knees, her eyes lighting with what seemed to be a startled recognition.

Kneeling down at her side, the older woman held out her hands. The girl took them and covered her ears with them. Frau Heller nodded.

"Don't hear it, daughter," she said, "Hear me." Drawing her to her feet, she glanced down at the girl's stockinged foot, found the flying boot, and helped her to put it on. "Come, let us wash that man off you," she said, briskly, then led her across the courtyard towards the commandantur.

Peter stood and turned to follow them as Leigh picked up the girl's RAF greatcoat, flinging the rope in a fury at the corpse of the French officer.

The doctor met them at the pass door. His face was set in a mask of anger, and he muttered angrily to Peter about violations of decency as he unlocked the door to the hospital wing. Eight rooms opened off this corridor, and Henning led them to the first, but Frau Heller walked past him without a word. The doctor stared after her, incensed.

"Mein frau," he called peremptorily, "Mein frau! This room. Here."

The woman ignored him and manoeuvred Tomasin West in through the seventh door. Radiating indignation, the doctor followed her.

The seventh room was a square, plastered and white-painted room, identical to the others. A standard hospital bed was centred against the left wall beneath a wall-mounted reading lamp. At the right side of the bed was a rolling table, and in the far corner of the room, next to the window, was an old armchair. Henning, nettled by the woman's defiance, was still complaining, and Peter intervened.

"Why this particular room, Frau Heller? Why must you have the good doctor travel so far to see his patient?"

"Because this is a healing room," she said, settling the girl into the armchair.

"They are all healing rooms," snapped the doctor. "This is a hospital wing."

"The other rooms are merely rooms in a hospital wing. This room is a healing room."

"Healing by what definition, Frau Heller?" asked Brandt curiously. He knew what he knew about this room, but he wanted to know what she knew. The woman fixed him with a piercing glance.

"Healing is healing. Does anyone have the means or the right to question its source? May I stay here with this girl tonight, Major Brandt?" Taken aback, Brandt glanced at the girl, who was sitting upright and rigid in the chair, her hands twisted into a knot on her lap. He nodded.

"If the doctor is willing to accommodate you, we can allow that. I'm sure she will benefit from your attendance."

The woman took Henning's willingness as a given.

"She will need a bath, and she must have a nightgown," she said firmly, "I will not put a man's pyjamas near her while she is in this state. May I send someone to my house for some supplies?"

Brandt hesitated.

"A guard will have to examine anything that is brought into the castle."

"Of course."

"Then I will arrange for a messenger."

Frau Heller gave him an address and a list of supplies, and he left the room as the doctor prepared to examine the girl, but he paused in the doorway and turned back. "You speak English, Frau Heller."

The woman lifted her head and looked full at him with peat-brown eyes, so dark as to meld the irises with the pupils.

"My daughter is married to an Englishman, Major Brandt, and she has lived in England since before the war. I learned the language in order to communicate with my son-in-law, and to ensure that he was treating my daughter properly, but you needn't concern yourself too much about that information; Major Steiger is fully aware of my circumstances."

***

The view from the window of the seventh room in the early hours of the morning was familiar to him, but now he stood on the threshold, observing the peace of the room as an outsider.

The girl was profoundly asleep. Frau Heller was sitting in the armchair with her back to the window, but Peter sensed that she was awake and watching him from the darkness.

"She's sleeping," he said into the silence, "how did you manage that?" The woman did not answer him, but stood up and moved to the foot of the bed. "You are aware, Frau Heller," he said slowly, "that the Reich forbids the practice of... subverting conventional medicine?"

"And you, Herr Major Brandt," came the woman's dark voice "Do you forbid?"

"As an officer of the Reich, I am required to forbid what my leadership says must be forbidden," Peter replied impassively, "So, it is fortunate that you do not engage in such practices." His eyes rested on the girl's face, hypnotised by the tranquillity that he saw there. "I am glad that Fraulein West will have some peace tonight," he said. "Good night, Frau Heller."

***

Tommie woke, shuddering, as memory overwhelmed the blissful darkness of sleep. The skin on her neck burned. She raised her hand, felt the dressings, and sat up in a growing panic.

In the darkness she heard a rustle of movement and felt a presence at her side. It wasn't a presence to be alarmed about. Gentle hands placed something on her forehead – something cool and damp and scented with bitter fragrances that painted a sour patch onto the back of her tongue. Gentle fingers removed the gauze from her neck and applied a fresh dressing as a voice came to her, low and calm.

"A man knows his enemy by the uniform he wears, but a woman must watch for her enemy in all men."

Tommie wept then; raging, tasting again the foulness of the hand over her mouth, and the panic of her own helplessness in the face of Joliet's assault. All of her unarmed combat training had not been enough to turn away his calculated act of will; it had taken another man with a gun to stop him. She laid her head on the woman's shoulder, and felt herself cradled and rocked gently until she had finished crying.

"It is in the nature of the human animal to conquer. To dominate. To control," said Frau Heller, wiping Tommie's face with a damp flannel, closing her hot eyes.

"What is in the nature of the female animal, then? To yield?"

The older woman smiled.

"Not at all. And I said the human animal, not the male animal."

"Then what?"

"The opposing forces are not man and woman, but aggression and passivity. Zeus and Poseidon were rapacious predators, but Hera, Eos and Circe were no better. They are the opposing poles of life, child; predator and prey, forever in opposition. But most of life lies between the two poles."

She adjusted the dressing again, and Tommie watched her movements through the darkness.

"I would like to learn from you."

"For now, you need to sleep."

"But I don't want to waste this opportunity; I want to listen to you."

The woman laughed softly.

"Then settle back down, and you will both listen and sleep."

Her voice wove itself into the darkness of the seventh room, low and lyrical, speaking names that brushed softly against Tommie's mind like the ghosts of moths. "Sigyn, Fulla, Hel, and Freyja. Kuan Yin, lady of boundless compassion, Diana the huntress, Athena the tactician,

Hestia the hearth-keeper; their stories are there, child, for those who wish to learn of them. Nanna, Rhiannon, Maia and Gwenhwyfar. Yemana, Zorya, Isis, Astarte," *Innana, Laima, Sarasvati...* Tommie shivered as another voice joined Frau Heller's litany, weaving in and out of the woman's words like a silver thread in colour-saturated cloth, and then more voices trickled in, speaking other names, telling other stories. *Dei-Greine, Sunna, Marisha-Ten, Saule, Innana Tara, Arinna, Estsanatlehi, Pele.*

The pungent scents of the herbs feathered together, loosening Tommie's thoughts, and she drifted and listened, and soon the voices were indistinguishable from each other; Frau Heller's dark voice speaking of Brigit, Laha, Artemis, Sif and Juno, wove a tapestry with the other voices, vivid and exotic or thin and querulous, that sang of Kali, Saule, Asherah, Sandraudiga, Nerthus and Var, Benzai-Ten, Chang-O, Ukemochi and Shapash. The names, some of them slightly ugly to Tommie's ears, some lyrical, poured over her shoulders like a waterfall, and she allowed herself to bathe in them, soaking them in as an endowment: "Lakshmi, Coatlicue, Shasthi, Oya, Shochiquetzal, Wawalak, Sulis and Ishtar, mighty Ishtar."

Mighty Ishtar.

***

Ushered by the guard through the pass door into the prisoners' courtyard the next day, Tommie felt as though she had been stripped and scoured by a sandstorm. Sensitised to every glance, she imagined that Joliet's attack on her was playing and replaying in the thoughts of every man there, to the accompaniment of Blauser's words.

With infinite gratitude she spotted Simon standing aimlessly near the steps to the British quarters. He had her greatcoat draped over his arm, and when he saw her, he hurried over, but stopped and spoke to her from a distance of several paces away.

"Tommie, I'm so sorry," he said, and his blue eyes were haunted, "it's my fault that this happened."

"Your fault?" The edges of the wounds on her neck rasped against the dressing as she spoke. "How is it your fault?"

"I... I... When you got here, I..." he hesitated, his eyes flinching away from the dried blood on her sweater. He tried again. "If I hadn't..." He stopped short and shook his head resolutely against some internal monologue. "If I hadn't been playing football yesterday..."

"What happened was Joliet's responsibility alone," she said flatly. He swallowed hard and nodded.

"Are you..."

"Alright?" she said on a broken sigh. "Am I alright? That's an interesting question. Whatever it is that I am will pass for alright until I *am* alright. And, Simon, I really appreciate your sensitivity in keeping your distance, but what would help even more right now is for you to give me one of your nicest hugs."

The opposing forces are not man and woman, but aggression and passivity.

He stepped closer and draped the greatcoat carefully around her. It slid off as she buried her face in his shoulder, but she felt herself encircled by his arms, and when she stood back from him, he retrieved it from the cobbles, brushed it off, and held it while she slipped her arms into the sleeves.

22
Germany bad, Russia good

"I envy your father his death, Peter." Beck's words, spoken in the elegant drawing room of the Wolf estate, connected with Peter like an electric shock. The resistance was being decimated, and this meeting was an attempt to regroup and re-assess. Hans von Dohnanyi had been arrested on false charges and removed from his post, and when Oster attempted to intervene in that process, he was dismissed. Dohnanyi's wife had also been arrested, along with Dietrich Bonhoeffer and others close to Oster. Hitler's distrust of Canaris had boiled over, and he had dismissed the admiral. Now Canaris, too, had been arrested. The company drawn together here was unsettled and wary, and taking the armchair next to Beck, Peter was shaken by the heavy sadness that now shadowed his former senior officer's face.

"Sir?"

"Your father gave his life for his country, and did not live to see this...this travesty of it" said Beck bleakly. "He died a hero, and he left a son who would carry his name with pride. No man could want for more, but it is better that I do not have a son who bears my name, because if we fail, Peter, our actions will count as treason, and that will taint not only our names but the lives of all those close to us."

Peter considered the older man's words soberly, and shook his head.

"To whom will our actions count as treason, sir? To those we are trying to remove? To those who choose to know no better? Surely, a man's honour doesn't lie in what is said about him by others, but in his actions and in the reasons for his actions."

Beck sighed deeply. "In times such as these, things are not so simple, Peter. My conscience is divided, and neither part can honour the resolve of the other. I am loath to die the dishonourable death of a traitor, to die like a dog, cudgelled to death by thugs." He stood and rested his hand on Peter's shoulder for a moment. "Perhaps it is not your father I envy, Peter, but you. Perhaps I envy you your certainty. Now, if you would excuse me, I must have a word with Tresckow and Olbricht before they start the meeting."

Peter sat with his thoughts for a long time. He would be flying to Geneva the following day, to attend a conference of Germany's military intelligence officers, and he expected to be contacted by Hendry. A copy of Goerdeler's constitution was already in his briefcase, along with an extensive selection of FHO documents. He would petition Hendry once more for allied recognition of the resistance, because without that, the movement would continue to do no more than tread water, like Vlasov's Army.

***

The soaring peaks of Switzerland's mountains were as pristine as ever, seemingly unpolluted by the clouds of intrigue that wreathed their feet.

There was a message waiting for him at his hotel when he checked in. Mr. Klamm hoped to meet him in the bar of the Hotel International at five o'clock that afternoon where, once again, Hendry categorically refused his petition.

Unsurprisingly, he already knew some of what Peter was handing him.

"They've had years to act against Hitler," he said quietly

when Peter broached the subject. "If they are so resolved, then why let so much time – and so much blood – pass? London will not get into bed with people who are likely to climb out the other side, and let me remind you that this is not your problem," he added, his voice neutral, and colourless as water. "Don't lose sight of the big picture."

"The big picture is pretty distorted from where I stand," Peter said harshly, and then anger tipped him over the edge of caution. "I'm working with them, you know; on the coup... on everything. I would do the job myself if they'd let me," he added savagely. "Assassination? I would do it tomorrow."

"Yes," said Hendry softly, "I believe you would."

Peter scrubbed at his face in frustration. "Did you give the powers-that-be my recommendation on the resistance?"

"No."

"You still haven't told them about me, have you?"

"No, and I won't," Hendry said bluntly. There was a long pause. "There are strange things happening over there, Peter," he said eventually. "Nothing is the way it should be. I'm very uneasy... the old instincts, you know." He slipped a pack of Swiss cigarettes from his pocket and pulled the last cigarette out, crushing the empty pack and dropping it onto the table. Watching Peter's face, he lit his cigarette, then reached down and tapped his leg with the lighter. The impact made a hollow, tinny sound. "Did you know I have an artificial leg?" He enquired casually.

"Yes, of course."

"You've never asked about it."

"It's your private business."

"Well, I'll make it yours now," said Hendry baldly. "Some time ago, I was an agent working in Russia. A very successful agent, actually. Without a shred of exaggeration, I can say I was bloody brilliant, but then I fell in love. She knew nothing of who I really was, but one day she approached the appropriate people, begging to be allowed to work with the resistance. She had heartbreaking reasons for her decision – they're always heartbreaking reasons – and she was adamant, because the cause was so..." the muscles in his face pulled taut, "... so poignantly right. So, did I agree to take her on board? What would your call be? Absolutely no go. Right? Breaks all the rules. But I thought – because I could see all the cards right there in front of me on the table – that I was in control of the situation, so I went ahead and allowed them to sign her up. I knew that she wasn't suitable, but who is?"

Hendry ran the pad of his right thumb along the edge of the table, pressing hard, then twisted his hand to examine the groove in the flesh caused by the pressure.

"She crumbled like chalk as soon as they began to work on her. She told them everything she knew, and then they killed her, of course. I found out about it much later, after our people somehow managed to pull me out of some gulag somewhere, and after they cut off my leg where it had rotted. Just as well for me, I suppose – the leg, I mean – it gave them an excuse to ground me instead of discharging me. They'll give a man the boot for making a fool of himself, but if he wears the DSM and he's crippled in the line of duty and has no foot to put the boot on, they pin him down behind a damned desk.

"But anyway, Peter, what I'm trying to tell you is that passion is a fact of life. Whether it's the love of a woman or the love of an ideal, it's a fact of life. You can't avoid it." He knocked two inches of grey ash from his cigarette, lifted the stub to his lips and inhaled, letting the smoke out slowly, softly, on a breath.

"When it's all you can see and hear and taste and touch, the passion overwhelms you. But underlying it all – underlying the passion – there is always the big picture, like a palimpsest, where the concealed image is infinitely more precious than what's painted over it. The passion is ephemeral. What's important is what lies beneath."

He signalled to the waiter to refresh their drinks, and when the man had left, he leaned forward and ground the stub of his cigarette into the ashtray.

"The powers-that-be do not see the big picture," he said

with a sudden, caustic bitterness. "They see only the paint that is daubed over it, and what they see is Germany bad, Russia good. 'We need Russia to help us win this war,' they say."

"But our need does not determine the Soviets' actions," said Peter, recalling Braun's judgement of Fromm.

Hendry shrugged.

"This is not the time for your friends to muddy the waters."

"Muddy waters are the natural habitat of the intelligence community," Peter said stubbornly.

Hendry shook his head.

"The department is quite unambiguously in accordance with the narrative, Peter; Germany bad, Russia good. No fine-shading, it's that simple. There's nothing I can do."

Peter watched Hendry through the curling cigarette smoke, allowing his thoughts to assume the same fluid, twisting movement.

"'Russia good,'" he said curiously, "how does that sit with you? It must get quite lonely in the coffee room."

Hendry grimaced. "If you're not wearing a fur hat you're improperly dressed. It would be comical if it weren't so dangerous. The department is like a prize bull; someone has stuck a ring through its nose and they're leading it wherever they want it to go. Right now, it's facing Moscow, so you know where the cow pats are falling."

"Who is leading the bull?"

"Impossible to say."

"And what about your nose ring?"

Hendry grinned, "I wear a clip-on. When nobody's looking, I slip it off and go my own way."

23
Voices get burned

"'Mighty Ishtar,' you called her," Tommie said, "Out of all those names, why Mighty *Ishtar*?"

Frau Heller had approached the castle's housekeeper about taking on the duties of a cook in the prisoners' kitchens one day a week after her domestic shift, and Tommie had signed up as a kitchen orderly to work alongside her. She cherished the woman's company.

"They are all mighty in their own right," Frau Heller answered, "but Ishtar has come amongst us; has been abducted, you might say, and it seems she has brought her affinity for war with her. We Germans found the pieces of the Ishtar Gate in the ruins of Babylon and brought it to Berlin, then re-built it brick by brick. It's only bricks, of course, but who can say what resonances such actions carry."

"I don't know anything about Ishtar."

"Well, she was the great goddess of ancient Babylon, but in one story about her, she wanted to lay claim to the realm of the dead, where her sister, Ereshkigal, was queen. Now, Ishtar had a handmaid – her closest companion – and before she ventured down into the underworld, she gave this handmaid detailed instructions about what to do if she didn't return; the handmaid should mourn the loss of her mistress according to custom, and appeal to the gods to rescue her. So, Ishtar set out, and at each of the seven gates of Hell, she was stripped of a piece of her finery until, at the last gate, she entered into the darkness naked and vulnerable.

"Predictably, she was taken captive by her dark sister, and up in the world everything languished – there was no music, no joy, no sex, no love and no procreation, so when her loyal handmaid did as she had been told, rolled in ashes, tore her clothes in mourning, and approached the gods, they were keen to make a deal with Ereshkigal. It was agreed that Ishtar should be released from the underworld, but she had to choose someone else to take her place in the world of the dead."

"She didn't choose her handmaid, did she?" said Tommie, horrified.

"No," chuckled Frau Koppel, "She chose her consort, Tammuz, because in her absence he had been living the high life, with no thought of mourning her, and Ishtar couldn't tolerate disloyalty. It turns out that she was keen on revenge as well as sex and war." She paused, staring out of the high window at the grey peaks of the castle's roof, "I think that story tells us that it's only when we have been stripped of what civilizes us, that we can experience the depths of our own darkness."

Tommie shuddered involuntarily.

"Someone just walked on my grave."

Frau Heller looked at her, startled, then laughed.

"You can mock, child, but I'd be careful if I were you; it seems you've already passed through a gate or two yourself. Before you know it, you'll be facing your own dark sister!"

***

"I, too, was an odd little person when I was your age."

They were sitting at a table in the canteen, taking a break. Weeks had passed, and the winter dragged on, taking its toll on the health of the prisoners. Remembering the yarrow poultice that Frau Heller had pressed to the wound on her neck in the hospital wing, Tommie had asked her how to prepare that poultice, and other remedies for the minor common ailments which troubled the men. The woman's response had sent an absent warmth washing over her.

What an odd little woman you are.

Missing Sam with a sharp pang, she finished up one of the two hard-boiled eggs that the woman had brought her, and dropped the other one into her pocket for Simon. All she ever had to offer in return was her chocolate ration, but it was invariably received with delight, and so she saved all of it to put on the table when Frau Heller brought eggs for her, or a jar of honey from her own bees, or two apples from her garden; always two, or enough for two, since Tommie had explained about Simon. She swept the peeled eggshell into her hand for the compost heap, and they returned to work.

"*Am* I an odd little person?" she said.

Cutting cooking fat into the flour in her mixing bowl, Frau Heller gave her a wry smile, "In the first place, it takes an unusual person to seek the sort of knowledge that you are seeking, and in the second place... one woman living amongst so many hundreds of men, and managing to keep them all at arm's length – *Lightly*; rub it in with your fingertips, not your hands – don't look surprised, I can tell when a woman is keeping herself chaste." She shook her head, "You tolerate their hostility and their petty insults, and yet you seek ways to treat their illnesses... Again, *lightly*; use the edge of the blade lightly, don't mash it. Are you an odd person? You had better be, or you won't survive this."

"After this past winter, they've all got coughs, and the pennyroyal doesn't always work," said Tommie, "but believe me, it is purely in the spirit of self-interest that I want to relieve their digestive complaints."

Frau Heller laughed, her solid body shaking, and Tommie's soul softened.

"No, child," the woman said, retrieving the rolling pin

from Tommie, "You're making pastry, not sawing a log. Is that how your mother made pastry? Like this; roll lightly then lift the pastry, turn it a quarter turn and roll again."

Tommie smiled at the thought of her mother – elegant in flawless linen or Chinese silk – rolling pastry. Frau Heller handed the rolling pin back and placed her floury hands over Tommie's to demonstrate the correct technique. "Next time I come, then," she said as she draped her own perfect pastry over the top of a pie plate, "I will teach you how to make a hyssop tea for their coughs."

Tommie had been trained by older midwives, who had, in turn, been trained by older midwives. The links in the chain went back a long way, and hints of the old remedies had filtered through, but only hints. Now, however, her sessions in the kitchen included how to make tinctures, salves and infusions.

Frau Heller had also left roots of meadowsweet, comfrey and hyssop at the gate of the exercise field for her to plant in her plot, and regularly brought little paper packages of her own dried herbs that Tommie smuggled out of the kitchen in her chest band, 'Because you'll not be able to dry any leaf in this cold, damp castle.'

Now she had a small but useful pharmacy that she kept lined up in little glass jars in the kitchen annexe of the dormitory; yarrow as a styptic for bleeding, and comfrey for skin and bone healing. 'How domesticated,' George Selby had sneered one day, peering at her growing collection, 'A veritable country kitchen.' But the potions were in constant demand, not only by the prisoners, but also by guards and orderlies working at the castle, who approached her through Bainbridge.

After a careful consultation with Doctor Henning, she had made herself available as an on-site nurse for minor disorders that didn't require the doctor's attention. Safeguards were necessary, of course; 'I won't look at anything between the waist and the knee,' she had announced to the officers, 'If you're concerned about anything that's going on in that zone, you can describe it for me… and by that, Harry,

I mean describe the *problem*, nothing else,' she clarified, forestalling what was certain to be an unsavoury comment from Harry Shaw. 'I might be able to give you advice, but otherwise take it to the doctor.'

'But if it starts in that zone, and falls below the knee,' said Shaw with a slow grin. 'You'd want to look at that, Tommie, wouldn't you?'

Sam had been right; she was Wendy to a bunch of lost boys. A den-mother. Hestia, the hearth keeper, had stepped in and taken the reins from warlike Joan of Arc. The anger and the dreams – especially that last dream – were history. This castle and its men had become her hearth.

***

"It all comes down to how stories are told," Frau Heller said, slicing into a comfrey root. "In the German pagan traditions, men worshipped the warrior gods, like Tyr and Woden, and the heroism of men like Hercules, Ulysses and Jason are revered across the western world, but all those heroes, even mighty Woden himself, were bound by the web of Wyrd; the web of fate spun by the Wyrd sisters. The Norns as we call them."

Into the void of an education in philosophy, Tommie was pouring a wealth of mythology.

"Like the Fates in Metamorphoses?" she said, "Clotho, Lachesis and Atropos. What did you call them? The Wyrd sisters? That's what Shakespeare called his three witches in Macbeth... the weird sisters."

"Yes, just so. The ancient spelling of 'word' was 'wyrd.' One word that represents all the power that words and stories wield. There is force and there is passivity, but there is also another element that exists in the no-man's land between them; the weird. The web of fate. The Wyrd. Stories. The hidden force."

"The Wyrd." Tommie frowned. "What's that saying from the Bible? 'In the beginning was the Word, and the

Word was with God, and the Word was God.'"

"Exactly! The sacred, the divine – the mystery of God – is the biggest and oldest story of all; the first and last battle. So, the forceful ones, the orthodox religions, try to seize its power for themselves. By investing 'word' with a capital 'W' – by planting God's flag on it – the priests claim divine authority to qualify all stories and so condemn, silence or extinguish their power." She paused and straightened her back, wincing, "Stories tell people about all the possibilities that life holds, this is why the orthodox religions insist that stories which don't conform to the orthodox are not the Word; they are heretical. Now we're back to force and passivity again; forceful people – and there are none more forceful than the adherents of the orthodox religions – attack opposing ideas head-to-head, like goats, and, of course, they easily dominate the passive ones, but the existence of stories in the no-man's land defeats them."

Tommie nodded; the dreams that had sent her to the British Library, and then to Hendry, had been filled with the consequences of force and passivity and... and what lay in the no-man's land between them. Frau Heller tilted her head. "There is something you want to say to me?"

Tommie hesitated, wavering.

Why, in my dream, did I step down from the stake and reach out to Hell?

She plunged in.

"Frau Heller, I have always believed that the witches in the Middle Ages were just women who followed pagan ways, or got on the wrong side of someone influential, but if some of them really *were*... Satan worshippers, well, can that sort of thing be in the blood?"

Frau Heller scattered two teaspoons of hyssop leaves into a pot.

"Labels!" she said sourly. "Labels only serve to quicken prejudice. Mankind cannot fight or kill without first pinning a label onto the chosen enemy. And giving yourself a label is just the same thing; it fixes you. Like a butterfly pinned in a display case – immutable." She picked up the kettle as it came to a rolling boil. "You want to know if you're a witch, and if being a witch makes you a healer or a devil-worshipper. Tell me this; how would you define a witch? I live alone, I talk to my bees and my cats, and I make potions. Does that make me a witch?"

She poured water over the hyssop leaves, covered the pot, and then stood for a moment, her black eyes glinting. "Digitalis can strengthen a heartbeat or stop it, Tomasin. Choosing how you use it and why; that's what matters." She patted Tommie's arm. "Learn from everything that comes to you, child. Don't burden it with a label, and don't be tempted to claim a label for yourself." She pushed the pot to her. "Now, have you been paying attention?"

Tommie nodded.

"Ten minutes for hyssop tea. No more, no less," she said, drawing the pot to herself. "I still can't believe that you don't have all your remedies written down; that they're trusted only to the oral tradition."

Lifting the lid, she stared into the bitter liquid, and a feather of steam brushed her face. In the depths of the pot the water gleamed like ink.

"Books get burned," said Frau Heller grimly.

"So do voices." The words emerged from Tommie's throat, hoarse and ghostly, and she straightened up, shaken. Frau Heller looked carefully into her face, then nodded.

"Let them burn what they can see, she said, "What lies in no-man's land is beyond them."

24
The enemy of my enemy

"Don't fret, Dmitri, we are not dealing with the SS here." Alexei Viniski was watching Peter's expression as he spoke. The Russian officers were gathered in the conference room, and Viniski was in a devilish frame of mind, not an uncommon state for him.

"The men of the General Staff serve Germany, not Hitler," he continued, "The good Major here is in the same boat as we are, my friends; waiting for the madman to fall. Is that not so, Major Brandt? Are you not waiting for the madman to fall?"

"Your opinions betray a considerable independence of thought, Major Viniski."

"Yes," the Russian answered with a wry smile, "and independence of thought is a currency that has been outlawed by the leaders of our two countries." Viniski stopped and looked into Peter's face. He seemed to find something there that satisfied him, and he smiled a tired smile, turning to the others. "That is what we are fighting for, my friends, for independence of thought. So, Dmitri, don't twitch with guilt over working with the Germans to that end. The enemy of my enemy is my friend. Well," he added with a grin, "if not a friend, then at least a useful ally in our cause."

The meeting continued to its conclusion, and when it

was over, Peter escorted the three men through the corridors of the west wing. At the stairway leading down to the lower corridor, Viniski, at the front, paused and stood back courteously for Frau Heller, who was coming up. The woman thanked him politely and acknowledged Peter as she passed on her way down the corridor, carrying her cleaning equipment. As Viniski started down the stairs, the voice of the sentry guarding the door at the bottom came echoing up the stone stairwell, speaking to the guard who had come to relieve him.

"...she must have been mouthing off about the Nazis again. I hear Steiger is asking questions about her." Peter stopped short, listening, and gestured for Viniski to halt. The Russians waited, watching him with interest.

"Working in this place, she should know better," said the new guard.

"And the English girl is allowed to work with her," continued the sentry. "The two of them sit and have coffee together, nattering away like they're in a street cafe. Let any two women spend time together like that and you might as well set a cauldron between them. Well, my grandchildren go to the same school as her niece's kids, and they've been instructed to report on anything those girls say."

The new guard sighed.

"The only one who can afford to speak out is the one who has no family and no friends to..."

Peter nodded to Viniski to continue down the stairs and the two guards fell silent.

With the Russians heading back to their camp, Peter made his way quickly to where a mop and bucket stood outside an office. He glanced around cautiously, but the place was empty except for Frau Heller, who was busy sweeping.

"Excuse me, Frau Heller, might I have a word with you?" The woman straightened up, wincing slightly, and Brandt spoke quietly. "It has come to my attention that the SS are showing an interest in you, and I think perhaps you might want to take care to avoid their attentions."

Frau Heller looked at him in surprise.

"Thank you, Major Brandt. I appreciate your concern, but I have sidestepped them more than once in the past, and since then I have become more... discreet in expressing my opinions."

Peter nodded curtly, then looked imperatively into the woman's eyes.

"I understand that Major Steiger's men have been asking questions this week about your grand-nieces at the Burgerstrasse school." The woman froze then, staring at him, and whatever it was that she was thinking made the hollows under her eyes turn grey. "You don't look well, Frau Heller," he added, taking the broom from her hands. "If you wish, I will inform the housekeeper that you were taken ill and had to leave. Immediately."

"Yes," she said slowly, "Thank you." Leaving the room, she paused and turned back, "Tomasin West, Major Brandt... please offer her all the protection that it is in your power to give."

***

The swifts were wheeling and squealing, high up in the blue dome of the sky, and the next generation of jackdaws had graduated from the roofline to the woods on the other side of the fence from where Tommie was digging. Occasionally, on some signal known only to corvids, they would rise up en masse, chacking loudly, and join other families from the town and from the fields all around, to converge in a raucous, ragged black vortex high above the plain, but inside Tommie, their noise fell on a heavy silence.

Soon, the swifts would leave again, taking their exuberance with them, but the jackdaws would stay, glowering over their hearth. Sam had left when the swifts were calling, and now Frau Heller had left, abruptly, with no goodbye. Sounding out the guards at her request, Bainbridge had been answered by indifferent shrugs; the woman had simply stopped turning up for work.

For Tommie, the castle now seemed like a ship adrift in a sargasso sea, while oceans of war boiled around them; to the east, Russian troops were driving German forces out of Crimea and advancing into Romania. Germany's new jet-powered flying bombs were targeting London. British and American forces were routing the Germans in Italy, and it was rumoured that a massive landing of Allied forces had swarmed up the beaches of Normandy.

The prisoners had a radio receiver concealed somewhere in the castle, and news was circulating, but it was a double-edged sword; cheering on the allied advances left them chewed up with powerlessness. The war didn't require their participation; they were surplus to requirements. Escape attempts were all but forbidden in view of the volatility out there, and in the hollow, waiting, torment of inactivity, the castle began to seethe like a crucible over a flame.

Tommie looked across at where Simon was picking up pebbles from the soil, examining them, discarding some and pocketing others.

"What are the pebbles for?" she asked as they walked back up to the castle. He shrugged.

"Just a little pastime."

25
One does not refer to dead men as friends

July 20th 1944

Hitler is dead.
Woken by a messenger sent from Renger, Peter hurried to the commandant's office, but the radio was broadcasting only martial music, and telephone lines were down. He left Renger, Henning and Hamm sitting in tense silence in front of the radio, and sped to Zossen on the Pioneer. It was the twentieth of July, and although the summer night had barely turned dark, it seemed that the horizon was preparing to split wide open and let in a new day.

Balancing on the edge of a chasm, the compound at Zossen was waiting to either topple in or settle back onto its foundations. Conversation was non-existent in the map room as the radio played the interminable martial music, and people wrapped themselves tightly in their thoughts.

Peter struggled with the impression that he was floating above Berlin, watching desperate figures in a living wargame. Beck was down there, in the Bendlerblock, anchoring the coup, giving substance and dignity to the inconceivable thing that was being done, but in this place, skulking in a pine forest, Peter felt separate.

Long after midnight, it came at last. The music stopped abruptly, and the announcer cried, "The Fuhrer speaks." A voice crackled into the room, faint and weak, barely audible above the static, but it was undeniably Hitler's voice, speaking of a crime that was without peer in German history.

Someone switched it off, and a brittle silence fell in the room as the men tried to absorb the implications. Wilfried Strik-Strikfeldt burst in with an update on events. General Beck, Colonel Stauffenberg, General Olbricht, Colonel Mertz von Quirnheim and Lieutenant Haeften, all executed on the spot by Fromm.

By Fromm. Peter's blood was lava.

Strik-Strikfeldt turned a tortured face to Gehlen, who had come to stand in the doorway.

"Our friends, Herr General, our friends..."

Gehlen stiffened.

"One does not refer to dead men as friends," he said in a flat voice, "one does not know them. Never forget that, Wilfried Karlovich. I have graduated through Stalin's school. This is only the beginning. Please, gentlemen, for all our sakes, let no man speak another word until I have left this room."

His core of officers, Manfred Kranz, Uwe Misch and Heinz Durer, rose and followed him out, but Peter stayed behind and spoke to Martin Seidel, one of those quietly necessary people that every organization has; a discreet master of administration.

***

He was waiting in Conrad's office when his friend arrived at work the next morning. He had ridden through the stifling dawn, and was conscious of being dusty, rumpled and wild-eyed.

The atmosphere in the law offices was oppressive, and Peter's anxiety had intensified by the time Conrad entered and closed the door behind him. Peter thrust an envelope at him. "Paperwork for you to fill in. It's already signed and stamped. Just provide photographs, and you will be on your way to Switzerland with your mother and Greta."

Conrad looked at the papers in Peter's hand without taking them, and shook his head.

"I won't run and hide, Peter. Not for myself, and not for my family. It is important that Germany understands why we did this thing and that we do not renounce our principles. What I did was right, and I will stand up and say that for the world to hear." His voice shook slightly, and he swallowed hard and took a deep breath, "I only hope that the world will indeed hear it. No, I will not shame myself, my family and my name by running, but please, Peter, take my mother and Greta to safety." He held out an envelope of his own, smiling weakly, "I too have papers ready because I knew you would come here, defying all common sense. I am asking you to take my place as my mother's son. In this envelope are all the photographs and documents that you will need for Greta and Mama."

A strange expression drifted across his eyes then, a wondering bewilderment that chilled Peter's bones. "Why did it fail, Peter? Why is it that he could not be killed? Does he really have God on his side? I was so sure it is the devil who stands with him."

He closed his eyes tightly. "Fromm turned against us in the middle of it all," he said. "He had them all killed on the spot to ensure that his own ambivalence remained a secret. Do you know about Beck?" Peter nodded, and Conrad turned to stare out of the window at the grey sky. "He asked them to leave him with his revolver, so that he could take the consequences of his actions upon himself. He shot himself in the head, but the bullet only wounded him. He wanted to try again, so they propped him up while he held the gun to his head. When he failed again, Fromm ordered a sergeant to haul him off into a side room and shoot him. That's what they're going to do with all of us, Peter, they will drag us through the dust, like dogs."

Peter leaned suddenly and heavily against the desk, his fingers scrabbling, trying to find a grip on the polished wood.

The images flung themselves at him; Beck, meeting his death slowly and sickeningly, forced to reflect on the futility of his betrayal of his pledge, on the corruption of honour, the mockery of dignity. He saw the fine hands twitching as oblivion came grudgingly, fixing the acute blue eyes in immutable despair. *I am loath to die the dishonourable death of a traitor, to die like a dog, cudgelled to death by thugs.*

"Peter?" Conrad's voice was pinched. Peter forced the spasms in his fingers to relax as he looked up blindly. His friend was staring at him in horror. "Damn it, Peter! You said you knew."

"I knew he was dead."

Conrad closed his eyes.

"Dead? Ah, Peter, death is not what matters. What matters now is the disgrace they will heap upon us, and the worst thing of all is that he will rise higher standing on the mound of our dishonour. Come, you have to leave now," he said, suddenly urgent, "you shouldn't be here. Please, Peter, keep yourself out of trouble, and get Greta and my mother out of Germany."

Forcing himself into a semblance of functioning, Peter answered bluntly.

"I will get Greta and your mother out, Conrad, of course I will, but after I do that, I will be going down too. When the Gestapo search through Gehlen's files they will see whose signature is on the requisition form for the British explosives, and then I will be joining you."

An angry light entered Conrad's eyes.

"You're a fool if you don't find a way to lose that evidence. For God's sake, don't you see that this is not your fight?" Registering the twist of pain his words caused, he shook his head and persisted. "This was your father's country, Peter; it is not yours. Damn it, it's not even *my* country. I have given my life for the memory of a Germany that no longer exists, but you... you still have your country to fight for. Don't throw yourself on this funeral pyre, because, make no mistake, your country will be next." He went to the door and held it open. "Go now. For your own sake, don't let yourself be destroyed, and for my sake, please get Greta and Mama out of Germany."

Walk through that door? Simply allow it all to happen, without a fight?

"No, Conrad. There has to be a way…"

"Peter, please," Conrad's voice cracked, and he cleared his throat. "There is certain to be no dignity in what remains of my life, so please grant me dignity in this moment."

Peter's lungs seized. That was good; if he refused to breathe again, he could die now without having to accept what was happening, without having to face the insanity, the screaming cruelty of all this. But it was not to be. "Goodbye, my friend," Conrad shook his hand awkwardly, then pulled him into an abrupt embrace, and Peter imploded like a lightbulb, sucking in ragged, unwanted breaths. He had only one fraction of a moment left in which to feel the physical presence of his friend, to feel Conrad's arms clamped around his shoulders, his chest pressed against his own. One fraction of a moment that would have to serve for the rest of his life, however long that would be. When Conrad released him, he walked away from the building into a world that was dissolving even as he passed through it.

26
This is a healing room

He stood in the hospital wing, in the seventh room, staring into the void beyond the window. The countess von Heiden and Greta had taken the papers from his hands and torn them up. 'You were not raised in this country, Peter,' the countess had said, 'But you have known Germany because you have known my son. Beautiful, brave, honourable and proud.' She closed her eyes, and the eyelids, veined and tired, clung to the aged roundness beneath. 'My son will give his life for Germany, and I will give mine. It grieves me to know that this will not be enough to cure the disease, but what happens next is not for us to know about.'

'Your Excellency, please,' he had pleaded, 'I gave Conrad my word that I would keep you safe. He... he asked me to be a son to you.'

The countess sighed. 'Your promise will enable Conrad to face his death with peace of mind, and that is of unimaginable importance both to him and to me, but I must act according to my own conscience.' She stood up, kissed his cheek, 'And Peter, you are already a son to me. All I ask of you, my son, is that you carry the memory of this family forward, to whatever will be left of Germany when all this is over.'

This is a healing room. If he were to turn away from this

window and take three steps... if he were to throw himself on the mercy of that bed, would he heal? No. Not when there were still wounds to be suffered.

He returned to his room and lay, fully clothed, on his own bed.

A disembodied hand took him and flung him against the wall. As he hung there, pinned, steel bars speared out from the stonework and sealed themselves into a cage around him. The wall crumbled behind him, disintegrating into nothing, leaving him floating inside the floating cage, touching nothing. The hand reached out, took hold of the skin on his left shoulder, and with a quick motion, twisted and yanked, peeling it cleanly from his frame. In a dreadful passivity he watched his skin, complete with face, disappear into the darkness through the bars of the cage.

He woke in a cold sweat and stared around his room. The clock was ticking softly on the bedside table, but he couldn't make sense of the figures on its face, and when he reached out to take hold of it there was no hand to grasp it with, just the empty sleeve of his uniform. A ghostly pain made him look down to see that his chest was splitting and gaping open, the two halves splaying wide in supplication, like two hands pleading. He lifted his head and cried out with grief and loneliness, and woke to the sound of his own voice rupturing the silence.

"Mamgu!"

Instantly there was another presence beside him, and a sigh of infinite sadness settled around his shoulders. Snakes writhed out of the troubled air and coiled themselves around his chest, gently but firmly closing his ribcage and holding his chest together.

"Honour and courage have always been with you, Peter," came his grandmother's voice, "allow common sense and humanity to embrace you now."

He lay there, lost. His grandmother's advice had never fallen so far short of the mark.

***

Late the following afternoon, General Gehlen requested his immediate presence at Zossen.

"Major Brandt, there can be no easy way for you to hear this news," he said when Peter arrived, "so I will be blunt. Count Conrad von Heiden was executed today at Plotzensee Prison." A vacuum formed around him, through which he barely heard the man warning him to distance himself from the situation. "And let me tell you a painful truth, Peter," he concluded, "Those men, noble, honourable, and brave as they may have been; they are failures." Peter flinched and stared at him. Gehlen returned his stare. "They are failures," he repeated firmly. "Regardless of what they did and why they did it, they failed. Tell me, Peter, what can those men do now to build the Germany they dreamed of?"

"May I be dismissed, sir?"

Gehlen's eyes narrowed. "Where are you planning to go?"

"To offer my condolences to the countess von Heiden in Berlin."

Gehlen sighed deeply and shook his head.

"I would strongly advise you against that, but it is not for me to stop you if you insist." He paused, glanced at his watch, and frowned. "You will have missed the last train into Berlin, but you may stay in this compound tonight, and if, after sleeping on it, you are still set on going, there is something else you can do while you are there. I would like you to attend the initial screening of Goebbels new instructional film, tomorrow at this address." He wrote the address on a notepad and handed it to Peter. "It is expected to be compulsory viewing for all officers, and I would like you to preview it for me."

27
Terrorize him

"What is this? And this? And this?" Tommie forced her eyes away from the naked light bulb that dangled on a cable from the ceiling above her. It wasn't lit, so there must be daylight somewhere, because she could see Steiger standing in front of her, brandishing a bunch of uprooted plants. "These were found growing in the plot that you have been cultivating at the castle," he snapped. "What are they?"

She squinted at them.

"Vegetables, Major Steiger, they're vegetables." Was the cultivation of vegetables a crime of such magnitude? She was disoriented. Strobing images played through her mind; she had been gagged, handcuffed and shackled before she had even woken up to the presence of SS men in her room... to the presence of Steiger in her room. It had been quick, quiet and efficient, and she had been carried out of the officers' quarters like a roll of carpet.

Thankfully, Simon had stayed asleep. Only Bainbridge had been awake, standing in their way; "Where are you taking her? Do you have the commandant's authority...?" A rifle butt had been swung at him. He had caught hold of the gun and wrenched it out of the man's hands, but a blow from behind knocked him off his feet.

Bainbridge, the big, disconcerting teddy bear, felled like

a great tree, lying stretched out and unmoving on the flagstones. Her muscles twitched, wanting to tend to him, but she wasn't there any more, she was here, wherever here was.

Outside the castle, she had been hooded, bundled into some sort of vehicle, and driven to this place. The hood had been removed, and the handcuffs and shackles were gone, but now she was tied with rough rope to a squat wooden chair in a bleak, square concrete cell with no windows, just a door in front of her that opened onto an equally bleak corridor. Between her and the door stood Steiger.

"Vegetables, yes," he snapped, "but this! This isn't a vegetable, so what is it for?" He pushed a fistful of meadowsweet into her face, "This is not for eating," he shouted. "Tell me what you are growing."

A sudden wave of rage broke over her at the sight of the delicate flowers, crushed in his grip, but their scent, cool and creamy, reached fresh little fingers out to her in the stale air of the cell, and, suppressing the futile anger, she drew a long, levelling breath.

"That's meadowsweet. It's a medicinal plant that I use for coughs, for an eyewash, and to control wound infections..." She stopped and shook her head, "Why am I here, Major Steiger?"

"You are accused of performing an illegal abortion on Katrianna Zahn, a young woman in this town."

Disorientation side-swiped her.

"An abortion? I am a midwife, not an abortionist, and how would I perform an abortion when I've been locked up in the castle..."

"The girl's lover – the father of her murdered child – is employed at the castle. He has testified that you provided him with a concoction made from your herbs. From pennyroyal, to be precise."

Relief swept over her; it was a simple mistake. "Pennyroyal is for coughs and colds. An infusion of Pennyroyal will not bring on an abortion. There is no safe remedy that will do that. There never has been."

Steiger's eyes took on a metallic glint. "'There never has been' you say. So, you have knowledge of the ancient practices; herblore and such?"

"It is the history of my profession."

"Abortion?"

"Not abortion. Herblore. Pennyroyal will not cause an abortion."

"On the contrary, I have done some reading on the subject, and I understand that pennyroyal oil is guaranteed to cause an abortion."

"Pennyroyal oil is lethal. It will bring on an abortion only by causing the mother an agonising death."

"Indeed, fraulein. That being the case, you will face the charge of murder."

She felt a stillness descending on her, the stillness of a small mammal in the presence of a predator poised to strike. "I have no access to Pennyroyal oil and it is not a substance that I can manufacture. If I am to be brought to trial on charges of murder, Major Steiger, it must be before a legitimate court."

He gave a rattling, phlegmy laugh. "A legitimate court? You should have been shot on the streets of Paris, but instead, you arrived on my doorstep, and I, in my ignorance, installed you in that castle, and now I must face the consequences of my actions."

"Are you going to try me for murder in this room?"

"No. The verdict on the charge of murder is a foregone conclusion; that would be a waste of my time. This trial is one that must be conducted under strictly controlled conditions."

"What trial would that be, then, Major Steiger?"

"Why, your trial for witchcraft, fraulein."

Witchcraft.

She had heard the word, whispered in her head, even before he said it, and now her dream was squatting all around her – *that* dream. The one where she faced the devil. What was happening here was not a dream, but it was what the dream had been all about.

So, Steiger wanted to cry 'witch,' did he? She had listened to Bainbridge translating the German newspapers that were distributed in the castle, and it seemed that Hitler had seized the reins of religion in Germany; between the pagan German Faith Movement and the Deutsche Christen, he had not only effectively made himself the High Priest of Germany, he had also overthrown the Pope. If Steiger had been raised as a Catholic – and the accusation of witchcraft and abortion was a pretty good indicator of this – then he was spattered all over with heresy. Did he really think conducting one furtive witch trial would absolve him of that?

Religion and superstition; where did the distinction lie? Not important right now, she would use them both on him. And science too; the first time she had seen Steiger, his fingers and eyes had been yellow, and the yellow was still there, more pronounced now; the signs of advanced gall bladder disease. Steiger was defying the laws of nature by even standing upright. She would drive him into a frenzy and induce a medical crisis before he could go much further with this.

"Witchcraft?" she said slowly, "Am I a witch because I am a midwife? What about you, Major Steiger? What were you? Catholic? What are you now?" Holding his eyes with hers, she shook her head. "I have seen that banner; the swastika first and foremost, and the sun in place of the Son. So very pagan! *Blood and Soil*, isn't that the slogan? Would you have the Son of God kneel before the sons of Thor and the daughters of Freya? And how does it feel to have your own church purged along with the rest of them?"

The muscles in Steiger's face twitched.

"The catechism is mistaken, and the Bible is corrupted. It must be re-interpreted within the parameters prescribed by the Fuhrer."

Tommie smothered her reaction, and gave him a moment to reflect on his words, because he had condemned himself. This could be over quicker than she had anticipated. She laughed lightly.

"'Think not of God, Faustus, think of the Devil,'" she said, "'And Faustus vows never to look to Heaven, never to name God, or to pray to him, to burn his Scriptures, slay his ministers, and make spirits pull his churches down.'" Steiger paled, his skin turning to sulphur, but he shook his head imperatively.

"The swastika marks the Aryan people as the chosen ones of God."

"So, the swastika has supplanted the cross, has it?" Tommie said, musingly, then chuckled. "'Repent, Faustus, repent.'" She paused, "Oh! Too late; there's no real church left for you, Major Steiger. No priest to hear your confession, nobody to grant absolution, nobody to intercede for you with God. Just the Church of Germany; a profane monument to national pride. A golden calf. You have taken the sacraments, Major Steiger, all except one... but can a heretic take the final sacrament?" Steiger's face lost its definition, slipping into an expression remarkably like fear. *Terrorize him.*

"Hitler's got it all sewn up, hasn't he," she said glibly. "Whether they're Christian or pagan, the German people get Hitler – and only Hitler – as their god." Inside her head she heard the crunch of flesh as her teeth met through the side of her mouth. The imprint of Steiger's hand burned its shape on her face as her mouth filled with blood, and she tried not to gag on the salty heat of it.

"You presume to mock the Fuhrer?" He shrieked, "The Fuhrer is a visionary! You are an abomination!"

She turned towards him, her eyes scorching with fury, and saw him double up, clutching his abdomen briefly, then straighten, wiping his mouth with his sleeve. She nodded and spoke softly, menacingly, as blood ran down her chin.

"That is the second time that you have hit me like that, Major Steiger. Be warned; your temper could be the death of you." Her instincts were true; Steiger wiped the hand that had made contact with her on his trousers. She saw that he, too, recognized the significance of this, and made a conscious effort to stabilize himself, but then he doubled up again, turned and hurried out of the room.

From the end of the corridor came the sounds of retching. The two guards stationed at the door glanced uncertainly at each other, but remained in position either side of the doorway.

Tommie closed her eyes for a moment and tried to steel herself for what was to come.

***

This was Berlin: shells of buildings which stared, shocked, upon their own entrails; a landslide of rubble with – half-way up – the leg of an elderly woman protruding. Winding blue veins meandered upwards from the swollen ankle in its felted wool slipper.

Peter closed his eyes, trying to form some sort of prayer, but a prayer wouldn't come.

This was Berlin: The von Heiden house being stripped, its contents loaded onto a truck. He approached an SS officer who was supervising the scene.

"Where are the people who lived here?" he asked.

"They have been shot, filthy bitches. They were to be arrested for treason, but they refused to leave the house, so they were shot where they stood, along with the man-servant."

A window was thrust open, and someone inside began to throw things into the garden below. Darkness filled Peter's brain as he recognized the paintings from the drawing-room. One by one, more paintings were tossed out, and there was a sharp crack as the corner of one frame burst through the canvas of another.

Peter caught the eye of the officer again.

"If you're not taking those, why don't you let me have a few? They might be valuable someday."

The man snorted.

"Nice try, but the valuable ones are in the truck already. What's left are just family portraits, and who wants portraits of such a family?"

"But the frames," persisted Peter, "they look like expensive frames. Won't you pass me a few? Even if they're only good for firewood."

The man grinned.

"An officer of the Wehrmacht, scavenging for firewood? I think you chose the wrong uniform, and I chose the right one." Stepping over the flattened shrubs, he pulled a few paintings from the top of the pile. The portrait of the countess' mother was in his hands. "Here!" he said, "Heil Hitler!"

This was Berlin: an SS lieutenant noting down names on a clipboard at the trial screening of Goebbels' new film. In the darkened auditorium, seventy-five officers watched as the rabid Roland Freisler presided over the People's Court.

On the screen, in the dock, stood men whom Peter recognized, and with a dull sense of inevitability, his eyes followed the line of faces to where Conrad stood, upright and composed.

The screen flickered, the eight defendants were sentenced to be hanged, and the proceedings concluded with the words "The army has purged itself of you and cries Heil Hitler! We all cry Heil Hitler!"

Peter lowered his head, but now the muttering in the room erupted into a collective gasp, and he looked up to see eight men dangling naked, each one kicking and swinging on a noose of piano wire suspended from meat hooks in the ceiling.

Peter was on his feet, but there was no breath to scream with as Conrad's body convulsed and swung from its wire noose.

Something happened to him then, but he was never to know quite what; only that he remembered being in the lobby, pinning the SS lieutenant to the wall above his head, and he had found breath to scream with.

Behind him, a colonel wearing the double bars of the General Staff was striding across the lobby, pulling off his name tag, flinging it to the floor. Then the swing doors of the makeshift auditorium opened again. And stayed open. The SS lieutenant had counted seventy-five officers in, and seventy-five officers advanced on him now in a tidal wave of outrage. Peter closed his eyes briefly, then opened them.

"The army says 'Heil Hitler,' does it?" he snarled. He jabbed a finger against the man's clipboard. "You had better start writing names." He dropped the man, picked up the portraits, clutched them to his chest, and left the theatre.

***

"Consider the book of Revelation!"

Tommie startled to wakefulness. She could not tell how long she had been asleep, or how long Steiger had been gone, but he was back, with Boehm standing behind him, and now he was armed with a long iron crowbar. Behind Boehm were two guards, stationed in the doorway.

"'Babylon the great,'" Steiger continued, "'The mother of whores and of every obscenity on earth... Fallen, fallen is Babylon the great! She has become a dwelling for demons, a haunt for every unclean spirit... Because of this her plagues shall strike her in a single day, for mighty is the Lord God who has pronounced her doom.'" He paused and stared at her, breathing heavily, a froth of spittle on his lower lip, "You know your Bible, Fraulein West. Have you not read these verses?"

More to the point, Major Steiger, Tommie thought to herself, *you* have read those verses, and most Catholics haven't, so it seems that you've been doing some research, and I know where that will have led you. I will guide you in the right direction, but just how far down this rabbit hole do we need to go?

"Yes, I have read those verses, Major Steiger," she said, calmly, "They foretell the self-destruction of mankind in its alliance with the antichrist and its rebellion against God, but I can't think that you brought me here to discuss theology."

"No, I didn't." Steiger gestured to Boehm, who stepped

forward, flipping open a straight-edged razor. "'Confess, witch,'" said Steiger, deliberately, "'for the Evil One is speaking with your voice.'"

This was a different tone, and one that sent a wash of fear over Tommie; those were not Steiger's own words, and he wasn't quoting from the Bible. Those words came from The Malleus Maleficarum, or some other, more obscure witch-hunter's handbook.

One of the two guards crossed the room to take Tommie's neck and jaw in a vice-like grip, and the razor passed in quick, practiced strokes over her head. Terror obliterated rational thought; this was too bizarre, yet too familiar, yet too extreme to be believed.

When Boehm had finished, she felt her pyjama jacket being ripped open, heard the buttons ping into the corners of the room, felt Boehm's hand pulling at the chest band, saw him flip open his razor again and reach for the bandages.

"Leave that!" snapped Steiger, and Boehm cursed under his breath, then slashed her pyjama legs and sleeves with quick, sharp movements. Finally, when the pyjamas were no more than tattered shreds, Steiger waved him away and stood before her, his eyes scanning her exposed flesh. He spotted the birthmark on her right shoulder, drew a knife from its leather sheath, and bent over her, applying it to the birthmark. Pain filled her body.

"'Renounce the serpent, who, even in God's own garden, drew the first – the only – pure woman into sin, defiling forever God's creation. Disown the serpent, who enticed the first man into contaminating himself with a craving for woman's filthy flesh.'"

The knife dug deeper, and she cried out, but urgent pieces of thoughts were flying at her, undercutting the pain; don't submit. He will not show mercy. Fly straight into the storm. Drive him to collapse.

Steiger's illegal homosexuality, the sacrilege of the Deutsche Christen, his Catholicism; these could not possibly co-exist in him. They were tearing him apart, but what she was doing – wielding religion and doctrine like a sword –

was dangerous for everyone involved.

Terrorize him.

Her teeth were chattering with pain.

Terrorize him or submit to him.

"If man and woman and knowledge were God's creations, Major Steiger," she said with difficulty, "then God created them to live in union, in whichever configuration..."

"Not in union!" he shouted, flinging out his arm. The knife, slick with her blood, flew out of his hand, grazing Boehm's leg. "Not in union. Not in union! Union is the machinery of our punishment, and I am being mangled by that machinery. The Grandmaster of the witches – you see, I have done my research – the Grandmaster of the witches, named for the antichrist, Simon, the Magus, has summoned me to be his pander, leading me, in my blindness, to set you up as whore to your people and consort of your master, but I will reverse my folly. Yes, here in this room I will redeem myself."

Incite him. Lure him deeper down the rabbit-hole.

"What does this... this trial have to do with Simon Magus?" she said, twisting against the ropes.

"You claim no knowledge of Simon Magus?"

"No, I don't claim that. I know he was the leader of one of the early Christian sects. He was called Magus; the magician."

"Indeed, and though the world in its ignorance will mock me for what I am about to do, I will accept that humiliation as my penance for having fallen into his thrall; for having united you with your master."

"My master?" Exhausted, Tommie retreated into a quiet, blurred place where the shrill alarm bells triggered by Steiger's words were muffled. *Whore to your people... consort of your master.*

***

Leaning his head against the window of the darkened railway station, Peter closed his eyes. The raging swell of fury that had carried him from the screening had subsided, leaving him in a place of desolation. The last train out of Berlin had left long before he had found himself here, so he sat and waited for the morning, watching the fractured skyline of the city glowing with the feverish, intermittent pulse of the fires that burned deep down in the rubble.

He was the angel of death. Everyone around him died. A prickling fog obliterated his memory of the past few hours, and he listened to the profound lack of breathing in the world.

The snakes that his grandmother had sent to hold him together had hardened into steel bands that bit into his chest. He had no further need of them; it was no longer necessary to stay whole, and yet still the bands held him together.

The promise he had made to Conrad, the one that had given him comfort as he went to his death, was broken, and his promise to the countess – to pass on the memory of her family to future generations – that obligation would soon be taken out of his hands because his signature was still right there on the explosives requisition form in Gehlen's office, and the Gestapo were agitating for access to FHO's files.

Before long, he would be seized, smashed, and drawn into that void along with the others, and how he yearned for that moment, but for now he adjusted his own breathing pattern; light, shallow and functional, in preparation for the moment when it, too, would cease.

All around him, a frail sky darkened to bruised purple, stretching across the horizon like a corpse with the heat of its life seeping away.

***

The scream brought her back with a shock that left her nerves shrieking in response. It was a man's voice, razored with pain as it rang out again, echoing down the corridor.

Steiger was watching her closely.

"The Magus," he said, softly, "Gnostic, heretic, disciple of Satan. Your familiar, your devil, your master." His thin lips curled. He made a gesture at Boehm, who was standing in the doorway, and Boehm called an order. Another scream, and Steiger shook his head wonderingly, "There is even beauty in his extremity; if I needed further evidence that he is not entirely human, there it is." He smiled again, "Your master. Simon."

Tommie's skin crept with a thin wave of horror. She remembered the stunned expression on Steiger's face as he first saw Simon in the interrogation room at the castle.

"Simon *Leigh?*" she said. They were words spoken in a nightmare. Not real. "You've brought Simon here?" No. It was a nightmare. Not real.

But then another scream echoed around the walls, and she woke up.

"For his *name*, Major Steiger? For his *name?*" Her voice rose on a shriek and Steiger's face settled into a smirk. "You would do this to him because his name is Simon?!"

Another scream tore through the air, and all the breath left Tommie's lungs in a primal grunt. It had been pure arrogance on her part to confront Steiger in the way that she had done – an unforgivable arrogance now that Simon was involved.

Terrorizing Steiger hadn't worked. She would humble herself. Maybe that would appease him. She would plead. She stared into his face and pleaded. "Please, Major Steiger, Simon has nothing to do with this. He's as innocent as a lamb. He has no knowledge of what we've been talking about."

"He doesn't know you're a witch?"

She allowed not even an eyelid's flicker of hesitation. "I'm not a witch." A deep, visceral thud sounded from the next room, and Tommie's insides became offal on a butcher's slab. Simon was being held in place, while Steiger's men put their whole, brutal weight into their task; she could see his body jolting, flung around like a rag doll, his vital organs rupturing. "Oh, God, no. Stop them, Major Steiger, please! Make them stop. I'll talk! Let me talk!" She choked, her words stumbling over each other. "Leave him alone. Please! Stop them!"

Steiger barked an order down the corridor, and silence fell, punctuated by a few diminishing groans. Tommie heard her own breathing, raw and ragged. If she confessed to being a witch, as Steiger wanted, then Simon would be implicated. The cell was lit by an eye-prickling, sulphurous glare, and she was balancing on a knife-edge. Impossible to take a step without falling into the darkness, pulling Simon down with her. Steiger leaned down and brought his face close to Tommie's ear so that his breath brushed her neck, and she flinched away.

"Is he cold to the touch, this... Simon, or is he warm?" Tommie shuddered at the silkiness in his voice as Steiger circled around behind her. "Is his skin smooth? Is it scaly?" His breathing was accelerating, "Is his skin warm, fraulein? Is it smooth and warm?" he persisted, "Is he warm, Fraulein? Is he warm to the touch? Or is he cold? Is his semen hot, fraulein?" he whispered hoarsely. "Tell me! Is his semen hot or is it cold?"

A ragged, gurgling scream sounded from the next room and Tommie echoed it.

"Ah! No! For God's sake, he's innocent. He's like sunlight. You only have to look in his eyes to see his soul. Just go in there and look at him, Major Steiger, just look in his eyes and see."

The words provoked a shocking transformation in Steiger. He backed away from her, lifting his hands in a muddled gesture of protection, a jumble of instinct and superstition, slashing his hands at her in a vicious sign of the cross.

"What you offer is evil, God-forsaken fiend!"

Fear.

It was as though a dark lantern had released a flicker of hope; Steiger had power over what happened to Simon, but he feared her.

Terrorize him.

She wanted to fly at him, claw her fingernails into his eye sockets, tear him apart, but she was bound to the chair.

"'God-forsaken?!'" she snapped. "Do you dare to speak for God, Steiger? Do you risk sacrilege for my poor sake? Which church do you claim authority from? The old church? The one that is so good at this sort of thing? No, Major Steiger, because in the eyes of that church you are a heretic. You have no power over me, Major Steiger. I do not give you the authority to deny me God."

"Then receive God's judgement from His own hands!" he snarled. White-lipped with fury, he snapped a command at Boehm, who stepped forwards drawing his knife.

The blade cut through the ropes, and Tommie's arms, abruptly released, swung down, flailing violently. Sheet lightning seared through her body, and she screamed as the tendons in her shoulders burst into flame.

"Now!" Steiger roared, "Now put your hands together, witch! Put your hands together and pray if you can! And if you can't, then know that God condemns you."

It was as though her arms had been wrenched out of her shoulders, and a pair of ungainly, fleshy wings had been jammed into the empty sockets. She had no control over them. Their tortured muscles bunched into peculiar, lumpy shapes, and they flapped wildly with the residual movements of the unholy creature they had been wrenched from.

"See?!" shrieked Steiger triumphantly, "The demons that writhe within her will tear her apart before they let her put her hands together in prayer."

She watched, strangely detached, as her left wing pulled itself along a protruding nail on the arm of the chair. The soft, pale flesh on the underside split open from wrist to elbow, and blood welled out, spattering around the room with its thrashing motions.

"Restrain her!" shouted Steiger, retreating in disgust to the corridor. An airless blackness filled Tommie's head. No thoughts troubled her, and she felt only a sensation of passive movement as her arms were taken and twisted once more behind her back. "So, now you are most assuredly godless, witch," growled Stieger, "Confess and repent before the scourge of God."

"The scourge of God, Steiger? Is that how you see yourself?" The voice should have been hers, but it wasn't. "No. You are just a sick man."

Wheezing with fury Steiger whipped around and shrieked to someone down the corridor.

"Spare nothing on him! No extremity he suffers may be cause for mercy, and death throes are not to be considered death throes until I myself have pronounced him dead."

This time there was no more than a hoarse grunt in response to a resounding blow, but it seemed that God's hand had punched itself through Tommie's chest. Could it be that Steiger was right? That God was with him? That God was nothing more than a spiteful, vindictive, *human* being; no better than the gods of Olympus and Rome?

"You are beyond redemption, witch," said Steiger, "That young man down the corridor, however, still stands a chance." His voice was suddenly, temptingly, coated with reason. "Would you deny him that chance? Your confession might persuade me to release him... if he is still alive by the time you come to your decision."

There was a God-sized hole in her chest. *Religion and superstition.* She lifted her head and struggled to think.

"But I'm not a witch, Major Steiger, and if I do as you want... if I claim to be a witch, then Simon will be condemned by his association with me."

"Perhaps not," he said slowly. "Perhaps I was mistaken about his involvement. I might still show him mercy."

"I don't trust you."

"That's a pity."

He lifted his hand and Boehm called down the corridor. A grating screech, barely recognisable as human, echoed from the walls and subsided into a bubbling gurgle. A fluid darkness soughed at Tommie's feet; a tar pool which dissolved the stone floor of the cell and plummeted down into nothingness. She stared into the blackness. Was that Hell, down there? As literal as it had always been depicted?

"'I therefore adjure thee, thou most foul spirit, in the name of Jesus Christ of Nazareth,'" Steiger's voice, chanting, yanked her back to reality. He was pacing steadily in a circle around her, pouring salt from a glass bowl to form a ring on the stone floor around her chair. "'Go out, thou wicked one, for God hath willed that man shall be His temple.'" He completed the ring of salt and stopped in front of her, squinting into a black, leather-bound book. "'Give place to the Holy Ghost, Who by His blessed Apostle Peter struck thee to the ground in Simon Magus...'"

Tommie stared at him. Had she somehow summoned him from Hell... or had he been drawn to something hellish in *her*? She blinked and cleared her mind. She had had a plan at one point, hadn't she? But it wasn't working; look at him... calmly chanting from the book. Her brain juddered sideways. Calmly? No. He was performing an exorcism, and no exorcism had ever been performed in a state of calm; exorcisms were performed by people who thought they were battling the forces of Hell. There was one more thing she could try. The thought of it frightened her more than she cared to admit, but she had nothing more to offer. Time to open the gates of Tartarus.

Tisiphone brought with her poisons of magic power: lip-froth of Cerberus, the Echidna's venom, wild deliriums, blindnesses of the brain, and crime and tears, and maddened lust for murder; all ground up, mixed with fresh blood, boiled in a pan of bronze, and stirred with a green hemlock stick.

She lowered her head and stared into the darkness that undulated at her feet. Soft fingers reached up, caressing her toes, her instep and her ankles and sliding shockingly up her legs. Fright prickled her body and she jerked back, but Steiger's ritual muttering rose and fell, and she knew that there could be no pulling back. There was force or passivity. Or no-man's land.

She let go and allowed herself to tip forward.

"'And the same Apostle, by his word of command, bade

thee come out of the damsel possessed with the spirit of divination...'" She could hear Steiger's voice intoning the ancient words, but he was far away. He was up there in the dank air of the cell, while Tommie knew herself to be in another place entirely. A dark place. A place of flames. She was hot. Her lungs expanded with air that licked her soul with tongues of fire. Oh, the power! Her chest rose with the heat of it, and her blood pumped lava.

She drank her fill of the flames, then rose up to meet Steiger, lifting her head slowly and smoothly, fixing him in her gaze. The red fire streaming from her eyes blasted his yellow skin and turned him orange. She grinned, because it was funny, then released a guttural roar that carried legion voices in it. When the roar had subsided, taking with it what remained of the colour in Steiger's face, she drew another breath and laughed loudly.

"You think your little salt ring will keep you safe, Steiger?" she said in a voice that was deep and strong and hot. "You think they are all in here with me? Wrong! It is you who have summoned them; you and your swastika. Look!" Her wrists were bound behind the chair, but she beckoned with her fingertips – tiny, teasing movements of each individual fingertip – and the shadows that crouched in his mind swarmed to her command.

Rigid, Steiger stood outside the circle of salt, his eyes shut tight over eyeballs that flickered and twitched. His lips moved, and she could hear the occasional sibilant as he muttered.

She laughed again, and the voices laughed in a hellish chorus with her.

"Where is your crucifix, Major Steiger? That nasty little crucifix? Oh, you threw it away, and now you have only the swastika, and they *like* the swastika. Here they come!" She shrieked in glee. "Here they come, Major Steiger, can't you feel them?" and she sucked up the blackness of the pit with her eyes and flung it around into the furthest corners of the room, hurling monstrous creatures at the man who stood, trembling, before her. The imps screeched with jubilation, cavorting around Steiger's feet, leaping onto his back and clambering onto his shoulders. She summoned up the hideous creatures from The Temptation of Saint Anthony, adding a few creations of her own, with scaly legs and plucked-bald, goose-pimpled bodies. Her voice was rising in pitch, and now she could see her words, inscribed in flame, burning in the air before her.

"Where is your precious salt ring now, Steiger?" she cackled, "Ah! Look! Look at them all; they are out there with you, charmed by those swastikas you wear. How do those swastikas feel now, Steiger? Are they burning? Yes, they're smouldering! Your flesh is charring!"

She laughed in delight, then allowed a moment of silence to drop into the room – a moment of silence that bared its fangs.

"You cannot drink the cup of the Lord if you sip from the goblet of devils, Major Steiger," she snarled, "You have summoned them and they have come, turgid from all the adulation, all the singing, all the torchlit invocations of your master. They have been given lebensraum! Oh! They love your master!"

She pressed her tongue behind her teeth and made a whining, hissing sound. Steiger screamed as the devils swarmed over him, squeezing their taut little bodies under his arms, between his legs, tweaking the soft skin of his thighs and poking at his scrotum, pushing their tongues into all his cavities, inserting fingers into his nose, thrusting unclean hands into his mouth.

He staggered and dropped the book, sweeping the creatures away with flailing arms, but they leaped back onto him, chittering and prattling in a demonic gibberish, lifting his hair and tweaking his eyelids.

Then, quite suddenly, there was a hush, and, with a sound like cartilage being separated from bone, another apparition materialized in front of him. Steiger fell very still, taking in the horns that protruded from the skull, the yellow goat-eyes and the cloven feet. With his eyes wide and staring, and spittle foaming at the corners of his mouth, he bent down, picked up the iron crowbar and swung it with all his strength at the figure. The bar passed cleanly through the apparition and connected with Tommie's left leg. Her scream sliced through the thick air in the room and everything fell quiet. Steiger grunted, retrieved his book, found his place and read, his voice thin and reedy.

"'The serpent is the place of thy habitation... The serpent is the place of thy habitation...'"

Barely conscious, Tommie writhed in pain. She had lost her gamble and condemned Simon with her occult theatrics. How long had it been since she had even heard a sound from the room down the corridor?

Swaying, Steiger turned to Boehm, who stood, transfixed, by the door.

"See? He is taking her now; possessing her with his damnable lust." He stepped forwards, scuffing the salt ring around the chair, and swung a vicious kick at Tommie's broken leg. "Witch! She sits there in front of an audience, joined in copulation with her cloven-footed master. She..." abruptly he fell silent and stared down at the broken ring, then turned, retched and stumbled against Boehm, fumbling at the man's uniform. Thoroughly revolted, Boehm pushed him away. Steiger reached out a clawed hand in a futile attempt to repair the ruptured circle, then raised his eyes to the girl, his face twisting in terror. "Now the goat. He has finished, and she gives birth to him. See him coming from between her legs..." He retched and convulsed and lay still.

28
Breathing

Peter entered the west wing and made his way up the stairs, brushing past the duty sentry who tried to approach him.

"Major Brandt! The commandant has left instructions for you to be summoned to his office the moment you arrive." Peter ignored him; he was in no fit state to be speaking to anyone. "Sir! Please, he says it is urgent." The man was at his heels, voice echoing up the stairwell, and Peter cursed violently to himself. Keeping his greatcoat on to discourage an extended visit, he made his way to the commandant's door, knocked and entered.

"Ah, Major Brandt, I'm glad to see you," said Renger. He lifted an arm towards the man sitting across the desk from him, then stopped and stared into Peter's face. Peter could only imagine what he saw there. In the silence, Colonel Gregory rose quickly and spoke.

"Major Brandt, as Senior British Officer at this prison I ask to be allowed to see Miss West. Where is she being held?"

Peter glanced at the commandant.

"Am I to assume that she is not in the British quarters?"

"Major Steiger came here in the early hours of yesterday morning and took Fraulein West," said Renger.

"He took her away from the castle? For what purpose?"

"He didn't see fit to consult me on the matter," said the commandant sourly, "In fact, he did not see fit to consult me on gaining access to the prison at all. He intimidated the duty guards into opening the gates, and took her before anybody knew what was happening." He paused, "You know nothing of this, then?"

"Nothing. He gave no indication of where he was taking her?"

"None. And, as you know, I wouldn't have had the authority to deny him – even if he had offered the courtesy of seeking my permission."

Peter rubbed his eyes roughly, then lifted his head.

"If he has taken her to Berlin then we will not be seeing her again," he said shortly. He was surprised that he could still feel something; a stab of sorrow, nothing more than a burning dart shot into a bonfire, but something. "If he presented no paperwork, though, then this abduction was for his own purposes, in which case he might have taken her to the town prison."

Renger shook his head.

"I have tried to contact the prison several times on the phone, but there was no answer."

"Then it is likely that she is there and Steiger has ordered the staff to keep it quiet. I will ride down there now if you wish, Herr Commandant, and phone from the prison to let you know what I find."

Action. Action might hold the horror at bay.

"Yes, I think that would be best," said Renger, glancing at Gregory. "Further than that, I think there is nothing more that we can do."

"Perhaps you would ask Doctor Henning to prepare himself for a trip," Peter said flatly, "If she is there, then we will have need of his skills."

"Colonel Renger, I would like to accompany the doctor, if it comes to that," Gregory's voice was quiet but firm, "Miss West is a non-combatant, and her status is…unclear, but as a British national she is, in some way, in my charge."

Renger was silent for a moment, and Peter watched as he considered the significance of Gregory's request. Incidents like this, particularly where they concerned the SS, were expected to be swept under the carpet. On the other hand, the girl's presence at the castle had left Renger responsible for her welfare in the eyes of the International Red Cross, and this was a burgeoning consideration. Renger met Peter's eyes with a hunted expression, then turned to the Senior British Officer and nodded curtly.

"Very well, Colonel Gregory, you will go with the doctor if it comes to that."

Heading towards the door, Peter realized that he was still clutching the portraits. The face of the countess' mother gazed at him with Conrad's eyes, and he gently leaned the frames against the wall. "May I leave these here for now, Herr Commandant? Will they be safe?" Renger nodded, distractedly, and Peter left.

The guard at the town prison denied any knowledge of a prisoner in the building, but his eyes flickered nervously down the corridor from which the cells opened, and as Peter headed in that direction, the man scowled and sat back down at his desk.

Each cell Peter passed was empty, but in the last one… he groaned at the sight of the figure slumped in the chair in the middle of the room. The girl's head, shaved and bloodied, had fallen forward, and her shoulders strained against arms that were pulled back and tied behind the chair. Her pyjamas had been slashed open to the groin, and her bare legs were tied to the frame of the chair. Below the left knee her leg projected inwards at a grotesque angle, and the skin stretched, shiny and purple, over the fracture.

The sight of the girl, broken and lifeless, sent him plummeting back into that ocean of brutality where other arms were fastened behind a back; where dangling legs twitched and kicked; where a wire noose tightened around a neck… Stumbling forwards, he fought to insert his fingers under the wire noose, but there was no wire noose.

He found himself kneeling next to the chair. The girl's

neck was warm, and the backs of his fingers felt a substantial pulse beating beneath the skin. Peter closed his eyes and lowered his head to her shoulder. She shifted and moaned, and the sound pulled him together. He stood.

"Fraulein." His voice echoed, dry and rough and loud in the cave-like silence of the room, and the girl flinched. He took a deep breath, "Fraulein," he said again, softly this time.

With difficulty she raised her head, and her eyes found his face. She stared at him for a moment, then looked around, searching the shadowy corners of the cell. Peter shook his head.

"They've gone."

She turned her eyes back to him, and in them was that odd, unfocused double-exposure look that he had seen on the day she arrived at the castle, but puzzled, as though she had been wanting to ask him something, and now found that she had the chance.

"Are you an angel?"

"No!" His voice cracked. Was she a seer, this young woman? Was she seeing the angel of death standing over her? He heard himself pleading for rebuttal, his voice grey and weightless; ashes blowing from a bonfire. "No, fraulein, it's Major Brandt, from the castle."

"I know who you are," she said, "But why do you shine?"

"Shine?" The world lurched back into perspective. Very carefully, he drew a breath. "How long has it been since they left you here?" She blinked the strangeness away, and now her eyes were hazed with confusion.

"I don't know," she answered thinly, straining against the ropes that bound her to the chair, "he hit my leg." Peter stood up, drew his pocket knife, and moved behind the chair to cut the ropes, but she stiffened and cried out. "No! Please don't. He did that too, and I couldn't... I couldn't...."

"I know it will hurt, and I am sorry for it, but the longer your arms stay tied, the more painful it will be when they are released. I will help you."

The pyjama jacket was torn and flapping open, revealing a wide bandage, wound several times around her chest, and her body was painted with dried blood. Other than the broken leg, it was impossible to tell what injuries she had sustained, but, kneeling behind her and slipping his left arm beneath her two arms, he held them firmly against his chest while he cut through the ropes. With the release of the strain, she cried out sharply, but he held her arms in place until he felt her relax a little, then, reaching around the back of the chair, he gently brought them forward.

He felt the stubble of her cropped head against the stubble on his cheek, and the dried blood where a razor had snagged her scalp. He heard her breath catching, and felt her body shuddering with the pain until finally her hands lay, mottled blue and livid red, on her lap. Cautiously releasing her arms, he moved around to squat in front of her. Her face was chalk white as she forced her hands out of her lap and brought them together, shaking violently, palm to palm, then whispered into the savagery of the world.

"No, you do *not* speak for God."

He watched her for a moment more, then unbuttoned his greatcoat and laid it over her, anchoring its shoulders to the back of the chair to keep her from falling forwards. Turning towards the door, he was whipped around with an almost physical wrench by the girl's hoarse shout.

"No! Don't go. He'll come back. Steiger will come back again if you go."

He knelt, bringing his face level with hers.

"I'm not leaving. There is a telephone at the front desk. I am going to phone for Doctor Henning to come here. We will take you back up to the castle."

She listened to his words blearily, and then her eyes widened as though he'd laid Eden at her feet.

"I can go back?" she said. "Simon. Simon too."

"Simon?" said Peter, puzzled. "Flight Lieutenant Leigh?"

"Yes," she said urgently, "They have him in the next room. The doctor should see him first; I don't know if he's…"

"There is nobody else here. Only you."

"No. They have him," she insisted. "They have him in there," She turned her head and stared at the wall of the cell as though she could see into the next room. "They were beating him. He was screaming. And I couldn't make them stop." Her eyes found his again. "He must be there, or where have they taken him? What have they done with him? He's innocent, Major Brandt, he's innocent! What have they done with him?" She shuddered suddenly, convulsively.

"Listen to me," he said firmly, "They were lying. Leigh was not taken from the castle. What you think was happening wasn't real. Do you understand? It wasn't real." The girl shook her head, and he tried again, "I will have Flight Lieutenant Leigh accompany the doctor down here, so you will know he is safe." But she was beyond hearing him now.

After a brief exchange with Renger, Peter replaced the handset and stood for a moment in silence. Henning and Gregory would be here soon, bringing Leigh with them. If only he could bring his own ghosts back from the dead with a quick phone call. If only that wasn't real. He pressed his fists against his temples, it was fortunate that the young woman, sitting bloodied and broken in that cell, could not know that the man they had sent to retrieve her was, himself, so close to collapse. He drew a deep breath and went into the tiny kitchen for a drink of water, then washed and filled the cup again and took it with him to the cell at the end of the corridor.

The girl was sleeping, her chin resting on the collar of his greatcoat, but she woke with a start when he entered the room. He offered her the cup of water, holding it to her mouth, and she drank thirstily.

"Enough," he said, withdrawing the cup, "any more and you will bring it back up." He took out a handkerchief, spilled some of the water onto it, and gently wiped some of the blood from her face. Her eyes drifted closed, and she was sleeping again before he had finished.

He hunkered down on the floor beside the chair and waited. The girl's breathing was slow and even, and he closed his eyes, drawing the sound into the echoing emptiness inside him. Outside of this unanticipated mercy mission, his existence was as pointless as that of a glass ball; he survived in a void, and within himself he encompassed a void. Soon they would come for him, and break him, and then he would be one with the void. He longed for this. Until then, though, the sound of the girl's breathing brought him a thread of comfort.

The arrival in the cell of the contingent from the castle came to him as a violation of some vital intimacy. He stood when he heard the voices approaching down the corridor, and stretched his stiff back as the doctor appeared in the doorway with Gregory and Leigh behind him. All three flinched at the sight of the girl slumped in the chair, and Leigh cursed bitterly, his face tight with horror as he crossed the room and knelt down beside the chair.

Peter gave a brief report to the doctor and retreated to the corner of the room to wait. Leigh was murmuring to the sleeping girl, and after a moment her head lifted and her eyes opened, focusing blearily on him. A soft smile lit her face, like a candle in a fine porcelain lantern, then faded as bitter disbelief snuffed it out. She turned away from him and stared bleakly across the cell. Seeing Gregory and Henning, her expression became uncertain. She searched further, and found Peter's eyes.

"Is this real?"

He swayed slightly, and swallowed hard, pulled back to the quiet moments when it had been just the two of them – out of time.

"Yes. This is real."

She turned back to Leigh.

"Simon, they didn't hurt you?"

"No, love," the muscles in the man's face pulled out of shape, "they hurt you." He stood up jerkily, unbuttoned his greatcoat, yanked the Wehrmacht greatcoat from the chair and flung it across the room at Peter. Without its support, the girl tipped forwards, and Leigh caught her by the shoulder. She yelped in pain, but there were no gentle words of comfort from him; he was frozen in shock, registering the shredded remains of her pyjamas. Gregory's eyes closed briefly, and the doctor winced, but his voice cut firmly through the silence in the room as, clenching his teeth, Leigh anchored the girl to the chair with his own greatcoat.

"Fraulein West, your leg is broken at both the tibia and the fibula. Unfortunately, the nearest good hospital is fifteen miles away, so I must give you chloroform and reduce the fracture here, to stabilize it before subjecting you to that journey."

There was an exclamation of horror from Leigh.

"That's ridiculous! This isn't the Crimea! You can't set her leg under these conditions."

"I will not allow her to be moved fifteen miles with these fractures," snapped the doctor.

"Fraulein West will not be going to a hospital," said Peter levelly, "she must return to the castle."

There was another eruption from Leigh.

"For God's sake, man, can't you stop thinking like a prison guard?"

Peter swept a look of contempt at him, and turned to address the girl, but she had drifted out of consciousness again. He spoke instead to Gregory.

"Colonel Gregory, if she is taken to a public hospital, whoever did this to her would be able to approach her again. Unfortunately, neither the commandant nor I have the authority to deny the SS access to her, but at least at the castle there would be a degree of accountability for her welfare. As Senior British Officer, do you agree to this?"

Gregory nodded gravely.

"Yes, Major Brandt, if it is in Miss West's best interests."

Peter turned to Henning.

"Karl, would it be better for this procedure to be performed in the hospital wing at the castle?"

Glancing down at the girl's leg, the doctor shook his head.

"The damage that we risk in moving her even that short distance outweighs the benefits."

Leigh swept his hand distractedly through his hair.

"But who is going to assist you? You're the only doctor here."

"One doctor is all that's needed," said Henning, borrowing Peter's knife to cut the rope around the girl's left ankle, "for the rest, it is strength that matters." He issued instructions, stationing Peter at the girl's feet, and Leigh and Gregory at her torso.

Kneeling in front of the chair, Peter heard a slight, gritty crunch, and glanced down to find salt scattered all around. Salt? His thoughts were interrupted by Leigh's voice, thick with hostility. The man was shaking with anger.

"I'll take her feet. She shouldn't have some Hun grabbing at her legs."

Peter stood up abruptly.

"Leigh!" Gregory grabbed his junior officer's sleeve as he took a bullish step forward, and Henning's voice echoed angrily in the cell.

"Major Brandt will take her feet, Flight Lieutenant, because neither you nor Colonel Gregory has the strength that will be necessary to pull the bones into place. Now, can we please get started?" Gregory maintained his tight hold of Leigh. "*Now*, I said!" snarled the doctor.

"Flight Lieutenant, stand down," snapped Gregory. Leigh met his eyes, then drew a quick, sharp breath and glanced down at the girl. His eyes flinched over her shaved and bloodied head, and then he crouched down and wrapped his arms around her torso, dipping his head against her shoulder. Gregory knelt too, but kept his eyes on Leigh. In the echoing silence, Henning glanced across at Peter, who was still on his feet, welded to the ground with anger.

"Major Brandt?"

Peter lifted his hand and pressed fingers and thumb across the bridge of his nose. Resuming his position, he felt once more the crunch of salt beneath his knees. Why salt?

"Who are you, Major Brandt?" Glancing up, he found

that the girl's eyes were open and watching him, unfocused again. She sighed as though trying to catch her breath, and suddenly another voice, insubstantial but insistent, was weaving itself with hers, like the wind breathing in summer trees. "Who are you?" the braided voices said, and, kneeling at her feet, Peter could only remain silent, staring into the strangeness of her eyes. "Why do you wear that uniform?" persisted the voices, "You are innocent of its crimes."

"As are many who wear it," he replied, his skin prickling. It was like having a conversation with a sleep talker. Perhaps he was imagining this.

"You hide the soul of an angel inside a borrowed uniform," she said quietly, and a sheet of ice draped him, melting instantly against the heat in his brain, "but I see you, Major Brandt. You are not the enemy. Who are you?"

"Tommie?" Leigh was taking the girl's face in his hands and turning it away from Peter's, towards his own. She blinked and her focus changed. "It's alright, love," he said, "you're not well right now, but we'll soon have you back to normal."

"Please, fraulein, we must start now," said the doctor, his face etched with concern.

"Yes, doctor," she said, "I'm ready."

Henning took a glass bottle from his bag, uncorked it and soaked a gauze pad with the contents. He held the pad over the girl's nose and mouth, watching closely as she went limp and sagged in the chair, then he stationed himself between Peter and Leigh, placing his hands gently at the fracture site. Gregory took hold of the young woman under her arms and around her trunk. Leigh wrapped his arms around her hips. Peter was ready at her ankle to do the pulling, and the doctor lifted her leg into the correct position.

"Now, pull," he said curtly. "Pull smoothly but pull as hard as you can. It is not possible for you to pull too hard. Do you understand?" Peter nodded and sat himself on the floor, bracing his boots against the legs of the chair. He took a firm grip of the girl's ankle and began to pull, carefully at first, but more firmly according to the doctor's instructions.

He kept his eyes fixed on the doctor, but Henning kept shaking his head. Suddenly, the girl's leg began to twitch and shudder with violent spasms, and Peter heard his own voice cry out in horror. The cell lurched and tilted drunkenly around him, and although he screwed his eyes shut, the images came anyway, assailing him from inside his eyelids; images of other legs that jerked and twitched, kicking in helpless, uncontrollable spasms.

"It's just muscle spasm." Henning's voice called him back, "Keep pulling!" Once again silence fell in the room until the doctor's voice rang out, "There! That's it. Colonel Gregory, please bring me that splint, and then take Major Brandt's position. Peter, you should step outside; you look as though you need a breath of air." Peter declined, and then moved out of their way as Gregory knelt where he had been. Again, Peter heard the crunch of salt. There was salt spread all around the chair.

A swift movement caught his eye too late, as Leigh barrelled into him, taking him down with a rugby tackle. Peter went down like a ninepin in an avalanche, and the quiet of the room erupted into chaos.

"Simon!" Gregory cursed, but was forced to remain in position, supporting the girl's leg.

Peter hit the floor, twisted his body around, brought his knees up into a jackknife, braced his boots against Leigh's chest and kicked out, sending the other man staggering backwards across the room. He unclipped his holster and drew his gun. He heard Gregory shout out, but shook his head and, with a flick of his wrist, sent the pistol sliding across the floor and into the corridor, out of reach. He was on his feet, braced and ready, as Leigh came at him again; if the man had a death-wish, then Peter was prepared to grant it.

Hearing the disturbance, the guards who had been stationed in the corridor scrambled into the room, taking aim, and the doctor's voice rang out, hoarse but authoritative.

"Put those guns away, idiots! You'll kill us all! Major

Brandt, Flight Lieutenant Leigh! For God's sake, hasn't there been enough violence done in this room?"

Peter barely heard him. The bitter crust of the volcano that had swelled at the screening of the film had ruptured, and Leigh had leaped into the crater with a can of benzene. He plunged into a blinding rage, finding satisfaction in every blow delivered and received.

Time evaporated and then manifested again, violently, as, with a savage uppercut, he sent Leigh crashing to the floor and threw himself on top of him. Pulling his fist back, he felt the muscles in his arm and shoulder stretching taut and hard, and Leigh, trapped, twisted his head away in anticipation.

Peter froze. The punch he was about to deliver would blast this man's head against the stone-flagged floor with a force that would fracture his skull, and although that thought did not deter him, something about the way Leigh's neck had twisted sideways brought him the memory of another neck twisting; a violence that had not been stayed.

His fist cramped then, as, keening through his rage and his grief for Conrad, came the memory of Tomasin West's voice mourning Leigh's death. What had been a fiction, he was on the cusp of making real. He lowered his arm, and one of the guards darted forward to thrust his rifle into Leigh's face. Peter knocked the weapon away and stood up, wiping his bleeding mouth. Leigh struggled to his feet, and the guards moved to seize him, but Peter ordered them to back off and cover the man's movements from the doorway.

"There will be no arrest," he said tersely, "there has been no incident here, do you understand?"

"But sir, an assault on an officer of the Reich... There must be a report... a court martial..."

"A report of this visit will be completed by Doctor Henning and myself. No other statements will be taken, will they, Herr Doctor?"

"As far as I am concerned, nothing beyond this young woman's deplorable condition requires reporting," replied the doctor without glancing up from his patient. The guards retreated, confused, and Peter turned to where Gregory was still kneeling, supporting the girl's leg.

"I want you to know, Colonel Gregory, that I had no part in this attack on Miss West."

Gregory nodded grimly, but Leigh's voice came darkly from the far corner of the cell, muffled by his rapidly swelling mouth.

"You are an intelligence officer. Interrogation is your business, and it looks as though you're very good at it."

"This is not how I conduct interrogations, and certainly not on Miss West."

"'Not on Miss West'?" Leigh repeated, his voice rising, "Why 'not on Miss West,' Major Brandt? Do you reserve special treatment for her? Is that why her pyjamas are torn to shreds? Is that an example of your special treatment?"

Peter's fists clenched again, and the doctor stood up quickly, looking as though he was undecided whether to restrain Peter or to lunge at Leigh himself, but Peter's anger had ebbed. He relaxed his fists and shook his head wonderingly.

"You are a remarkably stupid man, Flight Lieutenant Leigh."

"When Fraulein West regains consciousness, I am sure she will leave us all in no doubt as to who is responsible for this situation," said Henning. "For now, I am more concerned with getting her back up to the castle. Do you two gentlemen think we can achieve that without starting another brawl?"

The castle's ancient Opel truck wound through the town and up the hill. Riding ahead, Peter arrived first and called for the duty sentry to unlock the door leading to the hospital wing. The truck arrived, and the orderlies carefully lifted the girl's stretcher down.

Mercifully, she was still unconscious as they carried her into the commandantur, her scarred head lolling. There was a scuffle as the duty sentry barred the way against Leigh who had tried to follow them. Leigh called out.

"Major Brandt, will you please tell this man to let me

through?"

Peter held his gaze coldly for a moment.

"Now why would I do that?"

Leigh stared in disbelief.

"You've got to let me go with her," he said, weakly.

Peter lifted his hand to his split lip and swollen face.

"Do you honestly believe that your conduct has earned you that level of trust?"

Leigh spoke stiffly.

"Alright, what I did back there was stupid. A mistake. It won't happen again."

Peter ignored him, turning to the Senior British Officer.

"Colonel Gregory, will you please accompany me to the commandant's office," he said, "I believe Colonel Renger will want to speak with you. The guards will escort Flight Lieutenant Leigh to his quarters." He turned towards the commandantur, but stopped and turned back as Leigh walked deliberately towards him. Gregory stiffened, but Leigh held his hands up, palms outwards, clearly resisting the desire to indeed let it happen again.

"I was stupid, Brandt," he said, pleading now, "but look at the state she's in... I was angry."

Peter rewarded the man with a moment's silence, and, predictably, the self-control failed.

"What is it? Do you think I'll try to escape? For God's sake! After what they've done to her, I wouldn't leave her if you gave me papers and held the door open for me! Let me stay with her, Brandt. Please. She's been through hell, and she's all mixed up. You heard what she said to you in that cell; her brain is scrambled." Until this moment, Peter had convinced himself that he had imagined that strange interaction, but Leigh nodded. "Yes, I heard it," he said quietly, "we all heard it. She doesn't know which way is up, Brandt. When she wakes up, she's going to be scared. She's going to need me there."

An absurd, adolescent impulse to shove Leigh aside possessed Peter; she *doesn't* need you. *I'm* the one who rescued her. She has put her trust in me. But he couldn't dismiss the memory of the girl's voice crying out for this man. He clenched his teeth. Leigh was right; she would need to see him and talk to him if she woke during the night.

He gave the guards new orders, then turned back to Leigh.

"Very well, Flight Lieutenant, you may stay in the hospital wing with Fraulein West, but you will not leave the room under any circumstances. There will be two guards posted at the end of the corridor. If you leave the room, you will be shot without hesitation. Those are their orders. Is this clear?" Leigh nodded. "Colonel Gregory, you have heard my instructions?"

"I have heard them," said Gregory, "Leigh..."

"Sir."

Peter drew a deep breath and turned to Henning. "Please, Herr Doctor, have your patient settled in the seventh room."

29
The rattle of scales

The black puddle at her feet palpitated, swelling and bulging into bubbles like boiling tar, then sucked back obscenely and pitched out a hairless, stoat-like creature which flew at Tommie and fixed oversized teeth into her cheek. She screamed and pulled on it, but the harder she pulled, the deeper it bit. She had done this to herself; she had reached out and embraced evil, and now evil was embracing her.

"Tommie."

She screamed again. It was a man's voice, and she lifted her hands to ward it off.

"Tommie, it's me, Simon."

"Simon Magus?" She could hear the terror in her own voice.

"Simon *Leigh*. Tommie, don't you know me? It's alright, love, you're safe now."

"Why can't I see you?"

"It's the middle of the night, and the floodlights are out because there's been a power cut." Something touched her hands and she flinched violently. "That's me, Tommie. I won't hurt you. You're safe now." He covered her hands with his, and this time she didn't pull away. After a moment she drew a long, shuddering breath. "Simon," she said, "your hands are warm. You're warm, you're not cold at all."

Religion and superstition. It's bad stuff, and you should leave it alone.

But she hadn't

She woke to daylight, still wearing the ruined pyjamas, but with a hospital gown covering them. Simon had gone, and the doctor was tapping softly on the door, ushering in a young woman who kept her eyes lowered as the doctor spoke. A report was to be made in front of witnesses, he informed her. This was Fraulein Eckard, a trainee nurse from the village. She was to assist Tommie with a bath and then act as a chaperone for the proceedings. He left, and the girl stood, staring down at her shoes.

She was young, probably no more than sixteen, and conservatively dressed in a white pleated blouse tucked into a navy-blue skirt, but around her shoulders was draped a scarf which pulsed with irrepressible vitality. Folky, deeply fringed, and saturated with colour, it was an explosion of roses – red roses on a red background – vermilion, carmine, ruby, cherry, crimson, and candy-red with a vivid splash of green, all defiantly crammed together and joyous. Tommie plunged her eyes into it.

As the silence stretched out, the girl looked up for the first time, and her eyes widened in horror. Tommie lifted her hands to her head, exploring the damage, and tears came to her eyes. Wiping them away, she took a deep breath and indicated that she was ready for her bath.

The girl supported her to the bathroom, where she poured salt into the water while the bath filled. Tommie's left leg, in its temporary splint, was propped up on the bath caddy, and she lay back into the salt-sting. The girl sat on a wooden chair in the corner of the bathroom, gazing at her own feet while Tommie washed, but after a while she stood up, filled an enamel bowl with water, added salt, and gently cleaned Tommie's ravaged scalp, before soaping her shoulders and her back, rinsing her, and wrapping a towel around her as she stood up.

When she handed her the nightgown that Frau Heller

had given her, Tommie buried her face in it, fighting another wave of tears. The girl watched her intently, and then, pointing at Tommie, she spoke slowly and clearly.

"Hast du Katrianna und ihr baby getotet?" *Did you kill Katrianna and her baby?*

"No," Tommie said. "Nein." The girl stared at her for a moment, then nodded. She glanced at Tommie's head, removed the scarf from around her shoulders, folded it to enclose the fringe, and draped it over Tommie's ravaged scalp, drawing it back, tying the knot gently at the nape of the neck, and adjusting it at the front to lie just above the eyebrows. The soft fabric of the scarf and the touch of the girl's fingers on her neck were infinitely soothing.

"Danke," Tommie said quietly. Fraulein Eckard nodded, put an arm firmly around her waist, and supported her down the corridor back to her room.

***

Peter closed his eyes. The tranquillity of the seventh room had been invaded, its serenity churned up now not only by his own turbulent misery, but by the grim resolve of the three men who stood with him. Visibly ill-at-ease, Henning, Gregory and the commandant stood around the bed where Tomasin West sat, and a sergeant had been stationed on a stool in the corridor with a shorthand pad.

The girl had acknowledged Peter as he entered the room, taking in, with a flash of curiosity, the bruising and puffiness of his face. She seemed undaunted by the proceedings, although her eyes were watchful as she regarded the men from beneath a brightly coloured headscarf.

Puzzled by the headscarf, Peter glanced at the young nurse who sat silently in the armchair in the corner, her hands tucked between her knees. She caught his glance and looked away quickly, and he turned back as Renger began.

"I understand that this must be a difficult ordeal for you, Fraulein West," he said, "But I must ask you these questions. Can you name the person who took you from this prison on Tuesday?"

"It was Major Otto Steiger, accompanied by Lieutenant Boehm and two soldiers whose names I don't know." She turned quickly to Gregory, "Is Doug ok? He..."

"Lieutenant Bainbridge is fine," Gregory said, "a mild concussion, but nothing more. Doctor Henning has checked him over."

She nodded and turned back to the commandant. The questions continued, and the girl became unsettled as the nature of her injuries was questioned and documented in detail. Finally, Renger sighed deeply.

"That will be all, Fraulein West. Karl, may I use your office for a moment?" They left the room and he drew Peter aside, "This is just another of Steiger's excesses, and I will not allow him to sully my command with his ridiculous fantasies. I must dispute this charge of abortion, but I don't know where to start; I'm an administrator, not a detective. Do you think you can use your intelligence connections to arrange for a sensible investigation into this business?"

"I'll do what I can, but..."

"Good. I will leave it in your hands."

Peter waited in the doctor's office until the young nurse, who had remained behind to settle her patient, stopped by to report off duty. He led her into the first of the empty rooms and gestured for her to sit in the armchair. "Ist Fraulein Eckard ihr name?" She nodded, and he switched smoothly to English, "Do you know why this happened to the English girl?"

She stared at him in confusion, and replied in German. "I do not understand English, Herr Major."

He reverted to German.

"Do you know why this happened to the English girl?"

"It is said that Major Steiger accuses her of performing the abortion that killed Katrianna Zahn."

"Do you believe that she is guilty of this?"

"It is not for me to judge, sir."

"Is it your headscarf that the English girl is wearing?"

The girl swallowed nervously.

"Yes, Herr Major."

"Why did you give her the scarf?"

"Because it is a shame for a woman to have to face the world with her head shaved like that."

"But if she is guilty of what she is accused...?" At his words, the young woman's head twitched slightly but she kept herself silent. Peter nodded, "You don't believe that she is guilty, do you, Fraulein Eckard? But you don't speak English, and Fraulein West speaks very little German, so she cannot have pleaded her own case to you. Something else has convinced you of her innocence. Do you know who performed the abortion?"

The girl turned pale.

"No, Herr Major."

He softened his voice.

"No, of course you don't." He paused, "But I come from a small town myself, Fraulein Eckard, and I know what it is like; there is always gossip. Most gossip is nonsense – but not all."

He walked to the window and stared out across the valley, "If you were to hear any gossip, any rumours about Katrianna Zahn's death, and were to report them to me then perhaps we could sift through the nonsense, find this murderer and bring him to justice. Rumours are public property, and anyone could have reported them; nobody would be able to point a finger at you for passing on the information. Do you understand?" He turned back to her, "And what a sin it would be if Katrianna's killer were to remain free to do this again."

The girl's face became haunted. Peter waited, and at length she took a deep breath.

"I don't need to listen to gossip, sir, I have some real information. Last year a girl died the same way, her name was Maria Anders. Her family told people it was a burst appendix, but it wasn't. Maria was pregnant." Her right hand found a belt loop on her skirt and her fingers rubbed away at it with unconscious, fretful movements. "Everyone knows that Maria's family paid for her to have that abortion," she continued, "but Katrianna... Katrianna wouldn't tell her parents that she was pregnant, and she didn't have money to pay for... for what happened." Her face twisted into a misery that sat unfairly on the soft, round cheeks as she stared up at him. "Katrianna was my friend, Herr Major. She was a nice girl. I can't tell you who did the abortion, but on the day before Katrianna died, I saw a silver cross in the window of the pawnbroker's shop on the Kirke Strasse, and it was gone the next day. A little cross on a chain. It was Katrianna's."

Peter frowned. "How can you be sure it was hers? One silver cross looks very like another."

The girl shook her head.

"It was Katrianna's. Her parents gave it to her last year on her sixteenth birthday. I know it was hers because it had a flaw in the silver, right in the centre of the cross. Katrianna used to say that it was a scratch from the spear that pierced the side of Jesus. She said that the cross was holy because of it. She said it had the power to protect her from harm."

***

Submerged in a thick, fuggy sleep, Tommie became aware of footsteps approaching down a long corridor, and thrashed out, fighting to wake up. Why had she allowed herself to fall asleep? She wasn't prepared for another assault. Lunging towards the surface, she pawed her way through the murk, and burst out into daylight.

She was in the seventh room, and Simon was standing in the doorway. She caught her breath and choked on it.

"For pity's sake, Simon!" she coughed, "don't come creeping up on me like that. You should whistle or something, to let me know it's you. Oh, God! What happened to your face?" Her head spun wildly as she scrambled again to escape the vortex of reality and hallucination. Had she dreamed seeing his face, unmarked, in the prison cell?

"My face? Oh, that." He shrugged and came to perch on the edge of the bed, "You know what it's like in this place; tensions build, fists fly..."

An incongruous happiness settled on her; she was home.

"No wonder Pickman calls you Scrappin' Simon," she said, shaking her head. "What started it this time?"

"I really couldn't say," he said awkwardly, "I was pretty shaken up after seeing you in that cell, maybe it was that."

"Well, tensions must be building up all over, then" she said as he helped her to sit upright. "Major Brandt looks just the same way you do."

He looked at her sharply, then pulled the bedcovers higher over her.

"Major Brandt?" he said casually, "When did you see him? Oh, that's right, Colonel Gregory said he was part of the inquisition this morning. Listen, Tommie, I think you'd do well to stay away from him."

She raised her eyebrows.

"Stay away from him? We're not at a country club, Simon, I don't have much say about who I do or don't see."

"I know, but you should try to avoid him if you can. Just because he has access to women outside this castle doesn't mean he wouldn't look at you too."

She smiled.

"Haven't we had this conversation before? When you warned me off Sam? Well, if it sets your mind at rest, I think he's just as much of a ladies' man as Ian and Don and Ken are."

"Really?" said Simon thoughtfully, "Well, I don't trust him, anyway. He's a clever man, and, alright, you say that it's the SS who are responsible for this," he said, indicating her injuries, "but who knows what Brandt's involvement is behind the scenes?"

She shook her head.

"This was uniquely Steiger."

"Oh, yes, about Steiger and the witchcraft stuff..."

She flinched.

"Witchcraft stuff?! How do you know about that?"

"You told me about it. Last night. You don't remember? Well, Colonel Gregory said that apparently Steiger collapsed in the middle of interrogating you, and had to be hauled off to hospital, so he must have been ill all along, and that's where this witchcraft thing comes from – he was obviously hallucinating."

Tommie listened to him soberly, recalling Kate's unease with the library books. It seemed that people don't like hearing about witchcraft; they don't want to know that the occult tides which shift beneath the skin of humanity have not, after all, been subdued. They don't want to imagine Saint George turning away from the slain dragon, only to hear the rattle of scales behind him.

Simon's voice was suddenly hesitant and awkward.

"Tommie, Steiger is deluded, isn't he? About your being a witch, I mean. Because you know so much about this nonsense. Too much. And those remedies you use... you're not some sort of witch, are you? Because there's no such thing as witches any more, is there?"

Tommie hesitated.

Labels.

"No, I'm not a witch."

Relief flooded his face.

"Ok. Good. Well, I brought you some of this..." He crossed the room and retrieved a bundle of meadowsweet that he had stashed out of sight in the corridor, "This is the stuff you spread around your room, isn't it? It looks and smells the same – I picked it in the exercise field this morning, I hope it's the right stuff."

She couldn't speak, but she pulled him into her arms, releasing the soft, fresh scent of meadowsweet around them.

30
A string of pearls

She opened her eyes to absolute darkness. The floodlights around the west wing were off again, although there were no bombers. Silence reigned, and she closed her eyes, waiting to fall asleep, but there was something stopping her. She opened her eyes again.

The quality of the darkness was impressive; anyone could be standing close enough to touch her, and she wouldn't know. The thought provoked an unpleasant shudder, and she made herself lie still, regulating her breathing and waiting for her eyes to see through the darkness.

There it was; not close enough to touch, but across the room, outlined against the summer night sky, a figure was standing by the window. A burst of fear swept over her skin, but as the tall figure of Brandt became identifiable, fear gave way to relief; a conditional relief, because she was, if anything, more vulnerable alone up here than she was amongst all the men down in the main castle, but this was Brandt, and he wasn't a ladies' man.

Also, although she hadn't had the courage to look in a mirror since Steiger's exorcism, she suspected that she now resembled nothing more than a child's rag doll after a tug-of-war with the family dog. She felt reasonably safe, but nevertheless, she held her silence, watching the man until he turned and left the room.

The following night she woke again, knowing with the same certainty that she was not alone in the room.

Tonight, the floodlights were on, and this time she could see Brandt quite clearly as he stared out of the window, gazing through the veil from the floodlights into the true darkness. Was he sleepwalking? Unlikely; the two doors opening onto this corridor were kept locked, and although he clearly had keys, she thought it improbable that a sleepwalker could negotiate two locked doors.

She remembered hearing Phil Cooper warning Taylor and Bainbridge about Brandt's late-night patrols. 'My guess is insomnia. Every night he comes drifting down that corridor like a ghost.'

Curious, Tommie watched her silent companion. There was an intensity surrounding the man like an aura. Most of the prisoners had it; a vaporous sadness, vague and nebulous, like a dark form of the haze around the moon, but tonight, in Brandt, it appeared compressed and quite clearly defined. She watched the apparition of the man until her eyes teared, and until he turned and quietly left the room.

**

Peter woke with a jolt and lay drenched in cold sweat. The images of the dream had already fallen away from him, melting into the darkness and leaving him with nothing but a mushrooming bitterness in his soul and the wrenching pressure of the bands around his chest. It was two o'clock in the morning.

Washing his face and dressing quickly, he made a circuit of the sleeping castle. He had always walked the corridors in the early hours of the morning, startling sentries into resentful alertness, but since Conrad's arrest, when the dreams had begun to seize him from his sleep and leave him weak and shaking, he had sought sanctuary in the seventh room; the one that Frau Heller had designated a healing room.

Despite this – or perhaps because of it – he had given instructions for Tomasin West to be taken to the seventh room when she was brought, unconscious, from the town prison. Despite this, or because of it? Had he given that order because the girl was in need of the room's supposed healing properties, or from a hope that her presence there might break his growing dependence on it? Either way, at first it had seemed to work; he had avoided going there, deterred by the impropriety, but he had quickly drifted back, drawn now not only by the healing room itself, but by the sound of someone breathing.

All was quiet as he finished his circuit and unlocked the pass door into the hospital wing. The floodlights were off again tonight, and staring into the velvet blackness of the sky, he could almost hear the faint whisper of the dark moon as it passed through the night.

"What is it about that window that has you hypnotised night after night, Major Brandt?"

He turned, startled.

"My apologies, fraulein. I had thought you would be asleep at this time of the night,"

"I don't sleep too soundly now."

"Of course. I have been thoughtless. I won't disturb you again." He turned to leave.

"Oh, you don't disturb me," she said lightly, "Not anymore. The first night I saw you standing there I just about had hedgehogs, but I'm used to you now."

He considered this statement carefully; it posed several issues, but he only felt up to addressing one of them.

"Hedgehogs?" he said, "Isn't the correct expression 'having kittens'?"

"Yes, it is, but kittens aren't spiky." There was a reflective pause before she added, "That wasn't very proper. I shouldn't have said that aloud. I've shocked you."

He covered a faint, unexpected snort of laughter.

"I am not so easily shocked."

"And I'm not usually so indelicate," she said, placidly, "Not with strangers, at least." Another pause. "I am curious about what you see through that window, Major Brandt."

"The window?"

"I have watched you for the past several nights, staring out there."

He hesitated.

"The hospital wing has the best views in the castle," he said slowly, turning back to the void. "If one looks straight ahead, neither up nor down, it is possible to imagine that this castle doesn't exist; that nothing exists." He stopped and silence fell thickly in the room.

"But for the past two nights there has been no moon to light the landscape," she said eventually, as though the last three words had not been spoken, "and yet you have stood there and stared out on... on what?" He could feel her eyes on him as he, in turn, gazed out into the blackness, and in the absence of a response, her voice became conversational. "Some say that the dark moon is a time when the darkest acts of men are conceived or committed, but you don't strike me as a man who enjoys contemplating the darkest acts, Major Brandt."

"The darkest acts of men originate within the minds of men," he said sharply, "not with the movements of the moon or the planets or the stars. There is no excuse to be made for our crimes." He paused, making a deliberate effort to erase the harshness in his voice, but when he spoke again it had been replaced only by weariness. "It is not the window that draws me here, but the room itself. Frau Heller once told me that this is a healing room, and perhaps that is why I come here each night; perhaps I am in need of healing." The silence became uncomfortable for him. "How is your leg now?" he asked solicitously, "Are you in pain?"

"No. Thank you, my leg is not giving me any trouble."

"I'm glad to hear that. Well, I will leave you to sleep. Good night."

"Good night, Major Brandt," she said, "and I hope you won't be turned away by my presence here. You must come to this room as often as you wish. We all need something to help us ward off the demons."

He paused in the doorway, unable to resist responding to this.

"Indeed. But tell me, are you not troubled by the presence of one of those demons in your room?" Instantly he regretted his words as he heard the quick catch of her breath. "Me," he said quickly.

She seemed puzzled.

"You, Major Brandt?" she said, "You are not one of my demons. You are someone who wards off my demons."

He considered her words uneasily.

"Please understand that I cannot ward off your demons, fraulein. While I will do everything in my power to keep Major Steiger away from you, I do not have authority over his actions."

She shook her head, and her response was woolly with encroaching sleep.

"You mistake my meaning. I don't need you to be my knight in shining armour. It's just that I can see you are a good man, and that alone wards off my demons." She sighed drowsily, "You shine, Major Brandt. Even through your dark aura, you shine. That's all I meant." He remained standing there for a moment, and as her breathing became slow and regular, the tightness around his chest eased slightly.

***

"Do you believe in ghosts, fraulein?"

"No, I don't. Do you?" Brandt had taken her at her word, appearing each night in the doorway, waiting to be invited in, and she found that she looked forward to their conversations.

"Do I believe in ghosts?" he replied. "No. In times like ours the ghosts of the dead would overwhelm the living. There would be a cacophony... intolerable. But..."

"But?"

"What, then? What happens after death? An atheist would say nothing happens. Lights out, then nothing. In that case, everything that he was – everything he thought and did and planned and cherished, his family, his ancestors – went to nothing. From such intensity, such vitality to... nothing. It doesn't seem right. It doesn't make sense. And what do the religions have to say about it? Well, take your pick; Heaven, Hell, Purgatory, reincarnation, nirvana, none of those make any sense as far as I see it."

Everything he thought and did... She filed that away for further consideration.

Her time in the hospital wing had become like a string of pearls; each long, inactive day was a large, milky pearl separated from the next by the small, bright spacers that were the odd, inconsequential conversations with Brandt. Tonight, his distress was palpable. The baleful drone of a bombing raid, trapped by a low-lying, over-stuffed feather-quilt of clouds, pressed against her eardrums.

What happens after death? He seemed to want a response from her, and so she spoke, her words picking their way around the irregular crump of the bombardment.

"I believe that when someone dies, they are instantly at peace," she said. "I once went night-swimming from a rowboat off Corfu. The sea was full of phosphorous plankton, and the sky was full of stars, and the water was body temperature; it was like swimming in a summer sky. There were stars above and stars below, no sense of heat or cold, no gravity, and that's what I think it must be like after death. That's where our dead are; in perfect peace. But we still feel their echoes."

"Yes, echoes," he said thinly. "Those echoes could drive a man to distraction."

"But those echoes are images from the past," she insisted. "It's painful for us to go forward without the ones we love, it feels as though we have left them behind, but it's the other way round; they have left this world behind and it is no longer their concern. They don't become ghosts, they don't come back to visit loved ones, or haunt hated ones, they don't fret about the things they didn't achieve, and they don't worry about how people remember them. We, the living, we still have to deal with life. But they don't. They are in perfect peace."

"And when we die, are we reunited with them?"

"We are no longer separate from them."

He remained silent for a long time.

"On what foundation do you base those ideas?" he asked eventually.

"On common sense," she said sharply. Was he going to deliver a judgement on her lack of academic citations? "You said it yourself; Heaven, Hell, Purgatory, reincarnation, nirvana... if none of that makes any sense, then find something that does. This makes sense to me. Why try to twist yourself around religious or philosophical teachings that make no sense to you, when, patently, no theory has a more legitimate claim on the truth than any other?"

He had nodded, made no further comment, and left with a polite goodnight. Perhaps he thought her an intellectual lightweight, a fluffy thinker, and now he would find it beneath himself to continue to engage with her. She shrugged. So be it. If she wanted the company of an intellectual snob, she would seek out George Selby.

***

He had taken the girl her at her word, continuing to visit the hospital wing on his nightly circuit of the castle in defiance of the gnawing awareness of impropriety, but now, instead of the silent comfort of staring into the darkness beyond the window, the visits had become like a masquerade ball; a concealment of reality. God knows that he was speaking from behind the mask of a steadfast, trustworthy officer, and if she saw behind it – and how could she not; what genuinely honourable officer would repeatedly visit her under such inappropriate circumstances?

– if she saw behind that mask, then she saw nothing more than a good man, but Peter was uncomfortably aware of the other masks that he lifted to his face in the seventh room; the mask that concealed their shared connection with Hendry, and the mask that covered up the shattered wreckage inside him. Still, he visited the seventh room. He glanced down at a book that lay on her night table.

"Ovid. Do you like the classics?"

"I'm afraid I was never given the chance to find out," she said, coolly. "Girls' schools – at least, mine did – pick their way very daintily around the more cerebral disciplines. We were taught sufficient Latin and Greek to impart a veneer of sophistication, and French, of course, and they were very progressive about science, but I would have liked to study philosophy. I wanted to go to university, but my parents didn't want a bluestocking for a daughter."

"Instead, they got a spy for a daughter."

"A nurse."

"A midwife."

"Midwifery was the icing on the nurse cake."

He smiled. "Where did you receive your education?"

"I went to a girls' boarding school, then to a finishing school in Switzerland."

"A *finishing school*?!" That was tactless. If he hadn't recognized this for himself, the cool lift of her eyebrows acknowledged it, and there was a brief, icy pause.

"You are incredulous, Major Brandt," she said, and now her tone was clipped and formal. "Do you find that I am not... finished?"

"Refined," he said, and winced.

"Ah. You find that I am not refined."

"No! No, I just... I... it was the term you used – "finished" – that couldn't possibly be the correct term. *Is* it the correct term? But that's really not pertinent." He floundered and grasped at a straw, "At Oxford I attended several debutante balls... not for students, of course; for their sisters." He cursed silently – where was this rank insensitivity coming from? – and ploughed on through the mire of his own making, "I've met many finishing school girls, but you are nothing like them." Some blessed instinct clamped a hand over his mouth then, while his brain ran on regardless...

You are wearing a borrowed old-lady nightgown, and that's only because you can't fit your men's stripy pyjamas or your army battle dress trousers over your plaster cast.

I know you trained with Hendry's people, and I know what that entails.

You jumped from a moving train.

You were discovered in a hayloft with a British airman.

You incapacitated an SS officer while you were shackled and handcuffed.

I watched you polish off three large pastries and two cups of coffee in less than ten minutes.

You crawled over bomb rubble to save the life of an enemy, and God knows how you survived that vicious bastard Steiger's interrogation. But you are miffed – yes, miffed is the only word that fits – you're miffed because I am incredulous to learn that you went to finishing school. And yet I am not incredulous. Surprised, but not incredulous.

He swallowed hard, cautiously optimistic that his mouth had re-connected itself to his brain, but there was nothing in there that wouldn't be safer left unsaid, so he remained silent, and she watched him. Eventually, with a dainty tilt of her head, and enunciation that rang with the ping of fine crystal and set his teeth on edge, she freed him from his discomfiture.

"I am entertained – as any finishing school graduate worthy of the distinction would be – by the spectacle of you trying to climb out of that hole, Major Brandt, but since I have always been disinclined to conform to any imaginable embodiment of a finishing school graduate, I am prepared to perceive a compliment in your incredulity. May I do so?"

"Please do," he said fervently. "Please do."

"My education did not circumscribe my curiosity," she continued primly, dismissing his awkwardness with delicate sang froid, "I have always read books on subjects that interest me, but when there is nobody with whom to discuss abstract ideas, whether in finishing school, in nursing school or on the streets of occupied Paris, one's ideas tend to remain sterile. In this castle, conversely, the knowledge exists, but not the willingness. Lieutenant Bainbridge kindly loaned me that book," she continued, "but he is taciturn by nature, and averse to wearing the mantle of teacher. Lieutenant Selby, on the other hand, taught philosophy before the war, and presents lectures for the other officers, but he has declined to cast his pearls before swine."

This last comment took a moment to process. He frowned.

"Your self being the swine before which he will not cast his pearls?" he asked.

"My self being the swine," she affirmed. "Or a bluestocking. Sometimes both in the same tirade."

"I still have some of my philosophy texts from Oxford... in English," he said, "would you consider it inappropriate if I were to offer to lend some to you? I wouldn't presume to teach you, but perhaps we could discuss what you read... if you wouldn't find it improper."

She was silent for a long moment, and he found himself utterly unable to predict how she might receive his offer. Eventually she spoke, and he was relieved that she had discarded the crystal-ping finishing school diction, if not the quaint formality of her delivery.

"I don't believe that the seeking or providing of knowledge could ever be improper," she said, reflectively. "If, on the other hand, you were to offer to bring me nylons, that *would* be improper, and I would be aghast."

He laughed.

"If I promise not to bring you nylons, will you accept the loan of some books?"

"I will happily accept the loan of some books, Major Brandt, and also your offer of a discussion partner. You are very kind."

***

The envelope that had been delivered to his office that morning bore a Swiss postmark, and the address was in Hendry's handwriting. The message inside was also in Hendry's hand, but composed with potential third parties in mind.

Dear Peter,

Because of this blasted war, I will not be able to communicate with you for the foreseeable future.

Michael Klamm.

At that moment he had felt an excruciating need to catch hold of something in a world that was disappearing around him, leaving him suspended in nothingness, like the Cheshire Cat's grin. *Catch hold of...* that had been his grandmother's expression; 'Peter, catch hold of this.' But what was left for him to catch hold of?

Karl Henning, appearing in the doorway of his office, brought him out of his reverie.

"Good morning, Peter, I'm glad I've caught you before you vanish into the depths of Little Russia."

Peter smiled.

"Well, you've only just made it, I was completing some paperwork, but now I've finished."

"So I see. I will wait while you finish." The inconsequential response made Peter glance up. Henning's attention was on a folder that was lying on the desk, open at the profile page, where the photograph of Tomasin West looked out with eyes that had not yet developed the shadows they now possessed. Her hair had been shoulder-length when the picture was taken, pushed back behind her ears in a defiant gesture that was mirrored in her eyes.

Peter felt the doctor's eyes on him as he finished sorting papers into the series of folders on his desk. There were no papers for that particular folder, so he closed it as casually as possible and put it with the others before turning to Henning. The doctor's face was creased into a frown as he spoke.

"Has there been an update on the Katrianna Zahn case?"

"Not since Tuesday. They're still trying to delay the girl's burial until the post-mortem results are complete." There was a slight, awkward pause, and Henning nodded, still frowning.

"Ah, because I came to see you about having Fraulein West discharged into the main castle. Colonel Renger referred me to you for a decision. Her wounds are healing well and showing no signs of infection, and since she will be wearing the cast for several more weeks, I don't see why she can't return to her own people while the bone is knitting."

Peter shook his head.

"No. I want to keep her where she is for a while. Not that I don't agree with you about her progress, she seems to be recovering well, but Otto Steiger is not to be trusted, and while the case is still wide open, keeping her in this wing makes her just a little less accessible to him."

By an unspoken understanding Karl had not asked about, and Peter had not elaborated on, his conversation with the nurse.

"Very well, as you wish. How long do you predict for the post mortem paperwork?"

Peter shot a glance at the other man. They both knew that, under current circumstances, paperwork could take two days or two years depending on who was processing it and what interests were served by the processing. "Who can say, Karl. The police are pursuing several avenues of investigation, and in the meantime, until she is cleared of the abortion charges, I wish Fraulein West to remain where she is."

***

"What do you love about your country, Fraulein West? Tell me about your home town."

Tommie sat up in the bed, suddenly wary. Brandt was leaning against the windowsill, gazing out into the night, but he turned towards her, catching her hesitation.

"Oh, please don't misunderstand me," he said with a quick dip of his head to conceal a smile. Like a schoolboy, she thought; it was an oddly shy movement that contrasted with his usual, seamlessly assured manner. She had come to enjoy that smile, when the stillness of his face shifted and his grey eyes lit in the same way that the dark landscape outside the window could be startled by sheet lightning.

"This is not an interrogation," he continued, "I assure you that the scope of Germany's military intelligence is not dependent on such conversations as ours."

His voice was lighter tonight, and the terrible burden that lay across his shoulders seemed to have eased. She had learned to recognize that burden too, and the dark flinch of pain that often jolted his body in response to some savage memory, but tonight was being merciful on him.

"There are times when I miss England," he continued, "I miss the gently eccentric characters. Germany doesn't respond too well to eccentrics, I'm afraid, and I miss the formidable old women. There's a popular story – one that circulates only in strictly limited company, for obvious reasons – about a Luftwaffe pilot shot down over the English countryside. An elderly woman who was walking her dog came across him, arrested him with the insistence of the dog, escorted him back to her house and made him a cup of tea while they waited for the police to arrive."

He laughed, "Now, a grown man in the peak of physical fitness and almost certainly armed, could easily take on an elderly woman, dog or no dog, so perhaps he was injured or in a state of shock, but nevertheless, there is something inspiring about a woman who will confront the enemy with nothing more than righteousness and a dog. And there is something equally inspiring in a man who declines to shoot his way out of that situation, standing down in the face of such a woman."

Tommie smiled.

"She sounds like everyone's Aunty Mary."

He laughed again, the drawn lines fading from his face. She also enjoyed making him laugh, watching the ashen anxiety dissolve, even if only momentarily. Unexpectedly, along with Brandt's laughter, she heard Sam's melted chocolate chuckle, and smiled, imagining what she would have had to say about this... this fraternization, or whatever it was.

"So, tell me, then," Brandt insisted, "Leaving out any state secrets, what do you miss about your country?"

She thought for a moment.

"The postman."

"The postman?!"

"And the milkman and the newspaper boy. An undisrupted way of life; the things we take for granted until they're gone. I really long for the mundane routines of a country in peacetime." A bitter homesickness hit her and she fell quiet, listening to the rattle of the letterbox and the pat of envelopes landing on the mat, the rhythmic roll of lawn mowers; the mild, mellow sounds of life.

She could feel him watching her, although now, with his back to the floodlights, his face was in shadow. She sat up straighter against the pillows.

"And now it's my turn, Major Brandt, I want to know what you love about your country."

"My country?" The question seemed to catch him off guard, and he turned away from her. For a moment she thought he was not going to answer, but then he spoke, his voice sounding strained again, and not for the first time she found herself wondering about his life in the world outside this castle; the circumstances that rendered his face so tense and bleak.

"What do I love about my country? Let me see." He stared into the floodlights, and in the glare she saw the muscles of his face tightening. "I love an old, sprawling, smoke-stained city, built – as all cities are – from the greatest aspirations and the worst wrongs of mankind. I also love another city, a city of intense learning, committed to the finite knowledge of our world. I love the wild lands; the places that care nothing for cities. I love the smell of coal on the wind, heavy clouds resting on the hills, and I love the freshness after rain, when the breath of God is in the air and everything is clean and alive and breathing."

He paused, and then his voice came again, but changed now – heavy and slow. "And I love a deeply honourable nation that is blessed with good and noble men and women, and cursed with plague-ridden rats." He stopped speaking, and rubbed his forehead as though erasing the thoughts. "So, fraulein," he continued after a while, and now his voice was lighter again, "no harm done; I have confessed to missing the formidable old women in England, and you have confessed to missing the milkman. But be assured, you have revealed no secrets. The special relationship between a British woman and her milkman is a well-documented phenomenon."

"No!" she said, her voice emerging as a squeak. "No! Not like that! *Really*, not like that! Oh..." She blushed into the darkness and shook her head, listening to his quiet laughter.

***

"Good morning, Peter. What brings you here in the daylight?"

Peter hesitated. The doctor had long been aware that the hospital wing was included in what he called Peter's night time patrol, but this morning there seemed to be a calculated intent behind his words. He let the comment pass, though, and handed the envelope to Henning. "I have just received the post-mortem results for Katrianna Zahn. It shows significant internal injuries – evidence that the abortion was caused not by ingestion of any substance, but surgically, with the aid of an edged instrument."

The doctor's face darkened momentarily, but he was a pragmatic man, and had priorities closer to home.

"Well. So, that exonerates Fraulein West."

"Not quite. Before she can be fully cleared of the charges, it will be necessary to find out who actually performed the abortion, and to prove that that person was capable of operating independently. Until then, Steiger can still claim that the procedure was done under Fraulein West's instruction. The post mortem results are encouraging but not conclusive. May I visit your patient and give her the news?"

The doctor gave him a searching look.

"Is there any reason why you shouldn't?"

Again, Peter hesitated, unsettled, but shrugged the comment off and headed down the corridor. In the seventh room Tomasin West was sitting up with a book open on the bed in front of her, but she was watching for him.

"I thought I recognized your footsteps," she said, "Is there trouble?"

"Not trouble, no. Some promising news." Despite Hennings' odd remark, there was a liberating sense of propriety in visiting her in daylight; a refreshing ordinariness, as though they had come across each other in the high street, and stopped to talk. Ordinary, that is, if he declined to notice the headscarf that covered the scarred scalp, if he ignored the lumpy outline of the plaster cast beneath the blankets, and allowed his eyes to skim over the long wound, uncovered now, and healing, that stretched from her wrist to her elbow.

She nodded when he told her of the post mortem results, and in her eyes he saw an acknowledgement of the tragedy that had ended Katrianna Zahn's young life.

"When the police have discovered who performed the abortion," he concluded, "they will formally pronounce you innocent of the charges that Steiger brought against you."

"Thank you for letting me know."

Reluctant to leave, he glanced down at the book she was reading.

"Shakespeare? Have you given up on philosophy?"

She smiled.

"No, I find it quite stimulating to have my brain pulled inside out, but I was in the mood for a little magic this morning."

"Magic. Let me guess... A Midsummer Night's Dream?

No; you have a contemplative air about you, Dream is too coarse for that. So, The Tempest?"

"Yes, The Tempest."

He nodded.

"Betrayal, deceit, ambition, control, redemption. Despite the magic – maybe because of it – I have always found The Tempest to be one of his more sobering works."

"Even compared with Titus Andronicus and Julius Caesar?"

"Why would those come to your mind?" he replied, resisting a smile.

She lifted her shoulders in a shrug.

"Shakespeare wrote political plays to please his queen, comedies and tragedies for the masses; presumably he wrote his military plays for soldiers."

"Perhaps," he said, "But I was not always a soldier. And surely Shakespeare's greatest appeal is in his exploration of human nature; its fallibility, its flaws, and its vulnerability to fate and circumstance. And in the poetry of his language, of course."

"That's true."

"My grandmother gave me a volume of his plays when I was ten years old," he continued, and his mind filled with memories; reading in the old armchair, the comforting tick of the clock, rain battering the windows, and a coal fire in the grate. "She told me, "That man's words carry more music than anything else written in that flat language." She had little regard for the English language. Compared with Wel..." he caught himself just in time. "Well, compared with her own language, she said that speaking English was like trying to fly with wooden wings or sing with a mouthful of marbles." He burst out laughing at her expression, "Why, Fraulein West, the strain of being polite is showing in your face. Come on, out with it! The truth! You think that the German language is ugly, don't you?" He tilted his head at her; this would be payback for the finishing school conversation.

"Not ugly so much as functional," she said slowly. "I like

the logic of it, and the honesty of it. English is functional too – they both grew from the same root after all, although I believe that the German language has remained mostly intact, am I right? While English has taken on board a heavy serving of the romance languages, a splash of Saxon, and so many others, and now it seems to be learning American. But I think your grandmother was quite right; it takes someone with the genius of Shakespeare or Christopher Marlowe or John Donne to make English sing." She looked up at him then, her eyes glinting with a challenge, "So what does it take to make the German language beautiful?"

He smiled, rising willingly to the challenge.

"But I haven't conceded that the German language is not beautiful. Perhaps you will permit me to demonstrate for you its hidden poetry. Try this..." he tempered his delivery, perfectly aware of how, by avoiding the more guttural sounds, and softening the pronunciation of the words, the language became more acceptable to English ears. "'Sie werden durch ihre fehler nur lernen.' How does that sound?"

She narrowed her eyes suspiciously.

"It sounds quite nice. Something about learning?"

"'By making mistakes, you will learn.'"

She rewarded him with an astute nod.

"You've argued this point before, haven't you?"

"More times than I care to admit!"

"Sic probo, Major Brandt, sic probo. My Latin is atrocious, but there's no better language for gilding a victory!"

Laughing, he took his leave and headed down the corridor, but the doctor intercepted him, appearing in the doorway to his office and raising an eyebrow at his good spirits.

"So, how is your prisoner this morning?" he said, the words settling on his shoulders like rank sea-foam on an advancing tide. "Take care, Peter," he added quietly, drawing him into his office and closing the door, "you're heading for trouble."

"Trouble, Karl? I don't know what you mean."

"You know perfectly well what I mean. You must stop visiting her unchaperoned."

Mulish defiance surged in him.

"Since when does your personal opinion dictate my professional duty?"

"It's not my personal opinion, and we both know that you are acting beyond your professional duty."

The defiance flared into anger.

"You're questioning my honour?"

"Your honour?" said Henning with a short laugh. "Oh, no, my uptight friend, you have me there. Your honour is beyond reproach. In that respect, one would almost think your blood was pure German. No, Peter, if adherence to honour was the only governing force in human behaviour, then we wouldn't be having this conversation."

"Why *are* we having this conversation, Karl?"

"Because I'm worried about you. You have known enough sorrow in these past months to drown a man, but you refuse to acknowledge it. You need to take some time off. Your nerves are strung far too tightly."

Peter turned away impatiently.

"We've discussed this before, on numerous occasions."

"No! That's where you're wrong," persisted the doctor heatedly, "we haven't discussed it. I have spoken about it while you listened with deaf ears." He shook his head, and now his voice was heavy with compassion, "You are tired, Peter, and you are in pain," he said, "and I may be an old man, but I remember very well the spell that can be cast by a soft voice and gentle eyes."

A sudden pulse of warmth flooded Peter's chest, and he covered his confusion with outrage.

"Are you implying..."

"No, I am not!" the doctor cut in, "Don't wilfully misunderstand me. I am not concerned about your honour, your ethics, your moral compass or anything else of that nature... or hers. I am not saying that there is seduction going on. I know there is no intention of wrong-doing at all, Peter, not on either side, I can see that. But the lack of intent doesn't make a blind bit of difference. You are on dangerous ground, my friend, I can sense it, and I have no wish to see you face a court martial over this business. One can never tell how these things will turn out."

There was a long, simmering silence, and Peter stared out of the window across the wooded plain that was shining in the clear morning sunlight. He resented the pall that had settled over him once more with the doctor's words. Like a premature shroud, he thought grimly. Perhaps he should confide in Karl, reassure him that he, Peter, would be swinging at the end of a noose long before any trouble over his interactions with Tomasin West might surface.

"I appreciate your concern, Karl," he said finally, "And it's good to know that I haven't lost all of my friends to this madness." He brushed the top of his cap awkwardly with his sleeve before glancing at the doctor. "As far as my contact with Fraulein West is concerned, though, I enjoy my conversations with her, and that level of communication is not outside the realm of my official duties, so I do not feel obliged to stop visiting her. But you mustn't trouble yourself about the situation. She is a prisoner in this castle, and the prospect of any impropriety..." He sighed deeply, forcing the invisible bands to expand, then put his cap on, adjusted it decisively, and coerced a smile onto his face, "well, it would be unthinkable for me. And I believe this uniform is a deterrent to any such indiscretion on Fraulein West's part, wouldn't you say?"

"Perhaps. If she didn't believe that the soul of an angel lies beneath it."

Peter felt a jolt pass through his body.

"She was hallucinating," he snapped, "she remembers nothing of what she said on that occasion. Good day, Karl."

***

"They've tried to kill Hitler!" Simon's face was bright with excitement as he delivered the news to Tommie in the hospital wing.

"Simon, we've been trying since 1939."

"Not *us*; *them*! The Germans. They tried to blow him up. A small clique of officers... here... I wrote it down... '... a small clique of ambitious, unconscionable, and at the same time irrational, criminally stupid officers... committing betrayal out of greed for power.' Good Lord, they even read out their names on the BBC! There's hell to pay now. Some of them have already faced the firing squad."

A German underground resistance to the Nazi regime. It was as though a jigsaw puzzle had been emptied out of its box in front of her, with the pieces falling into place before her eyes; Brandt's aura of isolation and loneliness, his appearance of more than half belonging in another world, his palpable grief. She thought of Count Conrad von Heiden, who had stood at his side in the courtyard that day, and the annoyance in Brandt's face as the man had mock-flirted with her. All the pieces of the puzzle were there. And there was a heavy black border around the picture. *Lights out, then nothing... everything that he was went to nothing. From such intensity, such vitality to... nothing.*

Simon misunderstood her expression and attempted to cheer her up, "So what if they failed, Tommie, they're all turning on each other now. Do you know how much suspicion and mistrust is generated by treason?"

"Treason?" she said, confused. *I love a great country, blessed with great and noble men and women and cursed with plague-ridden rats.* "But look at what they were trying to do, Simon; they were trying to get rid of Hitler. We shouldn't be cheering at their fate, we should be honouring them."

"Honouring them?! Honouring the enemy? They were traitors; they took up arms against their leadership!"

"Took up arms against Hitler!"

"They betrayed their duty."

"Duty to an evil man."

"Duty nonetheless. He is their leader and they swore an oath to him."

"So, they are bound to obey evil?"

"If they elected an evil leader, then yes."

"Let me get this straight; the Germans are the enemy because they have an evil leader, and if they try to remove that leader, they are traitors?"

The argument quickly reached stalemate, and Simon left, visibly aggravated. Tommie's thoughts immediately returned to Brandt. A small clique of officers. There was no doubt in her mind that Brandt had been involved somehow, and that he had lost the man he loved in the process. So, this was the nature of his turmoil. And he, too, might soon face a firing squad. She was startled at the wave of sorrow that passed over her at the thought.

***

Peter shrugged off the stubborn rigidity in his shoulders as he unlocked the pass door to the hospital wing that night. He didn't need Henning to warn him about the impropriety of visiting the girl like this; it was wrong in just about every context there was, yet still he did it, and intended to continue doing it. This must be the streak of rebellion that Conrad had detected in him.

In the doorway of the seventh room, he paused, disoriented. She wasn't in the bed. She was sitting on the windowsill, perched over the void.

"How did you get over there, fraulein?"

She glanced across at him.

"By hook and by crook."

"You're not supposed to be putting weight on your leg yet."

"I didn't put my weight on it. I have devised a safe technique for perambulation, and although it owes more to Bela Lugosi than I could wish, it really does work."

"Nevertheless, you must not risk further injury."

She turned back to the window.

"Some things are worth the risk," she insisted. "It's a full moon. Look at this room, it's glowing. I just had to see the moon that could do that."

Crossing the room, Peter glanced up and felt the muscles in his face relax into awe as the light bathed him, its cool silence singing softly in his head.

"Have you ever seen a moon like that?" she demanded.

"I don't remember the last time I even looked."

"I walked on a mountain road in Greece once," she said, "and a moon just like this one hung in the sky right in front of me. So big and so bright it was impossible to look at anything else. I almost believed I could step right off the road and be inside it, but the road wound away around the mountain again, and all I could do was stand at the corner and stare at it."

Still hypnotized by the moon, his words spoke themselves.

"Tell me... where would you choose to be right now, if you could stand for one moment in any spot in the world?"

There was a brief pause before she answered.

"On a mountain in Scotland."

He was surprised.

"Not in England with your postman? Not in Greece, swimming in the stars and stepping into the moon?"

"You said 'for one moment,'" she replied soberly. "If I had only that one moment, then I would choose to spend it standing in the mountain winds in Scotland. The memories of all the centuries that have ever been are in those winds, and when they blow through you, they put everything into perspective."

He watched her face as she spoke. He had become familiar with her various moods; the prim correctness, the dreadful finishing school archness, and the teasing gleam that often provoked his own willing laughter, but now she was unguarded, unveiled by the unearthly light, so he watched and waited, and after a while she spoke again. Slowly and awkwardly.

"I have tucked myself away in a drawer and put myself to sleep, waiting until a time when it will be safe to live, but, in that cell, with Steiger... well, there are no guarantees that

that time will ever exist." She stopped and sighed. "There are places in this world where you can be closer to the essence of life itself," she continued, "I have felt it. In Greece you can see it; the light shimmers with it. In Scotland you can feel it in the wind." She closed her eyes, lifting her face to the mountain winds, "I know I can't – mustn't – wake up in this castle, but in this room, for the one moment that you have offered me, Major Brandt, I want to feel life blowing through me again. I want to wake up."

The charged silence following her words unsettled him, and he flexed his shoulders.

"Sleep, and feel nothing, fraulein," he said abruptly. "That is best."

***

"Will you tell me, Major Brandt, are you in danger?" If she had known that she was going to say that, she would have stopped herself, but it came out of nowhere. He blinked and turned to face her, and for an instant she saw the world tumbling in his eyes until he composed himself, and the familiar, imperturbable shell sealed itself around him, but she'd had her answer.

"Why, fraulein, are you trying to interrogate me?" he said lightly. "I must say, I admire your methods," he added, indicating the beam of moonlight that pierced the window like a searchlight. The moon was just a shaving past full now, and the perfect sphere was beginning to distort.

She smiled.

"Oh, I wouldn't presume."

He moved out of the light and came to stand in the shadows before her.

"Ah, but of course, I'm forgetting," he said, "you don't need to interrogate me; you already know my deepest secrets."

"I do?"

"Oh yes. You told me so, in the town prison, before the

doctor set your leg. I remember the moment vividly because Flight Lieutenant Leigh nearly pounded my brains out of my skull for it."

"Simon fought you?" Her heart thudded once, solidly, like a lead punching bag in her chest, "Oh, God! Striking a German officer; isn't that punishable by death?"

"Indeed, it is," Brandt replied carelessly. "Your friend certainly has a hasty temper, considering the penalty." She hated him, even as she lurched off the windowsill to beg, but he lifted a mollifying hand, "No, there will be no such punishment for Leigh; I'm ashamed to say that I derived sufficient satisfaction from responding in kind. It was highly undignified, but most therapeutic. Now," he added, "since we're on the subject, won't you tell me what it is that you claim to know about me? I want to know why you said those outlandish things."

She sank back down, her heart still labouring.

"Outlandish things?" she said cautiously, "What did I say? My memories are... somewhat fragmented."

"Let me see now, I believe you told me that I 'hide the soul of an angel inside a... a borrowed uniform.' Very cryptic! So, what did you mean?"

"I said that?" she said with a short laugh, "I must have been delirious."

"That was my assumption," said Brandt, "but on reflection," he added quietly, "I wondered if, perhaps, you have what used to be known as the sight."

His words tightened around her like a straitjacket, and she stood up again in one jerky motion. She was going to be burned as a witch after all, and Simon would be shot. How had she allowed herself to trust this man?

"I'm sorry," he said quickly, his hands reaching out to steady her, then pulling back again, "I have frightened you. Please... don't be afraid of me."

"Don't be afraid of you?" she echoed, "What you have just said is enough to have me burned, and you tell me not to be afraid of you? I'm not a witch, Major Brandt." She shuddered convulsively, "I am not a witch." The suddenness of her own disintegration astounded her; the room was jangling with her terror.

"A witch?" he said. "And... burned? We are not in the Burning Times."

She spat out a harsh laugh.

"Are the rumours not true, then about those extermination camps?" He swayed at this, like a skyscraper in an earthquake. "And why do I look like this now?" she persisted, with a flourish of her hand that encompassed her bruised and ravaged body and her shaved head. "And what about Frau Heller? Why did she disappear so suddenly?" Tommie was frightened and angry, but not too frightened and angry to notice that Brandt's shell was cracking. With the wariness of a man venturing onto thin ice, he spoke carefully.

"Frau Heller was under investigation for her intemperate disposition towards the Reich."

"'Intemperate disposition,' yes, of course!" Shock had twisted her laugh into a cackle, and she angrily slapped aside the too-late voice of restraint inside her head, diving into the flow of lava. "Major Steiger is not an incautious man, and I can only imagine that 'Witchfinder' doesn't read too well on one's military record. So, Frau Heller's official charge was 'intemperate disposition,' was it? Well, mine was 'performing a fatal abortion,' but now you know that I did not perform the abortion, and no, Major Brandt, I am not a witch. I'm grateful that your methods of investigation – so far, at least, – are gentler than Major Steiger's, but I must give you the same answer that I gave him," she felt her throat beginning to close up, "I am not a witch."

His face had seized into a mask of horror.

"Major Steiger accused you of witchcraft? Why didn't you say this when the report was made?" She stared at him in confusion. He surely had no motivation for continuing with the charade, but everything was out of control now in her head, and she knew only that she must not say any more. Faced with her muteness, he pressed her. "Fraulein, why did you not report this?"

"Report it?" she burst out, "Report that I was accused of witchcraft?!" He was clearly expecting her to take his question seriously. "When someone cries 'witch,'" she said eventually, "people generally grab a pitchfork. And you have just suggested that I might have the sight..." He squeezed his eyes closed, and she saw that she had misunderstood him.

The fear had been like a trident; one prong for the accusation of witchcraft, one prong for Brandt's betrayal, and one – the central one – for what had opened up in that cell; the malevolent cauldron inside her, now sealed, but where darkness still rippled across the face of the deep.

The fear dissipated, but she was deeply shaken. Not least because her fear had been matched by hurt at what she had perceived as his betrayal, and betrayal can only come from someone who is trusted.

The wound in her shoulder where Steiger had gouged at her birthmark began to ache, and she crossed her left arm over her chest, pressing her palm against it. Brandt caught the movement and his eyes sought hers with a question. She swallowed hard, because the act of speaking the words brought the grit of wood ash to her mouth.

"He was looking for the witch's mark."

His face was quite still.

"And your broken leg?"

"He was performing an exorcism on me, and..." she hesitated, and then lifted her head defiantly. "And the images I provided for him caused him to be overcome by his own fear."

"The salt ring around you," he said, but this time it wasn't a question. He reached out for her left hand, turning it palm upwards, tracing with his eyes the healing wound that carved a line from her wrist to her elbow.

Standing over her with his head bent and his arms outstretched, he awakened the ghost of a memory – a stone angel – but his hands were warm, and the stone angel faded. He lowered her hand.

"Please, sit down, fraulein, your leg..." She drew a deep

breath and sank down onto the windowsill. "I have to confess a degree of curiosity," he said eventually. "You have knowledge of traditional remedies, and... I understand that Major Steiger collapsed suddenly in the cell that night and was taken ill." He left the implication unspoken and she met his eyes, unflinching.

"Major Steiger has a chronic illness, and on that day his condition spiked and was becoming critical. I provided him with the phantoms that he feared most, to help him on his way." She stopped speaking, and a disquieting thought stepped out from the shadows of her mind where it had been lurking. She looked up at him, and the suspicion claimed centre stage. "Now it's my turn to ask questions, Major Brandt," she said quietly. "How is it that you know of the Burning Times?"

He blinked and rubbed his face vigorously, then glanced up over her shoulder into the face of the moon.

"My grandmother was a midwife," he said, "She knew of the old ways. She told me of the witch-hunts, the tortures... the Burning Times. She said it would happen again and again, because it's dormant in people, and she wanted me to be able to recognize it."

"Yet you joined the witchfinders!" she said, her voice crackling like kindling as she stared at the eagle on his chest. He shook his head sharply and leaned forward, lifting her chin with firm fingers, drawing her eyes from the eagle.

"First of all, this is not the uniform of a witchfinder. You know that. And now look at me. Look at me with your eyes that see, and tell me... Do you see a witchfinder?"

"I have looked," she said, "But I don't understand what it is that I see."

He released her abruptly.

"You understand enough," he said, "don't look further." He turned to leave, then turned back and spoke rapidly, "It is my understanding that Frau Heller's disappearance was engineered by her own hand, not by any other agency. Good night, fraulein."

***

"You remind me of my grandmother."

Since that raw night, they had been careful to confine their conversations to safer subjects. He had listened with interest each night to her commentaries on the philosophy texts. She had seized hold of many of the ideas and applied them to practical situations, others she had explored with a stoic determination, and some she had dismissed airily as too abstract to be worth consideration. Sometimes he would watch her fall asleep in the middle of a thought.

You remind me of my grandmother.

Although his words had been impulsive, he genuinely saw no incongruity in them until her response came to him from across the room.

"You might want to avoid using that line in conversation with a real woman, Major Brandt," she said drily.

He was mortified.

"I'm sorry, I..."

She laughed. "No apology necessary. In this place I'm not a real woman."

"Nevertheless, it was a personal observation that..."

"...that I am inclined to take as a compliment. Another one to add to the list. Should I?"

"Yes. Yes, of course!"

"Why, thank you, Major Brandt," she said archly, "you are gallant. What was your grandmother like?"

He sighed.

"She was small, and feisty... and warm. Even when I was only eleven years old, she barely reached my shoulder, but when she took me into her arms, it was like being held by the world. And she laughed like an earthquake – we laughed a lot – and she was soft, and comfortable..." There was a pause. A gaping pause. Dismay. Such a quaint, old-fashioned word, but none more fitting; he was dismayed. What had he just implied? *You remind me of my grandmother... small, and feisty, warm and comfortable.* Maybe she hadn't made the connection. He ventured a glance at her. There was a softness in her expression – probably a response to his last words – but it failed to fully conceal the mischief and amusement there. He rubbed his forehead vigorously.

"And I have just... well, I don't quite know what I have just said." He blinked. Twice. Had there been just the sketchiest suggestion of a long-lost Welsh lilt emerging from beneath the king's English and the clipped Teutonic diction? He shook his head wonderingly. He was stumbling all over this conversation like a new-born deer. Those long-ago men who believed they had been bewitched suddenly didn't seem so misguided. She was laughing again.

"It's my turn to apologise, Major Brandt; that was an ambush. I couldn't resist it. I'm not used to seeing you with your guard down."

"It doesn't happen often."

"I can imagine."

"It's because she was a midwife!" he said abruptly, lifting an explanatory forefinger, "... maybe also because of how you understand philosophy – she would have responded the same way to those books – but mainly it's because she was a midwife. That must be where the association came from. She made remedies. People in her town used to say she was a wi... a wise woman." He hoped he had managed to modify the vowel undetected, but of course she had heard it, and flinched. He was uncomfortably aware that this explanation might not be an improvement on his tongue-tied confusion, but the girl was interested.

"Your grandmother was a wi... a wise woman?" she said, "How was that perceived in Germany back then?"

"In Germany?" he said blankly, and caught himself with a jolt. Just how unguarded could he be? "How was it perceived?" he continued, bringing himself firmly under control, "Well, it was just there, I suppose. I believe that most people thought it was an anachronism; dark and arcane, but they didn't mind it being there as long as it sat quietly in the corner, just in case they might have need of it one day. And now I think I had better be going. Good night, fraulein."

***

"You speak of your grandmother and your mother, but you don't mention your father."

Their conversations had become increasingly, though still cautiously, candid and searching, in a way that reminded Tommie of her early interactions with Sam; curious and exploratory, and as innocent as Eden.

"My father was killed in the last war. I have no memory of him. My mother also died when I was young, and I was raised by my grandmother – when I wasn't in boarding school."

"Raised by a wisewoman."

He nodded.

"She had an unorthodox approach to life, and a woman's natural lack of appreciation for the codes of honour that men are steeped in."

She took a quick, outraged breath. "You think women don't understand honour...?"

"No, I don't. And that's not what I said!"

"It most certainly is!"

"It most certainly is not. I didn't say 'understanding,' I said 'appreciation,' and I meant 'appreciate' in the sense that some women – alright, I should have qualified that point; *some* women – see no common sense in the abstract forms of honour that hobble so many men." He held up a hand, fending off her objection, "Let me give you an illustration of what I mean; on a street in Moscow one day, years ago now, I saw people queuing for bread. The line stretched away down the street and around the corner. After working a long day in the factories, there they were, standing for more than an hour, waiting – hoping – to buy a loaf of bread. Now, that was not an unusual sight at the time, but what struck me was that every person on that line was a woman. Every one. Without exception. I asked one of them why there were only women in the queue, and I was told, 'For a man it is an insult to his honour to queue for bread.' 'But not for a woman?' I asked. She shrugged and said, 'A woman has to feed her family.'"

Tommie nodded thoughtfully.

"In Ibsen's play, A Doll's House, Torvald says to his wife, 'No man would sacrifice his honour for the one he loves,' and Nora says, 'It is a thing hundreds of thousands of women have done.' That interaction has always stayed with me."

He spread his hands.

"So, you see what I mean? My grandmother used to say that honour can only be honourable when it embraces common sense and humanity, and I think most women would instinctively understand that, but most men I know perceive honour as an abstract concept that must remain independent of all other circumstances. Such a man will tell you that honour cannot be assayed by anything quite so base as common sense." His eyes closed briefly, and she saw the dark pain stab at him. He drew a long, deep breath, then continued. "I knew a man whose whole life – his whole existence – was bound to his understanding of honour... until circumstances cleaved that concept of honour cleanly down the middle. When that happened, he was like a great oak tree split by lightning, and his soul began to die at that moment."

She remained silent until she could see that he had processed the pain.

"And you?" she said then, "Do you live your life bound to your honour?"

He sighed deeply.

"As far as I have been able to understand it, I think that honour and duty are not entities that exist independently. They should be used like a decoder; you should perceive life through that decoder, hold it up against difficult decisions, but if it causes a distortion – if life itself doesn't make sense when perceived through the decoder – then you should be prepared to set it aside and work from instinct. Otherwise, nature is betrayed, and you are lost." They remained together in thoughtful silence for a long moment, and then he smiled slowly, "No, fraulein, even if I did believe that women don't understand honour, I would not be so foolish as to engage you on the subject. I have seen how excitable you can become over a mere swede."

She blinked, taken by surprise, and then blushed.

"That was no mere swede, Major Brandt, as you well know," she said primly, "that was both a swede and a principle, and I wasn't about to relinquish either one of them."

***

He brought her a copy of a new book, published in France, that had intrigued him, and he was interested to know her thoughts on it.

"The Myth of Sisyphus," she said, then read the quote in the front; "'There is but one truly serious philosophical problem, and that is suicide.' That sounds a bit dark."

"Perhaps. Perhaps not," he said, "let me know what you think when you have finished it." She held the book in her hands, running her fingertips over its cover. "I have my own copy," he said in the face of her hesitation, "I bought this for you to keep." That caused her to glance up at him, but she remained silent, and eventually she handed it back to him.

"If I were to keep the book," she said slowly, "which I would very much like to do, I'm afraid the cover would have to be cut off."

He cursed his insensitivity. Those were the rules of the castle – for prisoners. And she was a prisoner.

"Of course," he said, and in grim silence he took out his knife and carefully sliced through the binding. She watched, a frown bringing a deeper shadow to her face.

"It hurts to deface a book."

"It does," he agreed, "but being able to read it is the important part." Handing her the book, he hesitated. "Needless to say," he said quietly. She understood; this wasn't a book that would have found its way legitimately into her possession.

"Needless to say."

***

"It can't be safe for you to be so... fragile."

There it was again; that hint that she understood at least the bones of his position. News of the assassination attempt and the fate of the conspirators had been broadcast on the BBC, and it was known that the prisoners had at least one radio set concealed somewhere in the castle, but for her to make the association with him was impossible. Even Gehlen was unaware of that connection. So far.

"I'm not fragile," he said sharply, then rubbed his eyes wearily and apologised for his abruptness. "I've been having trouble sleeping," he added, as though she might not have noticed that, for the past few weeks, he had spent the untethered hours of every night talking with her. These hours were a lifeline for him; a sanctuary from the dreams, but in the daytime a tidal wave of exhaustion would rise up behind his shoulders and loom over him.

He stared out of the window. The floodlights were on tonight, and there was no velvet blackness out there in which to rest his eyes, just a harrowing electric glare, so he turned his eyes to the girl sitting up in the bed.

"Can you suggest something that helps with sleep?"

"Do you use a hot water bottle?"

"A hot water bottle?"

She reached under the bedcovers and drew out a rubber hot water bottle. He stared at it and she shrugged, "If it takes more than a hot water bottle to get you to sleep, then a sleeping draught won't do you any good."

"It's the middle of summer."

"But it's always chilly in the castle. Anyway, it's not about the warmth, it's about the comfort."

He tried to smile, but the smile was dragged beneath the

surface and drowned.

"Getting to sleep is not the problem; staying asleep is the problem."

"Dreams?"

"They don't feel like dreams." He closed his eyes… and jolted awake. He had almost fallen asleep standing there in front of her. "Can you help me?" he said gruffly, "What about this?" he bent to pick up one of the creamy flower-heads that had fallen from her bed, "You sleep with these around your pillow."

She gathered up the rest of the flowers and pressed them into his hands. Soft and cool and frothy against his palms, they released a faint honey-almond fragrance.

"This is meadowsweet," she said, "it is thought to induce a death-like sleep." He knew he had failed to conceal the flicker of hope in his face at this, and she nodded. "You can take those with you if you like. Flight Lieutenant Leigh brings them to me fresh almost every day, or, if you would rather gather your own, it grows in the hedgerows. I could recommend valerian or camomile or lavender or hops, but all of those remedies are only effective for someone who is within the normal parameters of stress, and, if you don't mind my saying so, Major Brandt, I think you are far beyond the normal parameters of stress. The only way for you to be able to sleep is to face the demons that are denying you that sleep. And you need to cry."

You need to cry. How strange that she should feel comfortable saying such a thing to him. And how strange that he found himself able to respond candidly.

"No. If I do that, I will break."

"And then you will heal."

"I can't afford to break."

"None of us can afford to break, but we all must."

"No."

"Then at least you must face your demons."

"That is not possible," he said shortly, then hesitated before venturing, cautiously, "Frau Heller helped you to sleep after the French officer attacked you. You were deeply asleep that night."

She nodded. "That would work."

"Can you do that for me?" he asked, grimacing at the hopefulness in his own voice. The image of her lying there that night, lost to the world, had remained with him as a vision of utopia. The girl didn't answer. "What did she give you?" he persisted.

"She didn't give me anything," she replied, composedly, "she let me scream out my anger, and then she held me while I cried."

He heard his own hiss of frustration, forceful in the silence of the room.

"Well, I thank you for your advice," he said, heading towards the door. "Unfortunately, I cannot act on it. Good night."

"Good night, Major Brandt. I'm genuinely sorry to disappoint you."

That stopped him. Still clutching the flowers, he turned back to her, shaking his head. "I am never disappointed by honesty." At his words, an odd expression passed over her face, and he sighed. "Have I said anything again?" he said, mentally deploring the contorted grammar. She smiled faintly.

"No, Major Brandt, but I think I just met your grandmother."

He frowned, replaying his own words back to himself, and nodded. "Yes, I believe you did. Good night, fraulein."

31
Kissing the angel

This was it. Soon the dreams would plague him no more. Summoned by Gehlen for a private meeting at the end of the working day, Peter swung the Pioneer around the last bend in the road and halted in front of the security barrier at Zossen. A lowering darkness was gathering over the compound, exhaled from the endless pines as they dripped into their muffled gloom.

His heart knocked against the inside of his ribs. This had to be it. Gehlen had complained just yesterday about being forced to allow the Gestapo free access to FHO's files; what possible reason could his senior officer have for ordering this meeting other than that he had discovered the explosives requisition form that bore, somewhat defiantly, Peter's own signature. He would confront Peter with the form, explaining, perhaps regretfully, that he was duty-bound to hand the evidence over to the Gestapo.

Pausing for a moment outside the door to Gehlen's office, he composed himself. He would leave here under arrest. The thought of Hendry and his big picture came fleetingly to his mind; after all the lives that had been thrown in front of Hitler's juggernaut, would there be enough left to stand against Stalin? What would Europe look like in the aftermath of that battle? Peter would never have to find out. In answer to his knock, Gehlen's voice called out.

"Komme."

Two SS officers were standing at the near left corner of Gehlen's desk. They turned and stared speculatively at Peter as he entered. Peter returned the stare. He didn't need to look down to know that their uniforms bore the poison-green police-pattern shoulderboards of the Gestapo.

Gehlen greeted him cheerfully.

"Ah, Major Brandt, here you are, thank you for coming so promptly. I believe these two gentlemen have all but completed their investigation and are about to leave."

The shorter of the two glanced back down at the file in his hands.

"The form that we mentioned over the phone is not here, Herr General-Major," he said, "You can conduct your business with this officer in our presence if you wish, but we will not be leaving this room without the requisition form."

"Yes, of course," Gehlen replied, "the requisition form for the British explosives... what a terrible business. Let me see now, where did I put it?" He opened and closed one or two drawers in his desk, then unlocked the top drawer on his left, drew out a sheet of paper, glanced at it briefly and handed it over. Peter felt his throat constrict. It was impossible that Gehlen had not noticed whose signature was on the form. Why would he engineer this humiliating scene?

The officer slid a finger down the page to the signature, then nodded, and gave a sour laugh.

"How many times can you hang a man?" He turned to Peter, "Major... Brandt, is it? Were you acquainted with Major Erich Lohse?"

"Yes, I know Lohse. He is a particularly capable intelligence officer," answered Peter.

"*Was*, Major Brandt... *was*," snapped the officer, not liking the reply. Maintaining his cold gaze on Peter's face, he slipped the incriminating form into his file, "And I suggest that you revise your assessment of the man."

"Why would I do that?"

"Major Lohse was executed yesterday afternoon after being found guilty of numerous charges of treason," said the other officer. "We came here today to tidy up a couple of loose ends that might have been woven into his noose if we had known about them earlier."

A pill of suspicion lodged in Peter's throat, dispensing sickness.

"May I see that form, please?" he said hoarsely. From the corner of his eye, he saw Gehlen stiffen slightly. The stocky officer hesitated, then drew the requisition form from the file and handed it to him. There, squarely entered on the line, was Lohse's signature in the place where Peter had signed his. He could feel the officers examining him; vultures watching a staggering animal.

"Do you have any comment on this business, Major Brandt?" said the taller one dangerously. Gehlen leafed noisily through a pile of papers on his desk and injected a tone of impatience into his voice.

"I'm sure that Major Brandt, in common, I should say, with everyone in this department, finds it difficult to comprehend that a fellow officer – someone with whom he has worked closely, someone in whom he placed his trust – could have been using his position for the furtherance of treason," he said. "Isn't that right, Peter? Now, if you will excuse us, gentlemen, as the Fuhrer himself has so admirably demonstrated, the business of the Reich must go on." He escorted the two men to the door, murmuring bland pleasantries.

Their departure was no consolation to Peter; the signature on the page had seared itself into his brain like a branding iron, threatening to ignite the tinderbox of his mind.

"They've gone," Gehlen said shortly. He was standing at the window now, watching the staff car as it left the compound.

"He didn't do it!" Peter exploded. Gehlen turned and set an expressionless gaze on him. "Lohse, Herr General-Major, he wasn't the one who requisitioned those explosives..." He stopped abruptly and shook his head. "That signature... how long have you known about me?"

Gehlen ignored the question.

"FHO has been decimated by this witch hunt, Peter, and I refuse to lose one more man for the sake of a foolish and marginal involvement. As far as I can see, this incident with the explosives is your one indiscretion. Am I correct in that?"

"Yes," Peter said bitterly, "apart from that, I did nothing."

"Then it has been erased."

"But it wasn't yours to erase. It was my decision. My action. Lohse answered for his own actions. I will not have him answer for mine."

"Lohse was found guilty of involvement in five known attempts on the Fuhrer's life, does it really matter if his signature on that one piece of paper is not authentic?"

"Of course it matters! This is dishonourable!"

"And what would salve your conscience, Major Brandt? Confessing? Throwing yourself onto the conflagration? That officer made a good point; how many times can you hang a man? The People's Court managed to turn those five attempts into almost a dozen charges of treason. Lohse hanged for each one, and each one was his own doing. You couldn't have saved him by confessing to your involvement, Peter, but his signature on that paper can save you."

"Save me from an honourable death?"

"An honourable death?" Gehlen stared at him, and as Peter held his gaze, his hard eyes seemed to soften slightly. "Let me tell you something that I heard recently," he said slowly. "In the anarchy immediately following the attempted assassination, Stauffenberg and others were arrested and immediately put in front of a firing squad in the courtyard of the Bendlerblock – that noble citadel of honour. At the moment the order to fire was given, Mertz von Quirnheim threw himself in front of Stauffenberg, presumably in a gesture of his dedication to the man and the cause. Mertz fell dead instantly, of course, but Stauffenberg had to remain there waiting for the firing squad to reload, take aim and fire again before he could reach his peace." Gehlen sighed. "Honour has become a very convoluted concept in this war, Peter," he said, "but nowhere in all those convolutions can it be considered an honourable death to be labelled a traitor to Germany by this filthy regime." He opened a drawer in his desk, drew out a printed form and, glancing at Peter's signature on the line, he struck a match and set fire to it, dropping it as it flared, into a waste-paper bin.

Peter went to the window, threw it open and leaned out. He wanted to take a deep breath of the pine-filtered, oxygen-saturated air, but he found that he couldn't. His ribs could expand barely enough to keep his body functioning. Europe lay around him, choking in its own smoke, and here he was, being kept alive against his will, steeped in clean air that he couldn't breathe. Defeated, he turned back into the room.

Gehlen had crossed to a walnut cabinet on the far side of his office, and was pouring brandy into two crystal glasses. He held one out for Peter, and indicated the chair on the far side of his desk.

"Take a seat, Peter." The air in the room was laced with the bitter smell of burned paper, and Peter shook his head, wanting only to leave. "This is not mere hospitality," said his senior officer sharply, "there is a particularly sensitive issue that I must discuss with you, and although I wish I could postpone it until a time when you are less... shall we say shell-shocked, I'm afraid that we cannot delay any further. So please take a seat and accept the brandy." Peter took the glass, but declined the seat.

Gehlen shrugged and settled himself in his own chair.

"I have resolved to preserve, intact, the files of FHO, and to present them as an offering to the Americans when this area is... liberated." It took a while for his words to arrange and rearrange themselves in Peter's mind in a way that he could grasp, and Gehlen, savouring his brandy, allowed the information to percolate before continuing. "Germany must lie in ashes for a long, cold winter, and it is up to us to carry its seeds to safety until spring returns," he said eventually, "America is the only power strong enough to stand for us against Russia."

"But surely the British..."

"The British have turned us down once already. I will not go to them again."

"Turned us down?"

"I made the offer to London some time ago. It was received enthusiastically in some areas, but in the end, it was squashed quite unceremoniously. This was not entirely unexpected; one can only come across so many practical men in an organization before a sensible proposition gets shot down by someone's unimpeachable ethics."

Peter heard very little else after that, and, recognizing this, Gehlen dismissed him with instructions to report back after the weekend. As he closed the door behind him the walls seemed to tilt suddenly away on both sides, and he side-stepped quickly, reaching out to steady himself. Rubbing his eyes angrily he regained his balance and left the compound.

The British have turned us down. How could that be true? What Gehlen offered was the jewel in the crown of Hendry's greatest ambition; the focal point of his precious big picture. It was the whole reason for Peter's being in Germany. What had happened to Hendry?

The tidal wave of exhaustion and futility hung over him, roaring in his ears, and Peter yearned for its swift, crushing impact. He had expected to be taken today – had *wanted* to be taken – by the same wave that had swept Conrad away, that had claimed Beck and the little girl, Malki, and so many others. Until now he had still been tied to them, and to their fate, by his signature on that piece of paper, but now the connection had been severed and he was stranded; truly alone.

With no pressing reason for being in one place rather than another, Peter found himself heading towards the castle. How improbable it was that he should anticipate even a whisper of consolation there, but in his imploding brain its soaring, grey walls were the closest thing to home.

He passed through the outer gates and stashed the motorbike in its shed. After that, flinching from the prospect of the dreams, he sat in his office as darkness deepened around him.

When lights-out had been called, he made his rounds mechanically, pacing like an automaton through the corridors. The bands were biting viciously into his chest, and he could no longer ignore the pain or the spatial disturbances that had plagued him since he left Gehlen's office. He couldn't possibly visit the hospital wing in this condition; she would take one look at him with those eyes of hers and know everything. She would see him. And now, with a shock, he understood that this was something he wanted very badly. He wanted her to see him. He wanted it more than he wanted to take his next breath.

Fumbling with his keys at the pass door to the hospital wing, he paused to stretch the bands around his ribcage fractionally. He needed just enough breath to keep him from fainting.

As the door swung open, he was confronted by a swirl of white linen beneath a smudge of dark hair. The world shifted, and there was Malki, her white dress blotted with the yellow star. If he turned around, he would see Conrad sitting at the café, hand in hand with Greta. They would still be alive – everyone would still be alive – and, somehow, together, they would be able to stop the nightmare. He lifted his hands to his temples, and his vision cleared.

It was Tomasin West that he could see, speeding up the corridor towards him on crutches, with Frau Heller's linen nightgown flowing around her legs. She stopped short, staring at him. She saw everything, and he was ashamed. What had he been thinking, offering his disintegration up to her like a child running to his grandmother's arms? He swept the disorientation aside and snapped at her, cold and peremptory.

"What are you doing out here in the corridor?"

She lowered her gaze and glanced down at her crutches,

and when she lifted her eyes again, they skimmed over the surface of him, reconstructing, with unbearable mercy, the shell of him; the uptight, composed officer.

"I'm practicing for my escape attempt, Major Brandt," she said, throwing him a lifeline, drawing him safely into their familiar banter. "When I get over the wire, I want to hit the ground running. Now that I have an extra pair of legs, what do you think of my chances?"

He caught hold of the lifeline.

"Every bit as good as those of your fellow prisoners," he replied evenly. She winced and rewarded him with a sour look.

"Tch! Uncalled for," she chided him gently.

"The crutches were provided to help you move around safely inside your room," he said, "not to allow you the freedom of the castle." That was better; he had regained control of himself. He lifted his arm and gestured for her to return to her room. "If you please."

Unchastened, she bent to pick up the headscarf, which had slipped off in her progress up the corridor, tied it around her head again, then turned and made her way back towards the seventh room.

"They're fun. Have you ever used crutches?" she asked.

"No."

"You should try them sometime."

"Are you threatening me?"

He followed her into the shadows of her room as, laughing, she turned around to reply, but the crutches were awkward, and one wedged itself in the frame of the bed, wrenching itself out of her grasp and clattering to the floor. Caught halfway through her turn, she twisted and spun, and the white gown fanned out as she flung her arms out for balance. The other crutch fell, and she pitched forward. He lunged and broke her fall, catching her against his chest just before she hit the ground, but now, with her good leg trapped underneath the plaster cast, she was unable to stand.

"Put your arms around my neck," he said urgently. She stiffened. "Put your arms around my neck," he repeated, "and hold on. I will stand up and lift you with me." He sensed her casting around for options and recognizing that she had none. Leaning her weight against him, she lifted her arms and anchored them around his neck, turning her face away from his. He grasped her around the waist and slowly stood up, taking her with him.

"Major Brandt...? Thank you, I'm alright now."

Time contorted. How long had they been standing here together? Everything was dark, and her voice came from somewhere near his right ear. He heard his own voice, toneless, responding.

"Can you stand?"

"No."

He cursed.

"You've damaged your leg!"

"No," she said again, "I can't stand because my feet aren't touching the ground."

"Ah. I see." He found that he was clutching her against him, *Peter, catch hold of this.* Her breath was warm on his neck and the weight of her against his chest was comforting. He had saved her, and the prospect of letting her go was inconceivable. "I should let you go." For a moment she didn't answer, then her voice came again, almost inaudible.

"Yes."

He nodded and released her carefully, lowering her to the floor, keeping his hands around her waist until he was sure she could stand independently. As he released her, she drew her arms down from his shoulders, then hissed. The long wound that stretched from her wrist to her elbow was welling with blood that bulged black against the white skin. Her eyes found the eagle insignia on his chest, which held the scab, stripped from her arm.

Bird.

Malki stared at the eagle on his tunic, and the blood ran down towards the crook of her elbow, towards the pristine fabric of her gown, as the room distorted around him again. He lifted her sleeve away from the wound, but the blood was spilling, and Malki was spinning, fading into the shadows, then she was gone, and the blood dripped to the floor, splashing up in a fine red spray over the white fabric.

Bird.

With its wings spread wide, the eagle gripped the scab in its beak, and Peter groaned, a guttural, alien sound, fumbled to unbutton his tunic, pulled it off and flung it away from him. He took hold of her arm and pressed his shirtsleeve against the wound, cupping his fingers around her elbow. Minutes passed in silence as they stared at their twinned arms, and when he lifted his arm from hers, his sleeve bore a crimson wound of its own. The blood welled again. She swayed slightly and he gripped her elbow.

"Are you going to faint?"

"No," she said, lifting her face defiantly. It was a violence to him that now, after all these nights, because of that eagle, she would see him as the enemy, but her eyes widened, and in them he saw, reflected, the glowing whiteness of his shirt. She drew a long, slow breath.

"Oh! You see? An angel." Then, just for an instant, she raised herself to stand on tiptoe, gently touching her lips to his, and he felt her breath against his mouth as she sank back away from him leaving him with no breath.

Because now there was no breath at all. The steel bands around his ribs had seized. He had yearned for death – still yearned for death – and yet now he reached out for life, pressing his mouth against hers, searching for her breath and sucking it into his own lungs. Miraculously, his ribs expanded, allowing it to happen. He felt her body stiffen, startled, and then soften with understanding, and he cried out with gratitude for her humanity, her forbidden mercy. He breathed deeper and deeper, filling his lungs. The pains that crushed his chest were gone, and he breathed.

Until the gently prohibitive pressure of her fingertips through the fabric of his shirt ruptured the oblivion, and he broke away from her. Her face was wet with tears, and remorse slammed into him.

"Ah, God, you are crying."

"No, Major Brandt, you are crying."

The words didn't make sense, but his face was streaming with salt water. He lifted his hands to sweep it away, but she took his wrists in a cool, gentle grip, restraining them. His new, unleashed breath was seizing in jerky, childish sobs, dredging up the most invasive roots of an intolerable grief, and she watched him, her face a pale gleam beneath the gaudy colours of the headscarf, her eyes holding his with infinite compassion as they stood together in the cavern of the wave. The long-anticipated concussion was coming, and the bands tightened suddenly, compressing the sobs into a grunt. He felt a gentle, precipitative pressure on his wrists.

"Cry."

"No."

"Cry, angel," she said, "I will hold you."

The iron bands snapped with the sound of a rifle shot, and snaked off into the writhing air.

He broke silently, clawing at the crumbling façade of his self, but when he understood – if this primitive instinct was understanding – that it was useless to cling to wholeness; when he found, with a cold horror, that his whole body was twitching and convulsing, felt his eyes staring, mouth stretched wide, retching with the unbirthable grief, then he dropped to his knees, buried his face in her torso and screamed. Again and again he screamed, until the veins in his face boiled. His lungs convulsed, releasing barely long enough to suck in another breath and do it all over again.

Every scream was a suffocation, emptying him. Each one was an echo he left behind to haunt nobody, because nobody was left. He screamed until his lungs, his ribs, the gristle of his joints, fused into one incandescent lump. And she held him. Pinned to the bed by his weight, she put her arms around his shoulders and held him. Her body shook with the violence of his grief, but she held him, and he wept.

He wept for Conrad, and for Greta and for their severed lives. He wept for the obliterated dreams of the countess, for Ludwig Beck and the man's slandered betrayal of his life's values. He wept for Malki and for himself, and for Germany.

When exhaustion had shrivelled him from the inside out,

and he understood that he had to get up and keep living, he withdrew his arms stiffly from around her, braced himself with his hands either side of her on the bed-frame, and stumbled to his feet.

Through the raw slits of his eyes, he saw that the headscarf had slipped to the floor, and that her head was dusted with a downy new growth of hair, a soft dark moss that covered the scars, but he remembered them – the jagged, cruel gashes. What right did he have to seek sanctuary in the arms of this bruised girl? To risk visiting his curse on her? He was the angel of death, and she had embraced him.

"I bring death to everyone I touch."

"No. You are tired."

The brutal grief came surging over him again, and he sobbed with its impact, but he was drained of tears, dried out.

"Help me," he said. Somehow there was a mattress beneath him, and his head was sinking into a pillow. But he mustn't sleep. He twisted on the bed, struggling to sit up, his arms flailing feebly. "Don't let me sleep."

She reached out to him, and her fingertips, as cool and soft as the flowers that bring a death-like sleep, hovered over his burning face, tracing intricate filigree patterns, then drifted over his eyes, closing them.

"Sleep," she said. "I will watch over you."

The ultimate comfort; to close your eyes to this world.

***

She had kissed him. *Given him a kiss*, she amended quickly, because this amendment seemed to disengage her from the act, or at least to defuse it. The kiss had been dream-like, but she had to acknowledge that – as it would have appeared to him – she had kissed him, and this one action had precipitated his catharsis.

And then he had kissed her. No amendment here; he had

kissed her. But his kiss had been the desperation of a drowning man, a man breaking the membrane of the waters for the third time. A kiss purely for the purposes of seizing breath. A self-resuscitation.

She had put her hands on his chest to steady him, had held his wrists as he struggled with the inevitable. She had held his eyes with hers when the terror in them detonated with the knowing that he must break apart, and when his arms had circled her body, gripping her, and his screams had penetrated her core like the searing blossom of a flamethrower, she had held him.

When the rigidity in his frame had subsided into a shocked passivity he had risen to stand before her. His eyes, almost fully eclipsed by swollen eyelids, had sought the bed, and she had stepped aside, allowing him to topple onto it and crawl to the pillows with blind instinct, his boots catching in the sheets.

She had stilled his last, frightened struggle against sleep, trailing her fingertips over his face, not touching, just close enough to feel the heat radiating from his skin. Close enough to banish the night terrors that she could only imagine. And now, listening to his breathing, she watched the ravaged man as he slept like the dead.

How many times had she been curious about him, wanting to look more closely into his face without drawing that countering, cool scrutiny? Now she had a chance to really see him, so she looked.

She took in his forehead, gouged with the ghosts of furrows which remained graven there even in the stillness of sleep. She followed the dark eyebrows, sweeping outwards towards the temples, lingered over the broad eye sockets where the fine, pale skin was deeply shadowed beneath the dark lashes, and along the deep grooves beside his mouth.

In the intensity of his sadness, he had seemed to her like a stone angel, but now the angel had disintegrated before her, cracking and exploding along hidden flaws to reveal an all-too-human man. She had offered her kiss as she once had to a stone angel in a graveyard, but this was no stone angel.

Drawing a long, slow breath, she turned around and reached out to untangle the sheets and remove his boots. Her hands closed around the form of his foot inside – and leapt away with a crackle of static. And then she stood very still for a very long time.

She had feared, at the moment of his catharsis, that Brandt would – in his absolute dissolution – seek more than was offered; it was the stuff of thousands of romantic fictions, after all, but she had been deceiving herself, because even before she kissed the angel it had been *her* blood that flared like sheet lightning as she put her arms around his neck. It had been *her* body that quickened when she found herself stretched against him. And it was her poor little locked-away heart that sparked now, longing to touch otherness. Not just *any* otherness, this was no base, biological urge for human contact; this longing was for Brandt, for his quick, quiet smile, his startling laugh, his self-contained silences, his honour and his dignity, for his tall, straight figure, for his chest, and his broad shoulders, and yes, for his moody eyes.

At what point had she known – and hidden the knowledge from her conscious mind – that Sam had been right about him, and she had been wrong? Because Brandt's kiss, although it had been a drowning kiss, had held an indefinable something... a something that wouldn't have been there if Sam had been wrong and she had been right.

How had this happened? She had blocked out every man here, except for this one. Quickly, she drew the sheet over him, boots and all, covered him with the blanket, picked up the crutches, and retreated to her chair.

***

Peter jolted from sleep to wakefulness in an instant, sitting bolt upright too quickly and drawing breath with a shock that scorched his throat. She was sitting in the armchair with the RAF greatcoat covering her. His brain contracted savagely, and he released the breath with a groan. "What time is it?"

"It's still early – five o'clock."

He wrestled himself free of the blankets, his boots catching in the sheets and pulling them loose from the mattress. Leaving them there in a careless tangle, he stumbled gracelessly off the bed, retrieved his tunic and his cap, and then crossed the room again to stand in front of her. Reaching out, he took hold of her hand and turned it over to examine the wound that his uniform had reopened. At some point in the night the bleeding had stopped, and the blood had dried and crusted, both on her arm and on his sleeve. He could feel more of it on the back of his shirt where, still bleeding, she had held him in her arms. He swallowed hard and lifted his eyes to hers.

"My conduct has been unforgivable, Fraulein West. I will not visit you again."

***

I must act according to my own conscience.

The countess' words had come back to him several times that morning. Hadn't Tomasin West used the same words when – so long ago now – he had questioned her about delivering the Frenchwoman's baby? Last night, in comforting him, she had again acted according to her conscience, but this morning he had taken her actions and contaminated them with his confusion. He felt his face twist.

From outside his head, in the meeting room, a prickling silence reached him. Stanislav Kuzachenko, who had been delivering his weekly report, had faltered and stopped talking, and now there were comments passing between the three Russians.

"Give up, Stanislav," said Viniski dryly, "you're wasting your breath on the man today." Kuzachenko shrugged and laid his papers on the desk. Dmitri Gevnady stretched his arms above his head, linked his fingers and leaned back in his chair, grinning.

"I could do with stretching my legs. Do you fancy a walk? We could leave the room and he wouldn't know."

"We could leave the castle and he wouldn't know," said Kuzachenko. Gevnady snorted with laughter and Peter snapped out of his reverie.

"Good morning, Major Brandt," said Viniski with a slow smile.

"Good morning, Major Viniski," replied Peter, choosing to ignore the sarcasm. "Now, where were we?" he said briskly.

"Well, *we* were listening to Stanislav Kuzachenko's weekly report," said Viniski, "but I can't speak for where you were, Major Brandt."

"That's right. Captain Kuzachenko, please continue."

The Russian's heavy voice began again, outlining the progress he was making in the prison camp at Dabendorf. New intelligence continued to filter in daily, from prisoners recently interned, of troop movements in Ukraine.

His shirt, stiff with her blood, was soaking in the basin in his room right now, but the repercussions of the night would not be so easily washed away. The girl had given him warmth and compassion in his moment of disintegration, but, with the knee-jerk reflex of convention, he had denounced their interactions – not only of last night, but of all the nights they had shared – as nothing more than a regrettable breach of propriety. He clenched his jaw. He had to explain his mistake. He would visit her one more time, if she would receive him, to set things straight. A soaring happiness surged in him at the thought of seeing her again, dispersing the hopelessness that had claimed him as he left the hospital wing. He closed his eyes and lost himself in the peace of the seventh room.

In the meeting room, Kuzachenko paused again.

"Looks like he had a rough night," he said grimly.

"More likely a smooth night," said Gevnady, "A smooth night out in Berlin," he added, with a lurid motion of his hips, "Ah, I could do with one of those myself."

"Think again," said Viniski. "Take a good look at his face. That's the face of a man whose soul is being turned inside out. The sort of women you're talking about will pull your insides out, but they leave your soul alone."

"Predatory, that's what those women are..." muttered Kuzachenko darkly.

"Which ones?" said Viniski, "The ones who work on your body or the ones who work on your soul?"

"All of them," said Gevnady cheerfully, "all women are predatory. They all want something from you, and they all make a fool of you."

"The only one who can make a man a fool is that man himself." Peter's voice startled the Russians, and he caught Viniski eyeing him with a new interest. "If you please, gentlemen," he added firmly, "Let us get back to the issues at hand. I assure you, you have my full attention now."

***

Tommie had worked herself up into a cold fury. Flying in the face of all his fair-minded posturing, Brandt had proved himself to be nothing more than a stuffed shirt. What insane impulse had led her to kiss him? No matter that the kiss could not, by any stretch of anyone's imagination, be mistaken as anything other than chaste; no matter that it had been offered as a gesture of compassion, it had violated the boundaries that should rightly separate them.

She could have lived with the indiscretion, would have smoothed it over somehow, but Brandt's reaction on waking up had shaken her to the core; not only had he taken it upon himself to assume responsibility for her actions, he had pronounced a sentence for the offence, promising not to return, and so she was to be denied the opportunity to throw his pompous morality back in his face.

It was now late at night, and she had been twisting and turning in the bed, jabbed by angry thoughts, unable to sleep despite her fatigue. Finally, she had thrown back the covers, retrieved her crutches, and begun pacing around the room.

The angry clumping of the crutches hammered her annoyance deeper, and now, from the end of the corridor, came the sound of the door being unlocked and opened. Familiar footsteps echoed from the walls, and she froze, her heart flipping in her chest. Suddenly she suspected that all her furious lucidity was going to tumble around her like nursery blocks the moment she opened her mouth, and she debated whether to make for the bed and feign sleep until he left. Instead, she stood her ground and met him with a stony expression as he appeared in the doorway.

"May I speak to you, fraulein?" he said quietly. She nodded, and he stepped into the room, removed his peaked cap and turned it between his hands, running his fingertips along the band. "I have to apologise to you..."

"You have nothing to apologise for, Major Brandt," she cut in harshly.

"Indeed, I do."

"No, you do not!"

"Last night..."

"Last night?!" she snapped. "Never mind last night. This morning you said you would not visit me again, but that was clearly a lie, because here you are. The lie is something that you may apologise for, but what happened last night is not for you to apologise for. That was precipitated by me, and you have no right to apologise for me. If you feel that you need my absolution for what happened, you have it, but I have no need of yours."

She confronted him square on, proud of her eloquence. "It was *not* a lascivious kiss, Major Brandt," she said, forcefully, "And I didn't take your boots off."

He blinked, and she fought to keep her face neutral after that inexplicable statement.

"I know it wasn't a lascivious kiss, fraulein," he said, "I know precisely what you intended the kiss to precipitate, and as you are aware, it was devastatingly effective." They stood in silence together, inescapably bonded by the memory of his dissolution, and on some level, buried deep beneath her anger, she recognized that his composure was a proto-shell that he was cultivating to contain what had spilled out of him last night. A ghost of the tenderness that she had felt for him in his torment drifted softly through her.

"Have you been alright?" she said, hesitantly. He didn't answer, and the humiliation that had festered during the day resurged. She turned and propelled herself towards the window, her crutches thumping on the flagstones. "Well, anyway, for me it really wasn't so unusual an act; I have always had a soft spot for a wounded animal."

"A wounded animal?"

The dart had struck home, but she was still vengeful. "Or a wounded angel," she amended sourly, staring out into the darkness beyond the floodlights. An intense silence held sway in the room behind her, and then she heard him draw a deep breath.

"I am not a wounded animal, fraulein, and I am certainly not an angel. I am a man, and an officer charged, however indirectly, with your welfare, and you have misunderstood my intention in coming here tonight, so please, hear me out."

She turned back to him as he stepped further into the room and set his cap on the foot of the bed, picked it up quickly, then clenched his jaw and set it down again firmly. "By the codes of military honour, my conduct has been unconscionable since the first night I came to your room... No! I will say it, because it is an inarguable truth, and for this transgression I will apologise, regardless of your sensibilities, because it is my transgression to apologise for, but that is not what has brought me here tonight."

He paused, and they faced each other across the room. "I have come here to apologise for the manner in which I left you this morning," he continued eventually, "My reactions when I woke this morning were instinctive, and offensive towards you, and I have had time to reflect on them since then. I have reflected that your... your compassion towards me last night was not reckless, and not impulsive, but part of a deeply-considered and very specific response to my..." he swallowed hard, "to my despair, which makes what I said to you this morning all the cruder and more distasteful. It is for those actions and those words that I wish to apologise; for the slight that they implied on your own honour."

She watched him for a long moment, and then breathed a deep sigh.

"Then your apology is accepted, and I must apologise for being harsh with you tonight, for attacking you with such spite after what you have been through." She looked down and tugged at the new bandage that the doctor had secured around her left forearm. "I have been thoughtless, Major Brandt; this room is important to you. You told me so, and I should have acted accordingly. I don't know why I didn't. I can see now that I have been standing between you and the healing properties of this room. I will ask the doctor to discharge me to the main castle tomorrow so that you can continue to visit this room with your conscience intact."

"No!" Naked distress, instantly masked, contorted his face. His voice was clipped and emotionless, but what he said tumbled out spontaneously, as though the control he exerted over his face and his voice had no power to censor his words, "There is no healing for me in this room without you. To come here in your absence would be to enter a vacuum."

The force of his suppressed intensity astounded her, reminding her of the condition he had been in at this time the night before, and the memory swept aside what was left of her anger. She sank, confused, into the armchair beside the window.

"Then, clearly, I do not understand what you expect, Major Brandt. Is it that you wish to keep visiting me here in defiance of your conscience? I have neither the strength nor the inclination to continue being a penitent for your unwarranted guilt."

He shook his head and swallowed hard again, clearly as confused and shaken by his own pronouncement as she was, but there was more to come.

"I don't know what I expect. I had intended only to apologize for my behaviour this morning and leave. Now I think that to leave and not return would be to tear my own heart out."

She closed her eyes, shutting out his tortured, desperate vulnerability.

"What happened between us last night has had no negative impact on my conscience," she said, "It is your conscience, not mine, that is the issue here, so tell me, Major Brandt, in all honesty, will your conscience allow you to continue to visit me?"

His face gleamed whitely in the darkness, and she was half afraid that he would collapse again, although his instability appeared to be evolving into a stubborn determination. He drew a deep, shuddering breath.

"With your permission, I will continue to visit you."

32
One of Hendry's people

He had come to long for the touch of her hand on his sleeve as she emphasized a point in their conversations. He would sometimes turn from the window to find her studying him, but in response to his attention she would lift her chin and the neat, demure attitude would slip over her like a veil.

In the daylight, in his office, musing on those visits, he was forced to accept that he was trespassing beyond mere gratitude for her compassion, and, amid the clamour of the warning bells in his head, he fought to reconcile with his conscience the tremor in the air that sensitized his blood cells. When his thoughts took him where they shouldn't, when his hands would imagine reaching out, cradling the softness of her face in his palms, he would force himself to acknowledge the absolute absence of flirtation in her, and he would smile wryly, recalling the way she was as he left her each night; shuffling comfortably down into the bed, pulling the covers up to her chin and around her ears.

He knew that he stood now in the place that Henning had warned him about, but he rebelled against caution, and hungered for the moments he could spend with her.

"How did you make me fall asleep that night?" he said, "And how did you banish the dreams? Was it...?"

"A spell?" she smiled, teasing him, "No, I did nothing out of the ordinary."

"But what about this," he persisted, drawing his hands across his face as she had done, following the pattern her fingertips had traced there, a pattern that he could still feel, like filigree lace on his skin. "Wasn't that a part of some... ritual?"

"No, but it worked, didn't it!" She shook her head, "You were exhausted," she said simply. "A very long way past exhausted, in fact. This..." she passed her hands over her own face, the way she had done to his that night, and his eyes drifted closed involuntarily, "was just an act of physical comfort that released your exhaustion and allowed it to overwhelm your resistance to sleep. As for the dreams, I told you that I would watch over you. Sometimes that's all it takes; knowing that someone's there to ward off the demons."

Once or twice, he had found himself wanting to tell her about Hendry. She was one of Hendry's people too, after all, and the knowledge that these precious, quiet hours with her were founded on a lie of omission rankled with him. He longed to let her know the truth, but each time he went to tell her, before he had finished forming the words in his mind, Hendry's voice would interrupt him, speaking about the woman he had loved in Russia; 'They killed her, of course...' and although Peter couldn't put his finger on who exactly he thought 'they' were, or why they would kill Tomasin West for knowing the truth about him, his still-fragile senses would scream at the thought of her joining Conrad and the others on the other side, out of his reach.

***

"Tomasin." Brandt's voice speaking her name startled her with an almost physical sensation, as though he had leaned across from where he sat on the far side of the windowsill and stroked her face. "It's a good name. A name worthy of a finishing-school graduate. Why do you have them call you Tommie?"

"If they think of me as a Tommy it helps with what your friend Conrad once called my camouflage." She watched the grief surface. "He's dead, isn't he?"

"They all are."

"You're not."

"No, I'm not," he said flatly, and the shadow of an unspeakable misery passed over his face. "That option was taken from me – dishonourably – the night... that night, when I...."

When he failed to finish, she rested a hand on his arm. "Dishonourably?" she said, "but it's not you who is dishonoured if the action came from somebody else."

He nodded and stood up, flexing his shoulders, and she withdrew her hand.

"So, Tomasin West, do you know my name?"

"Yes, I do. It's Peter. Peter Brandt."

The schoolboy smile, the quick dip of his head. "Regrettably, it must remain 'Major Brandt,'" he said, "And I must adhere to 'Fraulein West.'"

"Yes, Major Brandt."

"God willing, this war will soon be over."

She looked up at him, stung by a barbed awareness that for the war to be over meant very different things to each of them, but he was gazing over her shoulder, out into the electric aura of the floodlights, apparently unaware of the incongruity of his words. "I must go to Berlin tomorrow," he said, "and I will have to stay there until Thursday."

"I will miss your company."

"You will enjoy an undisturbed night's sleep for once."

"And you will enjoy a rather more stimulating nightlife."

"Ah, no." He shook his head. "Not so. My habits are those of an old man these days. My evenings will be spent reading in the hotel lobby..." He stopped short and regarded her thoughtfully.

"I apologise," she said quickly, "It was not my intention to pry into your private life. Why are you smiling?"

"Come with me."

"Where?"

"To Berlin. I could smuggle you out of the castle, and we could go to the opera together, or go dancing. Your choice."

Her stomach flipped, and she laughed, surprised and delighted.

"Now wouldn't *that* pose a lively cocktail of practical and ethical issues!"

"Would you come dancing with me, Fraulein West?"

"In my nightgown? With my fuzzy hair?"

Something new was playing across his face; images formed, dissolved, dispersed and re-formed in his eyes, like the random patterns in falling snowflakes, and when he spoke, the patterns invaded his speech with an odd blend of hesitance and recklessness.

"If there were no war, then, and we were not... not *here*, in this castle. Or, when the war is over, if I were to come and find you in England, would you spend time with me? Not in this uniform, of course, but when there are no more uniforms. If it were simply me – Peter Brandt – would you go dancing with me? Or sit in a coffee shop with me, or share a picnic in the park with me? Or would you be ashamed because of who I have been in this war?"

"Ashamed?" she said softly, "*Ashamed*, Major Brandt? I would be honoured to be with you." He stared at her for a moment, as though he was seeing her for the first time, then, with a quick movement, he leaned down and kissed her very briefly, straightened up immediately and lifted a hand to cover his eyes. Indignation surged in her.

"Are you going to apologize again?"

He shook his head, and she saw that the swirling patterns had settled. That something had changed in him.

"No," he said. "No, I won't apologise again." He took her hands, drew her to her feet, and kissed her again, first gently, then, taking her face between his hands, more deeply. There was nothing brief or chaste about this kiss, and the gentle intimacy of his mouth sent a soft heat coursing through her body. If she thought she had crashed through barriers by kissing the angel, his kiss blasted them into match-wood.

He straightened up then, but his palms still cradled her face, keeping it tilted towards his, and his voice was like a shadow in darkness. "And, in case of any confusion, Fraulein West, this is not despair."

"There is no confusion, Major Brandt."

He closed his eyes, drew a deep breath.

"And now I really must leave." Retrieving his hat from the foot of the bed, he headed for the corridor, then turned back. "I will miss your company tomorrow night," he said, with the slightest of smiles, "while I am sitting, alone, in the hotel lobby."

***

The morning light, sifting through the woods beneath the castle, shredded the early mist into glowing organza ribbons and brought a gleam to her skin as she peered into the mirror over the sink. She regarded her reflection critically.

The soft fuzz of her hair's new growth was like a shadow clinging to her head, and her eyes were watchful. She resembled an elf or a pixie; a creature of some fantasy half-world, maybe even a hobbit, she thought, unkindly. She was an odd little woman. A pit-pony. She slid her hands over her hips... a sturdy little pit-pony.

She blinked and shook her head; in the face of all the raging inappropriateness of their situation – in the midst of all the ethical and moral rubble that lay scattered around them – is this really what was concerning her most? That she might not be attractive to him? What should be worrying her was the fact that, outside this room, he was the enemy.

Magic had been going on here. He had been bewitched by something – or she had been bewitched – and he had kissed her. And this time it hadn't been despair. And she had woken up to him.

He had offered to take her dancing, but men like him did not take odd little women dancing in Berlin, and tonight he would be surrounded by the sort of women who *did* go dancing and attend the opera with men like him, and those women wouldn't look like hobbits or pit-ponies; they would be thoroughbreds, tall and willowy. They wouldn't have scarred, shaved heads, and they almost certainly wouldn't lecture him on the merits of hot water bottles. Oh, God! Had she really shown him her hot water bottle? She squeezed her eyes shut.

At some point tonight, in Berlin, distanced from the magic of this room, he would remember what he had said and done last night, and he would be mortified. He would scrabble for an escape route. How could she face him when he came back? *If* he came back.

Maybe he would visit her this morning, early, before he left, and then she could laugh with him, let him know that she knew it had been nothing more than banter; provide him with an escape route that salvaged her pride. Before he realized his mistake. Before he had to cringe.

There was a noise from the open door and she turned to find the doctor standing in the corridor, watching her with an expression of frank dismay. Tommie dropped her hands from her hips and retreated to the far side of the bed.

"Good morning, Doctor Henning."

Henning lowered his head and rubbed the back of his neck vigorously.

"Good morning, fraulein. I have excellent news. The investigation of Katrianna Zahn's case has been concluded, and you have been fully exonerated. It seems that a doctor in the town was in the business of providing abortions for young girls who would pay him in barter. The police found receipts and goods in a pawnbroker's shop, which incriminated the doctor, and his assistant panicked when rumours of witchcraft were connected with the case. She gave the authorities all the information they needed."

"Does Major Steiger know all this?"

"I believe that Major Steiger is still in hospital, I don't know if they have told him, but it makes no difference. The police have formally cleared you of any involvement, so now you can move back into the British quarters."

Tommie was taken by surprise.

"But Major Brandt..." She stopped short. The muscles in the doctor's face had twitched, and after a moment he spoke stiffly.

"Where do you think the order comes from, fraulein?"

Her stomach dropped through the floor. Problem solved; quick and unequivocal.

"Yes, of course. When do I leave?"

"As soon as you are dressed. I will call for a guard to escort you down."

33
Tanchelin, the Magus and the Whore

If he should visit the seventh room again tonight, he would find it unoccupied, as it had been every night since his return from Berlin, but still he went there to stand by the window in the dwindling moonlight, and he would go again tonight.

Dropping himself heavily at his desk, he picked up his pen, made a few notes in the Dabendorf folder, then put the pen down again. Not for the first time, he reached out for the girl's file, but Henning had claimed it. He stared up at the ceiling. How innocent those nights had been, despite his misgivings about their propriety, but that last visit had changed everything. It would have been very wrong for him to continue to visit her in the light of what now existed between them.

Karl had made the right call in discharging the girl to the prisoners' quarters, there could be no arguing, but her absence was like an open wound in Peter's spirit. She had been taken away from him... and delivered back to Simon Leigh. At this thought he slammed shut the Dabendorf file, stood abruptly, stretched the stiff muscles in his back, and stepped over to the window.

The sun was sinking down behind the west wing, gliding over the black staff car that stood in the commandantur courtyard, its SS insignia hanging limply. Steiger's car. Fear exploded in him and he ran, bursting out of his office, sprinting down the corridor, and taking the steps flight by flight. Hearing his precipitous approach, the sentry at the door to the prisoners' courtyard had the pass door open before he reached it, and he forced himself to slow down to a more casual pace as he stepped through.

On the far side of the courtyard, Tomasin West was standing with her back to him, but Peter could see the tension in her body as she faced Steiger and two of his lieutenants.

"My dear Fraulein West," Steiger was saying as Peter approached, "don't look so frightened, I am here for pleasure today, not business. Or is it the other way around?" He laughed, "It's so easy to get them confused."

Other prisoners had gathered in drifts around the scene, and Peter passed between them to stand at the girl's left shoulder. Registering his presence with a frank hardening in his eyes, Steiger continued, "I regret that our last meeting was interrupted, fraulein. Unfortunately, I had to leave before I could finish what I had started. I understand that your guard dog here – or might I say, your lap dog – came and carried you away."

"The Katrianna Zahn investigation has been concluded, Major Steiger," Peter heard his own voice, cold and measured, betraying no trace of the harrowing fear he felt at the unrestricted authority this man had over the girl's fate. "Fraulein West has been exonerated from all charges. If you have any business here it is not with this prisoner. Shall we talk in private?"

"Would you whisk me away to your spartan office so quickly, Major Brandt?" replied Steiger without removing his stare from the girl's white face. "Perhaps you are afraid that I will do it again; carry off your little paramour here for my own pleasure."

Peter's response was forestalled by a quick comment, called out in French.

"Pfah! Who does he think he's fooling? Of everyone in

here, she is the least likely to bring him pleasure."

There was muffled laughter from the circle of onlookers, and Steiger turned pale.

"You will find out who made that comment, Major Brandt, and have him shot!"

"What comment?" said Peter mildly.

Steiger opened his mouth, closed it, then opened it again. "Dismiss these prisoners immediately!"

A dangerous silence reigned. Steiger's face twisted into a sneer. "Perhaps you lack authority over them," he said, and then the sneer evolved into something more volatile. "Or perhaps you are bribing them with leniency in the hope that they will return the favour should the Reich fall?"

Now the only sound in the courtyard was Steiger's laboured breathing as Peter examined the treasure that the man had placed in his hands; was it a trap, or was Steiger genuinely losing his grip? He looked into the yellow eyes and found his answer.

"'Should the Reich fall,'" he echoed. "Surely that's treason, Major Steiger, and spoken in front of witnesses. What can have... possessed you?" The slight pause, and the inflexion that Peter placed on that particular word, erased the menace in Steiger's face, and an eyelid began to twitch.

There was a scuffle of shoes on the cobbles then, and Simon Leigh arrived, eyes blazing, to stand at Tomasin West's other side. Without removing her gaze from Steiger's face, the girl stretched her right arm across Leigh's chest, whether for protection or restraint, Peter couldn't tell. The glow from the setting sun, reflecting off the stones behind Steiger, burnished Leigh's complexion to a bright gold, and fury was radiating from him with the force of a furnace. Steiger appeared to slump slightly, and he stared at the man, his lips moving in a whisper around incongruous words.

"How art thou fallen from heaven, o Lucifer, bright morning star." The girl's hand clenched into a fist.

"Major Steiger?"

Steiger jumped at the sound of Peter's voice, and the yellow tinge to his skin deepened perceptibly.

"There was a man once," he said in a hollow voice, "Simon Magus – Simon the magician. He appeared for all the world as one of the holy ones, an angel of light, but he had thrown his lot in with Satan. You don't know what you're dealing with here, Major Brandt..." He stopped and his tone became speculative, "Or do you? Perhaps you do. Let me see. Brandt... Brandt; I know several families of that name in Antwerp, the city that was once gripped in the claws of Tanchelin." He backed away several steps and appeared to gather his strength. "Tanchelin; the heretic who strove to overturn the One Authority. That sounds not unlike the ideal of communism, I would say; defying the authority of an ultimate leader." He swayed slightly and blinked, his yellow gaze focusing and unfocusing. "How are your pet Russians performing these days? I understand that your work with them is uncommonly secretive. Have you betrayed God, Major Brandt, to work against him with the profane host?"

There was a hiss from the girl.

"It is clear that you have not yet fully recovered from your illness, Major Steiger," Peter replied smoothly, "I suggest you seek professional help."

The rattle of Steiger's breathing was becoming more laboured.

"Satan and his host gather for battle, roused to wakefulness by the burning glory of the Fuhrer," he croaked, and his eyes flickered from Peter to the girl and then ricocheted fearfully off Leigh. "I am confronted by Tanchelin, the Magus and the Whore. So be it. The battle is on."

Beside Peter, Tomasin West drew a long, slow, deep breath, and he glanced down to see a strange, intense malevolence tightening the muscles in her face. Suddenly, she lifted her head, and her voice rang out, clear and loud.

"If you seek to prevail against such an unholy trinity, Major Steiger, you should have been more careful in choosing your men," she announced. "Who can say what manner of..." she paused and gave a sensuous, luscious tut with her tongue, "unhallowed fiend might have already corrupted them. Isn't that right, Lieutenant Boehm?" With the slightest lift of an eyebrow, she turned a luridly knowing gaze on Boehm, parted her lips with her tongue, and then flashed Steiger a broad smile. "Your lieutenant here was quite... stimulated by your performance in that cell, Major Steiger."

Steiger whipped around, stumbled sideways, and fixed the horrified Boehm with a yellow stare. Turning back to the girl, his head wobbling, he blinked owlishly.

"And so, the day of reckoning is upon us," he said in a thin voice. He stalked to the staff car, and his lieutenants followed uncertainly.

With his departure, the girl began to tremble, and Peter turned to her, but Leigh had already stepped in front of her, blocking her view of Steiger and taking her hands in his.

"So, who's this chap... Tanchelin?" he asked.

She shook her head and glanced quickly at Peter.

"I don't know."

Leigh shrugged.

"I'm the Magus," he said, "But who is the Whore?"

"That's me," she said stiffly, "The Whore of Babylon."

"*Babylon*? I thought you said you're from Marylebone."

Peter had to acknowledge a grudging admiration for the man's strategy here as the girl snapped out of Steiger's thrall with a shaky laugh, but then Leigh wrapped her in a bear-hug, and Peter looked away.

"Thank you for your intervention, Major Brandt." Her voice came to him, cool and neutral now, and he turned back to see her watching him from Leigh's arms. The taut malevolence was gone from her face, but the sun, lowering itself behind the tiled roof, cast the shadow of the castle over her, and in its half-darkness her eyes glittered strangely.

END OF PART ONE

If you have enjoyed reading *The Seventh Room*, please consider leaving a review with your retailer.

If you would like to read further, look out for Book Two of Ishtar's Gate:

Coming soon: Book Two of Ishtar's Gate:

Tisiphone Walking

Made in the USA
Middletown, DE
02 July 2025

About the author

Nicola Belluomo has been an archivist and a nurse, and was once almost a midwife. She also worked as an au pair, before earning a BA in English and Drama from Loughborough University, after which she became a magazine editor in New York City. She now teaches English as a Second Language, and lives on the Devon/Somerset border in the UK.

Acknowledgements

I have been encouraged and supported throughout the process of writing this book by my wonderful husband, Salvatore, who has also given me valuable input, notably on the mysteries of truck transmissions. Thanks also to my daughter, Holly, who listened with endless patience to the story, provided tech advice – also with endless patience – helped me to occasionally step back into the twenty-first century, and designed the breathtaking cover.

Historical characters mentioned in this book.
(Military ranks and political roles not given here, as they altered during the timeline of the story.)

Beck, Ludwig
von Blomberg, Werner
Bonhoeffer, Dietrich
Canaris, Wilhelm
von Dohanyi, Hans
von Fritsch, Werner
Fromm, Friedrich

Gehlen, Reinhard
Gisevius, Hans Bernd
Goerdeler, Karl Friedrich
Oster, Hans
Strik-Strikfeldt, Wilfried
Vlasov, Andrey
von Witzleben, Erwin